P9-ECX-210

"Who writes the best romance fiction today?
No doubt it's Jayne Ann Krentz."
—*Affaire de Coeur*

The answer is repeated over and over again...

"Ms. Krentz has deservedly won the hearts of
readers everywhere with her unique blend of fiery
passion and romantic adventure.... One of the
great pleasures of reading Ms. Krentz is the
marvelous symmetry between characters and
plot.... It is this gratifying intricacy that makes
each and every Krentz book something to be
savored over and over again."
—*Rave Reviews*

"A master of the genre...nobody does it better!"
—*Romantic Times*

"...Jayne Ann Krentz is a must for those who
enjoy romantic novels."
—*Brooklyn Record*

"The heroine sparkles, the chemistry sizzles, and
the hero leads the way—pure Krentz."
—*Romantic Times*
THE PRIVATE EYE
Harlequin Temptation

"A fun, witty romp...extremely entertaining...
quality of writing one expects from Ms. Krentz."
—*Rendezvous*
TOO WILD TO WED
Harlequin Temptation

"Have you ever risked something really important on a twist of fate?" Hannah asked

"You've become jaded, Mr. Cage. Everything's too easy for you now. Moving in on my brother's firm will provide no new sport, only the same temporary shot of adrenaline. You need a bit of real excitement in your life and I'm going to provide it." Hannah waited, her own adrenaline pumping furiously into her bloodstream.

Gideon stared at her and then he laughed. "I do see the novelty of it, Hannah. But the stupidity is far more evident. You must be out of your head."

"Two out of three wins. If I win, you give up your plans to take over my brother's firm."

Carelessly, as if nothing at all were riding on the outcome, Gideon shuffled. Then he handed back the cards. His eyes never left Hannah's face as she fanned the pack out in a giant arc across the white tablecloth.

She looked up. "You can go first."

Gideon kept his expression blank as he reached for the first card. Hannah had marked the deck— she was going to cheat him. He felt the stirrings of the first excitement he'd felt in a long time.

He didn't play fair, either.

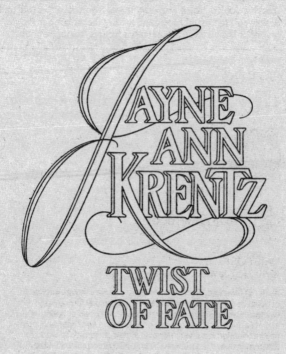

JAYNE ANN KRENTZ

TWIST OF FATE

Harlequin Books

TORONTO • NEW YORK • LONDON
AMSTERDAM • PARIS • SYDNEY • HAMBURG
STOCKHOLM • ATHENS • TOKYO • MILAN

If you purchased this book without a cover you should be aware
that this book is stolen property. It was reported as "unsold and
destroyed" to the publisher, and neither the author nor the
publisher has received any payment for this "stripped book."

 HARLEQUIN BOOKS

TWIST OF FATE
© 1986 by Jayne Ann Krentz

All rights reserved. Except for use in any review, the reproduction
or utilization of this work in whole or in part in any form by any
electronic, mechanical or other means, now known or hereafter
invented, including xerography, photocopying and recording, or in
any information storage or retrieval system, is forbidden without
the permission of the publisher, Harlequin Enterprises Limited,
225 Duncan Mill Road, Don Mills, Ontario, Canada M3B 3K9.

ISBN 0-373-83268-0

First Harlequin Books printing June 1986

Reprinted February 1993

All the characters in this book have no existence outside the
imagination of the author and have no relation whatsoever to
anyone bearing the same name or names. They are not even
distantly inspired by any individual known or unknown to the
author, and all incidents are pure invention.

® are Trademarks registered in the United States Patent and
Trademark Office and in other countries.

Printed in U.S.A.

Prologue

I dreamed of the island again last night. Strange how vivid the memories are after all these years. Perhaps that is the way it is with the image we retain of the turning point in our lives. We feed and nurture it, keeping it fresh and green so that we may continue to draw strength and power from it.

Even now I can still recall the stunning thrill of discovery. The aftermath is also as fiercely alive in my mind as it ever was. I have no regrets but occasionally, late at night, I do have some questions.

I made my choice and I will never have the answers to the questions. But the line of descent remains unbroken. It would be interesting to know how Hannah will handle her choices. In some way that I can't quite define, she is the strongest of us all.

—From the *Journals of Elizabeth Nord*

Chapter One

THE LAS VEGAS ILLUSION was so good at times that it was almost possible to believe the Powers that controlled the huge hotel-casinos also controlled the outside air temperature. Almost but not quite. Hannah Jessett stood on the chilled side of the plate glass doors and gazed out at the hotel swimming pool. The gigantic, whimsically shaped oasis with its meandering curves and unbelievably cute little bridges lay glittering beneath a broiling summer sun. The present difference between the gambling hell inside and the desert hell outside was approximately forty degrees.

On the whole, Hannah would have preferred to stay indoors. She was not fond of deserts. She was from Seattle. But time was running out.

Her cane skidded on a small patch of wind-tossed gravel as she shoved open the door and stepped outside. Pain shot through her left leg when she grabbed for the wrought iron railing that lined the wide steps down to poolside. For an instant she closed her eyes against the lancing agony and then she drew a deep breath.

"Damn it to hell."

It struck her that the oath was probably somewhat redundant. She considered the philosophical ramifications of the question while she waited for the pain to subside. She should have taken that midday tablet after all.

For a long moment she leaned against the ornate railing and wondered if the painkiller would have dulled her awareness any more than pain itself did. It was probably a toss-up. In the meantime she was grudgingly grateful for the fact that there were very few people around the pool to witness her less than graceful entrance. A couple of showgirls, all thoroughbred legs and classically contoured bosoms, drowsed beneath sunshades at one end. Hannah decided they either hadn't gotten the word that tanning was no longer considered healthy or else they were going for the short-term cosmetic benefits and consigning the future to oblivion. Hannah wondered what sort of future a Las Vegas showgirl had. Professional lives were probably short in that line of work. Might be a crying need for good career counseling here in Vegas.

Hannah forced her tense muscles to relax while she replaced the determinedly cool smile she had let slip a moment earlier. Forget the showgirls. Her goal was the other end of the pool where a man sat at a table beneath a fringed umbrella. Even from where she was standing Hannah could tell he was suffering. He had loosened his tie, opened his collar, and rolled up his sleeves, but the heat was taking its toll. There was a grimly determined expression of concentration on his face as he bent over a folder full of papers. Hannah got the impression that he was committed to the project at hand and would complete it even if required to do so in temperatures that hovered around a hundred and ten degrees. The dedicated type. As Hannah studied him, he glanced up and saw her. The intent look congealed into a considering frown.

He probably knew right off who she was, Hannah decided. She didn't look much like a showgirl. And she wasn't wearing a bathing suit. The man got to his feet and started toward her.

Her left leg grudgingly agreed to move again as Hannah tentatively leaned on the cane and took a few purposeful steps. She made it to the halfway point around the pool. Then she stood composing herself while she waited for the man to reach her. It wouldn't do to startle him by confronting him with a grimace of agony. People were very uncomfortable around someone who was in obvious pain, and the last thing she wanted to do was to make Gideon Cage uncomfortable. The leg was manageable now. Just as soon as this was over, she promised herself, she would go back to her hotel room and swallow the painkiller she'd put off taking earlier. As she consoled herself with that thought, the man reached her. Now she could clearly see the sweat on his brow and the dampness that marked the front of the once crisp white shirt.

"Mr. Cage?" She summoned a truly brilliant smile for the intense man with the slight paunch who stood before her.

"I'm Mr. Cage's administrative assistant. Steve Decker. I assume you're Miss Jessett?"

Decker removed his heavy-rimmed glasses and polished them with an automatic gesture as he waited politely. He appeared to be in his mid-thirties and obviously was not following the Yuppie trend toward physical fitness and a lean figure. In this era of fitness madness, a flabby physique could hurt his chances for career advancement. Hannah wanted to tell him that just sitting in the heat was not going to take off weight, regardless of how much he sweat, but she didn't.

Sometimes it was hard to resist handing out free advice. But Hannah reminded herself that just because she had a natural talent for advising, she couldn't expect everyone she encountered to appreciate it. There were plenty of people who played kazoos with concert level precision, but not everyone cared to listen. Free kazoo playing and the free dispensing of sound advice—especially career advice—were rated at about the same level on humanity's scale of values. The secret was to make people pay for both.

Without even thinking about it, Hannah picked up the stray clues that Decker gave out through his appearance, his manner, and his job. With a skill that was second nature she began assembling an interior puzzle, which, if she ever got around to completing it, would have enabled her to predict his actions very accurately. It was a knack she had, one that made her very good at her work. Hannah's bright smile became genuine. She liked people such as Steve Decker. They were generally decent, hardworking, loyal types. Unfortunately for them, it was their lot in life to need bosses. They were the kind of people who could hold an organization together but who would never dream of trying to assume control over it. "Administrative assistant" was a loose term that covered a lot of territory in some companies, but Hannah had a hunch that in this case she was looking at a valuable cog in Gideon Cage's powerful wheel.

"I have an appointment with Mr. Cage. I'm Hannah Jessett."

Decker blinked at the cane and replaced his glasses. "Ah, yes. Gideon's expecting you. This way, please."

He was on a first-name basis with Cage. That was interesting. It suggested that Decker might be one of the few decent, hardworking, loyal types who had been lucky enough to end up with a boss who appreciated him. It also said a few things about Cage, himself.

As Decker turned to lead her toward the table where he had been sitting, Hannah saw that he was developing a slight bald spot on the crown of his head. He could still comb the side hair over it but not for much longer.

"Gideon will be finished in just a few minutes, Miss Jessett. You're welcome to wait over there under the umbrella."

There was no sound from the pool, and it took Hannah a second to realize that it was being used. A man was swimming deep under the water. Hannah wished she'd been left to wait in the air-conditioned casino lobby. Out here the oppressive heat of the Nevada summer was dampening in more ways than one. She didn't know if the wet marks in the fabric of the rakish khaki bush shirt she wore with her jeans were from the heat or from nerves. She should have put on the olive camp shirt instead of the khaki bush. Olive didn't show perspiration stains so obviously. A little something to keep in mind if she ever found herself in this sort of situation again.

"If you'll excuse me, I have to be going. I was just on my way back inside when you arrived." Steve Decker smiled politely, concerned eyes going to the cane one last time. "Unless there's anything else you need?"

Hannah shook her head. "I'll be fine, thank you." She started toward the table under the umbrella, willing herself to move at a reasonably even pace. She would not betray any more signs of weakness than she could help. She would not, for example, start screaming immediately for the waiter who tended the poolside bar, even though she could use the alcohol to dull the ache in her leg. She would handle this with aplomb. Gideon Cage was a man who preyed on weakness. The first order of business was not to display any. "Goodbye, Mr. Decker."

Decker nodded, hesitated a moment as if having second thoughts about leaving a wounded creature alone with the man in the pool, and then left. Hannah's attention focused on the bar set up beneath the canopy on the other side of the pool. First things first. With care she lowered herself into a webbed chair and lifted a hand with what she hoped was casual demand. A waiter dressed in white shorts and a polo shirt detached himself from the bar and headed in her direction. Hannah hoped Gideon Cage would stay underwater a while longer.

"Two margaritas, please," Hannah said with her most winning smile as the young man from the bar reached her. "From scratch. On the rocks, not turned into snow, and made with real limes, not that yucky sweet mix." She slid three dollar bills across the table. "Any problem?"

The young man smiled in a friendly fashion and pocketed the bills. "No problem. The bartender generally uses the mix and turns the drinks into green snow but I think I can convince him to squeeze a few limes."

"Thank you. You can put the drinks on my tab." She displayed her room key. The young man nodded and headed back to the bar. Hannah watched him go, feeling a strong sense of elation. She was a good tipper because she had worked a couple of summers in a restaurant, and most people who had once waited tables were notoriously big tippers. But this was the first time she had ever tried outright bribery, and she was fascinated to find that it apparently worked. Slipping people a few bucks, she had heard, was the way to get what you wanted in Vegas. Hannah's only concern was that the three-dollar advance on the margaritas wouldn't be sufficient. Or perhaps she'd overdone it. Perhaps two dollars would have done the trick. There were obviously nuances to be learned.

The margaritas arrived in perfect condition a few minutes later. Hannah was sampling hers with what an ungenerous soul might have termed indecent haste when she became aware of being watched. Automatically she glanced up and found herself looking into the eyes of Gideon Cage. He studied her while standing chest high in the water, his arms folded on the concrete edge that surrounded the pool. Water glistened on his shoulders and slicked his heavy, dark hair.

Hannah's first impression was that he didn't appear to be as big as she had expected him to be. Somehow one always thought of predators in large terms. That sort of thinking tended to ignore spiders and snakes, she realized. Although it was only a tiny error in the mental image of him that she had fashioned, it bothered Hannah. Little mistakes, small pieces missing in the puzzle, could lead to much bigger and more dangerous mistakes.

"The cane is an interesting touch, Miss Jessett. A little theatrical, but interesting."

At least his voice fit her preconceptions. Soft and gravelled—the voice of a man who never had to shout to convince the phone company it had made a mistake on its monthly bill.

Hannah toasted him lightly with her margarita. "I'm glad you approve, Mr. Cage. My whole purpose this afternoon is to whet your interest." She took a long swallow of the refreshingly tart drink, wondering how much alcohol it would take to equal one of her pain tablets. Dangerous thinking. Rather like concentrating on images of wolves and lions while forgetting about the menace of spiders and snakes.

"You should have done your research a little more thoroughly. I'm a simple man. Not real kinky in my sexual tastes. The image of a lady in bed with a cane doesn't do a whole hell of a lot for me."

"I'm afraid you misunderstand the situation, Mr. Cage. It's not your sexual interest I'm going to try to whet."

"My sympathy?"

"No." She paused, thinking about that. "Have you got any?"

"Sympathy? None that I'd let get in the way of a business deal."

She nodded, satisfied. "That fits."

"With what?"

"The image of you that I've been building in my mind. I'm a guidance counselor by profession, Mr. Cage. It's my business to construct images of people that give me reliable information about how they function and what they need."

"And you're going to tell me what I need?"

She slurped determinedly on the margarita before answering. It would take a hell of a lot of it to equal one of her tablets. Then she smiled. "Come on out of the pool, Mr. Cage. You can't hide in there forever."

Something unpleasant flickered in his eyes and Hannah guessed he didn't like the implication that he was hiding from her. She would have to be careful to push him only so far or this whole thing would explode in her face. There were still too many unknowns in the puzzle that was Gideon Cage.

The pool water made a soft, rushing sound as Cage ignored the steps and hauled himself out the hard way. Upon quick reflection Hannah decided that he wasn't trying to impress her. It was the way he always left the pool. A moment later he was walking toward her, reaching down to scoop up a fat, white towel that lay on a lounger.

Not only was he under six feet—probably more in the neighborhood of five-ten, and built along lean, unbulky lines—he was also considerably less attractive than she had expected. A man who commanded the kind of financial power Gideon Cage did ought to look more like a graduate of Harvard Business School. There should be classic East Coast preppy refinement here, rather than this assortment of raw, blunt-edged features and hairy arms and legs. Hannah made another quick adjustment in her mental construct of the man. It was important to stay flexible.

"All right, Miss Jessett," Cage said mildly as he threw himself down onto the chair across from her. He cocked one bushy brow as he saw the second margarita glass and then reached out to pick it up. "Let's have it. Why did your brother send you?"

"He didn't send me. I got here all on my own."

With grave patience he inclined his head as if congratulating her on her ability to board an airplane by herself. "Again: why?"

Hannah smiled and set down her glass. "You're in luck, Mr. Cage. I have come to offer you a measure of salvation."

"Oh, Christ."

"Not that kind of salvation, I'm afraid. We guidance counselors try to stick to our areas of expertise. I'm offering professional guidance, not theology."

He gave her a level look, night-dark eyes examining her face warily. Then he tried the drink in his hand. Cool surprise flickered in his gaze. "How the hell did you get them to mix a decent margarita?"

"Bribery."

He nodded. "Congratulations. Going to try that tactic on me?"

"No, Mr. Cage. I'm not going to try bribery on you. It wouldn't work."

"You're playing games with me, Hannah Jessett. It would be better if you didn't."

"Better for whom? I have nothing to lose. For that matter, neither has my brother. Your group of investors is moving in on his firm like Attila the Hun. You've made it very clear that you're going to take over Accelerated Design."

Cage shrugged and lounged back against the webbing of the chair. "Any reason why I shouldn't? The firm has some excellent, highly marketable software products but it's a mess financially. Your brother is only twenty-nine years old, Hannah. He may be brilliant at software design but knows nothing about management. Accelerated Design is a sitting duck for me."

"Precisely my point." Hannah's leg protested angrily as she shifted position in the chair. Her fingers tightened around the glass in her hand. Pain control this afternoon might require more than one margarita.

"Pardon me, but I think I may have missed your, uh, point."

"A sitting duck. What do you need with another sitting duck target, Mr. Cage? Surely you're more of a sportsman than that? Where's the challenge in launching an assault on a small, badly managed software house such as Accelerated Design? You're a creature of habit. That's your problem."

Cage paused thoughtfully and then said very gently, "Habit?"

"Ummm. You've been on a roll for the past nine years. Ever since you demolished that company in California. What was the name? I remember reading about it in the *Wall Street Journal* recently when they did a profile on you."

"Ballantine Manufacturing."

Hannah marveled at the perfectly neutral tone of his words. Whatever had happened with Ballantine Manufacturing could not have been a neutral event for him. It had set him on the course he had followed unerringly for the past nine years. "You were only about thirty or thirty-one at the time, weren't you? After that, there was, apparently, no stopping you."

"I've been reasonably successful."

"You've been a steamroller. There's a difference, I think."

"No, Miss Jessett, there isn't. Being successful in my line of work means being a steamroller."

"As a professional guidance counselor, allow me to disagree. You're just in the habit of launching victorious assaults on companies such as my brother's. Habit, Mr. Cage. You're not moving in on him out of necessity. You don't need his firm. You just saw it sitting there looking vulnerable and decided to grab it.

I'd think you'd want more challenge, but that's your problem. I'm not here to alter your entire way of doing business."

"Lucky me."

Hannah gritted her teeth against the pain in her leg and kept her smile intact. "I'm here only to persuade you to lay off my brother's firm. As you, yourself, said, he's young. He needs time to bring the management situation at Accelerated Design back under control. If you take over the firm, he'll be out in the cold. You'll have obtained a company with some interesting products, it's true, but you hardly need one more of those. You've got lots of them already."

"I'm supposed to walk away from such easy pickings just because you've flown down here to plead your brother's case?"

"Oh, no, Mr. Cage. I wouldn't dream of appealing to your compassion or sympathy. You've already confirmed that you're short on both commodities, remember?"

A curious smile edged his mouth. "I remember. So what are you offering that will tempt me to forget about Accelerated Design?"

Hannah gathered her courage. "A simple game of chance."

"A game of chance." He took a slow swallow of the margarita, his gaze on the pool. "That wasn't quite what I expected, Hannah."

"Yes, I know. As I said, you've become a creature of habit. The habit of victory, whether in business or here in Vegas. I'm taking an educated guess that after nine years of hollow victories, you've become rather jaded, Mr. Cage. Everything's too easy for you now. Moving in on my brother's firm will provide no new sport, only the same temporary shot of adrenaline. You need a bit of real excitement in your life and I'm going to provide it." Hannah waited, her own adrenaline pumping furiously into her bloodstream.

"Excitement. That's an interesting thought. I take it you can do some fairly exotic things with that cane, then?"

"I said a game of chance. I meant cards, Mr. Cage. I'm proposing that you let your future hinge on the luck of the draw. You come to Vegas for a few days every summer, but have you ever risked something really important on a twist of fate? Have you ever won or lost a business deal on a bet? Think of the novelty of it."

He stared at her and then he laughed. "I do see the novelty of it, Hannah. But the stupidity is far more evident. Jesus Christ, lady, you must be out of your head. Are you serious?"

"Very."

"Even a guidance counselor couldn't be that naive."

Hannah leaned forward earnestly. "Gambling is apparently your one form of recreation, Mr. Cage. You're here now because you always come here at this time of year for a break. You're in the mood to gamble and I'm offering some interesting stakes. How can you resist? We draw for the highest card. Two out of three wins. If I win you give up your plans to take over my brother's firm. If you win..." She lifted one shoulder fatalistically.

"I take over? I can do that already. Any way you look at it, all I get out of the deal is a shot at losing."

She shook her head slowly. "No, you get a break from doing business in the same, habitual fashion.

You also get a break from your habitual form of rec-reation. I'm offering you a gamble with very large stakes. You see, I loaned my brother some money to help him start Accelerated Design. I took the repay-ment in stock. I now own a sizeable chunk. If I lose, I'll hand over my shares to you. It will make your takeover infinitely cheaper and less troublesome be-cause you will hold more than enough stock to put you in control. Surely that's a more interesting proposi-tion than a game of blackjack inside the casino."

There was a pause and then Gideon asked, "Just out of sheer, unadulterated curiosity, how did you know about my annual trip to Vegas?"

"I'm aware that you come here once or twice dur-ing the summer. Personally, I can't see why anyone would leave Tucson to come to Vegas in the summer. They're both deserts. But you've been doing it for years. My brother heard it from someone on the Ac-celerated Design Board of Directors. He said you limit yourself to one or two trips every twelve months or so and stay only a few days each time. But while you're here, you're rumored to bet very heavily. Not my idea of an annual vacation, but to each his own."

"Thank you for your tolerance. Vacation is the right word, by the way. Vegas isn't business for me. I don't do business the way I take a vacation." He spaced the words out carefully, as though she weren't very intel-ligent.

Hannah ignored the warning. "Think about it, Mr. Cage. Think about the unique opportunity I'm giving you. Have any of your other sitting ducks ever of-fered you a chance to win or lose on the draw of a card?"

"None have been quite that idiotic," he admitted. "What did your brother say about all this?"

"I didn't tell him exactly what I had in mind."

"I'll just bet you didn't."

Hannah smiled meaningfully. "That's all I'm asking, Mr. Cage. That you make a bet. An important bet. Try it; you'll like it. It will give you a break from the monotony of your usual mode of business. I think you need a break." She reached for the cane and started to get to her feet.

Automatically Cage got up and grasped her arm. He frowned slightly as he took in the wince she couldn't quite hide. "How bad's the leg?"

Startled by the question, Hannah glanced up at him. "Bad enough. I was in a car accident a few weeks ago. They're going to have to operate on my knee the day after tomorrow."

"Then what?"

She smiled. "Therapy for a while and then I get to go on *my* annual vacation. I'm going to walk along a Caribbean beach and do a lot of swimming. It's supposed to be very good for getting the leg back into shape."

"I see. You don't spend your vacations in Vegas?"

"No, Mr. Cage. I don't find gambling very amusing. It's your style of recreation, not mine. At a wild guess I'd say gambling appeals to you because it seems to provide an alternative to the precision and calculation with which you normally operate, but I doubt that it gives you a real change of pace. As a form of recreation it probably doesn't work very well for you in the long run."

"What makes you say that?"

"Because you probably play the way you work: lots of skill and concentration. It's not really a change from business for you. All gambling does is inject more unknowns into the situation. Still, that must provide some diversion. My little game of chance will do more for you because the stakes are more meaningful."

He kept his hand under her arm for a few steps as they walked back toward the hotel entrance, dropping it only when Hannah calmly pulled away. He continued to pad barefoot along beside her. "I take it you wouldn't get the same charge out of this, er, game of chance you're suggesting as you think I would?"

"I'm afraid not."

He eyed her assessingly. "I think you're lying. I believe you would find it very exhilarating. Otherwise you would never have proposed it."

She came to a halt at the glass doors and turned to face him. She was leaning very heavily on the cane now but she managed to keep her expression aloof and reasonably serene. "I don't really care what you believe about my motives. My only concern is to talk you into taking the chance. I'm staying here in the hotel. Room 432. Call me this evening after you've had a chance to consider my proposal. All or nothing, Mr. Cage. Win or lose, for once the House doesn't get a cut. How can you resist?"

"Are all guidance counselors this bizarre in their approach?"

"Nope. Some would give you a twenty-page test to determine your true interests and abilities. Then they'd tell you what you already know: you're a born genius at business and you like the occasional bit of gambling—as long as the stakes are high enough to make it interesting.''

Cage opened the door. ''Tell me, Hannah Jessett, are you really very good at your work?''

''One of the best. I have a talent for it.'' She moved the cane cautiously onto the step, avoiding the gravel that had proven so treacherous earlier. ''Call me, Mr. Cage. I'll be at the hotel until tomorrow afternoon. Then I leave for Seattle.''

''That sounds like an ultimatum.''

''It is. I'm giving it because I've got one hanging over my own head. I have to be in the hospital the day after tomorrow. I don't have time to string this out.'' She didn't look back as she made her way into the air-conditioned hallway. The glass door hissed shut behind her.

Before she turned the corner at the far end of the hall, Hannah glanced back once. Cage was still standing on the step, watching her. Her first thought as she rounded the corner and disappeared from his sight was that Gideon Cage looked surprisingly interesting in a swimsuit. Not at all like a spider or a snake.

Her second thought was that if he did call that evening she would suggest they eat at one of the half dozen restaurants in the hotel. It would save having to drive some place. She was getting better about driving, but Hannah still avoided it whenever possible, especially in a strange environment. Since the accident, it had taken a great deal of nerve just to be a passenger in a car. It took even more to get behind the wheel herself.

She was getting better. The butterflies in her stomach had only fluttered lethargically during the cab ride in from the airport that day. But there was no sense adding any additional strain to the evening. If Cage agreed to the bet, she would be nervous enough as it was.

Then her attention switched to the tablet waiting for her in the room. One thing at a time. Pain definitely took precedence over sexual attraction or her progress in recovering her driving nerve. Pain, when it struck, took precedence over just about everything, she had discovered.

GIDEON DRESSED FOR DINNER with absentminded attention. He'd phoned room 432 an hour before and calmly told Hannah that he would be there at six-thirty. He'd apparently awakened her from a nap.

"Does this mean you've agreed to my bet?" she'd inquired in a sleep-fuzzed voice.

"It means I'm taking you to dinner. One thing at a time, Hannah."

"Just what I told myself when I left you a couple of hours ago. See you at six-thirty. Would you mind if we ate in one of the hotel restaurants?"

"Suit yourself." She probably didn't want to venture far on that leg, he decided.

Gideon buttoned a white, open-throated shirt and fastened a belt on his dark slacks. The Vegas life-style tolerated anything from Bermuda shorts to a tuxedo. He chose the middle ground. Tie and jacket would be sufficient for this evening.

The classiest of the six hotel restaurants was done in a typically overwrought Vegas style. Greek pillars, splashing, lighted fountains and a staff dressed in togas. But the food was surprisingly good for a casino restaurant. It was one of the reasons Gideon returned to that hotel year after year. He frowned in the mirror, remembering what Hannah had said about his predictable habits. Her comments had been bothering him all afternoon.

Something about Hannah Jessett had gotten to him. Gideon knotted his tie, mildly irritated as he remembered the image of her sitting by the pool. She had worn the khaki bush shirt with its epaulets, button-studded pockets and dashing, quasi-military air with a certain defiant panache. She was not built like a Vegas showgirl on top. The outline of her breasts beneath the shirt had been small and gently curved. A wide, heavy leather belt with a sturdy brass buckle had defined a slim waist and emphasized the nice shape of her rear, which was encased in a pair of snug-fitting jeans.

The thought of the petite breasts and rounded derriere stopped Gideon for a second and then he found himself grimacing wryly at himself in the mirror. This evening hardly qualified as a dinner date. It was really more of a business skirmish.

But there was no doubt that it was going to be supremely entertaining. And it had been so long since he'd really enjoyed himself for an evening. Perhaps he should date more guidance counselors. He was curious to know how she would respond to the final act of the little farce she had staged.

He was curious about other aspects of Hannah Jessett, too, Gideon decided as he picked up a light sport jacket and started toward the door. She'd been oddly on target that afternoon when she'd accused him of finding that his victories were growing hollow. How had she known of the increasing lack of satisfaction in each new triumph? How had she guessed at something he hadn't even wanted to confront himself?

Maybe it was curiosity that had made him phone
room 432 and tell her he'd take her to dinner. Hannah Jessett was a new and unexpected element in his
world. His mouth crooked upward at one corner as he
fished in his pocket to check for the room key. On the
other hand, he might have been motivated strictly by
the soft, round shape of her tail in that pair of too-
tight jeans she'd been wearing.

Actually, she'd been pleasantly soft looking all over.
Her loose khaki shirt hadn't revealed a lot of detail but
he'd been able to tell that she wasn't wearing a bra.

Her hair had been soft, too, a cascade of little curls
rather than a sleek businesswoman's cut. Even her face
had seemed soft, except for a certain tightness around
the mouth that he knew betrayed the pain in her leg.
The lady had good eyes, Gideon reflected, as he put
his hand on the doorknob. The wide, hazel-green gaze
was direct and probably far too honest for her own
good. He liked that. It gave him one more advantage.
It was his nature to operate from a position of advantage.

All in all she looked a bit like an ex-liberal-arts grad
student. He pegged her age at around thirty or thirty-
one. He guessed she did her guidance counseling at a
college. When the phone rang, Gideon was reflecting
on the fact that he hadn't ever received any professional guidance counseling in his life.

For an instant he contemplated ignoring it, and then
the thought that it might be his new counselor made
him step back into the room.

"Gideon? It's Steve. I'm about to leave for the airport."

"Don't let me hold you up. If you miss the flight
back to Tucson, Angie will sure as hell blame me."

The polite, running battle Angie Decker conducted in defense of her husband always amused Gideon. She was convinced that Gideon was far too demanding and that her husband should be more assertive. She never quite grasped the fact that Steve Decker preferred to follow orders in the business world rather than give them.

"I checked with the office an hour ago. Mary Ann was on her way out the door but she said there was a message from Taggert. It was about Ballantine."

Gideon glanced at his watch. It was getting late. "Okay, let me have it."

"Not much, really, just that Taggert says he's on the move. Rumor has it that Ballantine really is going to go after Surbrook."

"Well, hell."

"I know."

"He doesn't stand a chance," Gideon murmured.

"No, but he knows you want the company and he can drive the price way up by acting as though he's interested in making a counteroffer. Hell, we've pulled that stunt ourselves a few times."

Gideon found himself staring at the framed reproduction of the 1569 world map by Gerhard Mercator that hung on the wall. Part fantasy, part reality, it was, nevertheless, a genuine effort to make sense out of that which was only partially known and largely misunderstood. That was the thing about maps, Gideon had always thought. They were monuments to the human need to comprehend and control the environment. He had found it astonishing that a Las Vegas hotel would have the taste to use such an item in its room decor. Reality was not a big deal there in Vegas. Gideon always asked for that room because of the map. Another habit. He'd more or less abandoned the collecting that had once been an important part of his life, but something in him still responded to an interesting map. "There's nothing we can do about it tonight. I'll call you in the morning. Make sure Taggert's available."

"All right. Just thought you ought to know Ballantine will definitely be challenging us."

No, Gideon thought, *not us. He'll be challenging me.* "Thanks for the update on the Marsden deal and the Jessett move, Steve. Sorry you had to fly here on such short notice. Make my apologies to Angie."

"I'll do that. Maybe it will get me off the hook for having to miss Terry's school play last night. Goodbye, Gideon. See you when you get back to Tucson."

Gideon tossed the receiver back into its cradle and started for the door. For a moment he allowed himself to dwell on the news about Ballantine. It was bound to happen sooner or later. The young cub was going to take on the full-grown wolf. The time to crush Hugh Ballantine was now, while he was still young enough and weak enough to be dealt with easily. Gideon opened the door and stepped outside into the thickly carpeted hall. Time enough in the morning to think about that. He had other things to do this evening.

He was going to give a certain career counselor a small but hopefully salutary bit of guidance.

HANNAH REACHED SURREPTITIOUSLY under the table and tried to knead her left knee as she munched on a bite of stuffed salmon. She had barely touched the glass of sauvignon blanc Gideon had ordered. She had to keep the alcohol intake down, she warned herself.

The last thing she wanted was trouble from mixing the painkiller with wine. She'd kept the afternoon dose to a minimum, though, and it hadn't been enough to completely dull the ache in her leg. God, she would be glad when this was all over. It was tough to appear casually chic under the circumstances.

"Tell me more about your vacation plans," Gideon was saying conversationally as he worked on his curried lamb. "Where in the Caribbean are you going?"

"To a little island near the U.S. Virgin Islands. It's called Santa Inez. My aunt had a home there."

"Had?" He glanced up politely.

"She died a couple of months ago. I'm going to go down there and pack up her things, especially her books and notes. According to her will, she wanted me to have them. She lived down there for several years, but she was always something of a recluse. No one but members of the family knew where she'd retired. She forbade us to tell anyone else. A fanatic about privacy."

"Were you close, you and your aunt?"

Hannah thought about that, remembering the vivid, intelligent woman she had seen only occasionally during her life. "I don't think my aunt was close to anyone, not even her sister, my mother. Aunt Elizabeth was rather a loner. Very brilliant in her field. She was a cultural anthropologist. Her best known work is probably *The Amazons of Revelation Island*."

Gideon looked surprised. "That rings a bell."

Hannah chuckled. "Which only goes to prove that somewhere along the line you must have taken a class in cultural anthropology. It's a classic text in the field. Still being used even though she wrote it in the forties. It was based on work she had done on Revelation Island in the South Pacific.''

''I don't really recall too much about it. I'm afraid my interests were more focused on business classes. I only lasted a couple of years in college.'' Gideon searched his memory. ''Something about a matriarchal society, wasn't it?''

''Yes. It upset a lot of theories about male-female relationships among primitive peoples. It was very controversial at the time. My aunt didn't mind being controversial, though.''

''As I recall the controversy was generated by the fact that no one could ever disprove her conclusions,'' Gideon said slowly. ''Didn't something happen to Revelation Island?''

''It became a strategic piece of ground during World War II. By the time the U.S. and Japan had fought back and forth across it a few times there wasn't much left of the original culture, let alone the inhabitants. After the war it became a long-range supply depot for ships. By the time anthropologists got back to Revelation Island in the early sixties everything had changed. There have been a lot of arguments about my aunt's work but no one has been able to discount it.'' Hannah grinned. ''A fact my aunt found vastly amusing. She was quite a character. Had absolutely no respect for the formal academic world even though she was a product of it. I think she saw herself more as a philosopher than an anthropologist.''

''Did she ever marry?''

''No. Followed a fine tradition of unmarried women, which litters my mother's side of the family. Back in the last century there was another female relative who was equally outstanding in her field. She never married either."

"What field?" Gideon asked.

"Mathematics. She did very sophisticated work in the area of number theory. And don't ask me to tell you anything about that. Math is not my strong point. I was strictly liberal arts in college. Then there was the artist. She lived around the turn of the century. Her work brings huge amounts at auctions today. There were a few other maverick ladies in the family whom I've heard about over the years."

Gideon surveyed her with genuine curiosity. "Are you going to follow in the tradition?"

Hannah's eyes gleamed for an instant. "Of not marrying? It has its merits."

"Somehow," he murmured, "I don't see you as the celibate type."

"Who said anything about celibacy?" She took another bite of stuffed salmon and wondered what had possessed her to order salmon in the desert. A mistake. She was spoiled by the fresh fish that was so available in Seattle. "Let's get back to the main subject here. I assume you're willing to take my bet?"

"Don't ever make the mistake of assuming too much about me, Hannah. I could be here simply because I didn't have anything better to do this evening."

"You *don't* have anything better to do. What's your alternative? Pick up some blond bimbo of a showgirl whose main concern is getting you to spend money on her? You can do that anytime. How often can you play a game such as the one I'm providing? Even here in Vegas, this will be a novelty."

"You seem awfully sure you're going to win."

Hannah sucked in her breath, knowing now that he was going to do it. "I have a chance. If I can't convince you to play then there's no chance at all. My brother will ultimately lose Accelerated Design. All he can do at this point is stall and make the takeover process as expensive as possible for you."

"Assumptions. You really ought to be cautious about making assumptions, Hannah."

She waved that aside. "I've got a pack of cards in my purse. We'll draw for high card when they clear the dishes. The staff will assume we're just cutting the cards to see who pays for dinner."

He watched her face for a long moment. Then he appeared to reach a decision. Hannah had the feeling that he always made decisions that way—quick and sure. It was another piece of the puzzle.

"All right, guidance counselor. I'll take the bet."

"Yes. I thought you would."

Without a word she removed the deck of cards from her leather shoulder bag while the busboy cleared the table. Her hands were trembling. Why on earth was that? She had nothing to lose. But her fingers were still shaking faintly as she handed Gideon the pack. Dear God, the man was no doubt very good at cards. Her only hope lay in the fact that he would not expect her to cheat. She knew her own image, knew how most people perceived her. *Pleasant* and *innocuous* were two common adjectives she suspected appeared frequently in the minds of other people when they looked at her. She didn't have the sort of face people thought belonged to a woman capable of blatant cheating. Guidance counselors tended to cultivate a sincere look. Or perhaps they were just born with it.

Carelessly, as if nothing at all were riding on the outcome, Gideon shuffled. Then he handed back the cards. His eyes never left her face as she fanned the pack out in a giant arc across the white table cloth. She looked up.

"You can go first."

He reached forward and unhesitatingly flipped over a card. "Three of clubs."

She had to do this without being obvious, Hannah told herself. Her palm was damp as she turned over a ten of diamonds. The relief was in her eyes. She knew it but couldn't disguise the emotion.

Mouth curving ironically, Gideon drew a six of hearts. Then he leaned his chin on his hand and waited.

Hannah was aware of an extra strong stab of pain from her knee. Tension, she assured herself. Pure, unadulterated tension. She put out her hand and removed the king of hearts. She didn't dare meet Gideon's eyes for several taut seconds. She tried to massage her knee again without being obvious about it.

"It looks like you've just won control of Accelerated Design for your brother."

He was so casual about it. "Is this the way you always play here in Vegas? As if it truly doesn't matter?" she whispered.

"I have a rule, Hannah. I never gamble on anything that really matters. Remember that when you go home." He got to his feet and handed her the cane. "Are you ready? You look a little wrung out."

"I feel a little wrung out." She stood awkwardly, not sure if the unsteadiness was from nerves or pain. Perhaps it didn't matter. She'd won. Silently she allowed herself to be escorted out of the restaurant. The clanging of slot machines and the low hubbub of the casino gaming floor greeted them. It was impossible to get anywhere in a Las Vegas casino without having to cross the gambling arena. Suggestive selling. But tonight Hannah wasn't buying. She'd already done her gambling for the evening.

She pushed back a curl that had escaped the tortoiseshell comb she was wearing. Something inside her was bubbling with unnatural energy. The relief she felt was almost overwhelming. It made her lightheaded. She halted abruptly and put her free hand on Gideon's arm.

"Thank you, Gideon."

He lifted a hand and coiled one curl around his finger, eyes pensive. "You're sure I'll abide by the outcome of that stupid game?"

"Yes," she said simply. "I'm sure."

"What makes you so positive, guidance counselor?"

She smiled tremulously. "I told you, I have an instinct for people. You've agreed not to take over my brother's firm. I know you'll honor your word. You know, if you give it some thought, you might learn something from what happened here tonight, Gideon. Trust me. I'm not even going to charge you for the advice."

He moved his head in a gesture of disbelief. "You think that by making me alter my plans for one business deal you've broken my bad habit of always winning?"

"It's a start."

"Christ, lady, you're an idiot. But an amusing idiot. You really believe what you're saying, don't you?"

"All you have to do is stop and think about what you did tonight," she told him earnestly. The ever present urge to put someone on the right path was breaking free inside her again. She wished she could restrain herself, but the temptation to try straightening someone out was too great to resist. She was so damn good at it. "You can use this experience as a turning point. From now on you can analyze future business deals in a different light. Decide what you really want and only go after the things that are important. You didn't need Accelerated Design. Winning just for the sake of winning isn't very satisfying in the long run. The high you get can't last, and it's never quite as good the next time. The only thing that makes winning work at all is the threat of losing. That threat hasn't existed for you for a long time. The adrenaline won't give you what you think you need. Not for much longer. You've been living off of it for too long. I think your life has become severely unbalanced because of it. Everyone needs balance in their lives, Gideon."

"At least in Vegas the dealers don't treat you to a short session of psychoanalysis after the game."

"No, I suppose they don't. Maybe they should. But I guess it wouldn't be good for business." Hannah stepped away from him, releasing the light grip on his arm. "I'm only trying to tell you that there are other things in life besides making the next business kill. You should start looking for them before it's too late."

"You're trying to save me from myself?"

She tilted her head to one side, studying him. "As a professional guidance counselor, I can't resist the challenge. I can't help giving advice sometimes. Occupational hazard, I suppose."

"I don't think anyone's ever tried to save me before."

"Someday you must let me know if I succeeded."

"Someday I will." He touched her shoulder as she started to turn away from him. "Hannah, there's just one other thing."

She froze. "What's that?"

"Could I have your deck of cards?"

Her leg began to throb in earnest. "Why?"

"Just as a souvenir."

She managed a smile. "I was going to keep them myself for that very reason."

He nodded and made no further comment. But much later that evening, alone in her hotel room, Hannah fished around in her purse for a pain tablet and noticed that the deck of cards was missing. The knowledge haunted her all the way back to Seattle.

Chapter Two

THERE WAS A CAR that she couldn't quite see in the blinding rain, a guardrail that couldn't withstand the impact of a swerving Toyota, the bite of seat belts as they took hold and then the odd feeling of weightlessness. The weightlessness lingered longer than usual.

For the third or fourth time Hannah swam up out of the anesthetic haze, and on this occasion she was able to stay awake long enough to register both her brother's presence in the room and the pain in her leg.

"I thought it wasn't going to hurt anymore."

The disappointment and resentment she felt at the continuation of the agony in her leg was almost childish. It was probably the remains of the anesthesia in her blood stream that made her sound as though she were near tears. Mustn't whine, Hannah thought. She had promised herself she wouldn't whine. She hoped Nick would ignore the precarious state of her emotions.

Her brother turned away from the window as he heard her voice, coming toward the bed with a concerned expression. In Nick the tawny hair that Hannah had inherited from their mother had come out almost blond. His hazel eyes leaned more toward true green than Hannah's did. He was a good deal taller than his sister, almost six feet, and built without her obvious tendency toward softness. At twenty-nine, he worked out frequently and took pride in his lean

frame. He was a natural for the successful Yuppie life-
style. It made Hannah tired just to look at him after
he'd been running.

Her younger brother was not a puzzle for Hannah.
She'd worked him out long ago as she'd watched his
sharp, technical mind evolve along with a healthy ambition. One of the new breed of incredibly young, incredibly bright men who had found their niche in the
world of high tech, Nick Jessett had come too far, too
quickly. He'd become arrogant during the past couple of years as his Bellevue-based firm exploded with
success, but Hannah had been tolerant, knowing that
sooner or later reality would catch up with him and
that he was intelligent enough to learn from the experience. She hadn't expected reality to take the shape of
Gideon Cage or to be so very nearly disastrous.

"How are you feeling?" Nick asked.

"Terrible."

"The doctor says that's normal."

Hannah stirred restlessly and then stilled as her
bandaged leg reminded her forcibly of its presence.
"He didn't mention that before the operation. Probably figured I'd cancel the whole thing. I might have
if I'd known it was going to be this bad. God, it hurts,
Nick."

"You'll be much better in a couple of days."

"Sure." She didn't believe it.

Nick's hand tightened on the bed railing. "Jesus,
Hannah, every time I think of you in that car and of
how bad it could have been. . . ." His voice trailed off.

"I know, I know," she soothed. "I realize I should
be counting my lucky stars that I got away with only
some bruises and this bad leg. It's just that right now

it's hard to count lucky stars. I'd rather count decimal places in a malpractice suit.''

"The nurses say Dr. Englehardt did a fantastic job," Nick told her anxiously.

"Don't worry, I'm not planning on suing the man." She managed a weary smile. "I must look awfully bad if you can't tell when I'm joking."

"Well, you're not at your best. Actually, you look pretty rotten at the moment."

"Honesty, thy name is younger brother." The dark relief of sleep was pulling at her again and the complaint came out slightly blurred. But there was something she wanted to ask before she surrendered again to the dreams. Something to do with spiders and snakes.

"Don't try to stay awake on my account," Nick said softly. "Get some sleep, Hannah. I'll be back this evening."

"Nick, what happened with Cage and the takeover bid? Everything's okay now, isn't it? He dropped the attack on Accelerated Design?"

"Let's just say he made his final move. It's all over, Hannah."

The words didn't sound right. They weren't sufficiently reassuring. With grim effort Hannah managed to stay awake a moment longer. "He's left you alone, hasn't he? He promised he would."

Her last conscious thought was that her brother looked unaccountably somber. "He's out of the picture, Hannah."

The relief she felt was marred by Nick's next sentence. "I just hope to hell you didn't sleep with him because then we both would have been had."

The next time she awoke with any alertness was the following morning. Hannah kept her eyes closed while she probed for sensation in her left leg. The pain seemed to be down to a dull throb. She decided to risk lifting her lashes. The first thing she saw was a bouquet of yellow roses and she grinned idiotically. If they were from Nick, they represented a great leap forward in his social development. If they were from her parents back East, they were appropriate and expected. If they were from someone on campus, they were very interesting. She reached out and picked up the card.

Be careful not to ask for what you want.
You just might get it.

Hannah's grin faded abruptly. Instinct warned her what the name on the card would be a split second before she read it. A local florist, apparently trying for an exotic touch, had used calligraphy to write *Gideon Cage* underneath the message. Nick's ominous words from the previous afternoon flashed into Hannah's bemused brain.

"Oh, hell."

A nurse popped into the room and caught the muttered words. "Leg still hurting? Only to be expected. You've got a long way to go before you're fully recovered. But each day will be a little better than the last and in a couple of months you'll be as good as new." The woman smiled the determinedly cheerful smile of the professional nurse who saves real sympathy for real suffering. She wasn't going to waste any on Hannah, apparently. She was wearing a name tag that identified her as Mrs. Broadcourt. "Doctor wants you on your feet as soon as possible. You're to start physical therapy this afternoon."

Hannah looked at her. "Are you kidding? I'll be lucky to make it from here to the bathroom."

The nurse smiled even more broadly. "If you need a bedpan, just ring for George."

"George?"

"He's on duty from eight to five this week. He'll be glad to assist you."

Hannah contemplated being assisted with a bedpan by a male nurse. She reminded herself of how wonderful it was that men were getting into nursing these days and discovering the nurturing side of their personalities. She thought about the young male sophomore she had guided toward a nursing career that spring, knowing instinctively that he would be happy in a caring profession. And then she assessed the distance from the bed to the bathroom.

"I think I can make it to the bathroom on my own," she advised Mrs. Broadcourt.

"Fine. I'll get a walker."

Hannah wondered how frequently Mrs. Broadcourt used George as a means of encouraging female patients to get on their feet.

Nick appeared in the doorway half an hour later, clearly on his way to work. He looked very up-and-coming in the gray suit and dark tie—ready to take his place among the movers and the shakers in the Silicon Valley North that was developing around Bellevue, Washington. Hannah took heart.

"Does that outfit mean you've still got a company to run?" she asked.

"Barely. God knows for how long." He came over to the bed. "Feeling better?"

"Thanks to George."

"George?" Nick cast a puzzled look at the flowers. "Is he the guy who sent the roses?"

"Not exactly. George is into bedpans, not flowers. The roses are from Gideon Cage." She gave her brother a level glance, waiting for an explanation.

Nick's mouth tightened. "Hannah, what happened down there in Vegas?"

"I tried a little salvation work. I haven't been able to figure out yet whether it was effective." Hannah struggled to a more elevated position on the pillows, wincing as the throbbing increased in her left knee. "Tell me what happened, Nick. I can't stand the suspense. Cage called off the takeover attempt, didn't he?"

"Oh, yes, he called it off."

"Then why all the cryptic comments? Why did I get that message on the card?"

"What message?" Nick leaned across the bed and glanced at the card that was still attached to the roses. He read it quickly and shook his head sardonically. "I think, sister dear, that you can forget about giving Gideon Cage any guidance counseling. He's way ahead of you. Way ahead of both of us." He straightened.

"Tell me what happened, damn it!"

"To put it simply, Cage never intended to take over Accelerated Design. He just wanted us to think he did. He bought a big chunk of stock and then made all the right moves to simulate a takeover bid. The activity in the stock market got everyone excited and drove the price of the stock sky-high. I and everyone else were properly terrorized. Yesterday he let it be known that he was willing to consider selling his stock back to us and bow out of the picture.''

A distinctly uneasy chill went down Hannah's spine. Perhaps it was just caused by incipient bed sores. Warily she eyed her brother. "I think I'm beginning to get the drift. By the time he offered to let you buy back his shares they were worth four times what he'd paid for them a few months ago.''

Nick sighed, running a hand through his neatly styled hair. "You've got it. Yesterday afternoon while you were sleeping off the anesthesia, I scrounged money from every source I could find. We had to liquidate a lot of assets, Hannah. Accelerated Design is now ass-high in debt. I cleaned out my own personal account and borrowed heavily on my line of credit at the bank.''

"Oh, my God." Hannah felt sick but it wasn't from the ache in her leg.

"Gideon Cage made a tidy bundle on the deal and then washed his hands of the whole thing. I'm stuck with a firm that will have trouble paying its light bill next month. But at least I've still got the company. It was a near miss, Hannah. We were lucky to survive. I think I'm going to have to pay a hell of a lot more attention to the management end of things. It may be time to leave the technical development to others. I should never have let Accelerated Design become so vulnerable.''

"He never intended to take over the firm and run it. He only wanted to make a quick kill." She touched the nearest of the yellow roses.

"He let us assume he intended a corporate raid and that's exactly what we did assume," Nick said quietly.

"He warned me about assumptions," Hannah murmured. Her fingers closed around the rose.

"Did you really go down there and talk to him about changing his career path?" Nick still couldn't believe it. There hadn't been time to argue about the trip after Hannah got back to Seattle. She'd been too busy checking into the hospital.

"You know me. A guidance counselor to the core. I really thought I knew what I was doing, Nick. I thought I had guessed what made him tick. Parts of him I could see quite clearly. But there are other elements in him that I couldn't quite grasp."

Nick shook his head. "He's hardly a liberal arts student floundering around looking for a career."

"I knew that." She made an impatient gesture with her hand. "But I thought I could make him see that he wouldn't be happy for long if he continues in his current direction."

"If you ask me, he's perfectly content with his current direction! It's made him rich. For Christ's sake, Hannah, whatever made you think you could offer guidance counseling to a man who thinks like a chess player?"

The rose started to come apart in Hannah's palm as she made a fist. "Just a feeling I had." She opened her hand and let the disintegrated flower fall into the wastebasket beside the bed. "The toughest part about being a counselor, Nick, is finding out that a lot of people won't take good advice. Not everyone wants to be put on the right path."

For the first time since Nick had entered the room, genuine amusement flared in his green eyes. "Well, at least I know for sure that you didn't sleep with him in an attempt to get him to stop his takeover bid."

"What makes you so sure?"

"This is the mood you get into whenever one of your counseled students fails to go in the direction you wanted him to go. You start fretting and worrying about his future. That's not quite the same way a woman scorned would act."

"How would you know? Scorning a lot of women these days?"

Nick started for the door. "Haven't got time for it. I'm too busy trying to save Accelerated Design. I'm barely making time for my workouts at the club. See you later, Hannah." He halted for a second, his hand on the door jamb. "Oh, by the way, Drake Armitage called me last night. He and his wife wanted to find out how you were getting along. I also got a call from the Andersons and the Barretts and a few others. You've got a lot of friends. Told them you'd probably be up to taking phone calls today and visitors tomorrow. That okay?"

"That's fine, Nick. Thanks."

"Armitage and his wife have joined my athletic club. They work out regularly. That Vicky sure does something for a leotard. If they'd made anthro instructors like that when I was in college I might have changed my major."

"Forget it," Hannah said with grave authority. "Most of the really fascinating anthropological sites are not conveniently located near fitness clubs or Alfa Romeo mechanics."

"You'd never guess Dr. Victoria Armitage didn't have access to a good fitness club all year long. Great pecs on that woman. See you later, Hannah." Nick disappeared into the hall.

He was right, Hannah thought briefly. Drake and Victoria Armitage, both visiting professors of anthropology who were scheduled to teach in the fall at the college where Hannah worked, were living testimonials to the value of physical fitness. They had introduced themselves to Hannah shortly after the local papers had carried an obituary on her aunt. The articles had mentioned that some of Elizabeth Nord's relatives lived in the Seattle area. Since they were on the faculty of the same college for which Hannah worked, it had been easy for the Armitages to locate her. She'd had coffee with them on a couple of occasions and had introduced them to Nick one evening when he'd accompanied her to a campus concert. Nick and the Armitages had found a common ground in their mutual interest in fitness.

Drake and Vicky were a pleasant enough couple if you liked the trendy, academic type, but Hannah wasn't all that comfortable in their company. She had decided it was partly because their chief topic of conversation around her was Elizabeth Nord's work. Their enthusiasm for it was overpowering at times, especially Victoria's.

But there was another reason why she preferred not to spend a great deal of time around Professor Victoria Armitage, Hannah admitted to herself as she gazed out the hospital room window. In some ways, Victoria and her respected work in cultural anthropology represented an alternate universe, one Hannah could have inhabited if she'd stuck to the path she'd originally chosen in college.

It had all seemed so clear-cut in the beginning: a straight shot from college freshman to Ph.D., then on to the faculty of some small but reputable college. At the start she hadn't really worried about which field to focus her energies on. It had seemed as though there was plenty of time. For the first three years she'd bounced cheerfully from the convolutions of history to the updated witchcraft of psychology. She'd experimented with philosophy and then with English literature. In between she had sampled a little radical politics, done a special studies paper on modern religious communes, and helped out in a local crisis clinic.

But somewhere along the line time began to run out. She'd reached the end of her junior year without having settled down to a particular field of study. Panic had set in. Then, in May of that year, Elizabeth Nord had made one of her rare visits to her sister's family and had casually inquired about Hannah's interest in cultural anthropology.

Embarrassed about the obviously undirected focus of her life, Hannah had immediately decided that cultural anthropology was as good a major as anything else. Fortunately she'd taken enough undergraduate courses in the subject to enable her to graduate with an anthropology major.

Telling herself that now she really had to settle down, she'd applied to graduate school and, thanks to a good, if somewhat eclectic academic record, had been accepted. The letter of recommendation from Elizabeth Nord probably hadn't hurt, either.

Determinedly Hannah had started out in the direction of a doctorate. She was pleased and somewhat surprised to discover that she had a genuine inclination for the subject matter of anthropology. She was fascinated by it. But she was also frustrated because so many of the people in the field seemed to become bogged down with the details of kinship theory and systems of religious behavior in various and assorted small tribes. Few of them took a step back to assess the long-range implications of their studies or the studies of others.

But Hannah had persisted for a while, even writing one or two well-received papers on the philosophical implications of anthropological work. More than one of her instructors told her she had a flair for writing about the subject matter of her field. All she needed was experience. She vowed to finish the Ph.D. program, do a little of the fieldwork so necessary to establish one's credentials in anthropology, and then settle down to a career teaching the subject. Since the name of the game was publish or perish, she figured she ought to be able to survive in the academic world because she could write.

It wasn't long, however, before she had once again found herself drifting, pulled in several different directions. One of the sidelines she found herself pursuing was counseling undergraduate students on what classes they should be taking to complete their majors. She proved to be astonishingly adept at it.

In the end she had simply run out of steam and surrendered. At the end of her first year in graduate school she had forced herself to acknowledge the fact that she wasn't ever going to finish. It had been a traumatic decision. There is nothing quite as pathetic in the academic world as the Ph.D. candidate who never makes it to the dissertation.

A different choice would have resulted in Hannah's having a Ph.D. and a career that would have put her at the heart of the academic environment instead of on the fringes where librarians, guidance counselors, coaches, and other assorted, nonacademic types were consigned. The papers she now wrote for the professional guidance counseling journals didn't count, at least not in the eyes of genuine academics.

Aunt Elizabeth hadn't seemed concerned by Hannah's decision. She had simply sent Hannah a brief note that said:

> Follow your instincts, Hannah. You won't go wrong. Women have such good instincts. It's a pity they don't act on them with greater intelligence.

There had been other occasional words of feminine wisdom from Elizabeth Nord down through the years but the comment about following her instincts was the bit Hannah had liked best. She did it on a regular basis when she was trying to guide others. When people had the sense to take Hannah's advice, they usually found themselves quite grateful to her.

She'd seen very little of her aloof, brilliant relative and knew that the rest of the family found her cold and distant. But Hannah had realized intuitively that Elizabeth Nord simply hadn't needed anyone else. She was complete within herself. A rare development in a human being. Sometimes Hannah wondered if Anna Warrick, the mathematician, had been like that. The family had only limited information on her. Her immediate relatives had found her something of an embarrassment. A woman who clearly did not know how to accept gracefully her proper role in the universe. About the lady artist who had scandalized the family at the turn of the century by running off to live in a Paris garret, even less was known. Her relatives had virtually disowned her. The fact that her paintings now brought vast sums would have been even more shocking to her parents.

From what little Hannah had learned, neither the artist, Cecily Sanders, nor the mathematician, Anna Warrick, had worried about what their contemporaries thought. Elizabeth Nord had been just as blithely unconcerned.

Hannah had opted to do as her aunt had suggested and had followed her intuition. She had decided that guidance counseling offered her the greatest opportunity for using her odd ability to direct others down suitable paths. It wasn't a talent that was in great demand anywhere except on college campuses, and even there it wasn't the sort of skill that paid very well. But Hannah liked the work. The part-time counseling job evolved into a full-time career. A lot of people egotistically thought they could give advice to others. Hannah knew for certain that she was brilliant at it. She was also fairly good at persuading others to act on her advice.

Knowing she was good at what she did, she was doubly dismayed when someone ignored her guidance. She glanced over the side of her bed and studied the crushed yellow rose in the wastebasket. One could live with the fact that one had failed. It was much harder to come to terms with having been made a fool.

She wondered how hard Gideon Cage was laughing.

GIDEON CAGE was not laughing. It occurred to him that he hadn't taken that kind of pleasure in a victory for a long time. There was usually, however, a certain sense of satisfaction that he had achieved the goal of his maneuvering. Even that seemed to be lacking this time around.

Gideon surfaced, drew a deep breath and shot back toward the far end of the pool underwater. It was the woman's fault, of course. Teaching her a lesson should have added an extra fillip to the final result of this particular siege, but it hadn't. He'd done her a favor, he told himself. He wondered how she'd taken the "good deed." And then he thought about how he would have reacted to her visit if he had really been planning on taking over Accelerated Design.

He reached the far end of the pool and hauled himself onto the edge, reaching for a towel. The morning sun was already threatening to turn hot even though it was only eight. There were no showgirls lounging by the pool at this time of day in Vegas. No one else at all, for that matter, except the waiter assigned to the poolside bar. Gideon heard the bar phone ring as he toweled dry and knew even before the waiter signalled that the summons was for him. He realized that there were times when he hated phones. Reluctantly he headed toward the bar. Without a word the receiver was handed to him.

"What is it, Steve?" Only Decker would be calling on this number at this hour.

"More news on Ballantine. The man's got some real money behind him this time, Gideon. He's done some wheeling and dealing with a few very high rollers, including the managers of a couple of pension funds. He's going to have the cash to put up a fight for Surbrook."

"Don't sound so astonished, Steve. He's Cyrus Ballantine's son, remember? Stands to reason he'd have inherited some of his father's ability. There's nothing to get excited about. We'll take care of him when the time comes. Did you give the message about the flowers to Mary Ann?''

Steve Decker hesitated, clearly not wanting to be distracted from his course. The problem with people such as Decker, Gideon decided, was that they had trouble adjusting to directional shifts. Sometimes you had to nudge them.

"I gave her the message. She had them wired yesterday. They should have been in the hospital this morning." Decker paused, as if just realizing something. "The cane was for real, then?''

"It was for real. The lady was trying to walk a thin line between painkillers and alcohol the whole time she was here."

"Well, at least she was different. She seemed sort of nice. I liked her. Now about Ballantine. What do you say I see if I can't dig up a pipeline into his office? There must be someone around who owes us a favor and who has inside information on that new investment group Ballantine's put together. Right now I'm having to work with a lot of second-hand information."

"Go ahead, Steve. See what you can find out." *But it won't be much,* Gideon added silently. "I'm coming back tomorrow, by the way."

Gideon nodded to the bartender as he hung up the phone. Ballantine's objectives were quite obvious. Gideon remembered a time when his own actions had been equally obvious. At least he'd developed some degree of finesse over the years.

Picking up the towel he walked back toward the lobby. That afternoon when he took his second swim of the day he'd try getting the bartender to make an-

other margarita the way he'd made them for Hannah.
A change of pace from Scotch. He almost always
drank Scotch. A creature of habit. He hoped Hannah
Jessett's words weren't going to haunt him much
longer. The more he thought about them, the more he
found them annoying. It was all very well to toler-
antly accuse Steve Decker of having difficulties adjusting to directional shifts. Somehow it wasn't the
same when it came to himself.

Two hours later he gave in to the impulse that had
been nagging him all morning. He picked up his room
phone and called his Tucson office. His secretary came
on the line at once. "Mary Ann, I want the name and
number of the hospital where you sent the roses."

"The hospital, sir?"

"Just do it, Mary Ann."

"Yes, sir." Middle-aged and looking forward to
early retirement, Mary Ann Cromwell did not question her boss's orders. She had the number for him a
moment later.

"Thanks, Mary Ann. I'll see you tomorrow." Gideon said and disconnected before his secretary could
say anything else. Then he redialed. A short time later
a groggy feminine voice came on the line.

"Hello?"

"I called to see if you got the flowers." He didn't
bother to identify himself and then realized belatedly
that any number of men might have sent flowers.
"The yellow roses."

There was a stark pause on the other end. "Message received and understood." The phone was
dropped abruptly back into its cradle.

Gideon sat staring at the dead receiver and tried to
think of the last time anyone had dared hang up on

him. He redialed very deliberately. Perhaps they'd been cut off.

Gideon was ready when Hannah's somewhat suspicious voice came back on the line. "Did they tell you in guidance counseling school that the work was easy? Sometimes it's tough to sell salvation. How's the leg?"

"In somewhat the same shape as Accelerated Design; down but not out. Please go away, Mr. Cage. I have written you off as a lost cause. Furthermore, you are not on my doctor's list of therapeutic exercises." Once again she hung up the phone.

This time Gideon didn't redial. Instead he sat staring out at the distant mountains and wondered why he was feeling vaguely disappointed that Hannah had so easily given up trying to save him. She had seemed so earnest about the matter a couple of days earlier. Then he reflected on how she might have received his call if he'd actually let her deflect him from his real goal.

He was behaving erratically. Vegas was no good to him in his present mood. He wouldn't be able to concentrate on the cards or the dice. That was where he worked out the few unpredictable quirks left in his nature, but even when gambling, Gideon never allowed himself to become too unpredictable. Habits. *Survival habits*. He might as well go back to Tucson.

He got up from his chair and opened a bureau drawer. Inside was the deck of cards he'd lifted from Hannah's purse when he'd helped her to the door of her hotel room. He removed the pack and fanned it out on the table, his fingers moving lightly over the slightly frayed edges that marked a few of the higher cards. He had felt those faintly tagged cards the night he'd shuffled them in front of Hannah. It had amused him to realize that she intended to cheat. She just didn't look the type. He'd actually experienced a twinge of admiration. The lady had guts. Very few people had the nerve to try cheating him these days.

Gideon was aware of a distinctly self-righteous sensation when he told himself he hoped Hannah Jessett had learned a lesson. Unfortunately, the feeling wasn't any more satisfying than the easy killing he'd made on Accelerated Design.

Hollow victories. Hannah had been wrong when she'd guessed that they had grown progressively unsatisfying over the years. The truth was they had been unsatisfying from the beginning. A career built on revenge was probably fated to lack much in the way of real intellectual and emotional satisfaction. Ambition, as a motivator, could probably be moderated. Revenge could not. It was either an all-consuming drive or it didn't warrant the label of revenge. Gideon entertained himself with the whimsical notion of giving Hugh Ballantine that piece of advice.

But it wouldn't do much good. Nine years ago, Gideon knew, he wouldn't have listened to such advice himself. Nothing burned more fiercely than the white hot fire of revenge. And after it burnt itself out there was nothing left but to keep going in the same direction.

Besides, Gideon thought as he restacked the cards and put them back in the drawer, there was no reason to stop doing what he did for a living. After all, he was damn good at it. The final analysis of the profits he had made on Accelerated Design proved it.

Gideon went to stand at the window, staring out at the broiling landscape from the safety of his air-conditioned room. He needed Vegas, but he wasn't in the mood to stay there any longer. He'd go back to Tucson for a few weeks and then try Las Vegas again.

After all, he usually made two trips each summer.

Habit.

THE WALK DOWN the stairs to the apartment house mailbox had been painful but manageable. Hannah felt a distinct sense of triumph as she opened the box in the charmingly ornate alcove that served as an entrance hall for the old red brick apartment building. It only went to show that triumph, like everything else in the world, was relative, she decided philosophically. Two months ago she hadn't thought twice about the freedom with which she went up and down stairs.

She'd gotten rid of the crutches after being home from the hospital for a week. Now she was back on the cane, but this time around it was a sign of progress. Dr. Englehardt had been pleased.

"How long until I can get around without the cane?" Hannah had demanded the last time she saw him.

"Patience, Hannah. You're moving along very rapidly. Don't rush things. I'm very pleased with the results. Very pleased, indeed. Dr. Adams, who assisted me, agreed that the damage was rather extensive." Dr. Englehardt was in his late forties and had the usual surgeon's ego. Hannah forgave him, because he was short and pudgy and quite brilliant. Also, she was objective enough to realize that Dr. Englehardt probably wouldn't have been a good surgeon without his oversize ego. Surgeons were similar to fighter pilots: they needed the right stuff. The *right stuff* implied style as well as intelligence and courage.

Style implied an ego. Dr. Englehardt had put her back on her feet. He was entitled to a little stroking.

"I saw the X rays." She'd smiled warmly, quite willing to offer his ego the petting it needed. "You did a fantastic job. I can't thank you enough."

He'd beamed. "Why, thank you, Hannah."

"But I still want to know how much longer I'll be on this cane."

Englehardt had sighed. "Probably a couple of months."

"Damn."

But here she was three weeks later hobbling around fairly well. Mustn't complain, Hannah told herself bracingly as she withdrew the contents of her mailbox. A positive outlook was important. And nobody liked a whiner. Too bad. She had a hunch she could get very proficient at whining and complaining.

The round-trip airline ticket to Santa Inez Island had arrived. Hannah propped her cane against the shelf in front of the mailboxes and leaned back to steady herself. Quickly she zipped open the envelope from the travel agent. Then she smiled. She would be on her way to the sunny Caribbean in less than two weeks. Visions of strengthening her left leg with long walks on the sandy beach in front of her aunt's home danced through her mind. Hannah decided she would buy a new bikini. She needed one. She didn't do a lot of swimming there in Seattle.

"Hannah!"

Closing the mailbox, Hannah glanced around. Through the iron gate that served as a security door she saw Drake and Victoria Armitage hailing her from the other side of the tree-lined street. They were jogging in full regalia. Victoria's mane of burnished cop-

per hair was held away from her classic face with a
green sweatband that coordinated beautifully with her
designer jogging pants. She wore a sleek, emerald
green tank top that emphasized the new style of well-
developed feminine musculature. Good pecs, Nick had
observed. Also good lats and triceps, Hannah decided as the familiar, ambivalent mood that Victoria
engendered settled on her. She stepped outside onto
the sidewalk, idly holding open the security gate.

Drake's outfit was black and white, right down to
his black-and-white wrist bands. He was a good-
looking man with blue eyes and light brown hair that
was styled, not cut, and just the proper amount of
dynamic assertiveness in his jaw. An excellent foil for
his wife.

Fashionable Nike sport shoes made virtually no
sound on the pavement as Drake and Vicky advanced
at a quick, disciplined speed. Handsome faces
gleamed with sweat even though the June day was
quite brisk.

They weren't alone in their athletic endeavors that
morning. Several other joggers had already gone past
Hannah's Capitol Hill apartment house. The whole
world seemed to be going fitness crazy. She watched
Drake and Victoria approach, trying to remember
what one offered a jogger in the way of refreshment.

"Good morning," she said politely as they slowed
to a halt in front of her. Somehow she felt obliged to
be polite. It was a small penance she paid for her irrational ambivalence. "Can you come in for a glass of
mineral water or something?" Was mineral water still
in for the fitness set? Hannah wasn't sure. These
things changed so quickly.

"Sounds great," Drake enthused, dashing the sweat off the back of his neck with his hand. "I think we've put in enough mileage today, haven't we, Vicky?"

"Definitely." Vicky stopped, hands on hips, inhaling deeply. "How's the leg doing, Hannah?"

"Much better, thank you." Nobody likes a whiner. Hannah forced a broader smile. "Come on up." She had a vision of their sweat-soaked bodies on her living room sofa and added brightly, "We can go out on the deck."

"Here, let me give you a hand." Drake put his fingers under her arm and propelled her forcibly back through the alcove and up the first three steps. The cane came off the ground entirely and Hannah grabbed for the rail.

"No, thanks! Please, I'm fine." Hastily she broke free of the grip before he could launch her to the top of the staircase. Not wanting to seem ungrateful she went on in a hurried mumble, "The doctor wants me to get as much exercise as possible."

"Maybe you should come down to the club," Victoria suggested, loping easily up the stairs ahead of Hannah. "We could get you in on a visitor's pass. Or your brother could arrange it, for that matter. You could work out on the equipment. Probably be great therapy."

"Uh, I don't think I'm quite ready for that." Hannah pushed open the door of her airy one-bedroom apartment and gestured toward the tiny scrap of a balcony. "Have a seat."

She watched them move through the tropical setting of her living room and could almost read their thoughts. Nick referred to the conglomeration of wicker, rattan, and ferns as Neo Import Shop. The

South Seas look was out, he'd informed her and had probably never really been in except among people who shopped at discount import shops on the wharf. But Hannah loved islands almost as much as Elizabeth Nord had loved them. She'd had no compunction at all about ignoring the trend toward Italian design in interiors in favor of maintaining her artificial island cottage.

Drake and Victoria Armitage contrasted sharply with what Hannah thought of as the island charm of her apartment. Two more Yuppies in a world that seemed to be filling up with the genus. Drake and Vicky were of the species *academia*. It was a relatively small but highly evolved example of the basic group. This species prided itself on being clever enough to see the subtle humor of ordering an expensive California zinfandel with roasted red pepper fettuccini. This species could also wage esoteric, academic, and totally irrelevant arguments while consuming both the zinfandel and the fettuccini.

Hannah saw Drake and Vicky quickly and expertly scan the heavily laden shelves of her bookcase. She knew they weren't terribly impressed. Her collection of books was highly eclectic, to put it mildly. It was unfocused, covering in uneven depth everything from the history of magic to basket weaving. Her personal library represented the kind of interests the academic world finds most amusing: a *layman*'s interests.

Hannah was still idly putting together her mental construct of Drake and Vicky Armitage. Most of the pieces were in place. Drake, she sensed, was going to make it up the academic ladder because he was good at handling academic politics. He got himself on the right faculty committees, went to the right teas, and managed to make himself useful at the right levels. He knew instinctively who held power in his world and he knew how to get close to those people.

Vicky, on the other hand, would climb the academic ladder using real brilliance. She would be the one whose publishing record would eventually guarantee her a slot on any faculty.

The marriage between Drake and Vicky, Hannah figured, would last as long as they were useful to each other. At this point Drake found that some of the gleam of his wife's intellectual abilities rubbed off on him in faculty meetings. His name had appeared alongside hers on a couple of monographs, although Hannah privately wondered how much he'd really contributed. Vicky, on the other hand, found Drake's understanding of how the faculty bureaucracy functioned extremely useful. It was an alliance made in academic heaven and would probably fall apart with little regret on either side the day they were offered good positions at opposite ends of the country. Hannah wondered who would get custody of the Armitage's wine collection.

"I'll help you with the drinks," Vicky said amiably, half way to the balcony. She swung around and came toward the kitchen. "You've got your hands full there. Here, I'll handle the mail for you."

She removed the letters from Hannah's fingers before a protest could be made. "Going on a trip?" Vicky indicated the tickets.

"Down to the Caribbean. I'm going to close up my aunt's house." Hannah opened the refrigerator and was relieved to find two bottles of mineral water that her brother must have left behind on his last visit. She couldn't stand the stuff herself.

"Oh, that's right. I remember you said something about it a few weeks ago." Vicky plucked the bottles from Hannah's arm and opened drawers at random in the white-tiled kitchen until she found an opener. "What a fantastic opportunity."

"Opportunity?"

Vicky shook her head in wonder. "Just think, the chance to see Elizabeth Nord's private library. All her notes and records; the books that she read and maybe even drafts of the ones she wrote. There might even be some unfinished work that hasn't yet been published. God, what I wouldn't give for that opportunity. What a shame she didn't leave it all to an academic library. I wonder why not?"

Hannah shrugged, watching in resignation as Vicky Armitage made herself at home in the kitchen. Short of tripping Vicky with the cane, there wasn't any way of stopping her. "She said in her will that she wanted me to have the stuff."

"You really should turn everything over to a qualified professional in the field, Hannah. Her papers and notes should be available to experts. They're academic treasures."

Unspoken, of course, was the implication that Hannah Jessett was no expert and was probably incapable of appreciating an academic treasure if it rose up on its hind legs and bit her. *I'm being petty and childish and mean-spirited*, Hannah admonished herself silently. Just the same, she decided it would be a cold day in hell before she turned her aunt's papers over to Victoria or Drake Armitage.

"I'm not sure yet what I'll find or what I'll do with her records," Hannah demurred.

Vicky glanced at her. "Your aunt's name was a household word in my home all the time I was growing up. My father had the greatest interest in her work. In fact, I believe he collaborated with her for a while on one project. Nothing ever came of it, unfortunately."

"Hey, are the drinks ready? I'm dying of thirst out here," Drake called.

"We're on our way." Vicky picked up the tray of chilled mineral water, ice, and glasses and started toward the balcony. "You know, Hannah, I think I'll massage that leg of yours for a few minutes. I've been studying the shiatzu technique and I've worked out a way of combining it with traditional pressure-point massage. It will really loosen up those tight ligaments."

Hannah protested politely as she levered herself down onto a lounge chair and stretched her feet out in front of her. "That's quite all right, Vicky. I'm already getting massage therapy at the clinic twice a week and I don't think..."

But Vicky was already leaning down, her hands closing around the injured knee just below the cuff of Hannah's safari-style walking shorts.

Hannah thought she was going to faint from the pain. For several seconds she couldn't even speak. The woman was every bit as strong as she looked. It was rather frightening. Even the professional masseuse at the clinic didn't have that kind of strength.

"Vicky, no! Please, that's enough. Leave me alone." She pushed at the other woman's hand, no longer worrying about being polite. "Stop it!"

Chagrined, Vicky straightened. "I'm sorry, did I hurt you?"

Hannah took several deep breaths. "It's all right. I know you meant well."

"Vicky's really into physical therapy," Drake explained half apologetically.

"Yes, I can see that." Hannah stifled a sudden, acute longing for a shot of tequila or a painkiller instead of the mineral water.

Life was a constant learning experience. A smart woman tried to pick up lessons along the way and apply them. Today was a case in point, Hannah told herself. This was the last time she would invite passing fitness fanatics in for a drink.

Chapter Three

HIS ATTENTION was focused on a deck of cards. Unfortunately, it wasn't the deck of cards being dealt in front of him. The mistake cost Gideon five hundred dollars in the blink of an eye.

Las Vegas was not working a hell of a lot better the second time around.

"C'est la guerre," he said easily to the dealer, who smiled back with well-feigned commiseration. "I'll try again later." He kept his disgust to himself as he swung around to slip through the milling crowds.

Endless rows of elaborate chandeliers that might have been designed for a Hollywood movie set cast their flattering light on everything from Bermuda shorts to tuxedoes. The continuous metallic clang of slot machines provided a background noise that somehow complemented the intensity around the card tables. It was nearly midnight and the casino was in full swing.

Gideon had arrived on the seven-fifteen flight from Tucson and had checked into the same towering hotel on the Strip where he always stayed. Then he had dressed in the dark evening jacket and slacks and the crisp white shirt he always wore at night in Vegas. Habit. The word was still haunting him, just as the memory of Hannah's deck of cards haunted him.

It was time to give the tables a break. Deprived of his normal concentration, his luck had become far too

erratic tonight. Something else was missing, too. The
small shot of adrenaline he usually got when he put
money on the line didn't seem to be taking hold this
evening. He could only hope that Hannah Jessett
hadn't ruined Vegas for him. Gideon headed for the
bar that overlooked the gambling floor. Maybe another kind of mood elevator would prove more help-
ful.

The twelve-year-old Scotch produced by a pretty
woman wearing a very small, sequined tutu did something, but fifteen minutes later Gideon wasn't certain
exactly what had been accomplished. The ambivalence was new. He didn't like it.

Vegas had always been the flip side of his daily life,
the alternative version of the war he waged in the
business world. It was supposed to offer more of an
element of unpredictability as Hannah had guessed,
but somehow the yearly visits had become as predictable as the results of a corporate raid. She had been
right. It wasn't that he always won here; it was that he
always came away with the same fleeting sense of excitement from the action.

Almost always. Tonight he wasn't even getting that
much out of it, and the knowledge was beginning to
eat at him. It was more than just the gambling that
wasn't working right lately, it was his whole life. For
the first time in a long while he wondered what would
have happened if he'd taken a different path nine years
ago.

There had been other things in his life then. The
cartography had been important. There was a woman
who had been important. There had been a sense of
adventure about the future, a feeling that he was
making progress. Tonight he could see only a flat,

endless road stretching before him; his business and his yearly visits to Las Vegas were the only destinations. Neither seemed able to draw any spark of enthusiasm or optimism from him this evening.

A little guidance counseling was a dangerous thing, Gideon decided.

He took his time with the Scotch, seeking the sensual pleasure he knew he should be getting from twelve-year-old liquor. But it seemed as elusive as the card-playing adrenaline. He wondered how much of a lesson Hannah Jessett had really learned from him. Gideon was contemplating that in great detail when he finally decided that the nagging feeling of being watched could no longer be ignored. Idly he leaned back in his chair and let his eyes sweep the crowd in the bar.

When he saw Hugh Ballantine lounging on a stool no more than fifteen feet away, Gideon acknowledged that there were some serious drawbacks to being a creature of habit. Ballantine's familiar blue eyes met his and the younger man smiled. The smile was vaguely familiar, too. So was the red hair. Hugh Ballantine was the reincarnation of his father.

Gideon lifted his glass half an inch in response and waited. Slowly, as though there were all the time in the world, Ballantine came down off the stool and started forward. He was very cool, very controlled, an element of caution in his riveting blue gaze. Gideon recognized the manner. He hadn't forgotten the feel of discovering the sense of power brought on by the first big hunt. A wise man respected that power and was wary of it. A fool rushed headlong into the euphoric fog and ended up at the bottom of a cliff. Ballantine was not a fool.

Gideon spoke first, deciding to spare Hugh the necessity of finding a brilliant opening line. Finding those lines was a strain at times when you were thirty years old.

"An acquaintance of mine warned me that I was becoming a creature of habit. You've just proven her point. Does everyone in the whole world know when I head for Vegas?"

Ballantine shrugged and sat down on the other side of the small, round table. "Anyone who wants to know. You come here a couple of times each summer. It wasn't hard to find out which hotel you favor, either."

"You find my life-style so fascinating?"

Hugh leaned his elbows on the table, his drink planted squarely in front of him. He smiled again. Gideon studied the feral expression and thought about how frequently he, himself, used it. It could be extremely intimidating to a potential victim. No one found it comfortable to look at a grinning shark, not even another shark.

"I find everything you think, say, or do fascinating, Mr. Cage. I'm sure you know the feeling."

"Admiration from the younger generation is always gratifying." Gideon tried some more of the Scotch. "Are you going to start following me around like a lost puppy?"

Ballantine shook his head. "I'm here tonight only because I wanted to talk to you for a few minutes. Alone. I would like you to know what I'm doing."

It was Gideon's turn to smile. "You don't have to spell it out," he said gently. "I know exactly what you're doing. Do you think you can pull it off?"

The brilliant blue eyes flared for an instant the way a predator's gaze flickers before the final leap. "I'm more interested in finding out if you think I can do it."

Gideon gave him a considering glance. "It depends."

"On what?" Ballantine was genuinely curious. A smart younger shark was always willing to learn.

"On how badly you want to win," Gideon said.

"I want to win, Cage. I want it very badly." Absolute conviction underlined every word. "I'm going to crush you."

"Practice the melodrama while you shave, not in front of the opposition."

Ballantine regarded him with interest. "That's a tip?"

"I took a guidance counselor to dinner a couple of weeks ago. She was fond of handing out tips. Thought I'd try it myself. It makes for light, casual conversation, don't you think? Especially when you know the other person probably won't act on it."

"You underestimate me, Gideon. I'm more than happy to learn from you. In fact, I want to pull this off in a style that will bring back some memories for you. I'd like you to be aware of all the subtle similarities between what's going to happen this year and what happened nine years ago."

"I'm sure your father would be proud," Gideon murmured.

"Yes." Ballantine waited for a heartbeat. "Too bad he isn't around to appreciate the final results."

Gideon read the fierce accusation in the other man's face and sighed. "Believe it or not, I'm sorry he isn't around, too."

"The hell you are."

"I didn't kill him, Hugh."

"You killed him. As surely as if you'd slit his throat." Ballantine stood up.

Gideon watched him. "Would you believe me if I told you that I'm beginning to think he's had his revenge?"

"Bullshit."

Gideon smiled thinly and swirled the Scotch in his glass. "Somehow I thought you'd see it that way."

Ballantine stared down at the table, following the movement of the amber liquid in the glass for a few seconds as if mildly fascinated by it. "I just wanted you to know. I wanted to tell you in person."

"It wasn't necessary."

Ballantine nodded abruptly. "I can see that now. You already know what I'm doing and why."

"You're Cyrus Ballantine's son," Gideon said. "I knew him better than I've ever known any other man. Therefore I know you. That's your biggest single disadvantage, Hugh."

"Because you think you'll be able to predict my actions? No, Cage. It may well turn out to be my ace in the hole. I'm not just a copy of my father, but if you believe I am then you'll make some interesting mistakes." He turned and disappeared into the crowd.

Gideon sat for a long time at the table. He finished the Scotch and ordered another. Halfway through the third one he decided to make a phone call.

Steve Decker was half asleep when he came on the line. Gideon almost envied him for a moment. Decker's wife, a warm, happy woman who was utterly devoted to her husband, was probably waiting impatiently in bed. She would undoubtedly have a few choice words to say about her husband's boss, who thought he could call at any hour of the day or night. Angie Decker was very protective of her spouse. It might be interesting, Gideon thought, to have a woman feel that protective about him.

"I'm sorry to get you out of bed, Steve, but I wasn't sure when I'd be able to call in the morning and I didn't want anyone trying to leave a message for me here at the hotel tomorrow. You know how Mary Ann panics if she can't find me when she wants me."

Steve's agile brain leaped to the most important question. "Where are you going?"

"I thought I'd go on up to Washington."

"Washington! But that Maryland project is under control. Why on earth do you want to go there?"

"State of, not D.C."

"Seattle? You're heading for Seattle? But why?"

"Thought I'd tie up a few loose ends with Accelerated Design."

Decker sounded utterly bewildered. "But, Gideon, there are no loose ends. There never are any loose ends!"

"I'm not so sure," Gideon said, trying to sound appropriately shrewd and businesslike.

"Well, I am. I put through the last of the paperwork yesterday. Gideon, you're supposed to be in Vegas for a week. You always go to Vegas for a week at this time of year!"

"Does it strike you, Steve, that I have become somewhat predictable?"

"Good God! Is that what this is all about? Are you worried about becoming predictable?" Decker's tone carried the profound shock of a man who values above all the comforts of a predictable life.

Maybe he'd value them, too, Gideon thought, if he were getting the comforts. All he seemed to have acquired from predictability was a sense of weariness. He almost wished he could relive the rush of emotion that he knew Ballantine was feeling tonight. "Steve, I really don't want to talk about this tonight. I just wanted someone to know that I'd left Vegas so no one would get overly excited tomorrow when he or she couldn't reach me. I'll check in with you in a day or two. In the meantime, hold the fort for me."

"But, Gideon . . ."

"There's one more thing, Steve."

"What's that?" Decker asked warily.

"I need the address of Nick Jessett's sister. The woman with the cane."

There was a long silence. "You need it tonight?"

"I'm afraid so," Gideon said apologetically. Angie was going to be furious.

Decker let out his breath in an unheard oath. "I'll have it for you in an hour."

"Thanks, Steve." As politely as he could, Gideon hung up in his assistant's ear. Then he started dialing airlines.

Back in Tucson, Angie Decker sat up in bed, frowning. "That was Cage?"

Decker finished replacing the receiver and nodded. He yawned as he ran a hand through his thinning hair. "That was Cage."

"Is something wrong?" Angie was willing to hold her fire until she determined whether or not the phone call had been generated out of a real emergency.

"Not unless you consider Gideon Cage going crazy as something wrong," Steve said thoughtfully.

To his surprise Angie didn't explode. "Actually," she said calmly, "it's a rather interesting idea."

HANNAH WAS STRUGGLING with the cane, her tote, an umbrella, and a bag of groceries as she approached her front door the next morning. A familiar morning drizzle had made the walk to the grocery store more of an event than usual. The cane tended to slip a bit on wet surfaces, and it had been impossible to keep the umbrella properly positioned while she carried the bag. In the end she had abandoned the rain protection in favor of concentrating on her footing. As a result her hair was damp and turning frizzy.

She was debating about the wisdom of trying for the mail on top of everything else, when she stepped into the apartment building entranceway and saw Gideon Cage lounging on the bottom step. He got to his feet at once.

Hannah said the first words that came into her head. "People in this building are getting far too casual about security. Who let you inside the gate?"

"A very nice man who looked like James Dean. He and his boyfriend said they were your neighbors."

"What are you doing here, Gideon?"

"Would you believe me if I said I came by for a little counseling?" He smiled at her as he reached out to take the sack of groceries but there was a strange wariness in his eyes.

Hannah brushed aside his dry question. She looked at him searchingly. "My brother said it was all over. He said you were out of the picture."

"There are a few minor loose ends," Gideon began carefully.

"I don't believe you. Have you changed your mind? Decided to try to take over the company after all?"

"If I said yes would you offer me another game of cards?"

"I can't make the offer, can I? You stole my deck." She realized that she was following him up the stairs to her apartment. There wasn't much else she could do. He had her groceries.

"I didn't steal the cards. I kept them as a souvenir." He paused outside her door, waiting for her to fish out the key. "Do you always dress as if you're heading out on safari?"

She chose to ignore the question. "Gideon, tell me what this is all about. I'm busy getting ready for my trip to the Caribbean. I don't have time for playing games with you." She shoved the key in the lock and twisted it with a vengeance.

"I don't need any more games. I've been trying to play them in Las Vegas for the past twenty-four hours. No fun." He unzipped the lightweight windbreaker that was all the protection he had against the rain.

"My heart would bleed for you except that I'm kind of busy at the moment." She dropped the leather and linen tote bag and sank down wearily into the nearest cushioned rattan chair.

"The leg still hurts?" Gideon put the groceries in the kitchen and came to stand in the doorway.

"Occasionally it hurts like hell."

"Is now one of the occasions?" he asked.

"I'll make a deal with you, Gideon. You don't waste any false sympathy on me and I won't waste any on you, okay?" She closed her eyes and reached down to lightly massage the knee through the fabric of her olive green bush pants. She shouldn't have tried walking to the store this morning. It was about one block too far for comfort. Now her leg would ache for a good hour.

She didn't hear Gideon cross the room but the instant his fingers settled in the vicinity of her knee she stiffened. Without opening her eyes, she said very evenly, "Touch that leg and you're a dead man."

He pulled away. "I get the feeling you mean that."

Hannah looked up at him from under half-closed lids. "The last person who tried to do me the favor of massaging my knee had a Ph.D. and she nearly killed me. Your qualifications aren't nearly as impressive. No telling what might happen if I let you try your hand at massage. I might never walk again."

"You don't trust me." It was a statement, not a question.

"About as much as I'd trust a junkyard dog," she agreed cheerfully. Hannah watched as he moved across the room to examine her bookcase. "What are you doing here, Gideon?"

"I'm not sure." He reached up and pulled down a copy of *The Amazons of Revelation Island*. "But if we're going to talk trust, it seems to me I'm the one who should be cautious." He glanced up from reading the inscription on the flyleaf of the book. It was to Hannah from her aunt.

Hannah had memorized the inscription long ago. It read: "To Hannah with a reminder that we must sometimes shape our own reality." She met Gideon's eyes. "If you're here to complain about the fact that I rigged the cards the night I invited you to draw for the shares, forget it. The game was irrelevant, anyway, wasn't it?"

"No sense of shame at all?" he mocked, closing the book and replacing it on the shelf.

"None, I'm afraid. I had my priorities that night. My honor as a gambler wasn't high on the list."

"Way behind your brother's best interests." He nodded. "I can understand that." Gideon took the large, fan-back wicker chair across from her, his mouth curving briefly in amusement as he dodged a huge fern that hung from the ceiling. He looked around at the rest of the furnishings.

"Gideon, for the last time, why are you here?"

"I flew in from Vegas early this morning."

"Oh, yes. The second trip of the summer."

"How well you know me," he murmured.

She rubbed her knee. "You always go to Vegas at this time of year."

"I know," he sighed.

"So why did you leave the bright lights of the Strip for the drizzle of Seattle?"

He leaned his head back against the fanned back of his chair. "I'm still not sure. I think it has something to do with getting a firsthand look at history repeating itself."

Hannah sensed the odd weariness in him and frowned. "Gideon..."

"Could I have a cup of coffee? I didn't get much sleep."

She gritted her teeth briefly. "Help yourself."

He uncoiled from the chair and disappeared into her small kitchen. Hannah listened to him opening cupboard doors and filling the kettle. He was going to make instant. At least he wasn't complaining, as her brother did, that she didn't own an espresso machine or keep unground coffee beans safely stored in the freezer to maintain their flavor. When he came back into the room a few minutes later Gideon carried two cups. He set one down beside Hannah, who had to bite off the automatic thank you.

"All right. Tell me about history repeating itself," she invited as ungraciously as possible.

"Are you really interested?"

"It might be the only way of getting rid of you." She stirred the coffee and tried to ignore the ache in her leg.

"It's great to feel so wanted." He resumed his seat and stretched out his legs.

Hannah drowned her comment beneath a sip of too-hot coffee. For instant the stuff wasn't bad. Gideon must have made a lot of it in his past.

"Someone's after me, Hannah."

She nearly choked on the thick brew. "After you!"

"A man named Hugh Ballantine. He's dedicating his life to crushing me. Do you think I should be flattered?"

"I realize that the business world, like the food chain, requires predators but it's much more fun for the rest of us when they hunt each other instead of people like my brother."

He winced. "Coming from a woman who was anxious to save me from myself not so long ago, that's a little harsh, don't you think?"

"I tend to be a little short-tempered when my leg is bothering me."

Gideon put down his coffee cup, an air of sudden determination in his eyes. "Move over to the sofa. I'm going to massage that knee for you."

"Over my dead body." She calmly sipped her coffee and ignored him.

"Hannah, if I hurt you, you can just tell me. I promise I'll stop."

"Ah, but I don't trust you, remember? What good is a promise from someone you can't trust?"

"You tell me. You're the one who was using a marked deck the night I took you out to dinner." He took the coffee cup from her hand and more or less hauled her to her feet.

Sensing the inevitability of the situation, Hannah surrendered. She allowed herself to be settled on the sofa, her leg stretched out along the flower-print cushions. Gideon went down on one knee and touched her leg through the khaki pants with a gentleness that was astounding.

All the difference in the world, Hannah thought in relief. Vicky's touch had been powerful and painful. Gideon's hands contained strength and power but he knew how to control both. Beneath his massaging fingers the tight muscles of her leg began to relax. The next thing she knew, Hannah began to relax inwardly as well.

"So tell me about the guy who wants to crush you," she heard herself say before she could think.

"He's the son of a former partner of mine."

"Former?"

"His name was Cyrus Ballantine. He was about fifteen years older than I was and he was a brilliant businessman. I learned a lot from him. Just about everything I know, in fact. We went into business together. We formed an investment syndicate."

Hannah closed her eyes as the warm relief of muscle relaxation took hold. This sort of thing could become addictive, she decided. "What happened?"

"It's a long story. I won't bore you with all the details. In the end, after a great deal of skillful maneuvering, my good friend and mentor, Cyrus, left me holding the bag of a bankrupt syndicate while he walked away with most of the assets and used them to set up another investment syndicate. The whole thing was really brilliantly handled," Gideon added reflectively as his fingers found the long muscle just above the knee and went to work on it. "I never knew what hit me until the dust had settled."

Hannah slanted him a curious glance. "Where's Cyrus today?"

"Looking out at me from his son's eyes."

"The father is dead?" she pressed.

"His son thinks I killed him."

Hannah thought about that. She felt the strength in Gideon's hands, considered the layers of steel in the man, and decided that Gideon might be capable of murder under certain circumstances. "Did you?"

"Cyrus Ballantine died of a heart attack a couple of years ago," Gideon told her shortly. "I never touched him."

"But the son thinks you did?"

Gideon moved his head in a slow nod. "He holds me morally responsible for the heart attack."

"Why?"

"Because after Cyrus left me behind in the mud of financial ruin, I decided to take revenge," Gideon explained. "At the age of thirty, I dedicated my life to it. I hounded the man, moving in on the companies he wanted and grabbing them first, even if it cost me far too much. I systematically destroyed his reputation as a man who could find the shrewdest investments. Within three years I was the one his clients came to when they wanted to hand their money over to someone who knew where to put it. Cyrus Ballantine filed for bankruptcy a few years ago. He never really came out of it. He was no longer a winner and he couldn't handle that.''

Another piece of the puzzle that was Gideon Cage suddenly fell into place. Hannah realized with a strange twist in her stomach that she had subconsciously never stopped working on the problem, not even after she had assumed she wouldn't see him again. Now, at least, she knew what had tripped the initial switch that had locked him on target. He had been like a guided missile for nine years, unable to veer off course even though the first target had long since been zapped. ''You achieved your goal.''

''It's not hard to achieve that kind of goal if nothing else in the world matters.''

Hannah shivered a little.

''Am I hurting you?'' Gideon stopped his work on her leg.

''No.'' She waited a moment longer before speaking. She turned the details of his tale over and over in her mind. She reached for one intricate piece of the puzzle after another, building a more and more complete picture of the man who was massaging her leg with such unexpected skill. But no matter how many elements she added, she couldn't bring the whole image into focus. Something eluded her. ''So you turned around and destroyed Cyrus Ballantine. You took your revenge for his betrayal.''

''Yes.''

''And now his son is coming after you.''

''Some people would call it justice,'' he said dryly.

"It's not justice, exactly. Merely a sort of internal logic built into the system, I think. The only way to break the pattern is to step out of the system." Hannah smiled briefly. "But I've already told you that. You're a captive of your own way of doing things. You've made it clear you don't particularly want to change. You've become addicted to the power and the constant winning."

"So I'm stuck with my fate?" he asked, looking amused.

"You're like one of those professional gunfighters of the Old West. You may be the best there is, but sooner or later someone younger and just as mean will be coming along. The only way he can prove himself is by trying to take you. Look at it this way. You may be able to crush Cyrus Ballantine's kid instead of being crushed by him. You'll probably come out on top again, Gideon. I have great faith in your predatory abilities. I've seen you at work. How old is the kid?"

"Thirty. The same age I was when I went after his father."

"Well, it should be interesting. Maybe I could sell tickets," Hannah mused. "This could be a real cock fight, you should pardon the expression."

His hands stilled on her leg. "I think," he said slowly, "that I came here looking for something more than that from you."

Hannah opened her eyes and found herself unable to look away from the night darkness of his gaze. There was a tension in him that she hadn't anticipated. How could he work such magic on her leg when he, himself, was almost vibrating with an inner tautness? Another piece of the puzzle. Her voice gentled slightly even though she refused to allow herself to feel any pity. This man had created his own world. Now he had to live in it. "Then you're out of luck, aren't you? What could I possibly do for you besides give you a discount on one of the tickets to the slaughter?"

"I'm not sure." His fingers flexed lightly on her knee. "Give me a little counseling?"

"Why? What's bothering you about this whole situation, anyway? It's the way your world works. You must understand it better than anyone. You've chosen it, you're good at what you do, and you don't want to change things. Why come to me for advice?"

She knew she was challenging him, pushing him harder than she should have but she couldn't seem to stop. The damned internal logic of the situation, she decided glumly. After having let him make a fool of her, she was compelled to reap what small retaliation might be available.

"Maybe," said Gideon slowly, "I came to you because I wanted an objective viewpoint."

"Objective! After what you did to me how could I possibly be objective? Try again, Gideon."

"Jesus Christ!" He released her leg, got to his feet and stalked across the room to peer out at the tiny balcony. "I don't know anyone else I can talk to about it. I wanted a little professional advice. Maybe I came to you because I don't want to have to crush Hugh Ballantine."

"Why not?" This was getting dangerous and Hannah sensed it. And she missed the soothing touch on her knee.

He swung around, his voice turning harsh. "Don't you understand? I know where he's coming from. I sat across from him in a bar last night and I knew exactly what he was thinking. I knew every emotion that was driving him.''

Hannah understood. She simply hadn't wanted to admit it. Understanding too often led to sympathy and she couldn't afford compassion with this man. "He's where you were nine years ago, isn't he, Gideon? You're seeing not just the image of the man who betrayed you, you're seeing yourself when you look at him.''

"Damn right!" He rubbed the back of his neck with his hand as if unknotting muscles that had bunched in preparation for a battle. "It's starting to eat at me. I know it's asinine to let myself think like this. Much simpler to just wipe Ballantine off the map. Safer, too.''

This time Hannah couldn't repress the flicker of compassion. Talk about asinine! She had long ago learned to accept the softness in herself even though there were times, such as now, when it was wholly unwarranted.

"I think it must be the season for it." She leaned her head back against the cushion.

"The season for what?"

"Seeing ourselves in someone else. You look at Ballantine and see a man at the same crossroads you were at nine years ago. It bothers you because you know what happened after the first big, satisfying kill. If it's any consolation, I've recently met someone who disturbs me in a slightly different way. I see her and I see the bright, professional cultural anthropologist I could have been if I'd taken a different path a few years ago. It's an odd sensation. Up until now I've always told myself I made the right choice when I dropped out of graduate school. But when I see Vicky

Armitage I'm not so sure. Maybe we're both going through a midlife crisis, Gideon.''

''Maybe we both need a vacation.''

''You've just had yours, remember? You were in Vegas,'' she pointed out.

''I mean a real vacation. A change of pace.''

Hannah ran her palm lightly over the arm of the sofa, unsure of where this was going. ''Personally, I plan on taking one. Tomorrow.''

Gideon gave her a whimsical smile. ''I don't suppose you'd invite me along on your trip?''

''Are you kidding? That would be rather like a goldfish inviting a shark to go swimming, wouldn't it? Not at all relaxing for the goldfish. Besides, you wouldn't enjoy it. There aren't any casinos on Santa Inez.''

''I don't feel like gambling this year. I just spent a day trying it and it didn't work.'' Gideon moved back toward her, sinking down on one knee beside her again. ''Is the leg any better?''

''Surprisingly, yes.''

''What's so surprising about it?'' He went back to work on the muscles, sending another wave of relaxation through her.

Unconsciously Hannah let out a long sigh of relief and closed her eyes again. ''I didn't think a man with your hands would have any gentleness in his fingers.''

''You think I wash my hands in blood every day?''

''No, just a couple of times a week.''

He let that ride, kneading and gentling for another few minutes before asking, ''How did the accident happen?''

''I don't have much recollection of it. The doctors said that was normal. I was unconscious for a while and probably lost a few minutes of memory. It's quite common, I'm told. I was coming back late at night from a friend's house. She and her husband live east of here, up in the mountains. I know it was raining and that I probably swerved to miss another car. The police said I may have drifted over the white line and panicked when I saw someone else's headlights coming at me, then overcorrected and sent myself off the road. I'll never know for sure, and the rain was so heavy that it made the accident difficult to reconstruct afterward. Wiped out most of the tire tracks. There is, however, a rather gaping hole in the guard rail where it happened."

"That's your Toyota parked on the street downstairs? The red one?"

Hannah nodded, not opening her eyes. The bliss of an ache-free knee was overtaking her common sense. Funny what pain, or conversely, the lack of it could do to you. Anyone who had the ability to remove physical pain must have some redeeming qualities. "That's it. The one with all the primer on it. Finally got it back from the body shop last week. They're going to paint it while I'm in the Caribbean."

"From the locations of the primer coating I would have guessed you'd been sideswiped," Gideon remarked.

Hannah found the energy to open her eyes. Her mouth tilted slightly at the corners. "That's what Tommy said, too."

"Tommy?"

"The guy at the body shop who pounded out the dents. But the police think I did the damage going through the guard rail and sideswiping a tree, not another car."

"Did the cops spend a lot of time on the case?"

"No. It seemed to them a pretty clear-cut example of a single-car accident. They were more concerned with whether I'd been drinking."

Gideon's fingers tightened fractionally, just enough to remind Hannah that underneath the new comfort zone there was still a lot of sore tissue. "Had you?"

"Only a considerable quantity of unfiltered apple juice. My friends in the mountains are back-to-nature freaks." Hannah wondered how long Gideon would be willing to go on massaging the leg. She would be willing to pay a very high fee for this kind of service. "You've got good hands," she murmured after a bit. "Maybe you missed your calling."

"That thought's been worrying me a lot lately," he told her. "Think I could have made it in the field of massage?"

"Either that or the field of hand-to-hand combat." She stretched luxuriously, sitting up with reluctance. "There's a fine line between the two. I'll give you credit for knowing where the boundary is. Vicky Armitage sure as hell didn't."

Gideon eyed her as she carefully swung her feet off the sofa. He sat down beside her. "Would you have dinner with me this evening, Hannah?"

She blinked owlishly, instant suspicion flaring in her. "I can't."

"Can't or won't?"

"Can't," she told him firmly. "My brother and some friends are giving me a bon voyage party this evening."

"You look grateful for the excuse."

"I am." She smiled faintly. "We goldfish learn early that when a shark invites one of us to dinner, chances are we're the entrée."

Chapter Four

He wasn't drunk, Gideon decided, considering the matter objectively as he pushed open the glass door and stepped out onto the sidewalk. He'd had enough Scotch to relax him, help him unwind, but he wasn't drunk. Unfortunately, he wasn't feeling particularly relaxed or unwound, either. Gideon shoved his hands into the pockets of his jacket and wondered how Hannah's bon voyage party was proceeding. Probably quite nicely. Hannah undoubtedly had a lot of good friends. Gideon reminded himself that he wasn't among them.

Behind him the restaurant's glass door hissed shut, cutting off the warmth and sophisticated ambience inside as neatly as if imprisoning it under a bell jar. Not a bad analogy, Gideon told himself as he turned and walked toward the street corner. The entire restaurant seemed to have been made of glass, although he hadn't gotten any farther than the stylish salmon-and-gray toned bar. The view had been spectacular, each gigantic glass window framing a scene of Elliott Bay at night.

From the cozy bar area with its gleaming machine that dispensed any number of exotic wines by the glass, Gideon had been able to watch the lights on the ferries that plied the night-darkened water. Occasionally a huge cargo ship had coasted slowly past, moving toward port with a litter of small tugs hovering anxiously around it. Very scenic and a little unreal when viewed from the safe confines of the upscale bar.

Now, if he wanted atmosphere with more of a touch of reality he could try one of the places on First or Second Avenue that he had walked past earlier that evening. Those places weren't made of glass. They tended to be black holes in the old buildings that were making a last stand against the downtown revitalization programs. Defiantly, the worn, brick facades held their own against the expensive condos and office buildings that were slowly but steadily encroaching. The black holes would provide lots of interesting, highly realistic atmosphere, all right. Gideon was willing to bet that Hannah had never actually been inside a place like one of those. It would be interesting to see her practice her guidance counseling techniques on some of the inhabitants.

There was a biting nip in the early summer air. A real change from the June heat of Vegas and Tucson. The lightweight linen sport jacket Gideon wore wasn't much protection. The garment would be just right for an evening out on a Caribbean island, however. Gideon thought about that, turning the idea over in his mind as he crossed the cobbled street that led through the Pike Place Market. It wasn't the first time the notion had slipped into his mind. A part of his brain had been playing with the idea all afternoon, ever since he had left Hannah's apartment. It was probably her import shop decor that had started him thinking about islands. That and the fact that he'd seen her airline tickets lying on the kitchen counter when he'd made coffee. It was easy to make reservations on an airline. All a man had to do was pick up the phone.

The cobbled street was lined with imported cars whose trendy owners were safely tucked away inside the equally trendy restaurants that dotted the Market. When said owners returned to their vehicles they would get inside, lock the doors, and drive quickly through the black-hole sections of town until they reached the welcoming security garages of their fashionable apartments or condos.

Gideon knew he had a lot of nerve being so damned condescending. After all, he drove an expensive import himself, and for a long time now he had patronized expensive, trendy restaurants, not black holes.

Gideon walked the length of the Market, passing the vegetable stalls that were closed for the night. There was a slight, lurching movement in a doorway. Gideon identified the cause: someone who in the past would have been referred to as a bum but who now came under the more socially acceptable label *street person*. Apparently the guy had missed the free city bus ride back to one of the missions in Pioneer Square. The mission doors were closed now. Anyone left out in the cold had to seek the shelter of a doorway or a stairwell.

Gideon mused on his own prospective shelter for the night. The hotel room was expensive, luxurious, and lonely. On the other hand, there was a nice lounge where he could have one more Scotch before going to bed. Once more he thought of Hannah at her party. He didn't really like parties, especially those filled with strangers, but if he were there with Hannah the two of them could ignore the others.

He wanted to talk to her again, Gideon realized as he left the Market behind and crossed First Avenue. There was something appealing about talking to

Hannah, even though she was more or less hostile toward him now. He'd like some more of her idealistic advice, even though he knew that he couldn't act on it. He was too far gone down another road. In the past nine years he'd closed off too many of his options and he knew it.

The morbid feeling grew as he walked another block toward the hotel. The morbid sensation turned grim and the grim mood turned aggressive and belligerent. Hands still thrust into his pockets, Gideon kept walking. There were others on the street. A few young prostitutes, male and female, watched him from the shelter of their doorways but something about him kept them from calling out. Gideon could smell the acrid scents of marijuana and cloves and urine as he passed the alleys. A couple of groups of cruising toughs sauntered past. They eyed him with the cold, voracious gaze of young piranhas but they didn't get in his way.

Gideon turned the corner at the next block, heading in the general direction of the expensive, luxurious, lonely hotel room that awaited him, and found himself on a much less active street. Here there were no prostitutes revealed in the streetlights, and the loose gangs of leather-jacketed teenagers weren't prowling. Gideon kept walking.

The man with the knife stepped out of the dark mouth of an alley next to a video rental shop that was closed for the night. Gideon felt the movement a second before he found the blade of the knife in front of him. The aggressive, belligerent feeling surged to the surface of his consciousness. Normally he got rid of the frustrated, angry sensations by swimming. But there were other ways to do it, ways he hadn't used in a long time. He stared at the haggard face of the man holding the knife.

"You want something?" Gideon asked very politely.

"Yeah, dude. I want something. A lot of things. I'll start with the wallet." He made a quick, upwardly arcing motion with the blade and held out his other hand. There was a glittering wildness in his eyes. "Let's have it."

"Don't let the sportcoat fool you. You're not the only one who's had the advantage of a street education. You want the wallet? Come and take it."

The glittering eyes narrowed. "This ain't no game, slick. I can cut you open 'fore you get a chance to yell."

"Show me."

"Son of a bitch. Give me the wallet!"

Gideon said nothing. He waited with a sense of gathering excitement. This was what he needed tonight. But the need must have been showing in his eyes because the younger man wasn't moving in on him.

"I ain't bullshittin', slick. Hand over the wallet or I'll..." The knife wavered as a car turned the corner and started down the street. The man glanced past Gideon, swore crudely and vanished down the alley.

Gideon didn't need to look around to know what kind of vehicle had turned the corner. He resumed walking. A few seconds later the police car cruised past. It slowed and the cop on the passenger side rolled down his window. He took one look at the expensive linen sport jacket and the Italian leather shoes and made his identification at once. Tourist.

"You lost, buddy?"

Gideon sighed. "No. I'm on my way back to my hotel." He named it.

"This isn't the best route."

"The hotel's only three blocks from here." He tried to keep the hostility out of his voice. His whole body was seething with unreleased tension and adrenaline.

"Walk up to the next block and then turn right. It's a little healthier than following this street."

"Thank you, officer. I'll do that."

The police car managed to stay within sight until Gideon had obediently walked up to the more active thoroughfare. It was a thoughtful gesture on the part of the Seattle police department but Gideon didn't feel much like thanking anyone. He wondered how he was going to get rid of this restless, frustrated aggression. The hotel didn't have a pool.

The hotel did, however, have that nice lounge, Gideon reminded himself as he walked into the heavily carpeted lobby. Without any hesitation he started toward it. One hour and two Scotches later he left the padded stool to find the lobby telephones. There was no answer in Hannah's apartment. Still partying. Gideon hung up and dialed the airline on which she was booked to Santa Inez. A man had a right to a decent vacation. There would be unlimited swimming available in the Caribbean.

HANNAH KNEW she should have been more astonished to see Gideon pacing the departure lounge at SeaTac airport the next morning. She couldn't quite figure out why she wasn't. She must have spent too much of last night thinking about him. She collected her boarding pass from the agent and hitched the strap of the many-buckled leather flight bag over one shoulder. She put her weight on the cane and walked toward Gideon with a sense of inevitability.

"I suppose you've got a good reason for being here." She planted herself aggressively in front of him. She was wearing a swashbuckling military-style shirt and pants in khaki twill. The clothing had arrived the day before from the mail order house from which Hannah ordered most of her things. Her favorite two-inch wide belt of British harness leather completed the rakish look. The clothes gave her a sense of bravado she found useful around people such as Gideon Cage.

He winced. "Could you keep your voice down? My head hurts like hell."

"Hangover?"

"Don't sound so damned pleased." He glanced pointedly at his watch. "Where the hell have you been? They're already boarding."

"I'm not much good at rushing these days." She tapped the cane on the floor to emphasize the reason. "And even when I am in good running form, I make it a practice not to run just because somebody else thinks I should. I'm perverse that way. I'd make a lousy corporate employee. You haven't answered my question, Gideon. What are you doing here?"

"Well, I didn't come to wave goodbye."

"I'm not surprised. You don't strike me as the sentimental type."

"Here, give me that." He took the flight bag from her shoulder and reached down to pick up his own leather carry-on bag. "Let's get moving. We've got a plane to catch."

"Isn't this pushing your desire for guidance counseling a little too far? Gideon, I didn't invite you along on this trip."

"On the other hand, you don't look real startled to see me." He led the way toward the boarding tunnel.

The man was a little too perceptive, even in his hungover state. Hannah trailed down the boarding ramp after him, aware that she was leaning too heavily on the cane. Her leg seemed especially uncomfortable and she guessed it was because she had spent too much time on her feet at the party.

"Here," Gideon said as he paused beside a row and began stuffing their flight bags into the overhead bins. "You can have the aisle seat. It'll be easier on that leg."

"Your thoughtfulness overwhelms me."

"Yeah, I thought it might." He slid into the window seat and reached for her elbow as she lowered herself onto the cushion. "Are you okay? You look a little beat."

"Since mornings are my best time, I'm not likely to get much better as the day progresses." Hannah leaned her head back and closed her eyes, buckling the seat belt blindly. "Talk, Gideon."

She had her eyes closed, so she didn't see him shrug but she sensed the vague gesture in his voice. "I told you. I need a vacation. I've never been to Santa Inez."

"And where do you propose to stay on Santa Inez?"

"There'll be hotels. There are always hotels."

"Just tell me why you're doing this, Gideon."

"If I knew, I'd tell you."

Hannah opened her eyes as the jet crouched at the head of the runway, its engines roaring to life. "You don't know why you're here? Other than the fact that you want a vacation?"

Gideon massaged his forehead, looking deeply pained. "Does there have to be more of a reason?"

She was about to tell him that there definitely had to be more of a reason, much more, but the jet was rolling very quickly now, straining for lift-off. Hannah didn't feel like pitching her voice above the grinding noise. She eyed him covertly as the green hills of Seattle dropped away beneath the plane. Gideon Cage did indeed look hungover. She found the thought curiously interesting. It didn't quite fit the mosaic she had mentally constructed.

"Do you get drunk often?" Hannah inquired politely as the jet leveled off.

He slanted her a hard-edged glance. "What do you think?"

"I think you don't do it too frequently," she responded honestly. "Being that out of control wouldn't fit your personality. Where did you go last night?"

"Some place near the waterfront. Lots of glass, great view. I don't remember the name. Then I walked back to my hotel and had a couple of drinks before going to bed. Hardly a wild evening."

"You walked from the Market back to your hotel? Alone?"

"Why not? Seattle is a very friendly town."

"Tourist luck," Hannah marveled. "You should have caught a cab."

"I'll remember that next time. How was your going-away party?"

"Lousy."

For some reason that got his attention. "Lousy? Did your leg hurt?"

"That wasn't the problem."

"Then what was the problem?" he asked with exaggerated patience.

"It took the form of am uncomfortable social situation. What might be called a scene." Hannah accepted a cup of coffee from the cabin attendant and waited as Gideon did the same. "I got into an embarrassing argument," she continued bluntly as the attendant moved on to the next row. "I hate scenes. Especially ones in which I humiliate myself."

"Are we discussing a scene with a man?" Gideon swallowed the contents of his coffee cup in two long gulps. He seemed grateful for the small comfort.

He really did look somewhat the worse for wear, Hannah decided. His hair had been combed with a too-careful hand, the severe style only serving to point up the grimness around his eyes and mouth. He was wearing a pair of tan pants and an open-necked cotton work shirt. Both garments looked a little crushed, as if they had been yanked out of a flight bag and not been given a chance to unwrinkle.

"No. A scene with a woman. Vicky Armitage. She's an anthro professor. I think I mentioned her. She knows I'm going to Santa Inez to deal with my aunt's library. Wants me to turn it over to someone who is competent to analyze it. Someone who can appreciate the true value of Elizabeth Nord's records and notes."

"And that someone isn't a guidance counselor?"

Hannah smiled wryly. "Sometimes you can be amazingly insightful."

"How did you humiliate and embarrass yourself?"

Hannah sighed, remembering the small scene. "I tried to hold my own in a field in which I am eminently underqualified."

"Anthropology?"

"Uh-huh. Normally I have sense enough not to get in over my head with the academic crowd, but Vicky really annoyed me last night. I found myself feeling what could only be described as hostile and aggressive."

"What a coincidence."

"I beg your pardon?"

"Never mind," Gideon instructed. "Tell me what happened."

"There isn't much to tell, really. I went a few rounds in the ring with someone who is way out of my league and I came away looking like an idiot. Vicky started going on and on about the importance of my aunt's papers to the scientific community. She said that Elizabeth Nord's work could be viewed as a prime example of the radical extremes to which participants in the old nature versus nurture controversy were willing to go."

"You're losing me," Gideon warned.

"During the first half of the century anthropologists were split on the issue of nature versus nurture," Hannah explained. "Some were absolutely convinced that heredity or nature determined all the various aspects of culture and human behavior. The other group was equally sure that culture molded human behavior, that a human being developed along whatever lines his culture dictated. Both sides were partially right and partially wrong, of course. Heredity and culture are intertwined, each contributing something to the formation of human personality. But back in those days anthropologists fought to the last ditch over the matter. Vicky claims that my aunt was on the nurture side and that she skewed her findings on Revelation Island to fit the claim that culture was everything. She thinks the Nord papers might prove that."

"And you attempted to defend your aunt?"

"I should have known better. It's been so long since I was in graduate school. I've forgotten the nuances of that kind of infighting." Hannah shook her head, regretting that she had made a fool of herself. "And I'd forgotten all the heavyweight names and the important monographs. I couldn't begin to remember the appropriate books and papers. Vicky brought out all the big guns."

"And you came off looking like a noncontender."

"Not unlike the way I looked after you'd finished with Accelerated Design."

Gideon groaned. "Could we forget that incident?"

"Are you apologizing?" she asked a little too sweetly.

"Would it do any good?"

"No, and I wouldn't buy it for a minute." She stretched out her weak leg, absently rubbing her knee through the fabric of her khaki slacks. "Are you running off to Santa Inez to escape the young gunslinger?"

"Ballantine? Maybe."

"That doesn't fit, either. Not like you to admit you're afraid of another man."

"Maybe you should quit trying to predict my actions on the basis of what little you know about me, Hannah."

"Perhaps you're right."

There was a pause and then Gideon asked cautiously. "What would you tell Ballantine if he came to you for advice?"

"You mean, what would I tell you if this were nine years ago?"

"Something like that," Gideon admitted.

"I suppose I'd give you a lecture on the futility of building a career based on revenge." Hannah finished her coffee. "But to tell you the truth, this morning I'm not sure my heart would be in my work. Quite frankly, after my little scene with Professor Armitage last night, revenge as a motivating factor suddenly makes a certain amount of sense."

"Feeling vengeful?"

Hannah's mouth curved in a faint grin. "Do you know what would really frost Vicky Armitage?"

"What?"

"If I were to write the big, revealing book on Elizabeth Nord's career myself. I know just how I'd do it, too. I wouldn't get it published through some high-class university press so that only academic types would read it. I'd send it to some huge, commercial New York publisher. Get it packaged as a hot, controversial, pop science best-seller. You know the type. The academic community scoffs at them but television picks them up for a big special. Since a lot of my aunt's work was on the role of women in society, I'm sure there would be an audience for a book about her. Women love to read stuff like that. I'd make it juicy instead of bone dry, go light on the science and heavy on the good stuff."

"Sex?"

"Precisely. Any book dealing with the role of women is bound to discuss a lot of sex, don't you think? Initiation rituals, marriage and divorce customs, all kinds of hot material. Then there's the personal side of things. My aunt was quite a character.

There were rumors that she was a lesbian. There was also some gossip about her getting involved in some of the rituals of Revelation Island.''

"You're not concerned with protecting your aunt's good name?"

"She didn't have a good name. She had a controversial name and she loved it. Believe me, it wouldn't bother her ghost in the least if I were to turn her life story into a sleazy best-seller. She'd get a kick out of it."

Gideon slanted Hannah a speculative glance. "Writing a book sounds like hard work, a long-term project."

"Sure."

"Take it from me, you're probably going to need a little more motivation than the memory of one embarrassing scene at a party."

"You're speaking from experience?"

"The trick to getting revenge, Hannah, is to make sure that nothing else matters as much as the revenge itself." Gideon's voice was flat, totally devoid of emotion. "That means the source of motivation has got to be pretty strong."

"As yours was?"

"Yeah. Got any aspirin?"

Hannah reached under the seat for her leather shoulder bag. "I was just going to take some myself."

They got more coffee from the flight attendant and used it to down the aspirins in a surprisingly companionable silence. When the small ritual was finished, Hannah leaned back in her seat and tapped one finger thoughtfully on the armrest.

"I have got a bit more motivation than one night's embarrassment, you know."

Gideon watched her profile. "Something to do with this Dr. Armitage reminding you of what you aren't?"

Hannah nodded. "It struck me this morning while I was brushing my teeth that it would be very pleasant to throw it all back in her face. Usually I don't let people, especially academic types, get to me like this."

"I don't think this is a good time to start."

"There's something different about Vicky."

"Forget her, Hannah."

Hannah raised her eyebrows. "You're handing out advice now?"

"Why not? I don't feel up to much else this morning. At least you've got a choice. If you don't act, nothing significant will change for you. Life will go on as it was before Vicky Armitage arrived on the scene. You said, yourself, that she was only a visiting professor. That means she'll be leaving Seattle in a few months, right?"

"Well, yes, but..."

"You're lucky. You can avoid her until then."

Abruptly Hannah realized where this was going. "Unlike your situation with Ballantine?"

Gideon's mouth twisted faintly. "This vacation to Santa Inez is only a small delaying tactic. I can't hide forever and hope he'll go away. Sooner or later I'll have to deal with him."

"And if you don't?"

"He'll destroy Cage & Associates."

Hannah heard the finality in the words and shivered a little. "You're sure?"

"Absolutely sure. It's what I would do in his place. What I did to his father. When I get back from Santa Inez I'll have to start fighting for my corporate life."

"You've built an entire career on revenge. It's incredible when you think of it."

"I try not to."

Hannah thought for a moment, playing with the puzzle that was Gideon Cage. "There was more to it than just the fact that Ballantine left you holding the bag nine years ago, wasn't there?"

"You don't think that was sufficient reason for crushing him?"

"I don't know. It might have been. It's just that I get the feeling there was more."

Gideon eyed her warily. "More what?"

"How close were you and Cyrus Ballantine?"

"He was my business partner."

"And also your mentor?" Hannah guessed. "They say a mentor is important in the corporate world."

Gideon shrugged. "I suppose you could say he was. He taught me most of what I know. The man was brilliant. I . . ." Gideon hesitated. "I respected him. Trusted him," he finished carefully.

"He was a father figure," Hannah announced.

"Jesus Christ, lady, do you have to analyze everything to death?"

"Sorry. Force of habit."

"You're supposed to be on vacation," Gideon muttered. There was a pause and then he said, "I never knew my real father. Disappeared before I was born."

"Where did you grow up?"

"On the streets of L.A. Quite an education."

"I can imagine," Hannah said, mentally plugging in another piece of the puzzle. "You're lucky you didn't wind up in jail."

"Not lucky. Smart."

Hannah hid a smile. "Is that your ego talking or is it the truth?"

"Who knows?" Gideon's mouth relaxed slightly. "A little of both probably. I did manage to stay out of jail and it wasn't because I was leading such a clean life."

"When did you discover your aptitude for business?"

"When I discovered you could sell a set of hubcaps back to the rightful owner without getting arrested for stealing them in the first place if you exercised due caution."

"Tricky. I take it you progressed from there?"

"I like to think so. Now I only steal companies. And it's all quite legal."

"When did you meet Cyrus Ballantine?"

Gideon looked at her. "Are you really interested in this?"

"Unfortunately, yes." It was the truth and Hannah rather wished it wasn't. She didn't particularly want to be interested in Gideon Cage.

"I got involved with Cyrus in my senior year in high school. The school had a work-study program that aimed at putting us so-called disadvantaged types into the business world for a while to give us a taste of legal employment. Ballantine got some sort of tax break for volunteering his firm. I took one look at Cyrus Ballantine's Mercedes and his five-hundred-dollar suit and I knew the corporate world was the racket for me. I dug in and went to work. Did anything and everything from fetching coffee to filing correspondence. I paid a hell of a lot of attention to everything Ballantine did. Tried to dress like him, eat like him, talk to people the way he did. Somewhere along the line, Ballantine noticed.''

''And saw something he liked?''

''Saw something he could use,'' Gideon corrected harshly. ''It was a fair swap for a while. He got my absolute loyalty and twenty-four hours a day out of me whenever he wanted it. In return I got a couple of years of college and an on-the-job education that was second to none. Cyrus taught me everything: how to buy a suit, how to entertain clients, how to manipulate people without letting them know what was happening, how to stay within the law while taking just about anything you wanted.''

''And then he pulled one last maneuver and left you standing in a pile of manure.''

''That's an accurate way to put it,'' Gideon agreed. ''And the beauty of it was that I never even saw it coming.''

Hannah felt an almost overwhelming urge to reach out and touch Gideon's big hand as it curled beside her on the armrest. Firmly she resisted the impulse. This man knew all about maneuvering and manipulating. She would be a fool to think he might not be herding her along right now in the direction he wanted her to go. The only thing she didn't understand was why he was bothering in the first place.

''So you're taking a vacation while you wonder how you're going to deal with Ballantine's son.''

''I haven't had a vacation in nine years.''

''What about those trips to Vegas?''

"Vegas doesn't count," he told her. "I can see that now."

"I won't go to bed with you for the novelty of it, you know," Hannah said quite conversationally. Inside her stomach was tightening.

Gideon looked at her. "If you go to bed with me, it won't be a novelty. It will be important."

Hannah wished devoutly that she'd kept her mouth shut. Because now she knew for certain. Those gold-flecked eyes had been gleaming behind his dark lashes, and there was a quiet awareness in him that Gideon wasn't troubling to conceal. The outlines of the puzzle altered again as a new piece was added. Hannah wasn't sure she understood the additional information, but she felt its impact deep in her body.

THE SWIFT CARIBBEAN TWILIGHT was darkening into night when the jet touched down on Santa Inez's single runway. During the past hundred miles the island had grown from a hazy green dot in the ocean to a painter's paradise of palms and sandy beaches. The lights of the tiny terminal blazed with welcome as Hannah and Gideon stepped out into the muggy tropical warmth.

"I've only been here five minutes and I feel like I need a shower already." Hannah headed for the car-rental agency at the back of the terminal.

"We'll acclimate," Gideon assured her. "Aren't you going to grab a cab?"

"I want my own transportation. I'm going to rent one of those cute little jeeps with the fringe on top." She pointed to a row of frivolous pink jeeps. "There's probably an unlimited number of cabs waiting outside," she added helpfully.

"That's all right. I'll share the jeep."

"Are you going to call a hotel?"

"Not just yet. I'll see you out to your aunt's place, first."

Hannah didn't bother to argue. She knew there was no point. Fifteen minutes later, Gideon shoved the keys into the jeep's ignition as Hannah climbed in beside him.

"Did you have to order one with pink fringe?" He backed the small vehicle out of its slot and found the narrow, palm-lined road that ringed the island.

"Don't worry, everyone will think you're a tourist."

"That's not what's bothering me. I am a tourist. I'm more worried that everyone will think I'm an idiot."

"Stop complaining about the pink fringe. Look, Gideon, isn't it beautiful?" Hannah inhaled deeply as the jeep swung around a corner to reveal a charming cove. Ahead of them the fading light revealed a perfect islandscape. A curving white beach met the froth of a gentle sea in an inviting scene that could have come straight out of an ad. All it lacked was an entwined couple strolling along at the water's edge. The warm evening breeze was scented with the sea. "I think I'm beginning to relax already."

"I'm glad *you* are," Gideon growled, jerking the jeep to the far side of the road as a dilapidated taxi came whizzing toward them. The car was straying dangerously over a very old white line that could barely be seen. The driver waved cheerfully and honked before disappearing into the darkness behind them.

Hannah's sense of relaxation vanished in an instant. She reached out to grip the edge of the windshield and took several deep breaths.

"Hey," Gideon said softly, "take it easy."

"I still get a little tense in a car. I've been doing quite well lately, but..."

"I can imagine how it feels." He eased his foot off the gas pedal, letting the jeep slow appreciably. Then he threw her a quick grin. "You're supposed to be navigating. Get to work."

"You're going to have to try to remember that I'm not one of your employees, Gideon." But Hannah pulled the small map out of her purse and leaned forward to study it in the light of the dash. She wouldn't admit it for the world but the small assignment did serve to distract her from the road, which was becoming increasingly twisty. Hannah didn't like the way it was rising above the sea, either. She didn't like roads that ran along the edge of cliffs, scenic though they might be. "My aunt's cottage is at the other end of the island. We'll have to go through town and then start watching for landmarks. You can keep an eye out for a hotel. If we pass one we can stop. You can run in and register."

"I'll worry about it later." Gideon's full attention was on his driving as they approached the small port town.

The conglomeration of colonial Spanish and Dutch style buildings was named after the island itself and reflected its varied past. Hannah delighted in the dusty pink-and-white architecture. To her right the intimate little harbour protected a collection of boats that consisted of everything from gleaming white yachts to rusty charter boats. On the single main street traffic inexplicably slowed to a crawl. People on the sidewalk called out to their friends in passing cars. Colorfully dressed tourists mixed with the equally colorful locals, meandering out of the shops that were closing for the day. The open-air bars were beginning to fill as darkness settled.

"I should pick up some food," Hannah said thoughtfully. "That looks like a small grocery store up ahead. Let's stop."

Gideon obeyed, swinging the little jeep into a convenient opening between two taxis. "I'll wait here while you go inside."

Hannah glanced up as she clambered out of the vehicle with her cane. "Don't you want to come in with me?"

"I'd rather keep track of the luggage. There's no place to lock it up in this thing."

"Oh. Good point." She glanced at the back seat of the completely open jeep. "I didn't think about that when I rented it."

"I know. You were too taken with pink fringe." He draped one arm over the steering wheel and smiled at her. "Run along, Hannah."

"Don't let anyone take the hubcaps, either."

There was a distinct pause and then Gideon said gently, "I'll keep an eye on them."

"It would be embarrassing to have to buy them back from the guy who took them."

"Do all guidance counselors have this perverted sense of humor?"

"Probably. See you in a few minutes."

She turned toward the small grocery store, feeling inexplicably lighthearted. Through the louvered door she could see an array of familiar looking potato chip

packages and soft drink labels. Once inside she found
an assortment of canned goods, although there was
virtually nothing in the way of fresh vegetables. She
picked up a carton of milk, some cereal, bread, and
tuna fish. Adding a few other items, she made her way
to the check-out stand where the clerk was chatting
with a girlfriend in the soft island patois. He glanced
up as Hannah approached and shifted into heavily
accented English.

It wasn't until Hannah emerged from the shop jug-
gling her sack of groceries and her cane that she allowed herself to admit she had picked up enough
supplies for two people. Gideon said nothing as he put
the jeep in gear and edged back out onto the crowded
street.

Elizabeth Nord's beachfront home was a graceful,
old-fashioned cottage, complete with an encircling
veranda. The wooden structure had been painted
white, and it sat amid a grove of palms. Lush banks of
exotic greenery sprinkled with oversize flowers grew in
a freewheeling riot of color around the house. The
jeep's headlights picked up only a hint of this wealth
of plant life as Gideon parked the vehicle in the cir-
cular drive. Hannah could hear the soft noise of the
surf in the distance as she opened her purse to search
for the cottage keys.

She said nothing when Gideon picked up both flight
bags as well as the sack of groceries and followed her
up the veranda steps. When she unlocked the graceful
double doors, found the wall switch and turned the
light on, the living room, which ran along the whole
front of the house, was revealed. She smiled with
pleasure.

"This," she announced, "is the way my apartment is supposed to look."

"The real thing." Gideon set down the bags and walked around the room, opening windows. The trapped, musty air soon began to dissipate. When Hannah switched on the overhead ceiling fan the atmosphere improved even more quickly.

White lacquered rattan furniture with exotically patterned cotton cushions were right at home in a tropical beach cottage. Bleached board floors and an expanse of windows had a cooling effect that was visual as well as physical. Between the windows, floor-to-ceiling bookcases were filled with journals, notebooks, and a lifetime's collection of heavy volumes. A huge, carved teak desk stood in front of one of the front windows, commanding a view of the sea.

Gideon uncranked the last of the louvered windows and halted beside a small teak cabinet. A tray of dusty glasses sat on the top. When he leaned down to open the door a variety of bottles glinted in the light. Gideon unhesitatingly reached inside to select one.

"Your aunt had good taste in Scotch."

"I'm glad you approve."

Hannah found herself trailing along behind Gideon as he carried the glassware and the Scotch into a surprisingly well-equipped kitchen. She watched as he rinsed the glasses in the sink and then proceeded to pour a healthy measure of Scotch into each. Her stomach was tightening again.

"To a real vacation." Gideon gravely handed Hannah a glass. His eyes held hers as she obediently raised the Scotch to her lips and tasted its mellowed bite.

"I didn't see a phone," Hannah heard herself say carefully.

"No."

"It's going to be tough to start dialing local hotels without a phone."

"Yes."

He stepped past her, crossing the living room to move out onto the veranda. Slowly Hannah followed, aware of standing on the brink of a very wide, very deep chasm.

Gideon's back was to her as he leaned against the railing and stared out to sea. Hannah realized just how powerful swimming had made his shoulders. She watched the smooth muscles bunch slightly beneath the fabric of his shirt as Gideon picked up the glass he had set on the railing and took another swallow.

"It's very different, isn't it?" Hannah ventured, feeling her way so cautiously she might have been trying to walk on hot coals. "It's not Tucson and it's not Seattle."

"Neutral territory."

"Is it?"

"I'd like to stay here with you, Hannah."

She took another sip of Scotch, hoping it would unknot her stomach. But all she felt was the fire. If she ever went to bed with this man, it wouldn't be a novelty. It would be important. Crucially important.

"Yes," she said and decided not to think about all that she might be saying yes to with the single word.

Gideon swung around and smiled slightly. "Why don't we go for a swim?"

Chapter Five

THE SEA WAS PERFECT. The frosting effect of the fat tropical moon on the soft waves created an illusion of alien reality. The warmth of the water was incredible to someone accustomed to the year-round bone-chilling cold of Puget Sound. Hannah stood at the edge of the light, foaming surf and wondered how she could be so far away, both physically and mentally from Seattle.

"What are you thinking?" Gideon came up behind her, dropping his towel onto the beach. He had changed into the snug, sleek swimming trunks he had been wearing the day Hannah had met him in Las Vegas. His dark hair was silvered faintly by the moonlight and in the scented shadows his strong, lean body seemed larger, more overpowering than she had remembered. Gideon, too, seemed strangely alien. But in his alienness there was an indefinable lure, a promise of excitement and wonder.

"Just that you were right. Perhaps this is neutral territory. It certainly is different. There's something about islands that has always appealed to me. They're fantasy worlds. I think my aunt felt that way, too. She always lived on islands when she wasn't teaching in the States. For a long time she made her home in the South Pacific and later, after she retired, here on Santa Inez." Hannah looked away from him, seeking the indistinguishable line where sea met night sky. "We could be all alone here."

"We are all alone."

He didn't touch her but she could feel his intent gaze as he examined her in the moonlight. The simple yellow bikini she had put on was not especially daring as such garments went, but Hannah felt quite naked in it now. The sensation made her uneasy. It also caused a ripple of anticipation. She set her cane down on the sand beside his towel and turned to glance at Gideon over her shoulder.

"What are you waiting for?"

"I don't know, but I sure as hell have waited a long time." He took her arm as she limped into the water.

"It's so warm," Hannah breathed.

"Almost as warm as you."

"Gideon..."

"Hush, Hannah. Let's swim." He tugged her gently down beside him on the far side of the lightly breaking waves.

The cove in which they swam was protected from the sea by a curving arm of tumbled rocks that reached almost half way around the sheltered water. The sea was gentle and silken and Hannah was weightless. For the first time since she had injured her leg, she felt graceful and mobile again. Here in the sea her weak knee was not the handicap it was on land. The pleasure of feeling strong once more made her laugh softly.

Beside her Gideon caught the laughter and smiled. He stroked slowly, luxuriously, leading the way. Hannah followed unquestioningly, feeling safe in this alien sea because of Gideon's presence. She was a fair swimmer but Gideon moved beside her like a sleek dolphin, playing in the liquid medium, slowing his pace to hers.

"Feels good?" he asked.

"It feels fantastic."

He touched her then, his big hand gliding across her slick shoulder. He wasn't trying to stop her or guide her or slow her movement. He simply touched her.

Hannah trembled and covered her reaction with a small burst of speed that carried her just beyond his reach. But when she glanced to her side he was there. He moved without noise or commotion in the water. For some reason she veered away again, and again she lifted her head to find him at her side. Once more she darted off, acknowledging now the rising excitement that was beginning to build as she found herself playing the age-old game.

This time Gideon reappeared to her right, staying a little behind her. Hannah felt his hand on the calf of her leg, the lightest of caresses, as if he merely wanted to ensure that she knew he was there. She was aware of him, all right. She knew that regardless of how long she played the game, regardless of how often she slipped out of reach, whenever she turned around she would find him beside her. It was inevitable. The flickering excitement filled her with a curious tension.

Hannah came to a halt, finding her footing on the sandy bottom. The warm sea foamed around her breasts. Gideon sliced through the water until he was in front of her and then he, too, stood. His eyes were dark with unmistakable desire, and the too-brilliant moon etched the hard angles of his face, revealing the masculine power that animated him.

"I've wanted you since that first afternoon in Vegas." The words were harsh, unvarnished truth.

She looked up at him, eyes wide in the silver light. "My brother said he was glad I'd had the sense not to go to bed with you."

"I wouldn't have taken you to bed as long as the business with your brother's company was in the way."

Hannah tilted her head to one side. "The Code of the West?"

"No. My code."

"My brother's business is no longer in the way?"

"It's over and done."

"For you," she said. "Not for him."

"If he's got the guts and the motivation, he'll survive. I taught him a lesson but I didn't destroy him."

"You could have destroyed him."

"There was no need."

She inhaled deeply. "You're so accustomed to power, so used to wielding it. You've even set up your own ethical standards, haven't you? You don't operate according to the standards of others."

"Is that so bad?"

"It makes you dangerous."

"Not to you." He lifted his hand and drew his forefinger along the line of her jaw. "Never to you."

"Why should I be an exception?"

"Because you understand me."

"Understanding doesn't buy safety," Hannah whispered. "Just a little advance warning of disaster."

His mouth curved slightly. "Do you feel you're standing in the path of disaster?"

"No," she said honestly, "but that's probably because I'm not thinking logically tonight. I haven't been able to put all the pieces of the puzzle together yet."

"Do you see me as a puzzle?"

"Yes."

He let his hand slide down to the curve of her shoulder. "Come to bed with me, Hannah."

"Because you want me?"

"Because I need you." His other hand closed on her shoulder and he pulled her to him.

Hannah felt the strength in him, but her body responded to it positively, glorying in it. The anticipation she had been feeling flared into a blaze of longing. When his mouth came down on hers she parted her lips.

Gideon groaned, the sound emanating from deep in his chest. His kiss was aggressive, not tentative; hungry, not seductive. He made no attempt to camouflage his desire, but the truly fascinating thing was that he made no effort to hide his raw need, either.

Perhaps that was one of the advantages of understanding and wielding Gideon's kind of personal power, Hannah thought fleetingly. Perhaps it gave him the freedom to exercise a kind of honesty other men wouldn't be willing to risk. Still, it astonished her. She hadn't expected him to make his need so clear. She had expected more finesse, more artful seduction, more deliberate sensuality.

His hands were gliding along her skin, down her back, compelling her closer to the fiercely masculine outline of his body. Through the thin fabric of his swimming briefs Hannah could feel the rigid length of him and the heavy weight there made her suck in her breath.

She tried to remind herself that there was another explanation for his bluntly honest approach tonight. Gideon could manipulate people so easily. It was very possible he had found the key to manipulating her without Hannah even realizing it. She would not have responded to a deliberate, teasing seduction. She would have been wary of any protestations of love at first sight. There were a hundred different approaches he could have used that would have set up her defenses.

But Gideon had claimed he needed her. He was making her believe that claim with every touch of his hand, every word he uttered. In her own mind she could find no explanation for his following her first to Seattle and now to Santa Inez. No explanation, that is, except the one he had given her. He needed her.

If Gideon were manipulating her with his need, he was too clever for her tonight, Hannah decided. Because she wanted, no *needed* him, too.

"Neutral territory," she murmured against his mouth.

"Our territory."

"Yes." And this time she meant yes to everything.

He must have sensed the surrender in her. Hannah felt his body tighten with restrained desire, heard the deep intake of his breath and then her bikini bra was free, dangling in his hand. Looping the strap over his wrist Gideon looked down at her breasts.

"You're very soft, my sweet Hannah." He flattened his hands on her shoulders and stroked slowly down her curves until her nipples were pressing into his palms. The sea frothed around his fingers, concealing and then revealing the shape of her breasts.

Hannah stretched her arms upward, circling his neck and lifted her face once more for his kiss. When his tongue surged eagerly into her mouth she felt him shifting position. The next thing she knew she was high in his arms, being carried back toward shore.

The night air was pleasantly cool on her wet body. Hannah clung to Gideon, the side of her breast teased and tantalized by the rough, curling hair of his chest.

He brought her through the surf and up onto the moonlit beach. Then Hannah felt herself being lowered to the towel. Already her skin was drying. Her breasts were tight and full and the need to be touched more intimately made her restless. She shifted her legs as Gideon came down beside her on the towel, one knee lifting a little in response to the tingling heat between her thighs.

"Gideon, I want you."

"I know," he said gently, the satisfaction deep in his voice. "I can feel it." He dropped the bikini bra and stroked his hand down her stomach to the edge of her suit. Then he inserted his fingers beneath the elastic and stripped the remainder of the bikini off her completely. When she curled toward him, he held her close for a long moment.

He rolled aside and pulled off his own swimming briefs. Hannah caught the gleam of pale light on his flanks, saw the tautness of his stomach. His arousal was blatant, fiercely demanding.

"I've wanted to touch you for days." He pulled her close again, his fingers gliding along her thigh, kneading, squeezing, stroking.

She curved her nails into the smooth muscles of his chest. "Please touch me, Gideon. I need it tonight. I've never needed anything so much in my life."

Hannah's eyes closed as he obeyed. The trailing, blunt tips of his fingers moved to the inside of her thighs.

"Open for me, sweetheart."

She did, a tiny moan accompanying the action. And then he was probing the hidden folds of sensitive skin, seeking the nubbin that was the center of feminine sensation. She gasped when he found it, clinging to him as her body flamed into full awareness.

"So hot, so wet and hot." His touch increased the damp warmth until Hannah thought she would go out of her mind under the sensual stimulation.

He became more insistent as he sensed her response. Without any warning his fingers moved lower. Hannah's own fingertips reacted to the intimate invasion. She clenched them, unconsciously letting her nails sink into Gideon's chest. With a sensual aggression that surprised her more than it did Gideon, she crowded forward, urging him onto his back.

Hannah could see the devil looking out at her from behind his lashes, a devil who was thoroughly enjoying himself.

"Gideon, please, don't laugh."

"How can I help it? You make me very happy, sweet Hannah." His hand continued to move intimately, teasing her into an exquisite sensitivity.

"And you're driving me out of my mind," she complained softly.

"I think I like you like this."

She arched her lower body against him. Then she reached down to cup him between gentle fingers.

"Ah, Hannah. Now you're going to push me over the edge." The devil in his eyes was no longer laughing. His mood had gone suddenly, wholly intense.

"Yes." Hannah pleaded with her body. "Yes, please, now, Gideon."

He tautened beneath her. The night sky spun overhead as Hannah found herself flat on her back. Before her whirling senses could reorient themselves Gideon was sliding heavily between her thighs. He cradled her with one hand, using the other to guide himself.

Hannah parted her lips on a silent cry of acceptance, wonder, and welcome as Gideon surged into her. The shock of his possession went through her entire body. She felt drawn too tight, filled too full, overwhelmed. Gideon went still for a tense moment, his face a mask of violent, barely controlled desire. With trembling fingers he stroked her hair, giving her a chance to adjust to him. Slowly she relaxed around him.

"All right?" he asked.

"Perfect."

He bent his head to kiss her shoulder. "This is what I've been needing. I've needed the feel of you in my arms, surrounding me, holding on to me. God, how I've needed it."

She clutched him, wrapping her legs around his muscled thighs. Hannah closed her eyes against the power of the moment. And then she gave herself up to it and the man who held her.

"Gideon, it's never been like this."

"I know, sweetheart. I know." Slowly he began to move again, thrusting deeply then withdrawing almost completely. Long, slow, heavy thrusts that stoked a new kind of fire.

The relentless momentum was forcing Hannah toward an unraveling infinity that promised a release she had never experienced. She followed the glittering promise of it, reaching for it with increasing eagerness until she was demanding it with all her strength.

"Take it, Hannah. Take it. It's all yours."

Hannah caught her breath as the spiraling tension broke without any warning, leaving her to toss about in a net of small shocks. Her soft cries echoed in Gideon's ears as she clung to him and her nails left the evidence of her need on his broad shoulders. She felt him shudder and then he, too, was crying out, a hoarse, masculine shout of satisfaction that thrilled her.

A moment later Hannah went limp beneath Gideon's weight. Remembered wonder and pleasure lingered in her eyes as she lifted her lashes. A small, private smile touched her mouth.

Gideon reluctantly rolled to one side, bracing himself on his elbow. He lifted a finger to touch the edge of her lips. "Now you're the one who's laughing."

"I know. It was just that it was such a surprise. I mean, by the time a woman reaches my age, she's aware she's missed something along the line but it's hard to know exactly what until it happens."

Gideon's shoulders blocked the moon as he loomed over her. "Are you trying to tell me in your own delicate fashion that you've never had an orgasm?"

"I wouldn't dare say that. It's unthinkable in this modern day and age for a woman to admit it. Furthermore, saying it would do unmentionable things to your ego."

"It's too late." He kissed the tip of her breast. "You've already told me."

"And your ego?"

"Is approximately twice the size it was half an hour ago," he assured her.

"I was afraid of that."

"If I play my cards right," he said, "I can go on from here to convince you that I'm the best thing that ever happened to you."

"It's not your card playing ability that interests me." Hannah drew a circle through the hair on his chest. She smiled.

Gideon groaned. "The trouble with aggressive women . . ."

"Yes?"

"Is that they're very exciting." He got to his feet and reached down to lift her up beside him. "But I think I've had enough of the great outdoors tonight. We'll spend the rest of the evening in bed."

They did. In Elizabeth Nord's wide, elaborately worked rattan bed to be exact. Before the night was over Hannah had deepened her knowledge of her own unique, very feminine power. It seemed strange to her that it had required this particular man to teach her about this aspect of herself. She wondered if he had learned anything from her. Her last thought before finally slipping into sleep in Gideon's arms was he had definitely been right.

Going to bed with Gideon Cage had been important.

Perhaps it was the most important thing she had ever done in her life. But her own words of warning, spoken while the sea cradled her during the first stages of desire, came back to haunt Hannah, too. Understanding a man didn't buy safety for a woman.

GIDEON CAME AWAKE with the first light of the sun. He stretched fully, enjoying the feel of Hannah's leg trapped under his. Experimentally he moved his foot. When she didn't wake he decided to be noble. Carefully he slid out of bed and stood for a moment, looking down at her.

She was all soft, sleeping woman lying there in the shaft of yellow light. Her tawny hair was a riot of frothy little curls on the pillow, tousled from sleep and the uninhibited lovemaking. The sheet had slipped, revealing the rosy tip of one breast. Gideon remembered the feel of the nipple as it had tautened more than once under his tongue. The gentle curve of her back made him want to stroke her again, from the delicate nape of her neck to the lush roundness of her bottom.

She wasn't just a soft, sleeping woman this morning, Gideon realized. She was his woman. He could feel the possessiveness flow with the blood in his veins. Half of him was almost amused at the intensity of the feeling. The other half, the primitive, not quite civilized half, took the sensation very seriously.

Gideon turned away as his body began stirring in response to his memories. If he didn't find another way to work off this excessive morning energy he would find himself crawling back into bed with Hannah. And then he would most definitely wind up waking her. Which was hardly fair, he told himself. After all, he was the one who had exhausted her so thoroughly in the first place.

That thought converted itself into a small grin as he padded, naked, out onto the veranda. His mood called for a swim. The sea beckoned with a lure that was far more powerful than any swimming pool.

As soon as he was in the water Gideon realized just
why the sea was so right. It reminded him of how
Hannah had felt in his arms. Silken, liquid warmth
that enveloped a man. But, unlike the sea, Hannah
gave herself completely, honestly, delighting in the
exchange of passion. Her pleasure in her discoveries
about herself had fed his own joyous excitement.
Knowing he had pleased Hannah was satisfaction
enough for this first day in paradise. Hugh Ballantine
and Cage & Associates seemed very far away. Nothing like being alone with his woman on a tropical isle
to give a man a different perspective on life.

God, he felt great this morning. He couldn't remember the last time he had felt this good. Hannah
definitely was in the salvation business, even if she had
been under the impression that her talent was limited
to giving advice. Gideon laughed aloud and then arced
deeply beneath the waves.

IN THE WIDE RATTAN BED Hannah came awake with a
sense of anticipation somehow mixed with wariness.
Eyes closed, she used her bare toe to investigate her
immediate surroundings. When she realized that the
bed was empty she sat up, blinking. Gideon was already up and gone. Swimming, no doubt. How could
he resist the world's largest swimming pool at his front
door?

Hannah pushed back the covers, reaching for the
cane that Gideon had left next to her side of the bed.
She stood leaning on the cane as she gazed out the
window at a huge frangipani bush that appeared to be
trying to climb into the room. Beyond it she could see
the grove of palms that ringed the beach. No wonder
her aunt had chosen to live out her retirement here.

What more could a person ask of life than the blue-green sea, the pure, white sand and the swaying palms? A land of fantasy—brilliant, colorful fantasy.

Last night, Hannah knew, she had stepped completely into that fantasy, allowing it to enclose her. The real world seemed very far away this morning.

Neutral territory.

Except that the way she was feeling this morning was hardly neutral.

Hannah made her way to the shower. Gideon still hadn't returned by the time she had dried herself and dressed in a pair of white linen trousers and a snappy white linen blouse that tied just above her navel. Both garments had been styled to look like sophisticated versions of a tropical naturalist's outfit, complete with pockets on the legs of the trousers and the sleeves. The linen was wrinkled from having been folded into a flight bag but Hannah reminded herself that the catalog had assured her linen was supposed to look wrinkled. That was the way it proved to the world it wasn't a synthetic. Hannah pinned her mass of curls back from her face with two tortoiseshell combs and decided she was ready for a major endeavor such as making coffee.

Actually, she felt good, wonderfully good, if she discounted the occasional twinges in the muscles of her inner thighs. With every step she received a small reminder of the night's activities, but she could live with that. Even her knee felt reasonably comfortable this morning. Hannah headed for the kitchen.

She found a teakettle and filled it with water. After she'd set it on the stove Hannah wandered out into the sun-filled living room. The window in front of the teak desk gave the best view of the sea. Leaning forward,

Hannah braced herself with both palms and narrowed her eyes against the brilliant morning light. No wonder painters had always liked islands. The light was incredible. As she watched the dazzle on the sea, she thought she saw Gideon's dark head in the waves. He was stroking back toward shore.

For a moment Hannah battled an odd uncertainty. She wanted to be cool and casual about the relationship that had flared to life last night. Gideon would be cool and casual about it, she was quite sure of that. A confidence in his own power as a man had always underlined his confidence in his power as an executive. Some of the faint wariness with which she had awakened that morning returned. People who wielded power as easily as Gideon did were dangerous. She would do well to remember that.

But it was a little late to be issuing warnings to herself. Hannah sighed and absently began opening the desk drawers. She had come to Santa Inez to sort and pack her aunt's library, not to have an affair with the man who had nearly ruined her brother.

The center drawer of the desk was locked but Hannah found the key on the ring she had brought with her. When she used it on the tiny lock, the drawer opened to reveal the expected assortment of pens and pencils, paper clips, and rubber bands. It also revealed a small, exquisitely carved wooden box. Curiously Hannah lifted it out of the drawer and opened it.

A pendant lay inside. It hung from a chain of heavy metal links. The stone in the simply worked setting was not particularly breathtaking or interesting. It was a dull greenish gray, opaque instead of clear, and it was unfaceted. The rounded surface had been cut, however. There was a design on it that was difficult to make out. Hannah turned her back to the window so that the morning sun fell full on the stone. The engraving was a series of graceful curves that flowed into the shape of a nude woman. The figure was holding something in one hand, perhaps a sword.

Glancing down at the box, Hannah saw a slip of white paper that had been lying under the stone. She unfolded it and found a handwritten note signed by Elizabeth Nord. It was dated shortly before her death.

> For you, Hannah. The future is yours and yours alone.
> Do not be afraid of it.

The stone seemed to grow warm in Hannah's hand. She blinked back a trace of dampness as she fastened the pendant around her neck. It wasn't as if she and her aunt had ever been close. But she had always felt a distant kind of link with Elizabeth Nord. Perhaps that was why she had come to love islands and why she had once almost made a career out of anthropology. The gift was unexpected and it touched her.

Gideon came through the double doors just as she finished locking the pendant in place. Hannah glanced up and then blinked as she realized that he was standing in front of her, unabashedly naked, his towel slung over his shoulder. His mouth curved with private male humor as he watched her efforts to keep her eyes firmly fixed on his face. Idly Gideon touched the stone in the pendant.

"Where did you get that?"

"I just found it in my aunt's desk. There was a note. She said it was meant for me. Like it?"

Gideon considered the object. "Not especially. Is it supposed to be valuable?"

"I have no idea. Probably not. I don't think Aunt Elizabeth was into jewelry. There's an interesting figure cut on the surface, though. She probably picked it up somewhere during one of her research trips."

"I can think of more interesting souvenirs." Gideon's faint amusement turned into a decidedly wicked grin as he leaned down to kiss Hannah.

Hannah tasted the salt on his mouth. The hard contours of his body pushed against her softness with the kind of aggressive confidence that came to a man who has assured himself he can satisfy a woman. Firmly Hannah told herself that such things worked both ways. She had satisfied Gideon, too. She put her arms around his neck and returned the kiss.

"Umm," Gideon muttered against her lips. "I was thinking of taking a shower and getting dressed for the day, but maybe I'll reprioritize things."

The whistle of the teakettle broke into his discussion of the change of plans.

"The hot water." Hannah stepped out of his arms. "Go back to plan A. I'll pour you a cup of coffee while you shower."

"Let's not do anything hasty here."

Hannah smiled. "I hate to mention little details, but I did come down here to work."

"You also came down here to take long walks on the beach," he reminded her.

"And so far I've done neither."

"Any complaints?" There was a hint of an edge to the words.

It occurred to Hannah that Gideon would want to establish and set the pace of the relationship. He considered it established after last night. Now he would control the pace. She must not forget that she was dealing with a man who was accustomed to manipulating everything to his own ends.

"No complaints," she said softly. "But I could use a little help packing books."

He relaxed, chuckling. "Don't worry. I'll earn my keep. See you in a few minutes."

She watched him stride down the hall to the bathroom, marveling at the easy strength with which he moved. He was whistling a nameless tune. A part of her was tempted to follow him right into the shower. She resisted and headed for the kitchen, instead. The battery that ran Gideon's ego didn't need any extra charging this morning.

She had cereal and toast and coffee ready when he emerged fifteen minutes later wearing casual cotton pants and a fresh cotton shirt.

"Just think," he said, swinging a chair around to face the kitchen table, "we've got a whole week of this in front of us."

"And then what?" Hannah regretted the words the moment they were spoken. You weren't supposed to discuss the long-term plans for a short-term affair. She was certain that somewhere there was an unwritten law about it. But it was too late to recall the question. Gideon looked at her as his white teeth closed around a huge chunk of toast.

"Then we take it from there."

"Sorry I asked." Talk about a nonanswer. Hannah bit into her own toast with a certain savagery. Then she summoned a smile. "No more dumb questions. I promise."

"It's not a dumb question," he said. "It's just that there aren't any answers yet."

"I know. I told you, it won't happen again."

"Hannah." He broke off, frowning as he tried to find the words he wanted. Then he gave up the task and switched topics. "What are you going to use to pack the books?"

"I don't know. I'll have to dig up some cartons. It'll cost a fortune to airfreight them back to Seattle, but I think that's what I'll do."

"You'll need packing boxes. We might be able to buy them from the airline or a freight handler here on Santa Inez. We'll drive into town later today and see what we can find."

Hannah grimaced. "I didn't exactly come prepared, did I?"

He shrugged. "It doesn't matter. I'm good at this sort of thing."

"Finding packing boxes?"

He grinned. "Organizing."

"Oh. Want to help me sort books after breakfast?"

"Should be interesting."

And thus, Hannah told herself bracingly, *we neatly pass over my little embarrassing faux pas.* She vowed not to make a fool of herself again. She was a big girl now. Big girls handled affairs with aplomb.

An hour later Hannah acknowledged aloud that the task of sorting through Elizabeth Nord's library was going to be far more involved than she had initially thought. One of the major problems was getting sidetracked by an interesting monograph or a fascinating bit of lore. Gideon wasn't immune, either. When Hannah glanced up from the folder of notes her aunt had made for a book, she found Gideon sitting cross-legged on the floor, an old, yellowed map spread out in front of him.

"What have you got there?" she asked.

He didn't look up. "A military intelligence map."

"Really? Of what?"

"Revelation Island. It was done in nineteen forty-two. Shows a landing strip that was the main objective of the Marines who were assigned to take the island. This would have been top secret at the time. I wonder how your aunt came by a map like this."

"She was doing her field work there in the early forties when the war broke out. I'm not quite sure when she left to return to the States."

"Maybe she helped do the military map. After all, she must have had a thorough knowledge of the island." Gideon bent over the faded, creased sheet of paper. "Military intelligence might have tapped her brain."

Hannah watched him for a moment and then smiled. "How long have you been into maps, Gideon?"

"For as long as I can remember. I used to do these incredibly elaborate maps of my neighborhood when I was a kid."

"Showing where all the cars with the best hubcaps were parked?"

"Cars with expensive hubcaps didn't park in my neighborhood." He continued to study the reconnaissance map. "I thought about becoming a cartographer for a while but Cyrus Ballantine's way of life was too tempting. So maps became a hobby. I had an idea I'd collect them seriously one day. Maybe build a really good collection around a couple of themes. You

know, military maps or nineteenth-century maps of
the States. Maybe maps of the world done before a
particular date. Then, after a while, maps became just
something interesting to hang on the walls." He was
treating the map in his hand as carefully as if he were
an antiquarian handling a rare book. Then he became
lost in his study of the island outlined on the yellowed
sheet.

Hannah was aware of a familiar sense of empathy
and compassion. She knew without any doubt that
Gideon should have nurtured his love of maps. He
shouldn't have allowed it to disintegrate. It was the
guidance counselor in her, she told herself. Too much
pop psychology. She ought to keep her mouth shut.
Gideon didn't welcome advice.

"Do you think you'll ever get back into your old
hobby?"

"Who knows? There's not much time for it these
days."

"Because you're too busy taking over other people's companies?"

He glanced up at that, eyes hardening faintly. "Or
threatening to take them over." He spoke much too
politely.

Hannah knew she had stepped over an invisible line
but she couldn't stop herself from finishing. "You
should, you know."

"Should what? Take over companies?"

She shook her head. "No. Get back into maps."

He tapped the edge of the sheet spread out on the
floor in front of him. "I already have another hobby,
remember?"

"Gambling? That isn't what you need. It doesn't provide the right kind of balance in your life. The maps might."

"I thought you weren't handing out free advice on this trip."

"I can't seem to help myself. Keep that map, Gideon. I have no use for it and you deserve something for helping me pack all these books."

"It belongs with your aunt's collection."

"I'm the one who decides what belongs and what doesn't." She waved a hand cheerfully to indicate the piles of documents surrounding them. "I won't miss one little map."

"You're sure?"

"I'm sure. Hang it on a wall in your home. When you look at it think about adding balance to your life."

He considered her words, challenge etching his expression. Hannah didn't like the look he was giving her. It made her uneasy, warned her she might have bitten off more than she could chew.

"Maybe," Gideon drawled, "I can use a woman to put a little balance into my life."

"You might use a woman for a lot of things, but I doubt you'd use her to keep your life on an even keel."

"Because I'm not bright enough to figure out how to do that?"

"No, because to do that you'd have to be willing to give up something of yourself. You'd have to surrender some of your sense of control. You're used to being the one in charge at all times. It would be hard for you to relax and let another human being have some room in your life. But the maps wouldn't present that kind of risk or threat. The trick with them would be to

teach yourself to turn your back for a while on the
fake rush you get from pulling off your business
coups. It would be good for you, though.''

''You think you know me so well.''

''I've already proven I can make large mistakes trying to analyze you,'' she reminded him.

He got to his feet in a lithe movement, advancing
across the room to confront her as she sat at the desk.
There was a restless gleam in his eyes and a touch of
grimness around his mouth as he leaned forward and
planted his hands on the teak surface. ''Do you think
last night was a mistake, Hannah? Worrying you
made a serious error in judgment by allowing me to get
into your bed?''

''No,'' Hannah said with complete honesty. ''I
don't think last night was a mistake. My life has lacked
something, too.''

''A man?''

She smiled at the arrogant satisfaction in him. ''No.
Risks. You're used to taking them and you're used to
winning. I hadn't done much of either until I met
you.''

''Getting the hang of it?''

''I'm getting the hang of taking the risks, all right.
Got off to a great start trying to cheat you at cards.
But I haven't had too much experience at winning yet.
On the other hand,'' she said evenly, ''I'm a good
student.''

''I can testify to that.'' He hauled her lightly up into
his arms. ''I enjoyed watching you learn a few things
last night. But now you're going to have to devote
yourself to practicing what you've learned.'' Some of
the sensual amusement faded as he studied her face.
''Hannah, whatever happens, don't ever doubt this is

a two-way street. I needed this trip and I needed you. I've never needed anything so much in my life."

Hannah smiled tremulously. The pendant seemed suddenly very warm as it lay between her breasts. She ignored the sensation and gave herself up to the more inviting heat of Gideon's kiss.

Chapter Six

HANNAH FOUND the colorful little map of Santa Inez
Island and the sea around it on the third afternoon of
her vacation. She knew it was the perfect gift the moment she saw it. Clutching her prize carefully so as not
to crease its heavy paper she made her way through the
crowded gift shop to the sales counter. A glance
through the open door showed that Gideon was still
occupied in the bookstore on the other side of the
cobbled courtyard.

It was Gideon who had insisted that they take a
break from the task of sorting and packing Nord's library. After lunch he had firmly bundled Hannah into
the pink-fringed jeep and driven her into town. She
was careful not to look down as they drove along the
cliff road, and that precaution, together with her trust
in Gideon's expert driving, made the trip almost en-
joyable.

Hannah had been grateful for the forced break.
Elizabeth Nord's papers and books were beginning to
ignite a kind of obsessive interest. The packing had
become slower and slower as each new item caught
Hannah's attention. Her fantasy of writing the book
that would infuriate Victoria Armitage was metamor-
phosing into more than a playful daydream. Hannah
was starting to think quite seriously about the project. The realization was intimidating. She had enough
of an academic background to know that Vicky was

right. Elizabeth Nord's library should be turned over to the experts. Hannah had no business trying to scoop the academic world. But she could no longer shake off the desire to do so.

Hannah and Gideon had found the cluster of tiny shops when they had explored a narrow alley that led off Santa Inez's main street. It was a picturesque collection of boutiques in an old courtyard shaded by heavy palms. Several other tourists and a couple of watercolor artists had already discovered the inviting scene. It had been a delight for Hannah and now she had found the map. She waited impatiently while the clerk carefully rolled it and wrapped it.

As she left the shop with her purchase tucked into a shopping bag, Hannah wondered if Gideon would bother to hang her gift on his wall alongside the huge, expensive maps he already had framed. It struck her then that she might never know what he chose to do with the chart. Hannah paused in the dappled sunlight under a palm tree and forced herself to deal with that fact.

She might never see Gideon Cage again after this precious week in paradise. It was as she stood there, staring unseeingly at the dusty pink walls of the courtyard that she began to acknowledge the truth of her feelings for Gideon. Before she could put the feelings into words, a movement at the corner of her vision caught her attention.

Automatically she glanced to the side and saw one of the artists, a thin man with a beard dressed in shorts, T-shirt and thongs, begin to pack up his paints and brushes. He nodded politely as she watched him. A little embarrassed, Hannah quickly looked away.

The small distraction had broken the spell of her incipient brooding and Hannah told herself she would not let the mood return. This was, after all, only her third day with Gideon. She had four left. Buoyed by the thought, Hannah hurried toward the bookshop where Gideon was paying for a weekly business newsmagazine.

"You're supposed to be on vacation," she reminded him as she saw his choice in reading material.

He grimaced. "I know. I've been feeling a little out of touch."

"By the time you get back to Tucson everything in that magazine will be old news."

"I'm aware of that." His long fingers clenched rather fiercely on the paper sack.

It was the force of his grip on the sack along with the edge in his voice that convinced Hannah to change the subject. "There's a duty-free jewelry shop up ahead. I want to see if they have any real bargains on watches."

But after careful perusal of the collection of Swiss and Japanese watches Hannah decided that she really didn't need anything to replace the twenty-dollar functional quartz watch she already wore.

"It does everything these fancy ones do," she explained to Gideon. "Tells the time and date and what's more, it uses real numbers. I don't understand this trend toward designing elegant watches and then leaving off the numbers. What's the point of a watch without numbers?"

"Only someone who was not destined to be eternally trendy could ask that. It's almost five o'clock. Let's go have a drink and discuss the matter. Looks like it's going to rain any minute."

He took her arm and led her out of the courtyard and back down the alley. By mutual consent they headed toward the main street of town, the one that overlooked the harbor and, after a little speculating, settled on an open-air, island-style bar shaded with a low-slung thatched roof. Under the thatched roof they found a pleasant collection of cane chairs and tables.

The rain came just as they were seated near the bamboo railing that encircled the bar. Hannah was growing accustomed to the frequent, warm showers that poured briefly from the clouds that built up overhead during the hot afternoons.

"I like the idea of warm rain. I think I could get used to it," she told Gideon. "You don't have to worry about getting wet because you dry out in a few minutes anyway. Seattle should consider switching to warm water instead of cold."

"The rain is like this in Tucson during the summers. Comes down like a waterfall in the afternoons. Cools things off for a while." Gideon's eyes were on the small boats bobbing in the marina that nestled in a corner of the harbor.

The last thing Hannah had wanted to discuss was Tucson. In a firm voice she ordered a frothy rum and fruit juice concoction from the hovering waiter. When Gideon ordered his usual Scotch she berated him cheerfully.

"You can drink Scotch anytime. Why don't you try something new? Live dangerously."

"I've already got enough excitement in my life."

Hannah wasn't certain how to take that. It was not, she felt sure, a compliment to her. Gideon seemed to have his mind on something else entirely. She was afraid she knew what it was. The dignified heading of the business newsmagazine was visible over the edge of the paper sack that lay on the table beside him. Determinedly she sought for still another topic.

"We should be able to finish packing my aunt's books by tomorrow."

"If you can stop taking time out to read as you pack."

Hannah winced. "I'm not the only one who gets sidetracked. Every time you come across a new map you take a break, too."

"It doesn't slow me down."

The drinks arrived before Hannah could seek still another conversational gambit. Gideon's mood was making her nervous. As usual, her knee seemed to react to the tension. Unobtrusively she stretched out her leg under the table, trying to relieve the tightness. Gideon's expression darkened.

"What's wrong? Leg hurting?"

"It's just a little stiff, that's all."

"I told you that you were overdoing the long walks on the beach in the mornings. You should stick to swimming for exercise."

"Yes, Gideon, you've mentioned that more than once."

"For all the good it does."

Annoyance began to replace the uneasy feeling. Hannah stirred her rum drink with a swizzle stick that had a tiny paper umbrella on the tip. "I'm the one who's in the professional advice business, remember?"

"Does that mean you don't take good advice, yourself?" There was clear challenge in Gideon's narrowed gaze. He cradled the Scotch between his hands and watched Hannah broodingly.

"Let's just say I'm probably better at giving it than taking it."

"That's not saying much, is it? The advice you give isn't all that useful except maybe to some dumb kid in college who can't decide whether to go into medicine or join the circus."

Hannah's fingers trembled slightly. She wrapped them more tightly around her glass. "I'm not sure the quality of my advice matters as far as you're concerned. You've made it clear you don't intend to take it."

"You haven't given me anything useful."

Just myself, wholeheartedly, for the past three nights. "You're in a hell of a mood, Gideon. Mind telling me why you're looking for an argument?"

He closed his eyes in brief disgust. "I don't know," he admitted finally.

Hannah took a breath and decided to try a tentative foray. "Is it because you've started worrying about your business and what's going on back in Tucson?"

"Just because I'm standing still on this island doesn't mean Ballantine is waiting patiently somewhere else."

"So?"

"So I'm out of touch. I don't know what he's doing. I started thinking about it this afternoon. If I know Ballantine, he's moving."

"Moving on what?"

Gideon moved a hand impatiently. "On a company called Surbrook. It's an aerospace manufacturing firm. Very lucrative but very strung out financially. A ripe target."

"Are you going after the same company?"

"I've told my clients we're going to take over Surbrook, install our own management to straighten it out, and then unload it at a sizeable profit."

"And Ballantine?"

"He's told his clients the same thing."

"I see." Hannah tried a sip of her rum drink, using the straw to siphon up the pineapple-and-guava flavored froth.

"I doubt it."

"What's so complicated that a simple guidance counselor couldn't figure it out? You're both going after the same firm. Only one of you will get it. The only question is which gunslinger goes down in the dust in front of the Bitter End saloon, the old pro or the new, young tough. The trouble with gunslingers is that they never figure out there's another alternative."

Gideon's face was set in harsh lines, but he couldn't seem to stop himself from asking, "What alternative?"

"One of the gunmen could simply walk away from the fight."

"Jesus Christ, lady. If that's your idea of advice, you'd better stick to handing it out to undergraduates."

"Well? Why can't you just walk away?" she demanded.

"Because in my business reputation is everything. If I start giving up on a project after promising my clients I'm going to make money for them, I'll very soon find myself without any clients. Is that simple enough for you?"

"I can't see why abandoning one takeover project should ruin your precious reputation."

"If Ballantine doesn't get the showdown he wants over Surbrook, he'll simply create another. If I don't show up for the next fight, he'll try again. And again. And with each new contest he'll be a little stronger, a little wiser, a little harder to beat. By the time my back is against the wall, he'll be a hell of a lot harder to deal with than he is right now. Sooner or later my back will be to the wall, Hannah. Don't you understand? He'll simply keep pushing, keep going after everything I want until he forces me to fight back. He can afford some losses. After all, he's young and everyone knows he's just starting to claw his way up to the top. People will expect a few losses from him enroute."

"But they won't tolerate losses from you?"

"I'm not supposed to make mistakes."

"You make the whole thing sound inevitable."

"It is," he growled.

"Then why keep pushing me for advice you can't use and don't want?"

Gideon took another long sip of Scotch. "Damned if I know."

Hannah had a flash of intuition. "It's because even though you say you have no alternatives, a part of you is still looking for a way out. You're hoping against hope that I'll come up with something really brilliant. Something that might give you an idea of how to handle Ballantine. Could anyone have stopped you nine years ago?"

"No."

Hannah let that hang in the air for a moment. The rain began to slack off as the late afternoon thunderstorm disintegrated. Water ran quickly off the streets into the open gutters that lined the roads and alleys.

Santa Inez had had its afternoon bath and was clean and sparkling once more.

"Have you considered," she asked cautiously, "abandoning the field even if it means giving up Cage & Associates entirely? Let Ballantine take whatever he wants."

Gideon stared at her as if she were out of her mind. "Are you crazy? I've spent nine years building that company. I created it out of nothing. I've spent every day for the past nine years making it what it is today."

"But you're not enjoying it. From what I can tell, you've never particularly enjoyed it. You get a few adrenaline highs from the skirmishes but that's about it. You know what your problem is? You've lived off power for so long you're not sure you can live without it. But there are other things besides power out there, Gideon."

"You don't know what you're talking about. You've been safely locked away in your liberal ivory tower, theorizing about the real world but never actually having to live in it."

"That's not true."

"It is true," he gritted. "You want proof? Only a fool who had no concept of the reality of the business world would have come down to Tucson and tried to beat me out of what I wanted with a deck of marked cards. And only an even bigger fool would have given me a lecture about changing my ways after she'd tried to cheat me."

Hannah had all she could do not to show how badly she was starting to bleed from the wounds he was inflicting. With all the dignity she could muster she reached for her cane and got to her feet.

"Where the hell do you think you're going?"

"Back to the cottage," she said quietly. "I didn't invite you to Seattle and I didn't invite you along on this trip. You have an incredible amount of nerve to sit there and chew me out for the quality of my advice. If you don't want it, you shouldn't keep hounding me for it."

Unsteadily she started across the plank floor. Her leg was throbbing now. Before she reached the door Gideon was at her side, taking her arm. In his hand he carried his own paper bag plus the package she had left behind.

"You didn't invite me to Seattle and you didn't invite me to Santa Inez but you sure as hell invited me into your bed," he muttered.

"I don't recall issuing the invitation."

"Then you've got a poor memory, lady."

Hannah was incensed. "Gideon, I think this *relationship* of ours has about run its course. It's obvious you're anxious to get back to the big showdown in Tucson. Don't let me stop you."

"I'm not going anywhere for another four days."

They were out on the sidewalk now, heading toward the jeep. The dissolving thunderclouds were reflecting the light of the setting sun in a magnificent sweep of burnt gold and peach. The breathtaking sunsets were as common to Santa Inez as the afternoon showers. Beyond the harbor the sea heaved gently under the receding line of rain.

"Gideon, I don't see any reason to spend four more days together. Not if you're going to spend them gnawing on me. This is my vacation and my cottage but this is not exactly my idea of a good time. I won't let you ruin . . ." Her knee gave slightly as she swung herself into the front seat of the jeep.

Automatically Gideon reached out to steady her. The package with the rolled map in it started to slip. He caught it just before it dropped into the swirling water of the gutter.

"What the hell's this?" He examined the curled sheet of paper.

"A souvenir. Here, I'll take it." Hannah made a grab for it and missed.

"Looks like a map." Retaining his hold on it Gideon walked around the front of the little four-wheel drive vehicle and climbed into the driver's seat. He sat behind the wheel and unrolled the chart. He spread it out carefully against the wheel and sat studying it for a long moment. Eventually he looked at Hannah. "You don't collect charts and maps."

"Gideon . . ."

"You bought this for me, didn't you?"

"Sometimes," Hannah said dryly, "I tend to act impulsively."

"Regretting this impulse?"

"Let's just say I am now thinking of having the map laminated. I can use it on my kitchen table."

"Like hell." Something flickered in his eyes as he leaned across the gearshift and caught her chin in his fingers. "Thank you, Hannah."

She said nothing, searching his face in silence.

"You're right about one thing," Gideon said.

"What's that?"

"I have no right to chew you into bits and pieces every time you offer some advice. The truth is, I want you to go on offering it."

Hannah shook her head. "Why?"

"Because I haven't got anyone else I can talk to the way I do to you." He rerolled the gift with great care and stashed it safely behind the seat. Then he twisted the keys in the ignition. "I like it when you try to tell me what to do."

"I doubt that." Hannah braced her hand on the side of the windshield as the jeep darted out into the disorganized traffic of Santa Inez's main thoroughfare. Two taxis honked loudly as Gideon cut them off but there was no real malice in the sound. It was more an acknowledgement that the pink-fringed jeep had won the small contest.

"It's true, you know," Gideon insisted above the noise of the traffic and the engine. "I do like it."

"There must be any number of people who would be quite happy to tell you what to do and where to go."

"Ah, but they all have axes to grind, preferably into my skull. I can't trust their advice." He grinned, his mood changing abruptly as he drove. The wind caught his hair, ruffling it.

"What makes you think my advice is so damned altruistic?" Hannah challenged.

"You've already learned the hard way that you can't manipulate me. But you still let me into your bed and you still hand out the advice. Must be out of pure, altruistic motives. You're sweet, Hannah. Gentle. Kind."

"Sweet, gentle, and kind are insults, coming from you. They make me sound weak, silly, and vulnerable."

"You are definitely not weak or silly. Just a little out of your depth when you start trying to tell me how to run my business."

"Do me a favor. The next time you're trying to come up with some compliments, keep them to yourself."

His grin broadened as he slanted a glance at her. "In addition to sweet, gentle, and kind you have the sexiest little ass I've ever seen."

"I can't tell you what your admiration means to me."

He laughed, his good mood fully restored. "Thanks for the maps, Hannah," he said again. "Both of them. I'll take good care of them."

"Hey, where are we going?" she demanded as he turned off the main road and started inland. The narrow track that bisected the island was known, appropriately enough, as the mountain road. It crossed Santa Inez at the island's highest point.

"To dinner. Remember that old plantation we read about? The one up on the mountain that's been turned into a hotel?"

"I remember."

"It's supposed to have great conch chowder."

"Is this a peace offering?"

"Honey, we're not at war."

Hannah thought about that. "I'd hate to be in the way if we were."

Two HOURS LATER Hannah was forced to concede that the "peace offering" had worked. By the time she had dined on conch chowder, lobster, and a heavenly coconut-and-pineapple pie she was willing to let bygones be bygones.

From the veranda of what had once been a plantation home back in the days when the island had been rich in cane and cotton, dinner guests could look out on the town and its harbor far below. Trickling down the hillside to the sea were scattered bits and pieces of gleaming gems, the lights of homes built along the mountain road. Many belonged to those living out their dream of retiring to an island as Elizabeth Nord had done. Most of those born on Santa Inez preferred to live in town where it was easier to participate in the casual round of community life. The locals took the breathtaking sea views for granted. Only the expatriates demanded beachfront or hillside property.

On the drive back down the mountain after dinner, Gideon made a few of the short, pithy comments he reserved for other drivers on the narrow roads, but his general mood remained complacent. Hannah felt relaxed and happy once more. She could almost ignore the twists and turns of the route down the mountain. Gideon's driving was smooth and competent. Whatever had been making him restless earlier in the day seemed to have faded into the background.

Four more days to go.

"I don't suppose you feel like packing one more carton of books tonight?" Hannah asked as she entered the living room of her aunt's house. "We're almost done."

"Not especially. But I wouldn't mind having a brandy and sitting on the sofa while I watch you work."

"You're too good to me."

"I'm glad you realize it." He headed for the kitchen.

Hannah walked over to the one set of bookshelves that had not yet been denuded. Cartons of materials, all precisely wrapped and labeled, were neatly stacked to the left of the door. The neatness of both packaging and labeling was one of Gideon's chief contributions to the effort. Hannah had discovered early on that his handwriting was a good deal better than her own. It was probably a legacy of his early interest in maps, she had decided. Or perhaps the precision and control of it were simply a reflection of his character.

Idly she plucked one of a series of slim, black, leather-bound volumes off the bottom shelf, opening it at random. Her aunt's now-familiar handwriting covered the pages.

"Gideon?"

"Yeah?" Glasses clinked in the kitchen.

"I think I've found something interesting."

"You're always finding something interesting." He gave her an indulgent smile as he came through the door bearing the snifters of brandy.

"I'm serious. This looks like a journal. It goes back to the very beginning of her career. Back to when she was a grad student." Hannah dropped cross-legged to the floor, spread the book on her lap, and scanned the pages with deepening interest. "This is going to be where the good stuff is. I know it. These are her personal journals and observations of her early studies. Not her formal papers and notes."

"What do you mean 'good stuff'?" He sprawled on the sofa, watching her. "Sex?"

"You've got a one-track mind."

"It wasn't me who was planning to write the sleazy best-seller exposing her aunt's exploration of bizarre sexual customs."

Hannah frowned over one of the pages. "Well, I may have to tone down the lesbian angle. Too bad. That would have been good for sales."

"Your aunt was straight after all?"

"There's definitely a man hanging around here at the beginning of her career. A 'Dear Roddy.'"

Gideon exposed his teeth. "Roddy?"

"No worse than 'Giddy.'"

"You ever call me that and you'll find yourself over my knee."

Hannah smiled, her eyes never leaving the page. "We haven't tried it that way yet. Might be interesting."

"Interesting for me. Uncomfortable for you. What's with Dear Roddy?"

"Looks like he was a year or two ahead of her in his studies. Went with her on this field trip to research a Southwestern Indian tribe."

"Does it look like they shared the same field tent?"

Hannah chuckled. "Nothing that indiscreet. But it's obvious she was very excited both about the study and about Dear Roddy. Listen to this:

> Dear Roddy agrees with me that the vocabulary the women use is different in some ways from that of the men. It contains words the men do not use. He understood at once what I have discovered. I'm not sure he has accepted my conclusion about the importance of this find, however. He did point out that the lower prestige associated with certain words in the women's vocabulary might help contribute to the stereotyped image the men have of them as fundamentally inferior. But he doesn't agree that the women themselves might be using the extended vocabulary as a means of establishing a significant bond of communication among themselves."

Gideon swirled the brandy in his glass. "So what's so important about the women's vocabulary?"

Hannah drummed her fingers on her knee, frowning thoughtfully. "Well, take *mauve*."

"You take it. I wouldn't touch it with a ten-foot pole."

"Exactly. Why wouldn't you touch it?"

Gideon narrowed his eyes. "It's a silly word. A word for dress designers and fashion freaks and a few other groups I won't mention."

"What other groups?"

"All right, all right. It's a woman's word."

Hannah grinned. "Now you've got it. Big, tough, macho types such as yourself wouldn't think of using a word like mauve or taupe."

"No reason to use them," he grumbled into the brandy.

"Are you kidding? Without them you can't begin to describe certain shades of purple or brown nearly as accurately as I can."

"There is no need to describe those particular shades of purple or brown," Gideon stated with absolute certainty.

"Face it, Gideon. Without the word *mauve* in your vocabulary, you're limited when it comes to describing colors. I could give you an example of other words you probably wouldn't use because they seem silly and female to you. But by using them I can communicate much more precisely with my women friends or with an interior designer, for that matter. The drawback to my using them is that it might make me sound like a woman."

"You are a woman."

"Very observant. Given that fact and knowing nothing can change it, why should I deprive myself of the word?" Hannah went back to the page she was studying. "Actually, this was a very astute observation on my aunt's part. She made these notes before the war, you know. Before linguistic analysis was as advanced as it is today."

"What's Dear Roddy have to say about all this?"

Hannah read a little further. "Apparently he was inclined to take a condescending attitude. Aunt Elizabeth gave him a detailed analysis of her findings and he just sort of patted her on the head and told her she was a bright girl. He's lucky she didn't kick him in the balls."

Gideon winced. "That's not a very feminine thing to say."

"My vocabulary isn't limited to just feminine words." Hannah read further. "Her basic conclusion is that the women's language is richer and is used to express whole concepts and emotions that the men can't understand. Here's the bottom line, though. The paper she wrote on the subject was accepted for publication. Dear Roddy's was not. Hah! Take that, Dear Roddy."

"The question is, was your aunt sleeping with him or not?"

"If she was, apparently he wasn't good enough in bed to change her mind about her research findings." Hannah closed the journal. "Darn. This is interesting, of course, especially if I can ever find out exactly who Dear Roddy was. Wouldn't it be great if he's now some honcho in the anthro world?"

"Revealing a leading academic's past indiscretions with your famous aunt might make for some of the sleaze you want," Gideon agreed musingly. "Probably would have more snap, though, if you could work the lesbian angle. A bit more shocking."

"I know. Well, we'll just have to wait and see what happens." Hannah scanned the row of thin black books. "No telling what other interesting tidbits are buried in these journals."

Gideon studied her quietly, the wry humor disappearing from his expression. "You're really starting to think seriously about writing that book, aren't you?"

"Yes," Hannah said simply. "I am."

"Out of a desire to get even with Vicky Armitage?"

Unconsciously Hannah fingered the pendant around her neck. "It's more than that, Gideon. Maybe I want to prove something to myself."

"Prove what? That you could have made it in anthropology if you'd wanted to go that route? Writing the book won't prove it. You've said yourself, it's not exactly going to carry the weight of anthropological expertise. You're going for titillation and controversy, remember? You might sell a million copies but the academic world will probably still tear it apart and hang it up to dry."

"Let 'em." Hannah's mouth curved. "Whatever else they do, they won't be able to ignore it. My aunt would have loved it."

Gideon set down his glass, clasping his hands between his knees. "What's the book going to do for you, Hannah?"

"I'm not sure yet."

"If you're going to step into the ring, you need to have your goals very clearly in mind. You need to know how far you'll go, how much punishment you can take, and whom you're willing to kill to get where you want to be. Most of all you have to know where you want to be.''

''Is that a warning from an expert?'' she asked calmly.

''Just thought I'd try my hand at a little guidance counseling.'' His mouth crooked wryly but his gaze remained serious. ''How am I doing?''

''I'm more accustomed to giving advice than I am to taking it.''

''I'm not used to taking advice, either. Maybe that's why I was so rough on you this afternoon. I'm sorry, Hannah.''

''I know. I figured you were when you decided to take me to dinner. It was your way of apologizing.''

''Still think you can read me like a book?''

''I'm getting more and more pieces of the puzzle together every day,'' she assured him.

''Come here, Hannah.'' He held out his big hands with slow, sensual intent. ''I'll give you something else to add to the total picture.''

She didn't move but she felt the ready stirring of desire deep in her body. ''You find this so easy, don't you?''

''Making love to you? Easiest thing I've ever done.''

''Because I'm a pushover?''

''No.'' He shook his head once. ''Because it feels so right. You fit me like a warm glove, Hannah.''

''I'm comfortable then? I'm not sure that's any more impressive than being a pushover.''

''Now who's spoiling for a fight?''

He came off the sofa in a smooth motion, bearing Hannah down until she was lying beneath him on the floor. She looked up at him, aware of the heat in his

eyes and the heavy weight of him sprawled along the
length of her body.

"This wasn't quite the fight I had in mind," she
whispered, eyes languid with the need he brought forth
so effortlessly.

"Yes, it is. I can feel it in you." He lowered his head
to her mouth, his hand closing over her breast. "And
I like the feel of it." His tongue slipped easily between her lips.

Through the thin material of the oversize fatigue
shirt she wore, Hannah felt her nipple tightening under his palm. She whispered Gideon's name far back
in her throat. He pushed his way between her thighs in
response, urging himself against her softness. She was
vividly aware of the heat in him, even though they
were both still fully dressed.

Gideon sighed in satisfaction as he felt Hannah
softening beneath him. Like the sea she gave way when
he pushed against her and then closed around him like
liquid silk. He wondered if he could ever get enough
of her. Deliberately he closed his mind to the fact that
there were only four days left on Santa Inez. There was
still too much to learn, too much to explore, too much
to experience with this woman. With Hannah he felt
new and revitalized. Going to bed with her was the
greatest refreshment he had ever known. She would
make him shudder with his need and afterward he
knew he would be satiated, thoroughly content for a
timeless interlude.

But the best part of all was listening to the way she
breathed his name when she trembled with her own
satisfaction. Gideon decided he would never in a million years grow tired of his name on her lips. Her re-

sponsiveness was a feast at which he could dine again and again.

He slipped open the buttons of her shirt. When he moved his hand inside to cup her breast his fingers brushed against the pendant. It was a cold, hard, worthless stone. He wondered what she saw in it. Then he forgot about the jewelry as his hand found a budding nipple. This was definitely not cold or worthless but there was a decided hardness to it that intrigued him enormously. Hungrily, Gideon bent to taste the firm peak.

Hannah's fingers clenched in his hair as he made the contact.

"Ah, Gideon. *Gideon!*"

"It's coming, honey. There's no rush."

"I'm in a rush," she complained, lifting herself achingly against him.

"Are you?" He reached down to unfasten the snap of her jeans and then he slid his fingers through the curling nest that shielded the tight, sensitive bud. "Then I'll give you a little something to tide you over until the main meal."

She gasped and twisted her hips as he began to stroke. Her fingertips tightened again in his hair and then slipped down to his shoulders.

When he used both hands to slide the jeans off completely she started to fumble with the buttons of his shirt. Laughing softly he caught her hands.

"Not yet. We're going to give you an appetizer first, remember?" Cupping her buttocks in his hands he went lower, seeking with his mouth the hot, fluid heart of her passion.

"Gideon!" His name was a soft scream of excitement and wonder. "Oh, my God, Gideon."

His fingers sank into her skin. "Don't fight it. Let it happen. Just let go. I want to feel you when it hits." The insides of her thighs were so warm, so very soft. The scent of her was filling his head, driving him half crazy with wanting.

Hannah tightened. He sensed the quickening tension, knew she was on the edge of release. Gideon deepened the intimate kiss and suddenly she was trembling in his grasp. The ripples of fulfillment moved through her like rain over the ocean. Gideon drank in her satisfaction as if it were his own.

"Gideon, I wanted to wait. I wanted to be with you when it happened." Hannah's protests were uttered before the gentle convulsions had faded. There was a wistfulness in her words.

Gideon moved up her body, eyes gleaming with anticipation. His mouth closed over hers, letting her taste herself on his lips.

"Now we'll go for the main meal." He saw the pleased astonishment in her eyes as he fit his body to hers and thrust forward. He entered her to the hilt and felt her fiercely feminine reaction.

"I don't think I can. Not so soon after. But I'd love it if you went ahead and had your wicked way with me," she murmured dreamily.

"Don't worry, you'll be there with me the next time. You've got all kinds of hidden talent."

Chapter Seven

THE DAWNING SUN seemed to fill the room with a light that was almost too clear, too fresh and new. The crimson frangipani that always appeared to be trying to grow through the louvers of the window could have been part of a painting. Acrylics or oils, Hannah decided. The red was too strong to capture with watercolors. The island had a way of making one think of trying one's hand at painting. For the first time in her life she was tempted to buy a brush and some paints and find out if she had any ability in that direction. Waste of time. She knew her own assets and abilities and art wasn't on the list.

Hannah lay still for a moment, blinking into wakefulness. Beside her Gideon slept in a magnificent sprawl that covered more than half the bed.

Turning carefully onto her side and bracing herself on her elbow Hannah looked at the man who, in the manner of a conquering army, occupied the bed. In the brilliant light he, too, was much too vivid and intense to catch with watercolors. The white sheet was twisted around one muscular leg. His other foot hung off the edge of the bed. Gideon lay on his stomach, his head turned away from her. The darkness of his hair was a harsh contrast to the pillow. Even in sleep the powerful contours of his shoulders spelled out the internal force in the man.

Hannah thought about the driving energy and will that motivated Gideon and wondered why he had followed her first to Seattle and then to Santa Inez. She was willing to bet this was the first time in his life he had let himself be distracted so completely while business was pressing. She didn't know whether to be flattered or wary. A little of both, perhaps.

It couldn't last, of course. She knew that. This week in paradise was a stolen one. She had resigned herself to that almost from the beginning, even though a part of her hadn't fully accepted the inevitable.

Gently Hannah pushed back the sheet. The brilliant light and her thoughts were making her restless. She felt strangely edgy. Naked except for the pendant, which she had forgotten to remove before going to bed, she walked to the window. Through the grove of palms that sheltered the cove she could see the hard, white light on the sea. Suddenly Hannah knew what she needed to work off this uneasy restlessness.

Gideon was still sound asleep as she slipped from the room with her swimsuit in hand. She dressed in the front room, slung a towel over her shoulder and opened the double doors to step out into the early morning light.

The small beach was extraordinarily pristine today, clean and white and untouched. The arm of the cove framed water that was too clear, almost unreal. Dropping the towel, Hannah waded into the sea.

This was the fourth day of her vacation. Hannah floated on her back and thought about what she would be doing this time next week. Gideon would be in Tucson. Would he call? She knew he wouldn't write. Men as busy as Gideon didn't write. The truth was that she would probably never see him again.

Hannah turned over and started stroking slowly toward the mouth of the cove. She had her own life to live and the odds were against Gideon ever being a permanent part of it. Unless he changed, no woman would ever be a permanent part of his life. He probably would never even notice what he'd missed.

Gideon wasn't unique. Aunt Elizabeth hadn't missed Dear Roddy apparently. There was no mention of him in her later notes. It would be fascinating to trace his story through the private journals. It occurred to Hannah that in some ways Gideon and Elizabeth Nord were alike. Both had achieved a large measure of personal power in the worlds they chose to occupy. Both seemed content to go through life alone.

It wasn't just that they were independent, Hannah decided as she tried to analyze the two people who had never met. Hannah, herself, was independent. She had been reasonably content with her career and her friends and her life-style. No, it was something else. There was something qualitatively different about the kind of aloneness characteristic of both her aunt and Gideon.

Hannah stopped swimming and treaded water as she stared out to sea. The dazzle of the light on the shifting water was almost blinding now. It hurt her eyes to look at it. She turned her head to study the rocky outthrust that formed one arm of the cove. Her eyes began to recover from the glare, and the jumble of granite, dark from sea spray, came into focus.

Focus. That was part of the key. Gideon and Elizabeth Nord had both been incredibly focused. Victoria Armitage was also focused, for that matter. And all three of them gave the impression they could, by and large, do without others in their lives. When they did have others around them, they tended to use them. There was no doubt in Hannah's mind that Vicky used Drake. There was also no doubt that Gideon was capable of using anyone who got in his way. There was no telling whom Nord might have used over the years. They were people who commanded vast reserves of ability and strength and they channeled all of it toward their respective goals.

What was it Gideon had said the night before? If she were going to step into the ring she needed to know exactly where she was headed and how much she was willing to sacrifice to get there. He'd put it more bluntly than that. He'd said she had to know whom she was willing to kill to get where she wanted to be. Most of all she had to know where she wanted to be.

Hannah groaned ruefully. It was ludicrous to remember how she had advised Gideon to add some balance to his life by resurrecting his old interest in maps. People such as Elizabeth Nord and Victoria Armitage and Gideon Cage didn't need or want balance in their lives. They had no room for it. All their energy was focused on their private goals. Perhaps they were the lucky ones. They didn't know or care about what they might be missing. For them, nothing was missing.

If she had stayed on the road to her Ph.D., would she have found that kind of personal strength and completeness? Hannah wondered. Thinking of the man still asleep in her bed, she decided for the first time that a part of her envied him. He didn't need her, except in a fleeting, physical sense. But she could so easily get to the point of needing him and her need would go far beyond the physical.

With the envy came resentment, and her general feeling of restlessness increased. Arching, she dove deep into the water and then surfaced, swimming strongly. Unconsciously she headed toward the mouth of the cove. There in the water her leg felt so much more normal. There was a slight weakness in her knee when she kicked, but her balance wasn't affected. Whatever else had happened on this trip to the Caribbean, it had had the desired effect on her physical recovery.

The touch of a hand on her ankle came just as Hannah was nearing the reef that guarded the cove's entrance from the sea. Gideon. He had awakened and come after her. Instinctively Hannah veered to the right, familiar now with the sensual game of water tag he liked to play.

But the fingers didn't fall away from her ankle. Instead, they gripped with sudden, totally unexpected fierceness. Startled, Hannah whipped around, her head just above the surface. Even as she told herself that Gideon must be submerged beneath the water, she realized that the man who had grabbed her ankle wasn't Gideon.

Her scream was short, cut off violently as the hand on her ankle dragged her back under the water. Panic lent strength to Hannah's thrashing attempts to free herself. The water churned and through the bubbles she could see the face of her attacker. He wore a diving mask and the top half of a black wet suit that covered his head. Hoses from the tank on his back fed into his mouth, giving him the appearance of some lethal visitor from another world. Relentlessly he stroked his fin-covered feet, pulling Hannah deeper.

Desperate fear gave Hannah the strength to resist for a painful moment. When she kicked out ruthlessly, trying for the mask or the hose, she gained her freedom for a few precious seconds. Long enough to surge to the surface and fill her lungs with air. It was a breath she didn't dare waste on a scream. The hand closed around her leg almost immediately and she needed every bit of air as she was hauled back under the water.

Some sense of lingering rationality warned Hannah that she stood no chance of simply pulling free of the lethal grip. This time when she was dragged beneath the waves she didn't even try. Instead she whirled under the water and reached out with both hands, trying to grab the mask or the hose. Her fingers caught the edge of the faceplate and she pried frantically. She must have loosened the seal because the man in the wet suit slashed at her arm and jerked his head aside. But she didn't succeed in breaking his grip on her leg.

As she struggled Hannah realized just how weak her injured leg still was. It was her strong leg that was caught in the viselike grip and the strength in the other leg was waning fast. Pain shot through her knee as she kicked again and again at her attacker's face. Pain was shooting through her lungs, too. The horror of drowning gave her another surge of adrenaline. She slapped at an air hose, twisting frantically to one side. Once more she managed to get her face above water long enough for one quick gulp. This time when she was yanked downward she knew she wasn't going to be allowed another chance.

They were near the edge of the reef. Hannah caught glimpses of a treacherous underwater world of sharp coral and dark recesses. Perhaps if she could get her hands on a piece of coral or rock she might have a weapon.

But her assailant seemed to be aware of the opportunities the reef might present. He pulled her steadily down toward the sandy bottom, using his free hand to fend off her weakening efforts to reach a vulnerable point. Hannah's lungs felt as though they were about to burst. She was going to die. In another few seconds she would be drowning. The agony in her knee was nothing compared to the fear and fury roaring in her veins. Damned if she would let her assailant escape without a mark. She curled inward, no longer resisting the relentless grip on her ankle.

Doubling over she drove herself into the wet-suited body, no longer caring what he did with his free hands. She felt a blow against her stomach and another on her face but the force of both was impeded by the water. Her fingers curved once more around the face mask and she yanked with all her strength.

For an instant her attacker's eyes locked with hers and she thought vaguely that his were blue.

And then, without any warning, she was free. Hannah had neither the strength nor the time left to assess what had happened. She kicked for the surface without a split second's hesitation. There was simply no air left in her lungs.

The sunlight above tantalized her with awesome cruelty as she fought to reach the surface. She wouldn't die this close to air. She couldn't. Desperately she kicked, clawing at the water as though it were a living thing that was trying to block her path.

It was as she broke through into sunlight and air that she sensed the lithe shape flash beneath her. For an instant she thought it might be a shark. Perhaps that was what had scared off her attacker. She floundered in the water, sucking air so deeply that she hurt in every corner of her body. If there were a shark in the cove it was her chance to make it to safety.

The water frothed behind her. She lunged for the rocks, fearful that the sea creature was turning on her instead of the man in the wet suit. She felt movement in the water and instinctively looked down.

There was a battle in progress but it was no shark tearing into her assailant. It was Gideon. Stunned, her breath still coming with a frantic heaving effort, she stared down through the crystal green water as Gideon's bare body flashed and curved around the black-suited man. Bubbles suddenly spilled from the regulator.

In an instant the attacker made his decision. He shot forward, the fins giving him a powerful advantage. He swam toward the reef and disappeared over the top of it even as Gideon surged to the surface beside Hannah. His face was stark and forbidding, his expression unlike any she had ever seen on him. For a dazed second she almost thought he was a shark.

"For Christ's sake, Hannah! What the hell... Come here. Just hold on and stop struggling. I've got you. Can you breathe all right?"

She tried to answer and coughed instead. She managed a weak nod as he caught hold of her, supporting her in the water. It was such a relief not to have to use the last of her energy just to stay afloat. Her arms went around his neck as she continued pulling air into her lungs in ragged gasps.

"Thought...you...were...a shark. Never been so glad to see a shark in my life."

"Don't talk, honey. Just breathe. We're almost there."

Gideon cut through the water, taking her to safety. A few minutes later Hannah felt him pause to find his footing. Then he scooped her up into his arms and carried her out onto the beach. She hung there against his chest, absorbing his strength as she tried to regain her own. He felt reassuringly solid. She clung to him with the same intensity she did when he was making love to her.

Carefully Gideon knelt on the sand, setting Hannah down on the towel she had left behind before entering the water. She lifted her head wearily, her relief making her light-headed.

"Your sense of timing is terrific," she got out between short gasps for air. Her body was beginning to believe she was going to stay out of the water for a while. It was relaxing slightly, her breathing becoming more regular.

"My timing is shit. What happened out there?" He cupped her face in his hands, his eyes savage. "You scared the living hell out of me. Where did that jerk in the wet suit come from?"

"I wish I knew." She was beginning to tremble. Shock, probably. Hannah wished Gideon would look a little less violent. "I just went for a swim. He came up behind me from underneath. I never saw him. Touched my leg. I thought at first it was you. And then I found myself trying to breathe water. Oh, God, Gideon, I've never been so terrified in my life." No, that wasn't right, Hannah thought. There had been another few moments of fleeting terror the night of her auto accident. But those seconds of stark fear were vague and blurred in her mind. Today's events were frighteningly clear.

"He was trying to kill you."

She shook her head in a ridiculous attempt at denial. Because, of course, that's exactly what the man in the wet suit had been trying to do. "Gideon, it doesn't make any sense."

"He might have thought you were living in the house alone. Maybe he had some idea of getting rid of you and then robbing the place."

"My aunt's house has been sitting empty for several months and there's been no robbery attempt. Why now?"

"Maybe the local police will have some theories." Gideon released her face. He touched her, stroking her arms as if assuring himself that she was alive. "You're all right?"

"Yes, thanks to you. I may give up swimming for life, but I'm all right. Oh, my God, Gideon! I was so scared." She reached out, hugging herself to his damp strength and burying her face against his chest.

"Easy, honey. Easy. It's okay. It's all right. You're fine now." He cradled her, his voice softening as he smoothed her wet hair. "Jesus. You think you were scared. I am now the world's leading expert on panic."

"How did you find me?" The trembling wouldn't stop. Hannah took several deep breaths, trying to control the involuntary spasms, but it didn't work.

"I woke up and realized you were gone. I figured you might have decided to take a swim. I was on my way down to the beach when I heard you scream. It was damn hard to see anything against the glare off the water. Fortunately you were making enough of a fuss that I finally spotted something going on there by the reef. Hannah, you little idiot, you should never have gone into the sea alone.''

''You do it almost every morning.''

''That's different.''

''Please don't yell at me, Gideon. Not now. Maybe later, okay?''

He leaned over her, holding her close. ''All right. Later. God, honey, stop shaking.''

''I can't.''

''Yes, you can, damn it.''

She smiled blearily. ''I'll bet you run Cage & Associates this way. Always giving orders.''

''It's the only way to run a company.''

''But I'll bet you don't do it naked like you are now very often.''

He muttered something into her wet hair. ''You have a way of putting a new twist on a situation.'' He began rubbing her back briskly as she nestled against him. ''Feeling better?''

''Much.''

''How's the leg?''

''It hurts but I've put it into perspective. Compared to nearly being drowned, a sore knee is a minor inconvenience.''

''Think you're up to getting dressed and paying a visit to whatever passes for the law around here?''

''All right. But I don't think it's going to do much good. Gideon, all I saw was the face mask and the wet suit. I couldn't begin to identify that man.''

''We've got to report it.''

''I know.'' She sniffed and pulled her head away from the comfort of his chest. ''This sort of thing can really take the edge off a vacation, can't it?''

He looked at her oddly, a dark frown pulling his brows together, but he didn't respond to her comment. "Come on, Hannah. Let's get back to the house."

THE ISLAND POLICE were polite, took the matter with an appearance of seriousness but were ultimately totally unhelpful. They did have a theory, however.

"I don't believe it," Hannah said fiercely as she climbed back into the jeep after the dismaying scene with the police. "That guy was trying to drown me, not rape me."

Gideon's hands flexed on the wheel. He sat staring through the windshield, his eyes hooded and unreadable. The only thing Hannah could be sure of regarding his mood was that it was not a good one. It hadn't been good since he'd walked into the police station with her two hours earlier.

"I don't know, Hannah. The captain may have been right. It fit with those other two cases he told us about."

Hannah shivered, remembering the discussion. In the past month there had been two rapes on Santa Inez. In each instance a female tourist swimming alone had been attacked by a man who had first weakened his victims by nearly drowning them. "But neither of those women said their attacker was wearing an air tank and a wet suit."

"Damn it, I know that." Gideon shoved the jeep into gear with controlled savagery and swung out onto the road.

The repressed ferocity in him was unsettling. Hannah didn't need any more violence this morning. She huddled down into her seat, staring bleakly at the passing scene. The low one- and two-story houses that flanked the small downtown area all had a certain similarity about them. No glass in the windows, only louvered shutters that were always open except during a storm. Small yards in which the frangipani, bougainvillea, and hibiscus ran wild. Appropriate for a life-style lived outdoors on the streets where one's neighbors were always willing to stop and gossip. Another world.

It was time to get back to her own world, Hannah decided. She glanced at Gideon's hard profile. "You nearly tore that poor police captain to shreds."

"I was annoyed."

"You're hell on wheels when you're annoyed."

He ignored that. "The man had a point, Hannah. You shouldn't have gone swimming alone."

"Not that again! You were the one who defended me to the captain, remember? You told him that was a private beach. Told him I had every right to swim there. As I recall you made quite an issue of his inability to control rapists on the island. You were on my side back there in the station. Chewed that poor guy up one side and down the other and then spit him out. Now you're buying his line?"

"You shouldn't have gone swimming alone."

"Why not, for heaven's sake. That cottage and the beach in front of it belong to me! I'm getting annoyed now. I have my rights, Gideon. Why is it that whenever a woman is attacked, men take the attitude that she invited it?"

"I didn't say you invited it. But you've got to face facts, Hannah. You're a woman. When you're alone or isolated, you're vulnerable."

"My aunt," Hannah informed him in a too-level tone, "lived in that cottage for years. Alone. No one ever bothered her. It's not as if it's a high-crime neighborhood, Gideon. I've lived by myself in Seattle for years and have yet to be assaulted. And I'm sure Seattle's crime rate is considerably higher than this island's!"

"You don't know this island as well as you know Seattle."

Hannah's head came around. "You know what the problem is here? You're angry with yourself because I was attacked this morning. You feel responsible somehow. And now you're unloading your anger on me."

"I'm not in the mood for a psychological analysis of my motives. I'm trying to get something across. Something logical and loaded with common sense. Back home in Seattle you don't walk around alone downtown at night, right? Here, you're not to go swimming alone."

Her own anger was having a bracing effect, Hannah discovered. It helped her shake off some of the bleak, shocked feeling she'd been enduring since this morning's disaster. "It's not necessary to yell at me. Believe me, I may never go swimming again in my life."

Gideon finally seemed to realize that she was not in a meek frame of mind. His expression softened slightly. "Honey, I'm not yelling at you."

"Is that right? What do you call it?"

He sighed. "Maybe I am. I haven't recovered from what happened this morning. I'm still cold inside. You're probably right. I'm short-tempered with you because I'm furious with myself."

She relented. "It was hardly your fault, Gideon. You saved my life, remember?"

"Jesus. I'd sell my soul to get my hands on that guy in the wet suit." Gideon made a visible effort to throw off his own foul mood. "I don't feel like going back to the cottage, do you?"

Hannah's anger was already fading, this time into a depressed acceptance of reality. "No."

"We haven't driven completely around the island yet. This is a good day to do it." He didn't wait for her agreement. He was already driving past the turnoff to Elizabeth Nord's cottage.

Fifteen minutes later, at the island's southern tip, he parked the jeep on a craggy bluff overlooking the sea and turned to face Hannah. The island's short, pleasantly warm morning was already giving way to the standard muggy afternoon. Overhead the first clouds were forming. A sailboat was rounding the island point, heading for the harbor. It was a peaceful, idyllic scene, a million miles removed from the violence that had shattered the image early that morning.

"Are you okay, Hannah?"

"I think so. I just feel a little strange."

Gideon leaned back against the door, studying her with the brooding look that was becoming so familiar. "Not surprising."

"I guess not."

Gideon shifted his gaze to the sailboat, his left arm resting casually on the jeep's steering wheel. "I don't think the local police are ever going to find out who attacked you this morning."

"I know. We'll be gone soon. Just a couple more tourists who lodged a complaint. As soon as we're off the island, they'll file it away in a very deep file cabinet. Out of sight, out of mind."

"Maybe that's what's eating me," Gideon said.

Hannah smiled fleetingly. "You're angry because there probably won't be any justice done?"

"That amuses you?"

"No," she said slowly. "I'm not exactly thrilled with the idea either. But somehow you've always seemed such a law unto yourself. It must be hard to find yourself having to depend on the formal criminal justice system."

"If there was any way in hell I could find out who did it myself, I would."

Hannah believed him. "Don't let it get to you, Gideon. There is no way and we both know it. I appreciate the sentiment, though."

He swore crudely. "It's not exactly a *sentiment*. I'm goddamned mad."

"I think," Hannah said quietly, "that the vacation is over."

Gideon's eyes snapped back to her. "What are you talking about?"

"I think it's time to go home."

"This is only the fourth day. We've got three more to go." His voice sounded different. Tighter somehow. Strained.

"It's time to go home, Gideon." Hannah was sure of it now. "Nothing will be the same here now. We both know it."

"The hell it won't. The only difference is that I'm not letting you out of my sight for the next three days. Hannah, listen to me. I know you're frightened and upset. But I'll see to it you won't be alone again. You'll be safe."

"But it won't be the same. No, Gideon, it's time to leave. Not just because of what happened this morning. You're getting restless. I knew that when I saw you buying that business magazine yesterday. We both know you're wondering what Ballantine is doing. Cage & Associates is your main concern in life. You can't afford another three days of being out of touch with it."

His eyes narrowed. "I can afford anything I damn well please."

She shook her head. "Maybe you can. I can't."

"What's that supposed to mean? If you're running short of cash, stop worrying. I'll pick up the tab for this trip."

Hannah's mouth curved wryly. "I'm not talking about money. The truth is that four days of you is about all I can afford."

Gideon went still. The unnatural quietness in him was unnerving. "I didn't realize you had any major complaints."

She flinched at the harshness in him. "No complaints, Gideon. You of all people should know that. It's got nothing to do with you. It's me."

"You're upset because of what happened this morning."

"It's more than that. I'm upset because of what's happening between us."

"What the hell is wrong with what's happening between us?" he rasped.

"Gideon, don't you understand? I'm not built the way you are. You're willing to live in the present when it comes to relationships. You're content to let the future take care of itself when it comes to dealing with other people. Cage & Associates is the only thing with a future you care about. But I'm not like that. Just look at the way I keep trying to give you advice even though I know you have no intention of accepting it. Don't you realize why I go on doing it? It's because I do think in terms of futures. I worry about yours and I worry about my own. I told myself I could have this week out of time and not pay for it, but I was wrong. There's a price on everything. Four days of you is all I can afford. Another three days will cost too much. I won't go home with lots of memories to cherish; I'll go home bitter. I don't want that."

"You're just feeling depressed and emotional," he told her grimly. "Hardly surprising considering what you've been through. By tomorrow morning you'll feel different. Stop thinking about things. Just try to relax and let the day go by."

"I can't stop thinking about things, Gideon. I can't turn off my emotions the way you can. I can't focus on one thing and tune out all the others. Believe me, I wish I could. Before the man attacked me this morning I was thinking about just that. Strange, isn't it? I was comparing you to Vicky Armitage and to my aunt. All three of you have or had the ability to focus on the one thing in life that's important to you. Everything else that goes on around you is dealt with on a more or less casual basis. Nothing gets to you except something that is a direct threat to the one thing you care about. In your case it's Cage & Associates. In Vicky's case it's probably her career. It certainly was that way with my aunt. A part of me envies the three of you. But another part of me finds that kind of talent frightening. It has something to do with the personal power it gives you. I feel helpless against it. I can't really explain it, Gideon. But I know it's dangerous. And it's time I got away from it."

"You're creating some kind of weird fantasy out of a perfectly normal approach to business. For Christ's sake, Hannah, stop brooding on it."

"But I can't stop brooding on it. That's the whole problem. I was ignoring it with reasonable success until this morning. Now, I can't ignore it. Don't you understand at all?"

His fingers gripped the wheel. "I understand that you're emotionally upset because of this morning. I can accept that. God knows you've got a right to be upset. But the rest of this talk about focus and power is bullshit."

She stared at him. He hadn't moved, had made no effort to touch her, but she realized that he was trying to overpower her in some way. Hannah could feel Gideon willing her to back down and accept his analysis of the situation. She couldn't move for a timeless moment. Then a weary amusement surfaced. "If you bottle that kind of bullshit, you'd make another fortune. Let's go back to the cottage, Gideon. I want to finish packing the boxes this afternoon and get them to the airport. I can make my return reservations while I'm shipping the books."

"Hannah, listen to me, damn it!"

"You're welcome to stay in the cottage for another couple of days."

"That's not the point," Gideon said roughly. "And you know it."

"I know. But I don't think there's much point in discussing the real point. Let's go, Gideon."

IT WAS TOO SOON.

The words kept hammering in Gideon's head as he loaded the last cartons of books into the jeep and drove to the airport. The same words prodded him, gnawed at him, consumed him as he watched Hannah making her return reservations for the following morning.

Too soon.

Five days wasn't long enough. He'd been promised seven. A full week. And now Hannah was going to leave on the morning of the fifth day. He should have had three more full days with her. This wasn't the way it was supposed to be.

The ludicrousness of his own logic was not lost on him, but it didn't seem to weigh against his sense of being denied something important, something he'd arranged for himself.

Gideon told himself she was running because she was scared after what had happened in the cove that morning. Didn't she realize that he'd take care of her? He wouldn't let her get ten feet from him now. He'd slit the throat of anyone who tried to hurt her. The bastard in the scuba gear wouldn't get close a second time.

At various times during the afternoon and evening Gideon tried to reassure Hannah on that score. But she wasn't interested. Calmly, methodically, she'd finished the packing and cleaned up the cottage. She was going to leave in the morning.

That night after dinner she stood on the veranda, drinking in the night sky and the moonlight on the sea. Morosely Gideon watched her. The Scotch he was drinking wasn't providing him with any creative inspiration. Earlier that day he had been sure he could talk Hannah into staying the full week. When he was intent on convincing someone to do things his way, he was almost always successful. Hannah shouldn't have been a problem. He had outmaneuvered her at every turn. He'd played games with her in Tucson, invited himself along on her vacation, coaxed her into letting him into her bed. This was the woman he could make shiver in his arms. She was responsive to his lightest touch. The woman who yielded beautifully to him, welcoming him with her tight, hot passion.

By the time he'd driven the last jeepload of books to the airport, Gideon had begun to admit defeat. It galled him because defeat wasn't on his private list of permissible options. Now he swirled Scotch in his glass and covertly watched helplessly as the woman he should have been able to lead and manipulate so easily planned her departure.

She was very quiet tonight. Possibly because every time she opened her mouth he used the chance to argue with her, Gideon admitted to himself. The balmy breeze was playing with the curling halo of her hair, making him want to play with it, too. There was a remoteness in the way she stood leaning against the railing. It bothered Gideon because it told him just how firm her decision really was. He had seen her in many moods from cautious to passionate, but he had never seen Hannah so distant.

"You don't have to do this, you know. In the morning I'll drive you to a phone. You can call and cancel the reservation."

"I won't be canceling it."

"Wait until morning to make up your mind."

She shook her head.

"Hannah." He put down his Scotch and went to stand behind her, his fingers settling on her shoulders as he inhaled the faint herbal scent of her hair. "Wait until morning. Everything looks different in the morning. You don't have to make the decision now."

"The decision is made, Gideon. It's best this way."

His fingers sank into her. He released her at once when he felt her wince. "Wait, Hannah. Just give it time." He found her ear hiding amid the curls and gently set his teeth to the lobe. "We'll talk about it again in the morning."

She didn't answer with words. Instead, she turned into his arms, lifting her face for his kiss. Gideon felt the trembling passion in her and responded to it unthinkingly. He was instantly taut and filled with wanting just as the sails of the boat he had seen earlier that day had been taut and filled with the sea wind.

He made love to her with an intensity that at times bordered on roughness. Hannah didn't seem to notice. She was too busy making her own passionate demands. It was as if both of them had decided to make the memory of this final night last a very long time.

But when it was over, the haunting words came back into Gideon's head, tormenting him until dawn.

Too soon. It was all over too soon.

The next morning Hannah sat silently beside Gideon for almost the entire flight to Miami. There they were forced to part. Gideon booked a flight on to Tucson and Hannah already had her ticket to Seattle.

She stood in the boarding lounge with him since his jet was scheduled to leave first. The silence was maddening but Gideon couldn't think of a way to break it.

It wasn't until the flight was called and he picked up his leather bag that Hannah finally touched his arm as if half calling him back. He turned to her at once.

"Gideon," she said quietly. "I owe you my life. The only way I can repay it is with some advice. I know you don't want it and I know you won't listen to it but it's all I have."

"I'm listening."

"Just remember that there is always a choice. Nothing is inevitable for you when you deal with Ballantine. You don't have to crush him. If you can't find any other solution, you can always walk away and refuse to fight."

"Hannah..."

"Goodbye, Gideon." She stood on tiptoe and brushed her mouth against his. "You were right. It wasn't a novelty."

Chapter Eight

THE FIRST BOX OF BOOKS Hannah had shipped from Santa Inez Island arrived on Wednesday. Hugh Ballantine was right behind it.

Hannah didn't notice the tall, red-haired man immediately. He was standing on the other side of the iron gate in the arched entranceway of her apartment building, watching curiously as she assessed her chances of getting the large carton of books up the stairs.

"Can I give you a hand?"

Hannah swung around, startled. The man was silhouetted by the bright sunlight behind him and it was difficult to make out his features. All Hannah saw for certain was the bright red of his hair. That and the expensively cut, dark pinstripe suit. Suits didn't make any difference, she told herself. Muggers came in all kinds of clothes. Automatically she smiled and shook her head. "No thanks, I'll manage."

"That carton is as big as you are."

Hannah gazed morosely down at it. "An acquaintance of mine packed it for me. I'm sure it's a convenient size for him to handle. Unfortunately he forgot to make allowances for the fact that I'd be dealing with it alone at the other end of the line. But it's no problem, really. My next-door neighbor will be glad to help me with it."

The red-haired man stepped closer to the gate and peered at the label on the box. "You're Hannah Jessett?"

Bad move, Hannah thought. Women living alone weren't supposed to let their names and addresses be connected by strangers. Still, it was hard to imagine this man in the pinstripe suit as a mugger or a burglar. He looked too much like her brother, too much of a businessman. She decided to gently take the offensive.

"Were you looking for someone here in the building?" she asked politely, not bothering to answer his question.

He smiled, an interesting, crooked little smile. Hannah saw that his eyes were of a rather intense blue and that they were set in a face that was handsome in a square-cut, open sort of way. This man could have been driving a tractor across a plowed field in the Midwest or carrying a football into an end zone. There was even a faint sprinkling of freckles to prove his silent claim to an All-American Boyhood. He'd probably been a Boy Scout. The overall effect was slightly marred by the alert, watchful expression in his eyes and by the strong line of his nose. The fit of the pinstripe suggested that whatever he'd done in the way of high school athletics, he hadn't allowed himself to become too soft in the intervening years. Hannah guessed he was somewhere in his late twenties or early thirties. Perhaps exactly her age.

"I was looking," the stranger said, "for Hannah Jessett. I'm Hugh Ballantine."

Hannah leaned back against the tile wall, folding her arms across her olive-gray fatigue sweater. The jeans she wore were the oldest pair she had. They had been put on for housecleaning. "Ballantine," she murmured. "Ballantine. Why do I know that name?"

"Possibly because you're interested in the financial world?" he suggested gently.

"*That* Ballantine?" Her fingertips played a short musical scale on her arm. Matters appeared to be about to complicate themselves and she was forced to wonder why.

"I'm flattered that you seem to recognize the name."

Hannah came away from the wall and bent to hoist the book carton. "Don't be. My interest in the business world is fleeting."

"I'll get that box for you." He waited expectantly.

Hannah sighed and reluctantly opened the iron gate. Ballantine moved to lift the carton before she could get a firm grip on it. "Up these stairs?"

Hannah nodded. At least he wasn't a mugger. "Down the hall. First door on the left."

"I promise I won't take up too much of your time, Miss Jessett. I just want to talk to you." He started up the stairs, carrying the carton easily.

"I can't imagine why." But she was very much afraid she could make a reasonable guess. She dug her keys out of her jeans pocket as she climbed the stairs behind him.

"You and I have a mutual problem, Hannah." Ballantine stopped at the indicated door and waited. His blue eyes swept over her profile as she unlocked the door.

"I wasn't aware that I had a problem. At least, not one that I can't handle."

"Does the name Gideon Cage mean anything to you?" He followed her through the door and set the carton down near one of the bookcases. Slowly he straightened, dusting his hands automatically as he took in the mock island decor. Whatever he thought about the interior design, he was polite enough not to comment. Hannah gave him credit for that much.

"Have a seat, Mr. Ballantine."

"Hugh." He took off his jacket and tossed it over the back of one of the wicker chairs with a gesture of familiarity. Then he took the fanback throne. "Please call me Hugh. You haven't answered my question. Does the name Cage mean anything?"

"I think you know the answer to that or you wouldn't be here."

He nodded, apparently satisfied with the response. "You're right. I know the answer. What I'm not sure of is what effect his name has on you."

"And that's why you're here?"

"That's why I'm here."

There was a moment of silence as Hannah took a seat and considered his words. "Mr. Cage's main effect," she finally said carefully, "was on my brother. Why aren't you seeing Nick?"

"Because Nick Jessett isn't in a position to do me much good, regardless of how he feels about Cage."

"And you think I am?"

"It's a possibility."

Hannah looked at him. "I think you've wasted your time."

"I rarely waste time. Coming to Seattle may prove to be a dead end but I won't consider the trip a waste of time."

Hannah grinned in wry amusement. "Because I'm so good at entertaining out-of-town guests?"

"Because of your connection with Gideon Cage. Any connection with Cage is worth checking out. I try to cover all bases."

"I'm crushed. Does this mean I don't have to take you to the Waterfront and the Space Needle?"

He smiled. "No obligation whatsoever. I would like to take you to dinner, however."

"So that you can ply me with wine and get me to talk about Gideon Cage? Why don't we both save some time. Tell me what you want to know and I'll tell you if I'm going to answer your questions."

"It's not quite that simple."

"I was afraid of that." Hannah curled her legs under her and winced as the still-healing knee protested the radical bend. Unobtrusively she tried to straighten out her left leg. "Mr. Ballantine, I'll be honest, forthright, and straightforward with you. I do not wish to be involved in whatever is going on between you and Cage. I am not into the financial world. I'm a guidance counselor. I know absolutely nothing about Cage that would be useful to you."

"If you did know something useful," he said, "would you tell me?"

She eyed him through narrowed lashes. "Probably not. I told you, I don't want to get involved."

"Because you saw how your brother got burned?"

"I take it you know all about that?"

Ballantine nodded. "It was a typical Cage & Associates operation. Appear on the scene like the Four Horsemen and send everyone into a panic with visions of a takeover. The resulting chaos drives up the price of the stock. Cage & Associates sell their stock at the top and back out, leaving a dazed and critically weakened victim behind in the dust."

"And you don't operate like that?"

Ballantine smiled his odd, crooked little smile. "I have no interest in your brother's firm. The one I'm after is Cage. All I want to know at this point, Hannah, is whether you're interested in a little revenge."

Hannah took a deep breath. "Revenge for what Cage did to my brother?"

"For what he did to your brother and for what he did to you."

The breath she had just taken got caught in Hannah's throat. "What do you think he did to me?" Stupid question. She sincerely hoped Ballantine wouldn't answer it in the vernacular.

"Cage is a strange man. Winning is so commonplace for him now that there are times when he finds ways to make a victory more interesting. In this case I think he found you an added fillip. I know he went with you on your recent trip to the Caribbean. What I don't know is whether you realize that you were part of the victory celebration. And if you do realize it, I don't know if you care about your role in things. Perhaps a brief affair with the man who nearly ruined your brother's firm doesn't strike you as risky. Perhaps you know exactly what you're doing."

"Perhaps I do," she muttered.

"Then again," Ballantine went on calmly, "there's a chance you thought you could handle him. You may have let him get close because you believed you could use his interest in you as a form of retaliation. If that's the case, I know it didn't work. And if it didn't work, you might be interested in another method of revenge."

"You don't seem to have much faith in my womanly wiles."

Ballantine shrugged. "I have considerably more faith in Cage's ability to use people. He's a shark. Only another shark has a chance of taking him."

"Don't tell me, let me guess. You think you're the shark who can handle him."

"I've worked hard and long to get to a point where that's a viable possibility." The blue eyes were calm, utterly sure. "Are you interested in helping me or are you satisfied with what happened down in the Caribbean?"

"You seem to know a lot about my activities lately. I'm not sure I like that. Did you have me followed, Mr. Ballantine?"

"No. But I keep tabs on Cage. No one followed the two of you to Santa Inez Island. I thought I knew what was happening and saw no need to invade your privacy by having you tailed."

"Gracious of you."

He ignored that. "I do know that Cage came to Seattle when there was no need; that he saw you while he was here and that he left on the same plane to the Caribbean. I know he's now back in Tucson."

"And you thought you'd come and see for yourself whether my heart was shattered or if I was lusting for revenge."

"Or whether you simply enjoyed a short liaison with a man to whom you found yourself attracted in spite of circumstances." Ballantine was casual. "It happens."

"No accounting for a woman's taste?"

"Something like that."

Hannah glanced at the carton of books, remembering the night Gideon had packed it. When he had finished sealing it he had taken her into his arms and made slow love to her on the flowered rattan sofa. She hadn't been thinking about her brother's firm at the time. She hadn't been thinking about the future. She hadn't been thinking about anything except the deeply sensual reality of the moment.

"I've already said it once, Hugh. But I'll repeat it. I don't want to get mixed up in the warfare going on between you and Gideon. Innocent bystanders might get torn to pieces."

Ballantine hesitated, but to her surprise he didn't argue. "I understand. I can't say I blame you. In your position I'd probably do the same."

"No, you wouldn't," she told him with a faint smile. "You'd start salivating at the prospect of sinking your teeth into Gideon. You hate him, don't you?"

"I see why you're in guidance counseling. You seem to know what makes people tick."

"Sometimes I even offer actual guidance."

"Do people follow your advice?" he asked.

"I have better luck with undergraduates than I do with members of the business world."

Ballantine tilted his head assessingly and then he gave her another of his small, twisted grins. "If you tried to give Gideon Cage guidance counseling I can understand why you might be feeling somewhat ineffective. There isn't much that can alter his plans once he sets them in motion."

"But you're going to try?"

"The secret to handling Cage is not to alter his plans, but to let him get so far along in them that he can't alter them either."

Hannah studied her visitor curiously. "You really think you can take him?"

"Sooner or later." Ballantine leaned back in the fan chair and glanced around the room again. This time he examined the wall of books behind her. "You are a woman of eclectic tastes I see. Does that come with the guidance counseling profession?"

"It comes with having changed one's mind too many times in college."

"I see a lot of anthro stuff." He got to his feet and wandered over to study the spines of some books. "I was interested in anthropology once a long time ago. I thought the idea of taking off to the far corners of the world to record vanishing cultures was just about the most interesting idea I'd ever had. Used to imagine myself working for *National Geographic*. I could see myself dressed in bush clothes and wandering through places like New Guinea or Central Brazil searching for undiscovered tribes."

"I know the image." Hannah felt a flicker of empathy. "I used to see myself dressed the same way. So I subscribed to *Banana Republic* and started ordering the right clothes, even though I knew I was never going to use them on any real fieldwork. Sometimes I get the feeling that nearly everyone has flirted with the idea of being an anthropologist."

Ballantine glanced at her. "I suppose we're all fascinated by different cultures."

"They show us patterns of survival that have worked for some segment of the human race," Hannah said. "The variety of those patterns is awesome. If we ever run into an alien race in space it may be anthropologists who will have to figure out how to go about making contact."

Ballantine came away from the row of books he'd been examining. "I accept your decision about not getting involved in the situation between Cage and myself. But since I'm here and I've come all this way, can I at least talk you into dinner?''

The open, farm-boy charm was surprisingly effective, Hannah decided. "All right.''

"We don't have to go to the Waterfront or the Space Needle.''

"How about one of the places on Broadway?''

"I'm in your hands,'' Ballantine told her.

Hannah considered that. It was an interesting thought.

GIDEON LOOKED DOWN at the short note that had just been placed on his desk by his administrative assistant. Then he glanced up at Steve Decker.

"What the hell do you mean, Ballantine's in Seattle?''

"Just what I said, Gideon. My contact over at Ballantine Investments told me he left for Seattle this morning. Thought you'd like to know.''

"The last word you gave me was that he was starting to move on the Surbrook deal.''

Decker pushed his glasses up on his nose and frowned. "That was before you decided to disappear for the better part of a week. Things have been happening while you've been sunning yourself on a tropical beach. Did you think it would all stand still and wait for you to get back to Tucson?''

Gideon crumpled the note. "Why Seattle?''

"Beats me. But I can take a guess.''

"So can I.'' Gideon swung around in his chair to stare out the window at the Tucson skyline. In the distance the Santa Catalina mountains were deep purple shadows meeting the endless blue of the sky. The city sprawled across the high desert valley floor; the more expensive homes such as his own trickling up into the foothills. The vista was about as different from Santa Inez's beaches as it was possible to get. Gideon had been back a week now, and the feeling that things had ended too quickly between himself and Hannah persisted. He couldn't shake it and it was making him restless.

"Won't do him much good, though," Decker said thoughtfully. "There's no way Ballantine can use Accelerated Design against you, no matter how mad Nick Jessett is. Jessett hasn't got time or resources to devote to anything except getting his firm back under control."

"I know."

Decker paused and then decided to be assertive. His wife was always telling him he should be more assertive with Gideon Cage. "And there's no way Ballantine can use Jessett's sister against you, either, is there?"

Gideon didn't move but he felt the tension in himself and was angry about it. "Hannah's a guidance counselor who likes to dabble in anthropology. She's hardly anyone's idea of a financial consultant."

"Anthropology, huh?" Decker closed his eyes, remembering some early notes he had in his file on Hugh Ballantine. "I think Ballantine was once briefly interested in anthropology. Seems to me he was majoring in it."

"Decker, your computerized brain never ceases to amaze me." Gideon swung around in his chair, planting his palms flat on the desk. "Go find out what you can on the status of Surbrook's last round of negotiations with Ballantine. I want to know how high the bidding is going to go.''

Decker eyed him. ''You think Ballantine has enough cash to outbid us?''

''I think the question is going to be how badly do we want Surbrook.''

''I thought we'd already answered that one.''

''I'll talk to you later, Decker.''

Decker knew when he'd pushed assertiveness as far as possible with Gideon. He nodded and withdrew.

Gideon sat for a while staring at the framed air navigation chart of the Tucson area that was hung on the wall. There was no doubt as to why Ballantine was in Seattle. He knew about Hannah. What made him think he could use her? Hannah knew the situation. She wouldn't allow herself to get drawn into the middle of the war. She wasn't that naive.

Then he remembered that her idea of deflecting a corporate shark was to challenge him to a game of cards. Ballantine might find her easy game.

Gideon dug Hannah's number out of his wallet. Then he picked up the phone and dialed it himself. No need to give Mary Ann another thrill. His secretary had been watching him with a smugly interested look ever since he'd come back from Santa Inez Island.

There was no answer. Impatiently Gideon replaced the receiver and decided he'd try again when he got home from work. Hannah was probably out shopping.

Three hours later he surfaced in his swimming pool, hauled himself out onto the rim, picked up a towel and padded over to the table where the phone rested. The sun was just beginning to set. Hannah should be home for the evening. He dialed.

There was no answer.

HANNAH FOUND Hugh Ballantine to be surprisingly good company. The man knew how to talk about something besides business and he didn't seem to mind doing so. They dined in a cozy little restaurant on Broadway, in the heart of the Capital Hill district. Around them a variety of casually chic people ordered vouvray wine and discussed the various aspects of success and how to obtain it. Out on the sidewalk, upscale evening strollers sauntered along in couples. Some of the couples were composed of opposite sexes and some were made up of the same sex. All of them were interesting. The intent was to see and be seen by the other cruising boulevardiers. To that end a wide variety of trendy clothing had been purchased and a lot of money had been spent on hairstyling. The long days of summer were particularly conducive to the good-natured parade. Broadway had a certain beat all its own.

"My aunt thought that the secret of the power of the women on Revelation Island had to do with the fact that they were seen as the sole intermediaries between humans and the gods. She mentions a certain ceremonial vessel that was used to contact the gods. The women had charge of the vessel and guarded it from all male eyes. Men had to go through a woman in order to ask for supernatural assistance. Lines of descent were reckoned through the females, too. Property was inherited that way. The women controlled the system of marriage. Aunt Elizabeth concluded that women held the ultimate power in the tribe, and that's not at all customary as you know."

Hannah grinned as she reached for a roll. "Just ask any woman."

"And now you've got Nord's original journals?"

Hannah nodded, pleased with Hugh Ballantine's obvious interest in the subject. "I'm going to use them to write a kind of history of her work. But I'm going to focus especially on the notes she made about the Amazons of Revelation Island. Of all the studies my aunt did, that one has always been the most controversial. I want to write the final, definitive verdict and since I've got her personal papers . . ."

"You've got the inside track." Ballantine smiled. "I understand. With that kind of data to draw on, you shouldn't have any trouble getting your work published. Did you tell Cage your plans?"

"I discussed them with him, yes." Hannah took a bite out of her roll.

"Sounds like the two of you got fairly close. Cage is good at that."

Hannah's eyes narrowed. "I'm discussing the same subject with you and I hardly know you."

"True." Ballantine looked apologetic. "Sorry. Sometimes I jump to conclusions."

"Have you spent your whole life hating him?"

"No. I've only hated him since he destroyed my father."

"I see."

Ballantine still wore his half smile but there was no humor in his eyes. "Did he tell you about that?"

"What happened between your father and him? Yes, briefly. He said your father betrayed him."

"Cage lied."

"Well, it makes no difference to me."

"Because you're staying out of this? You may be right. Unfortunately, I don't have any choice."

Hannah shook her head in exasperation. "I've heard that before. And it's nonsense. You've got a choice. But you've already made it, just as Gideon has. I wish you both joy in your battles."

"Is that the truth? You really don't care if I succeed in taking him or not?"

"Nope."

Ballantine chuckled. "I almost believe you."

"Why almost?"

"A part of me can't help wondering how you felt when you went down to Vegas to beg Cage to lay off your brother's firm."

Hannah looked at him with mocking admiration. "My goodness, the corporate spy business is certainly alive and well, isn't it?"

"Again, I wasn't having you followed, I was just keeping tabs on Cage. When you showed up in Las Vegas we had to assume you were there to make a plea for your brother's firm."

"Well, just to set the record straight, I didn't exactly beg. Nor did I sacrifice myself on his bed."

"Good. Because neither would have worked with Gideon Cage. He would have let you beg or let you make the ultimate sacrifice and then gone ahead and done exactly as he wanted."

"What about you?" Hannah asked calmly. "What would you have done?"

He had the grace to wince. "The same as Cage, I'm afraid."

"That's what I figured."

"Let's go back to discussing the Amazons of Revelation Island. I'm beginning to feel that I'm in the presence of one, anyway."

Hannah glanced past him at the woman who had just entered the restaurant. She smiled grimly. "No, my friend, you're not. But I can introduce you to one."

Ballantine lifted an eyebrow in surprise. "An Amazon?"

"Uh-huh." Hannah kept smiling as Vicky Armitage spotted her and came forward down the row of tables. Energy and determination fairly sizzled in the air around her. Drake followed in her wake, looking faintly embarrassed. "Hannah! You're back. How was the trip?" Vicky came to a halt by the table and smiled brilliantly at both Hannah and Hugh Ballantine.

"I had to cut the trip a little short. But other than that I think you could say it was a very productive vacation. The knee is much better. Vicky, this is Hugh Ballantine. Vicky Armitage and her husband, Drake."

"My pleasure," Hugh said, accepting Vicky's handshake. He glanced down at her hand when he felt the strength of her grip but he said nothing. Instead he flicked a small, amused glance at Hannah who hid a grin.

"Did you find the library intact?" Vicky demanded, turning to Hannah.

"Oh, yes. It was all there. Quite a collection. I packed it up and shipped it back in boxes. The first one arrived today."

"When are you going to invite me over to see it?" Vicky demanded lightly. "You know I'm absolutely dying of curiosity."

"Maybe later when I've had a chance to unpack and get things in order." Hannah was hedging and she knew it. She didn't care. She might ultimately let Vicky browse through some of the papers and books but the other woman was never going to get her hands on the personal journals.

"I can't wait. I'll give you a call later on this week." Vicky tugged on her husband's wrist. "Let's go, Drake. I'm starving."

Drake nodded at Hannah. "Glad to see you're back. Why did you have to cut the trip short?"

"Something came up."

"I see. Have a good evening. Nice to meet you, Ballantine."

Hugh inclined his head politely and then turned back to Hannah. "That's the Amazon?"

"I sometimes think of her that way. She's a visiting professor of anthropology and she's been hounding me for a chance to work with my aunt's papers and notes."

"Understandable, I suppose."

"Mmmm." Hannah took a sip of her wine.

"So what did cut your trip short?" Hugh asked.

"I had a swimming accident. Nearly drowned. Kind of took the fun out of the trip."

"My God, I didn't realize. No wonder you came home early."

Hannah thought about how much Ballantine hated Gideon Cage. Next she thought about how Hugh knew so much concerning Gideon's activities. Then she thought about all the possible reasons why someone might have wanted to attack her that morning in the cove. The list was quite short and none of them made much sense. But one fact did stand out if one were inclined to be paranoid. She had been staying on the island with Gideon. Someone who wanted to get at Cage might conceivably have decided that Hannah would make a useful hostage to use against Gideon. What if the man in the scuba gear hadn't intended to drown her, but merely kidnap her?

Hannah nearly choked on her wine. As Hugh watched in concern she collected her breath and apologized.

"Sorry about that. Went down the wrong way," she murmured.

"I know."

Paranoia was an odd thing, Hannah decided. It could be based on absolute nonsense. Ballantine and Gideon were engaged in a corporate battle of wills. Such battles took place in the boardroom, not out in the field. What was the matter with her anyway? She pushed the unsettling thoughts out of her head. Ballantine might conceivably try to tap her feelings of revenge, but that would be as far as he would go. Just to be on the safe side, Hannah decided to make one thing clear.

"It wouldn't do you any good, you know," she began conversationally.

"What wouldn't do me any good?"

"Look, Hugh, even if I were a woman scorned or a sister incensed, there's not much I could do for you against Gideon Cage. The man didn't confide any top-secret business information to me and I think you know he's not likely to do so in the future. We have no plans to see each other again, and if we did you must realize that he's not the kind of man to allow a woman to be a weakness for him."

Ballantine sighed. "It would have been worth a try. I need to find some weaknesses in him, Hannah."

"If you want to know how he works and where he's weak, you should probably take a good look at yourself. The two of you are very much alike, you know."

Hugh gazed at her, startled. "You think so?"

Hannah nodded. "And what's more, Gideon knows it."

Ballantine blinked owlishly. "He's wrong. But that's something, isn't it? Cage is very seldom wrong. Maybe I'll eventually find a way to make that work for me."

Hannah groaned. "Give me nice, malleable undergraduates any day."

THE PHONE in Hannah's apartment started ringing just as she closed the door behind Hugh Ballantine. Hugh had been a very pleasant date in a lot of ways. And he certainly hadn't expected anything from her after dinner, not even a cup of coffee, she reflected as she picked up the receiver. He had deposited her very politely at her door and then departed. The perfect image of the nice, polite country boy who had moved to the city, bringing his old-fashioned country manners with him. It was hard to remember sometimes that Ballantine was from California.

"Hello?"

"Christ, it's about time you got home. Is Ballantine there?"

Hannah nearly collapsed onto the sofa at the sound of Gideon's voice. Unconsciously her fingers went to the necklace her aunt had left her. It hadn't done much for the dashing padded-shoulder, khaki trench dress Hannah had chosen to wear that evening, but for some reason she hadn't wanted to remove it. She was growing accustomed to the warmth of it at her throat.

"Gideon! I wasn't expecting you to call. What on earth do you want?"

"I want to know if Hugh Ballantine is there," Gideon repeated with a patience that sounded extremely tenuous.

"No. And if that's all you were calling about, I guess the conversation is finished." Hannah replaced the receiver and sagged back against the couch cushions. The phone rang angrily.

"Someday," Gideon began without preamble as she picked up the receiver, "I'm going to break you of this nasty habit you have of hanging up on me. It's bad for my image. Now tell me about Ballantine. You've seen him?"

"I've seen him."

"But he's not there now?"

"I've already answered that question."

"What did he want?"

"What do you think he wanted, Gideon?"

"To use you."

Hannah closed her eyes. "Funnily enough he implied that you might have had the same intentions. Are all you corporate gunslingers just naturally inclined to think the worst of each other?"

Gideon swore softly. "Are all guidance counselors naturally naive?"

"Oh, I wasn't naive about the situation, Gideon. I explained right off that I wasn't the femme fatale he needed to get to you. Not that it isn't good for my ego to be told I might have a certain influence over you, of course. But I know how to draw the line between fan-

tasy and reality. I told him I was staying out of the
war."

"Good. So what did he say?"

"He accepted the news like a gentleman and then he
took me out to dinner."

"And you went with him?" Gideon exploded.

"Had a very nice time. Look, is there anything else
you wanted, Gideon? It's getting rather late and I
thought I'd do some more reading in my aunt's journals before I go to bed."

"Hannah, listen to me. Stay clear of Hugh Ballantine."

"The only rule I've made is to stay out of the war.
Other than that, I have no hard and fast rules. I plan
to make 'em up as I go along. Good night, Gideon.
And thanks for calling. It's always nice to have a man
call to thank you for a vacation fling. Makes a woman
feel useful."

"Hannah, wait—"

She cut him off in mid-sentence, yanking the plug
out of the wall jack. Then she sat broodingly on the
couch for a while thinking about the fact that the first
time Gideon had bothered to call her after his return
to Tucson had been for the purpose of finding out
what Ballantine was up to. Obviously the man was not
exactly pining away for her.

It was unfortunate that she had been thinking about
him so much during the past few days. She was determined not to pine for him.

But the last thought Hannah had before falling
asleep that night wasn't about Gideon Cage. It was a
memory of blue eyes behind a diving-mask faceplate.
Eyes the same color as Hugh Ballantine's.

Chapter Nine

DEAR RODDY HAS ASKED ME to marry him. Why do I now find the prospect unappealing? A year ago I would have thought it the perfect match of minds and interests. Lately, however, I find myself questioning his motives in almost everything. This marriage proposal, for instance. While it is an honorable and gentlemanly offer, I cannot shake the knowledge that it comes so soon after notice of acceptance for publication of my paper on the Manatash Islanders. Roddy suggested that the paper be published under both our names as so many of our last papers have been written as a collaboration. I refused. Selfish, perhaps, but I feel I must establish my own reputation. I find myself wondering whether Dear Roddy believes that if we are married I will no longer have any objection to sharing authorship of my work. Surely he would not propose marriage for such purposes, would he? But there is no denying that he has been receiving less and less attention from the academic press lately, and there has been talk of revoking some of his university research funding.

Hannah sat back in her chair, lifting her eyes from the pages of Elizabeth Nord's journal to the square of framed tapa cloth that hung on the wall above her desk. So her aunt had gotten to the point of considering Dear Roddy's marriage proposal and immediately began questioning it. It was clear to Hannah from her reading thus far that "Dear Roddy" was changing from a condescending mentor into a leech. His protégé was rapidly overtaking him both in ability and in academic sophistication. Hannah was a year into the journal by now and the young Elizabeth Nord was showing indications of her later brilliance and maverick independence. Such an intelligent and motivated woman would not be patient for long with "Dear Roddy." It was no surprise that she was having doubts about accepting the offer of marriage.

Hannah got to her feet and wandered into the kitchen for a cup of coffee. The cane remained where it was, leaning against the side of the desk. For short distances she no longer used it. Her knee was definitely improving. Perhaps it would be a good idea to join her brother's athletic club for a while. Physical therapy was good for the leg but it was getting to be a bore going into the clinic for it. Hannah didn't feel ill any longer and the atmosphere of the clinic was hardly cheerful.

The sun was shining with unaccustomed intensity outside her kitchen window. Hannah glanced across the street and saw that several neighbors were taking advantage of the late afternoon warmth to frantically work in their tiny gardens. She filled the kettle and wondered if Hugh Ballantine had returned to California that morning. After last night he must know there was no real point in hanging around.

For a few moments she allowed herself to wonder what Gideon Cage was doing. It would be interesting to know how he'd learned that his rival had come to

Seattle to see her. The obvious corporate spying made her shudder. How did those two men tolerate lives of such tension and manipulation? It was clear that nothing was going to stop Hugh Ballantine. He could think only of revenge and wouldn't be satisfied until he got it. His open, friendly face had not concealed the depths of his anger.

Gideon, Hannah had allowed herself to hope, had reached a different point in his life, a place where he could view his situation objectively and opt out of the warfare. He seemed to understand what was happening to him and to Ballantine. But he showed no real evidence of being willing to take the risk of stepping back. Hannah had been fooling herself by thinking that he might be able to change.

She waited for the water to boil and poured it over a heaping spoonful of instant coffee. Then, limping a little, she wandered back to her desk. The journals were fascinating and they served to take her mind off Gideon Cage. She was becoming more and more enthralled with them. She sat down at the desk, eager to see exactly how her aunt had handled Dear Roddy's proposal.

May eighteen. The most unusual package arrived today. It was sent by my sister in the States, who says it came in a large bundle of belongings received from the estate of our Aunt Cecily. I have little recollection of Aunt Cecily but apparently she wanted me to have a certain necklace that has long been in the family. It is not a particularly beautiful or valuable piece of jewelry but I find it interesting. I also find its history quite fascinating.

It belonged at one time to Cecily's aunt, Anna Warrick, a mathematician in the last century. Anna did not marry. She died in 1890, leaving her estate to Aunt Cecily. Before that it seems it belonged to another ancestress, a writer of some renown. Perhaps one day I will leave it to another female relative. It is good to maintain some sense of connection with the past, and since I'm beginning to believe I will not have the time or interest in having children of my own I will have to consider carefully to whom I will someday leave my possessions. It is strange to think about such things.

By far the most interesting news of the day is word of a small group of people living on Revelation Island. Apparently they have not yet been studied and I have requested funding from the University to do so. It would be an absolutely marvelous opportunity. Roddy is opposed.

The phone rang and Hannah reached for it as she turned the next page in the journal. The voice on the other end was her brother's.

"I'm glad you called, Nick. I've got a favor to ask. Can you get me into your nice yuppie athletic club on a guest pass? I'm thinking of finishing my physical therapy in more stylish surroundings. I'd rather wear a snazzy little leotard than a hospital gown. Besides, you've got that great restaurant downstairs in the club."

"You just want a guest pass so that you can eat in the restaurant on a club discount."

"You know me so well, brother."

"Not well enough to guess where you were last night."

Hannah grimaced. "Why does everyone want to know?"

"I don't know why everyone else is interested but I was calling to see how my poor, limping sister was doing."

"Your poor, limping sister was living it up on the town. I had a date with Hugh Ballantine."

"Ballantine?"

"The man who's bound and determined to make Gideon Cage eat dust," Hannah informed him melodramatically.

Nick chuckled. "Well, I wish him the best of luck. I can't say I'd spend much time crying if he succeeded. Why was Ballantine dating you, though?"

"Good question. I think he was just checking out possibilities. He knew I'd spent a few days in the Caribbean with Gideon."

"Ah-hah. And Ballantine wondered if you were a secret weapon he could use to get past Cage's defenses? I never pictured you as the Mata Hari type."

"You don't have to make it sound so amusing," Hannah said. "I might have potential you don't know about."

"Do you have any potential in that direction?"

She sighed. "You mean could I make it as a corporate spy? No. I'd burst out laughing in all the wrong places. Those men are playing such ridiculous games and they take them so damn seriously."

"Cage is taking Ballantine seriously? That surprises me."

"Seriously enough that when he found out Ballantine was in Seattle he called me to find out what was going on. First time he's called since we parted company in Florida."

"Be careful, Hannah, you may find the games amusing, but I'll bet neither Cage nor Ballantine does. I wouldn't want to see you get crunched in the middle between those two."

"I've informed both that I'm a nonparticipant. I never was much good at games. I lack athletic prowess. Speaking of athletics..."

"Yeah, you can have a guest pass. I'll leave it at the front desk of the club for you. When will you pick it up?"

"How about this afternoon?"

"Will that give you time to buy the appropriate outfit? You can't wander into these places wearing safari shorts, you know."

"Don't worry, I'm on my way downtown to Nordstrom's. I'm picturing something yellow and black. Does that sound snappy enough?"

"Sounds like a giant bumble bee. Talk to you later. Got to get back to work. I haven't even had time to go to the club myself since Cage finished chewing up Accelerated Design."

Hannah winced. "Nick, about that trip I made with Gideon. Does it upset you? I mean, I know it must look rather odd, me going off with him after what he did. But I guess I told myself that what had happened between the two of you was all over."

"It was. And whatever I felt about Gideon Cage before you went with him changed drastically the minute I found out he'd saved your neck that morning you went swimming. Don't worry about it from a business angle, Hannah. You've got other reasons to worry about getting involved with Gideon Cage."

"You mean Hugh Ballantine?"

"I mean," Nick said carefully, "that you should probably ask yourself why Gideon went with you to the Caribbean. The man likes his little victories."

"And you think he saw me as a way of topping off his victory over Accelerated Design?" Hannah's fingers tightened on the telephone.

Nick groaned. "I should have kept my mouth shut. The truth is I don't know why he went on vacation with you. Vacations to anywhere except Las Vegas are definitely not normal for the man, from what I've heard."

"But pursuing victories is normal behavior?"

"Yeah. On the other hand, who knows. Maybe the guy has fallen for you. Just think, Hannah, you could be the one to bring the conquering hero to his knees."

"Uh-huh. Not likely. Thanks for the guest pass to the club, Nick. Go back to salvaging Accelerated Design."

"That's all I have time for these days."

Hannah hung up the phone, aware of an uneasy feeling in the pit of her stomach. She wanted to believe that Ballantine and Nick were wrong about the reasons for Gideon's interest in her. There might not be much of a future with Gideon Cage but she didn't want to believe that the past had been a lie. She didn't want to feel used.

Somehow she couldn't bring herself to accept the worst possible interpretation of Cage's actions. She remembered his uncertainty about how to deal with Ballantine, the way he had provoked her into giving him advice even though he had no intention of acting on that advice. At times there had been almost a desperation in his lovemaking, as if he wanted to forget the past and the future and concentrate only on Hannah and the moment. And in the end he had saved her life. It was difficult to believe the worst of a man who had saved your life.

Hannah went back to her aunt's journal. The question of "Dear Roddy" was still unresolved.

STEVE DECKER found two bottles of Dos Equis beer in Cage's huge refrigerator and carried them along with a couple of glasses out to the pool. He walked along the edge watching Cage slip silently under the water, swimming toward the far end with his usual powerful strokes. Sunlight danced on the surface of the pool, dazzling the eye and making it difficult to see the man underneath. Decker sat down in a chair under the umbrella and loosened his tie. It was hot out there even though it was six o'clock in the evening. He should be heading for home in a few minutes. His wife would be waiting with dinner.

"What do you think, Decker?" Gideon hauled himself effortlessly out of the water. "Did you have a chance to do an analysis of the situation?"

Decker handed his employer a glass of beer. Gideon stopped drying himself and took a long swallow before sinking down into the other chair. "It doesn't take much analysis, Gideon. Backing out of the Surbrook deal won't cost us much in the short term. It's the long term that's our problem."

"You mean because of what it will do to the reputation of Cage & Associates?"

"Any way you slice it, it's going to be interpreted as backing down from a fight. Ballantine will just keep coming at us."

Gideon nodded absently. He already knew the truth. He took another swallow of beer and leaned back in the chair, gazing morosely at the faceted water in the pool. "Taking Surbrook from him won't hurt him too badly. He's still at the stage where his backers expect him to lose a few battles."

"You're not at that stage. People expect you to win every time, Gideon."

Gideon rolled the cool bottle between his hands. "Do you think it's possible to get tired of winning, Steve?"

"For you? No."

"You sound sure of that."

"I've worked with you for a lot of years, Gideon. I'd hate to see you if you started losing. You'd be enraged with yourself and everyone else around you."

Gideon's mouth crooked wryly. "You don't think I'm the kind to accept defeat with gracious equanimity?"

"Frankly, no. What did you find out about Ballantine's visit to Seattle?"

"Not much. He saw Hannah while he was there."

"She admitted it?" Decker looked slightly astounded.

Gideon frowned. "She admitted it. Even said he took her out to dinner."

"Jesus. He's trying to get at you through her, Gideon. You know it."

"Hannah says she assured him she wasn't the femme fatale type. Said she had no influence on me and that she wanted to stay out of the war."

Decker smiled briefly. "I can see her saying that. Ballantine was probably only casing the situation, looking for anything he could use. When he found out you'd gone on vacation with her he probably thought he had a handle of some kind. I'm sure he told her that you had been playing games with her, using her to make the victory over Accelerated Design a little more interesting."

Gideon studied the Dos Equis label. "I guess someone could make a case for that interpretation. On the surface it could look that way."

"The real question is whether or not Hannah now sees it that way. What else did she say when you asked her about Ballantine?"

"Not much. She hung up on me."

Decker raised his brows behind his glasses but was wise enough not to comment. "I think maybe I'd better be getting on home."

"You didn't finish your beer."

"You drink it." Decker nodded goodbye and left.

Gideon finished his own beer and then reached for Decker's untouched bottle. At the bottom of the second Dos Equis he was finally able to put his finger on what had really bothered him about the way Hannah had hung up on him.

The message he had been getting from her since they had parted in Florida was that she no longer considered him worth saving. Gideon wasn't sure he liked being written off by a guidance counselor.

He got to his feet and padded through the open sliding glass door to the living room. The cheap little map of Santa Inez Island that Hannah had given him lay on an end table. Gideon had decided to send it out to a frame shop and have it put under glass. It would look good in his bedroom. Not exactly a fine example of the cartographer's art but interesting in its own right. It would serve as a souvenir of the only real vacation he'd had in years.

IN THE END Hannah had decided on a yellow leotard and turquoise tights rather than black tights. She had spent nearly a hundred dollars on the proper athletic gear before walking through the front door of her brother's club. Once inside she had been put in the hands of a professional physical therapist who had immediately worked out a paced program for her knee. The therapist had worn black tights and a silver leotard. Hannah wondered if she'd made the wrong choice when she'd opted for yellow and turquoise. The silver was really quite striking. There were so many fine points to learn about trendy, upscale living.

She hadn't had time to ponder the question for long, however, as she soon found herself in the center of a huge machine designed to systematically destroy human muscles and ligaments. Within three minutes Hannah's new leotard was soaked under the arms. The machine methodically and somewhat obscenely spread her legs and left Hannah with the task of trying to draw them back together. She began to wonder if she should have gone back to the clinic instead.

"Hannah! When did you join the club?" Vicky Armitage's astonishment was evident in her voice as she came through the door. She was wearing green on green. It went beautifully with her red hair. "I had no idea you were even considering it."

"Just a whim," Hannah assured her, gritting her teeth as she struggled to get her legs back together. "One I'm already regretting. Thought it might be good for the knee. I'll be lucky if they don't have to amputate after this machine gets through with me."

Vicky settled into another machine nearby and threw herself into a workout that emphasized her smooth, female musculature. "You'll get used to it after a while. Any more of your aunt's books arrive?"

"I got another carton today. There are still a few more enroute."

"Have you had a chance to ready any of the more interesting papers?"

"Just some journals she kept." Hannah took a deep breath and wondered if she could manage another battle with the machine. It was a temptation to simply let the thing have its way. If it weren't for the embarrassment of sitting there with her legs spread apart Hannah would have quit fighting.

"Do the journals cover the early years of her career? I'd like to see some of her notes on some of the more controversial studies. Before she became such a celebrity there was often a lot of disagreement over her findings. Several of her contemporaries argued with her about her linguistic analysis of the language of the Manatash Islanders, for instance. And she made some major errors in her interpretation of the marriage customs of the Topan Islanders."

Something clicked. Hannah had just read a section of her aunt's journal that morning concerning the Topan Islanders. She struggled with the leg machine while she tried to remember exactly what she had read. "She felt that the rituals used by the Topans to prepare the young girls for marriage were designed to give them more power as women and wives."

"Nothing of the kind," Vicky assured her, not even breathing hard as she leaned into her weight machine.

"The tattooing was done for purely cosmetic reasons. It had no religious significance."

"My aunt says in her journal that she was able to talk to the women alone and they claimed they only allowed the men to think it was done for cosmetic reasons but that every woman in the tribe understood the true meaning of the tattoos. It was a shared female secret."

"That's not how other anthropologists on the scene interpreted it," Vicky said firmly.

"The other anthropologists were male," Hannah informed her, remembering the notes in her aunt's journal. "The women of the tribe simply told them the same thing they told all males: that the tattooing was a beauty treatment, nothing more."

"Hannah, your aunt was a very young woman at the time she was involved in those studies. She probably wanted to make some original observations to get started building her reputation. I expect she had to invent a, shall we say, more interesting point of view in order to get herself into print."

Hannah's ankles came together with a snap. "You're saying my aunt lied to further her own career?"

"Calm down. I said nothing of the kind. Elizabeth Nord was perfectly entitled to her opinions. And they did get her published. They also drew a lot of attention to her over the years because they usually conflicted with the opinions of more-established authorities. In the case of the Topans, as in the case of the Amazons of Revelation Island, we'll never be able to prove anything one way or the other. The last full blooded Topan died years ago."

"You professional anthropologists must be getting nervous about the growing lack of undiscovered tribes to study. What will you do for fieldwork when there aren't any mysterious primitives left? Even baboons and chimpanzees are getting scarce. You might not have them to fall back on in a pinch."

Vicky ignored the sarcasm. "We were talking about your aunt. She seemed to enjoy arguing with the authorities in the field, you know. She never displayed any respect for the great thinkers of her time."

"Some of those so-called established authorities who disagreed with her analysis weren't much older than my aunt was at the time. Maybe they took the other point of view just to further their own reputations, or because they thought it would be easier to get published." Hannah was getting angry and it showed. All of a sudden it was easier to work the leg machine.

"Hannah, the Topan marriage customs are just a small example of the areas of disagreement. Your aunt's journals could shed some valuable light on those areas. I'd like to see how she justified her interpretation of the female initiation rites among the Manatash. She claimed that the women originated the ceremony as a way of ensuring fertility and safety in childbirth."

"Seems like a couple of reasonable things to try to ensure."

"Yes, but it wasn't anything of the kind. It was simply an adaptation of the male rites and as such didn't carry any great symbolism of its own."

Hannah stopped struggling with the machine and immediately found herself sitting with her legs wide apart. "That's why I don't think I'll turn my aunt's papers over to the academic community."

Vicky straightened away from the weight machine and frowned at her. "What do you mean?"

"Just that every one of you probably has an axe to grind, and you'll use my aunt's papers to prove what you want proven. She deserves an impartial interpretation, and it's becoming obvious she won't get that from other anthropologists!"

"You think you're capable of writing this impartial interpretation?" Vicky demanded.

"I'm going to give it a try." Hannah unchained herself from the machine and tottered to her feet. "I'll see you later, Vicky. I think I've had enough for one day."

GIDEON·WAS ON the third bottle of Dos Equis when he remembered the other map Hannah had given him, the one that had been done by military intelligence for the landing on Revelation Island. He dug it out of the desk where he'd stashed it and carefully spread it out on the black glass surface.

He no longer tried to fool himself into thinking that his interest in maps that evening was simple curiosity on his part. The maps were a way of brooding over Hannah, and after three bottles of beer he was enjoying his brooding in a perverse sort of way.

The heavily creased military map was fragile. He'd have to get it properly preserved or it would soon fall apart on him. Gideon sat studying the sketched-in details of Japanese fortifications and bunkers. It had probably cost a few lives to get those details. Many more lives had been spent during the landing. All for a chunk of South Pacific rock that, before the war, had been home for only a small group of islanders.

Gideon let his mind play with the dramatic events that had taken place on Revelation Island and then reached for one of the many atlases on a nearby shelf. It would be interesting to see how accurately the terrain pictured on the simple intelligence map compared with a pre-war rendering.

It took him a while to find a chart that showed Revelation Island as anything more than a pinpoint in the ocean but eventually he came up with a map that depicted Revelation and a few neighboring islands. Military intelligence must have had to rely chiefly on dangerous aerial surveys because there simply hadn't been many decent survey maps of the area available.

The terrain corresponded in a rough way with the one small pre-war map Gideon could find. The airstrip that the Japanese had built—one of the major reasons the Marines had been sent to take the island—was missing from the pre-war map, of course. The Japanese had constructed it after they arrived.

Revelation was a typical South Pacific volcanic formation with a towering peak in the center of the Island. The beaches that must have been used for the American landing assault were wide expanses with little or no natural cover that the Marines could have used. They would have gone ashore under a barrage of fire from the Japanese bunkers situated above in the rocks. A costly assault.

The map would have been both a talisman and a bane to the captain who carried it. It was a guide through hell and, at best, it would have been excruciatingly inaccurate. One mile on paper might easily have translated into two or three miles on the ground. In a battle where progress was measured in inches and yards, the difference between a one-mile estimate and a three-mile reality would have seemed enormous. The estimate of the number of Japanese bunkers had probably been way off, too. For every one visible from the air, there could have been five or ten hidden in the rocks. Gideon lost himself for a moment in contemplation of the captain's frustration and dogged determination to do his job. It was all there in the map.

The map was marked with a small circle on the east side of the island. Gideon hadn't paid much attention to it when he'd first noticed the mark, but now he speculated on what it might have indicated. There were other notes on the map, but the ink used to make them was of a different color. He had the impression that the mark had been made by a different hand, although he couldn't be certain. It was something about the shape of the circle. Too precise. Not like the scrawl that characterized the other notations. A careful search through his post-war atlases for maps of Revelation Island didn't turn up any indication of what the circle might have been intended to mark. It probably meant nothing now.

A thought crossed Gideon's mind. What if the mark had been made by Nord, not the captain who had probably led his men to the airstrip using the map?

Hannah might find this stuff interesting.

Gideon went to the refrigerator for another Dos Equis while he tried to decide just how interested Hannah might be in his random speculations. It was an excuse to call her and he knew it. It was humbling to realize that he was reduced to using excuses to make a telephone call to a woman with whom he'd shared an affair so brief that it probably came under the heading of "fling."

Even as he dialed the phone he knew the real reason he was placing the call. Some part of him wanted to be reassured that she hadn't given up on him completely. He didn't like the idea that she no longer considered him worth trying to save from himself.

He didn't realize that he was holding his breath while the phone rang until Hannah picked up the receiver.

"Hannah?"

"Still checking up on me? Relax. Ballantine is no longer around as far as I know."

He heard the bite in her voice and took a grip on his own emotions. "I was just calling to talk about your aunt's journals and papers. I've been studying the map you let me have. The one done by military intelligence before the landing."

"What about it?"

"Well," he was floundering already. "There's a mark on it that I'm sure indicates something reasonably important. And I don't think it was made by the man who carried it ashore. I have a feeling it might have been made by your aunt after she came into possession of the map. I just thought you might find it interesting."

Hannah hesitated on the other end of the line, and when she spoke again her voice was softer, suspiciously neutral. "I'll keep it in mind while I go through the journals. Perhaps she'll mention marking the map for some reason."

"It's probably not important now. Probably means nothing." Already he was running out of words. "How are things going?"

"Just peachy when I'm not being pumped for information by you or Ballantine. I can tell right off that

I'm not cut out to be a corporate spy. How are things going there? Preparing for the big confrontation with Ballantine Investments?''

"Among other things. Cage & Associates does have other irons in the fire besides the Surbrook deal.''

"Ah, yes. You're a professional wheeler and dealer. Well, don't let me keep you from your appointed rounds. I'm sure planning the attack on Ballantine is a lot more interesting than talking about a bunch of islanders who no longer exist. Thanks for calling, Gideon.''

She hung up the phone before he could think of anything brilliant to say. She really had written him off, Gideon thought.

The knowledge no longer depressed him. It enraged him.

Chapter Ten

HANNAH FOUND GIDEON waiting in the entrance hall along with the last carton of books from Santa Inez Island. It was raining and the sun wasn't due to show its face until late in the afternoon. Given the fact that it was already noon and there had been no sign of the rain lessening, Hannah doubted the forecast. Weather in the Puget Sound region was tricky to forecast. The actions of Gideon Cage were equally risky to predict. She didn't bother to ask how he'd gotten through the iron gate this time.

"What in the world are you doing here?" Hannah came to a halt at the bottom of the stairs and stared at him. The look on her face wasn't quite open-mouthed surprise, but it probably came close. He was dressed in the kind of casual clothes he had worn on Santa Inez, a pair of slacks and a white, long-sleeved shirt. The only addition was a slate-colored windbreaker that was soaked from the rain. "You're supposed to be busy saving the reputation of Cage & Associates."

Gideon looked at her, water dripping from his dark hair. There was a puddle of moisture spreading around his feet. "I came to see *you*. You could look a little more delighted to see *me*."

Hannah blinked and then realized what was going on. "Oh, I see."

"What do you see?"

She bent to wrestle with the carton of books. "You're here to find out what Ballantine's been up to in Seattle. Sorry, I can't help you. Haven't seen him for a week. Not since that night he took me to dinner." She tipped the box slightly in order to get a better grip on the underside. "And even if I could help you, I probably wouldn't. As I keep telling both of you, I'm out of your war."

"Hannah, I said I came to see *you*." He moved forward, gently edging her aside. "Let me get that carton. How many have arrived so far?"

"This is the last of them." She brushed aside a stray strand of hair and narrowed her eyes as Gideon shouldered the carton and started up the stairs. He had no right to show up like this, not when she'd been successfully concentrating on other things besides him for nearly two weeks. It wasn't fair but, then, she had already learned that men such as Gideon often didn't play fair. They played to win and they played the game by their own rules.

"Is the door open?" he called from the top of the stairs.

"Yes."

She shook off the feeling of disorientation and shoved her key into her mailbox to collect the rest of the mail. Grabbing the handful of envelopes and advertising flyers she closed the box and started up the stairs. She had come down without her cane, and on the way back up she didn't pay as much attention to her still-awkward sense of balance as she should have. Hannah stumbled a little on the first step. Belatedly she reached out to grasp the handrail. On the landing above Gideon disappeared inside her apartment door.

Hannah took a deep breath and paused in the middle of the flight of stairs. Unconsciously she touched the necklace she wore over her khaki naturalist's shirt. She would stay in charge of herself and of the situation.

"Where shall I put it?" Gideon swung around to face Hannah as she came through the door.

"There on the floor beside the bookcase will be fine. Thank you, Gideon." She closed the door behind her.

He eased the carton down onto the floor and then straightened, his eyes moving over her with shuttered interest. "I see you're not using the cane."

"Only when I go out."

"Does the leg ache much?"

"Rarely."

"Still taking physical therapy?"

"I go to my brother's athletic club three times a week."

"Hannah, for God's sake, stop looking at me like that. I was awake half the night making the decision to come to see you. My administrative assistant is practically foaming at the mouth because he's been left to handle everything for another couple of days. The flight was delayed and I wound up killing two hours at LAX. I get to Seattle and it's raining and I get to my woman's apartment and she acts as if she can't quite remember who I am. It's only one o'clock and already it's been a very long day."

Hannah took a deep breath. "It rains a lot in Seattle."

"Christ, lady, I'm in no mood for jokes." He moved, gliding forward and reaching for her before she could step aside.

"Gideon . . ."

But he was already wrapping her close, folding her into his wet clothing until she felt the underlying heat of his body. His mouth came down on hers with an urgency that brought back all the intimate memories of the time on Santa Inez. Hannah closed her eyes, torn between allowing herself to remember and her decision to not look back.

"Kiss me, Hannah. It's been too long. Too damn long."

Gideon tightened his hold, seeking to overcome the passive resistance he felt in her. Slowly Hannah let herself relax. Whatever she'd had with Gideon had been good and physically satisfying. It would do no harm to taste the memories. Her mouth opened beneath his and she heard his stifled groan of satisfaction. His hands slid down her back, urging her closer. It wasn't until water dripping from his hair splashed onto her nose that he reluctantly lifted his head. His dark eyes gleamed with a hint of satisfaction and relief as he looked down at her.

"That's better," he murmured. "Much better. Now you're almost as wet as I am. Got a towel?"

"In the bathroom."

He released her, heading for the hall. "I'll be out in a minute. How about some coffee?"

Hannah watched his back. "I'll put some on." She waited until she heard the bathroom door shut and then she started slowly toward the kitchen. Halfway there she realized that she was still holding the bundle of envelopes in her hand. She dropped them on an end table.

Gideon was here. She hadn't expected to see him again, had convinced herself it was better if she didn't. But now she had to deal with the man and his effect on her. She also had to deal with the real reasons he had come back to Seattle. The affair had ended almost before it had begun. Gideon wasn't the kind of man to chase a woman. So why was he here?

Hannah had the kettle boiling when she realized that Gideon was standing silently behind her in the kitchen doorway. She turned to glance at him and saw that he was holding a long white envelope. It was from the stack of letters she'd left on the end table. His gaze no longer held satisfaction or relief. He was studying her with a narrow intensity that immediately put her on the defensive.

"Maybe you'd better open this." With a quick, casual movement of his hand he sent the envelope sailing onto the counter beside her.

Hannah glanced down and saw that the return address was that of Ballantine Investments. Her blood chilled for an instant at the implications and then cool anger took over. She was not a pawn for these two men. Defiantly she reached for the envelope and tore it open.

"It's probably a thank you letter for the dinner we had." She scanned the contents, keeping her face impassive.

"It looks like business to me."

Hannah smiled grimly. "I imagine it does. But that's probably because everything looks like business to you."

"What does he want now, Hannah?"

She considered her response as she finished reading the short letter and then decided to tell Gideon the truth. "He says he'll be happy to set aside a piece of the action on the Surbrook deal for me if I reconsider my decision about involvement in the war." She tossed the letter back onto the counter and picked up the kettle. "How about that, Gideon? My chance to get rich quick."

"And all you have to do is feed Ballantine some interesting news about me."

"Unfortunately I don't know anything that interesting about you, do I?"

"Would you tell him if you did?"

She swung around as the inner anger rose to the surface. "I've told both of you that I have no intention of getting involved and that's exactly what I meant. It's not my fault that neither of you seems capable of comprehending a simple statement. You're so locked into your stupid macho confrontation that you can't believe someone else might not give a damn about the outcome, but that's how much I care about who wins the Surbrook war. Not a damn. Try to get that through your head, Gideon. You've come a long way for nothing. Ballantine and I are not conspiring against you. I can't give you any more information about him than I can give him about you. And I wouldn't even if I could. With all your corporate spying you seem far more aware of his activities than I am, anyway. I'm sure he's keeping tabs on you, too. The two of you can play your silly games until hell freezes over. I want nothing to do with them. Do I make myself clear?"

He watched her broodingly for a long moment. "The whole problem, Hannah, is that I want you to give a damn."

She stared at him and then slowly shook her head. "Why?"

"I'm not sure. Maybe it's because I want you and I would feel far more secure if I knew you cared a little about what happens to me."

"I tried caring, remember? It didn't do any good because you weren't willing to change. You've chosen your own path, Gideon. You're going to have to walk it alone."

"I didn't think guidance counselors were allowed to write off recalcitrant cases."

"We do. All the time." She turned to pour hot water over the coffee. "And you're not just a recalcitrant case, Gideon. You're an inflexible, immovable, unalterable case. I've decided I'm not going to waste any more of my time on you. I've got more interesting things to pursue at the moment."

"Your aunt's papers?"

"Exactly. I'm learning a great deal from Elizabeth Nord's library. I intend to start putting some of it into practice. Here's your coffee."

He took the mug from her, his eyes never leaving her face. "I didn't come to see you because of Ballantine."

"Really?" She kept her voice careless.

"You don't believe me, do you?"

"Let's just say I have enough respect for your abilities to know that you're quite capable of pursuing two objectives at the same time. You might be willing enough to go to bed with me again, but I doubt that you'd come all this way just to do it unless there was another compelling reason to make the trip. As it happens, there is another reason. You're curious about what Ballantine has been doing here in Seattle. So you've decided to kill a couple of birds with one stone."

"Does it occur to you that I might be jealous?"

She tilted her head to one side. "It occurs to me that your ego might be slightly outraged at the idea of Ballantine taking me to bed so soon after you've finished with me, but that's about as far as it would go."

"Did he take you to bed?"

"What do you think?"

Gideon took a swallow of his coffee. "I don't think he did."

"Fine. Now that's settled, you can smooth your ruffled feathers and head back to the airport. You must be awfully busy these days, Gideon. I doubt you can afford this time to check up on me."

"I didn't come all this way to be kicked out the door fifteen minutes after my arrival. Could you please calm down for a few minutes and give me a chance to talk to you?"

Hannah sighed and stepped deliberately around him. Walking into the living room she settled herself on the sofa. "Talk, Gideon. You're too big for me to kick out the door and my left leg still isn't functioning at full capacity."

He sat down slowly in the fan back chair, taking his time setting the coffee mug down on the end table. "I know you don't believe me, but I'm here to see you. That's the only reason I came."

Hannah didn't argue. There was no point. She didn't know what to believe. She only knew that with Gideon she had to be very careful. "You're going to find it very inconvenient trying to maintain a long-distance affair with me, Gideon. Even if you don't, I will."

"How far have you gotten into your aunt's journals?"

The question took her by surprise. She had been expecting more denials. "I'm at the point where she's just reached the village on Revelation Island. She's established her first contacts with several informants."

"Informants?"

"That's what anthropologists call the members of the tribe they actually question about customs and meanings. They try to set up friendships with them and get them to talk freely. My aunt makes it clear that she's going to follow her usual procedure of relying primarily on female informants. She feels that women are usually neglected by researchers. Male anthropologists assume that men dominate the social and political life of the societies they study."

"There's no mention of what the circle on the map might be?"

"Not yet."

Gideon nodded. "Yeah, well, it's probably not going to turn out to be very important. Just a minor curiosity for someone like me who's into old maps. Have you started making notes for your book?"

Hannah was still wary, but she felt on more solid ground now that they were talking about Nord's papers. "Oh, yes. I think I've finally got a handle on the focus of the book. My aunt was vitally interested in the rituals and customs that affected females of the various groups she researched. She made several observations that were at variance with the mainstream interpretations. She was primarily interested in the subtle applications of female power in a tribal society."

"I can see you're finding it fascinating."

"Infinitely more fascinating than studies of male power."

Gideon smiled faintly. "All right. You've made your point. I will say this once more and that's the last time. I am not here because I'm trying to use you to maneuver against Ballantine. This is not exactly a power play."

"Oh, good."

"Hannah, you're going to try my patience."

For an instant she gazed at him in utter astonishment and then her sense of humor overwhelmed her. "I'll try to be careful."

"Do that."

"How long are you going to stay in Seattle?"

"I can't afford more than a couple of days."

"Where are you staying?"

He picked up his coffee cup. "Here?"

"No, not here," she said very firmly.

"I'll have to think about it, then. Will you have dinner with me this evening?"

"What would you do if I refused?"

"Keep asking."

Hannah nodded. "Until you got the answer you wanted. All right, Gideon, I'll have dinner with you."

"Thank you, Hannah." He put down his coffee and got to his feet.

Startled, Hannah looked up at him. "Where are you going?"

"I have a little business to attend to this afternoon."

Her smile thinned. "Of course." She'd known all along, hadn't she?

"I'm going to see your brother."

Hannah grabbed the arm of the sofa and hauled herself to her feet. "The hell you are. You've done enough to him. Leave him alone, Gideon."

"We're just going to talk. Don't worry. He's expecting me. I phoned him from the airport."

"I don't trust you, Gideon."

He stared at her for a long moment. "I saved your life once."

She flushed. "That's got nothing to do with business. When it comes to business, I don't trust you. If you've come to Seattle to do more damage to my brother, I swear I'll slit your throat. You gave me your word you were finished with Accelerated Design."

"What good is my word if you don't trust me?"

"Gideon!"

"I'll see you tonight. Six-thirty."

He was out the door before Hannah could think of a way to stop him. She rushed for the phone and dialed her brother's number.

"Nick? I just saw Gideon Cage. What the hell is going on? He says he has an appointment to see you?"

"He does." Nick sounded overly casual. "Don't worry about it, Hannah. I'm just going to talk to the man."

"Why?"

"I don't know. He hasn't told me yet. I'll let you know afterward."

"Nick, I don't like this."

"I'm safe enough at the moment. There's nothing he can do to me now. He's already done his worst."

"Then why meet with him?"

"Because I'm curious, I guess. The guy's a genius in his own way. I want to hear what he has to say. Besides, I can hardly deny the request for an appointment after what he did for you, can I?"

THE OFFICES of Accelerated Design were just off Interstate 405, north of Bellevue. The entire region on the eastern side of Lake Washington was filling up with modern glass-and-steel office buildings. The movement of high tech industry into the area brought with it the familiar California-style architecture. If Bellevue wasn't careful, Gideon decided as he parked his rented car in the Accelerated Design lot, it was going to find itself surrounded by a mini Silicon Valley. From his point of view that was hardly a problem. The high-flying, unstable computer industry provided rich pickings for someone in his line of work.

He walked through the lobby of the building, not particularly surprised to find that the receptionist looked as if she'd been a cheerleader once upon a time. It was typical of young entrepreneurs to go for looks instead of brains when it came to hiring receptionists. He was pleased to see, however, that Nick Jessett's secretary appeared to be a little older and infinitely more competent. She nodded him into her boss's office and he felt her curious, wary gaze on his back as he went through the door.

Nick got to his feet behind the glass-and-steel desk. He was wearing a shirt and tie but his jacket was hanging in the closet. This was the first time Gideon had seen him in person, and the first thing that struck him was that the young man's eyes reminded him slightly of Hannah. A darker shade of green, perhaps, but they had that faint upward tilt at the corners. He took the hand Nick extended and sat down.

"If you've come to view the remains," Nick said dryly, "you're a little early. Accelerated Design is not quite under the rug."

"I don't have any morbid fascination for the remains of companies that get in over their heads," Gideon said.

"Then to what do I owe the honor of this visit?"

"I'm thinking of selling you a product you might find interesting."

"I didn't know you sold any products for computer firms." Nick smiled politely, his eyes watchful.

"It's a new line. You'd be my first customer."

"I'm waiting for the kicker."

Gideon gazed around at the expensively designed office, noting the stacks of papers and binders piled on every available surface. "Would you be interested in some management consulting, Nick?"

"From you?" Nick looked startled.

Gideon smiled briefly. "What I have to sell is expertise. I can save you from having to do a lot of things the hard way. I can make sure you survive."

Nick absorbed the information. "I'm still waiting for the kicker."

"The price? It's negotiable."

"Not if it includes a chunk of Accelerated Design stock."

Gideon smiled again. "It doesn't."

Nick absently tapped the end of a pencil on the desk. "I'm not sure I can afford you, Mr. Cage."

"We'll work out something. The details can be left for later. Right now I'm only here to find out if you're interested."

"I'd be fool not to be interested, wouldn't I?"

"Not necessarily. You'll probably make it on your own. I learned a great deal about you during our last encounter. You held things together when another man might have given up and abandoned ship. You have potential."

"That's what my sister says." Nick hesitated. "Is that why you're here? Because of Hannah?"

"Hannah doesn't approve of my coming to see you."

"She's a fairly good judge of human nature."

"Not right now she isn't. She's too wary of me to be a good judge. If we agree to work together you'd have to trust your own instincts."

"I'm willing to back my own judgment."

"You wouldn't be heading up your business if you weren't. Are you in the market for some consulting?" Gideon asked.

"I'm in the market. As I said, I'm just not sure I can afford you."

"It can be arranged."

"I'll bet. I'd want a contract. One that guaranteed you'd keep hands off Accelerated Design in the future. I'd want your fee tied to verifiable improvements in standards of operation and profits. And I'd want a trial period to see whether we can work together before we agree to any long-term arrangement."

"You're a cautious man, Nick."

"I recently learned caution the hard way."

Gideon shrugged. "It's a good lesson to pick up early in life."

Nick smiled slightly. "I paid a high price for it. I don't want to wind up paying that much for anything again. Especially not consulting work."

"As I said, we can work it out."

"Have you had lunch, Gideon?"

"Yes. On the plane."

Nick considered the man in front of him. "Got plans for the afternoon?"

"No. Not until this evening."

"My sister tells me you swim. There's a large pool at my club. I'm going to work out this afternoon. If you'd like to come along, you're welcome."

"Fine. We can talk."

Some of the casualness went out of Nick's eyes to be replaced with grim directness. "I owe you for what you did for Hannah. You saved her life."

"Is that why you're taking the risk of talking to me?"

"That and simple curiosity."

HANNAH WAS ANNOYED to find herself pacing the floor at six-thirty that evening. She had been dressed for half an hour, her uneasy restlessness putting her much too far ahead of schedule. The black-and-white tropical safari dress she was wearing was of linen, and she was afraid to sit down for fear of wrinkling the fabric before the evening had even begun. Hopefully the linen fashion craze wouldn't last long, she told herself. Not everyone looked good rumpled.

Pacing with a still-healing knee was not the most comfortable exercise in the world. She was relieved when Gideon arrived. She went to the door still feeling a sort of generalized irritation. The fact that he was looking very good in a conservative light-tweed jacket and slacks didn't appease her.

"You're late."

He glanced apologetically at his watch. "Only five minutes. I had trouble finding a parking space."

"But you had no trouble finding my brother?"

"No. Where's your coat?"

"In the closet."

"You'd better get it. It's getting chilly out there, although the rain has stopped."

She frowned. "The coat will just make my dress wrinkle more than it already intends to wrinkle."

He grinned. "It's all right. I'll pretend not to notice." He walked to the closet and pulled out a black trench coat trimmed in khaki. "There. We'd better get going. I've got reservations at seven."

"Where?"

"A place your brother recommended down on the waterfront."

Hannah slanted him a long glance as they walked toward the stairs. "Well?"

"Well, what?"

"What did you talk about with my brother?"

"Business."

"Gideon, if you don't give me some straight answers, I'm going to call the evening to a halt right here."

He sighed. "Okay. I offered to do some management consulting for him."

"Management consulting! You don't do management consulting. Your firm is an investment company."

"Do you think it's too late for me to explore other areas of business?" There was a thread of wistfulness in his voice that startled Hannah.

"No, of course not," she said automatically. Guidance counselors always took the positive approach when people talked about making changes. "It's just that I don't see you going into a new field like that. Not unless there's something in it for you."

"There's something in it for me. A fee."

"Something more than a fee. My brother couldn't possibly afford much for management consulting right now, so how is he going to pay you?"

"You're a suspicious woman, Hannah."

"Can you blame me?"

"Yes. I've never lied to you. Never given you cause to distrust me. You don't have to worry about your brother. My arrangement with him is straightforward and aboveboard. Stop worrying about it. Relax and enjoy the evening."

She would gain nothing more by questioning him, Hannah decided. In the morning she would pin Nick down. "Maybe you're right. I'm just not convinced that you're genuinely thinking of branching out into another kind of business."

"I'm not convinced of it either. This is an experiment."

"I'm not sure I want you experimenting on my brother."

"You, Hannah," he told her gently, "don't have anything to say about it."

The restaurant was a traditional fish house located on one of the old piers that lined Seattle's downtown waterfront. The huge container ships that docked regularly in Elliott Bay were too large for the old port facilities. They used the modern ones farther to the south. The old wharves had been turned into restaurants, shops, and parks. From the window Hannah could watch the ferries arriving and departing for their regular excursions across the bay.

The evening was turning out more pleasantly than she had expected. The salmon was excellent and so was the chardonnay. On top of that, Gideon was going out of his way to be a good host. Half way through the meal Hannah realized that she was doing all the talking. She closed her mouth in the middle of a sentence and eyed him thoughtfully.

"What's wrong?" Gideon asked.

"I just realized I've spent the whole evening telling you about my aunt's journals."

"So? I'm enjoying it. I have a vested interest. Finish what you were saying about the women's cult of the goddess on Revelation."

"Well, I'm just getting into it, but it's clear that my aunt recognized the cult immediately as the basic power structure for the islanders. Nord was obviously quite fascinated with it. She goes on for some length about it in her writings. The goddess was associated with the sea and with fertility. Only the women could appeal to her or ask her blessing. There was a special vessel used during ceremonies in her honor."

"From that she assumes the women ran things on the island? I seem to remember that in her book she made a big point of interpreting all the customs as female oriented."

Hannah nodded. "I've also come across some notes about my own ancestresses. This necklace has been in the family for generations, Gideon. It belonged to the relatives I told you about. The mathematician and the artist. It also belonged to a female member of the family who was a writer during the generation before the artist."

"I remember. The women in your family who never married."

"And who were very successful. Now the necklace belongs to me."

"And you don't consider yourself worthy of wearing it because you're just a guidance counselor." He grinned lazily and forked up another bite of salmon.

But Hannah took him seriously. "It's true, you know. The women who have worn this necklace have wielded considerable personal power of one kind or another. People like you take power for granted, Gideon. But I don't. Writing the definitive book on Elizabeth Nord would be a start in the right direction for me. It would give me a chance to do something important. Something that would make me successful."

"You've said yourself, your talent is in guiding people."

"It's a talent that people like you and Vicky Armitage don't take seriously."

His grin faded. "You want to be taken seriously by Vicky Armitage?"

"Is there anything wrong with that?"

Gideon considered the matter. "Nothing wrong with it, I suppose. I've never met the woman, but offhand it doesn't sound like much of a goal."

"You're laughing at me, aren't you, Gideon?" Hannah smiled wearily. "You see what I mean? You don't take me seriously, either. I would like to find a man who did take me seriously."

"Hannah, this is nonsense. I don't know what got you off onto this chain of thought, but it's a sure-fire conversational dead end. You know damn well I take you seriously. Do you think I'd leave Tucson in the middle of this mess with Ballantine to take off on vacation with you if I didn't take you seriously? Do you think I'd be chasing up here to Seattle now, if I didn't?''

"It's not me you're chasing, Gideon. You're looking for some answers in your own life. Answers about the situation in which you find yourself with Ballantine. Answers about the mid-life crisis you seem to be battling. Business answers. Who knows? For some reason you think you might find some of those answers by hanging around me. But you won't.''

He watched her narrowly. "How do you know that?''

"Because I've stopped giving advice to people like you, Gideon. I'm going to concentrate on following my own advice.''

"Is that so?'' he challenged. "Just what sort of advice are you feeding yourself these days?''

Hannah thoughtfully put her elbows on the table and laced her fingers together. Resting her chin on her folded hands she looked at him. "I'm going to stop worrying about other people and worry only about myself. I am not going to let either you or Hugh Ballantine use me. I'm going to make myself worthy of the necklace I'm wearing. I'm going to discover my own personal kind of power, Gideon, whatever it may be. And then I'm going to exploit it to the fullest. I have suddenly become very ambitious.''

Chapter Eleven

SHE WAS SERIOUS. Just how serious Gideon was finally beginning to realize. Hannah was no longer interested in saving him or anyone else. She was concentrating on herself.

It came as a shock because in the back of his mind he'd known that the restlessness he'd been experiencing could be assuaged in Hannah's presence. The cure might be temporary, lasting only as long as he was with her, but it would bring some peace of mind. Perhaps he had come looking for the answers he already knew he couldn't accept. Knowing he couldn't accept an answer didn't necessarily keep a man from wanting to hear it.

"Just how ambitious are you, Hannah?" he asked.

"I don't know yet," she said. "But every day lately I get a little more so. It's curious, Gideon. I feel as though I've just discovered something in myself, something quite useful, quite powerful. All I have to do is focus and aim it and live for it. It must be the same sensation that people such as you and Vicky Armitage take for granted. A kind of single-minded devotion to a goal. I've never felt so single-minded before. You're looking at the woman who changed her college major so many times she lost count."

"But you eventually concentrated on a career," he pointed out. "Guidance counseling."

"I think," she said musingly, "that guidance counseling was really a way of not having to choose a career at all."

"That's ridiculous. Helping people is a skill, a talent you have."

"No, I think in my case helping people choose different paths was just a way of making up for my own inability to choose a field and rise to the top."

"Hannah, that's idiotic." He was getting angry now, maybe a bit desperate. Grimly Gideon clamped a lid on his emotions. "I'm not suggesting that you shouldn't write this book on your aunt, but you're wrong to think that you've been wasting your life up until this point. What are you going to do? Go back to graduate school and get that damn Ph.D. in anthropology?"

"It's a possibility."

"The world has enough anthropologists. Too many of them. Just ask any lost tribe that's tried to stay lost in the twentieth century. I'll bet a lot of anthro grads can't even find decent jobs."

"I'll have an edge over most of them. I'm Elizabeth Nord's niece, remember? I now own her personal library. I can build on that. If I make a big enough splash with the book I'll be off and running. But I may not go back to school. I may decide to do this on my own terms and in my own way. There's more than one book to be had from Elizabeth's library. It's a treasure trove of information, not only about herself but about the people she studied. Any anthropologist or linguist who wants to do research on Nord or her writings will have to work through me."

"I get it. You'll be the one in charge, the one with the key to the library. Hannah, think about it. Do you want to spend the rest of your life guarding her secrets?''

Her eyes widened. ''When I decide how I want to spend the rest of my life, I'll let you know. If you're still around, which I doubt. I'm sure you'll be heading back to Tucson very soon. That Surbrook deal sounds as if it's getting hot.''

''Hot enough for Ballantine to try to bribe you with a piece of it.''

She smiled. ''That bothers you, doesn't it?''

''Naturally it bothers me. The man's making a blatant attempt to use you. He tried to appeal to any lingering notion of revenge you might have and when that didn't work, he tried outright bribery.'' Gideon struggled to keep the deep anger out of his voice. ''By the way, what did you tell him when he asked if you were interested in revenge?''

''I told him the same thing I'm telling you. I don't want to get involved in the battle.''

Gideon shook his head once, impatiently. ''You must have said more than that. Didn't he try to arouse some sisterly sense of protectiveness in you?''

''Unlike you, Ballantine didn't push. He asked his questions and accepted my answers.''

''What kind of answer did you give when he asked about our trip to Santa Inez?''

''He didn't ask about the trip. He already knew about it.''

Gideon inhaled deeply, a fierce sense of satisfaction fighting to take command. Ruthlessly he held it under control. ''He knew we'd spent the time together? In the same house? That we had an affair down in the Caribbean?''

"I think it was a fling, not an affair," Hannah said seriously.

"If he knew we'd had an affair," Gideon pursued, ignoring her comment, "then what made him think you might still be in the mood for revenge?"

"He implied that by now I must realize you had taken me to bed only as a way of topping off your little victory over my brother," she said easily. Too easily, Gideon decided. "He said you did things like that to add a fillip to your wins."

"The bastard." Gideon studied her intently, trying to see beneath the cool, flippant facade. "Did you believe him?"

"I thought he had made a logical assumption under the circumstances." She reached for her wine.

"I asked if you believed him." His anger was getting hard to control and he thought Hannah knew it. The knowledge didn't seem to bother her. He was beginning to wonder if she was enjoying herself.

"I don't see why it matters to you, Gideon, but, no, I didn't believe him. I've already decided that the reason you find me interesting is because you're trying to work something out in your own mind and occasionally I make a good sounding board. The victory over my brother was too minor, too unimportant for you to be bothered with trying to augment it by taking me to bed."

He felt frustrated and stymied. She was sitting there, just out of reach tonight, baiting him. Gideon tried to take heart from the knowledge that at least she hadn't bought Ballantine's interpretation of the situation. But he sensed that he was fighting a losing battle this evening, and he was beginning to feel a little savage because of it. He had to find a way past the defenses she

had in place. Gideon didn't question the necessity of
finding a breech in the facade she had erected. He just
knew he needed to do it.

"I'm glad you didn't buy what Ballantine was selling. He'll use anything he can to get at me. Using you
wouldn't bother him at all."

"I know. As you said, he's a lot like you."

"Hannah! Damn it, do you have to twist everything I say? I have never used you."

"Are you sure of that, Gideon?" Her eyes were almost wistful. He didn't trust the expression one bit.

"Of course I'm sure of it. The old business between your brother and myself had nothing to do with
you."

"You played games with me over it."

He paused with a forkful of salmon and aimed the
prongs at her. "No, Hannah, you tried to play games.
I only went along for the ride. You're the one who
came to Vegas and tried to maneuver me into agree-
ing to leave your brother alone."

"I was out of my league with you, wasn't I?"

He shrugged and swallowed the salmon. "You're a
guidance counselor, not a financial consultant."

"As a guidance counselor I'm out of everybody's
league. That's one of the reasons I'm getting ambitious."

"Christ, you're getting paranoid."

She nodded. "Possibly. I prefer to think of it as
ambitious, though."

He glared at the necklace around her neck. "You
know, that thing gets uglier every time I see it."

"I love it. I wear it with everything now. I think I'm
ready to go home now, Gideon."

His mouth hardened in frustration. He didn't know how to reach her verbally. She was beyond him tonight, dancing just out of reach and determined to stay there. That left only one other approach. "All right, Hannah, I'll take you home."

The drive back to her apartment was made in silence. Gideon's rented Ford climbed the hills through the financial district, past the high rise office buildings. The rain was returning as a light mist, forcing Gideon to use his wipers about every third block. They crossed over Interstate 5, which cut through the heart of the city and then they were into the quieter neighborhoods of Capital Hill. Here, grand old brick apartment buildings reigned, their windows warm with light. Gideon frowned to himself, trying to remember the layout of the streets. He wasn't that familiar yet with Seattle. Many more trips like this one, though, and he'd soon know his way around. There was definitely a question as to how many more trips he'd get. He had to do something about that tonight.

He hadn't been able to reach Hannah with words, but he doubted that her body would let her forget what they'd shared physically. It had been almost three weeks now since they'd returned from the Caribbean. As far as he could tell there was no other man in the picture. Surely she must be a little hungry for him tonight in spite of her shiny bright facade of indifference. He sure as hell was starving for her.

Gideon found a parking space in the same block as Hannah's apartment and slipped the Ford into it with a skill he took for granted. Without a word he opened the door for Hannah and waited while she climbed out.

He couldn't just jump on her the moment she opened the door. Maybe she would give him the opportunity he needed by inviting him inside for an after-dinner drink. She didn't say a word as she walked beside him along the tree-lined sidewalk. Gideon decided he'd give a great deal to be able to read her mind at that moment. He was struggling for some comment to break the silence when he spotted her Toyota.

"Did they get it painted for you while you were down in the Caribbean?" In the street lights he paused to examine the vehicle.

"Yes. It looks decent again." She fumbled for her key and kept walking.

Gideon had to take a few quick steps to catch up with her. The mist was getting thicker. Soon it would turn back into real rain. "Here, I'll take that." He reached for her key as they walked into the entrance hall of the apartment building and started up the stairs.

"It's all right."

"Hannah, for pete's sake, I'm supposed to open the door for you after a date. Let me have the key."

"I said, it's all right, Gideon. I can manage my own door."

She promptly stumbled slightly on the stairs, and Gideon reached out to take her arm and the key. He had both before she could protest further. At the top of the stairs he opened the door and pushed through behind her even as she was turning with a polite good night on her lips.

"Hannah," he whispered, shutting the door behind him, "you don't want to send me away." Gideon tugged her into his arms, determined to find the response he'd tapped that afternoon when he'd arrived. Once he had it he was sure he could build on it.

"I'm not interested in going to bed with you tonight, Gideon. If you've come all the way from Tucson expecting a casual roll in the sack, you've really wasted your time."

"Nothing is ever casual with you." She started to respond, but he cut off the cold words as he bent his head and kissed her.

She didn't actively fight him. Instead she merely remained passive beneath his attempts to find the answers he wanted. Gideon gripped her arms, pulling her closer. He could feel the soft thrust of her breasts beneath her dress and when he slid his hands down below her waist he found the lushness of her hips.

"Kiss me, Hannah," he said against her mouth. "You remember what it was like between us. You can't have forgotten." Gideon didn't wait for an answer. He moved his lips coaxingly on hers, urging her lower body against his. He wanted her tonight and he wanted her to know it. She had responded so beautifully to his need for her during their stay in the Caribbean. He couldn't believe she wouldn't respond that way again.

He had left Tucson convinced that in this one area, at least, their communication was almost perfect. Gideon had been certain that regardless of what passed between them on a verbal level, taking Hannah to bed was a sure thing. Once he had her in bed he could relax and give himself up to the satisfaction he found so easily with Hannah.

Slowly he felt her mouth soften under his. With a rising sense of relief and anticipation, Gideon tightened his hold. He flicked his tongue along her full bottom lip and then probed intimately between her teeth. She lifted her arms almost reluctantly to encircle his neck. Hannah didn't want to surrender, Gideon realized, but she was as much at the mercy of the passion that rose between them as he was. Triumphantly he groaned, cradling her completely against him. Memories of her lying nude beside him in the darkness had been haunting him for three long weeks.

She was responding more fully now, her body soft and pliant against his. Her tongue slipped delicately into his mouth, seeking to return the intimate, probing kiss. Gideon felt her shiver in his arms and took harsh pleasure from the knowledge that she was falling back into his hands at last. He should have taken this approach the moment he arrived that afternoon. All the talking at dinner had achieved nothing. The way to handle Hannah in her present mood was to take her to bed. Catching her gently by the nape of the neck, Gideon used his free hand to find the fastenings of her dress.

"No, Gideon."

The words shocked him with their clarity and certainty. She didn't try to pull away. She simply refused him access to her clothing.

"Hannah, you want this as much as I do."

"I told you earlier I won't go to bed with you."

"Why?" he asked softly, drawing his hand gently down over her breast. He could tell she wasn't wearing a bra. "Why fight something this good, honey? We're lovers. There's no need to send me away tonight."

She looked up at him, her arms still circling his neck, and it seemed to Gideon that her hazel green eyes were deeper and more unfathomable than he had ever seen them. Her lips curved very slightly.

"I'm not going to get involved in an intellectual debate on the subject. The answer is no."

"Are you afraid of me, Hannah?"

"Maybe."

He stroked her cheek lightly. "You know there's no need. I'd never hurt you."

"I'm afraid that I'm still not in your league, Gideon. I'm getting tougher and I'm getting stronger, but I'm not quite ready for you yet. I took a risk down in the Caribbean and I lost. I won't take any more risks for a while."

He stared at her fiercely. "What kind of risk did you take?"

"I thought you were changing, softening. I thought you were beginning to need me and that we could find some common ground together. But you're never going to change, Gideon. You're always going to be as hard as nails. Until I'm also as hard as nails I can't afford to get involved with you. Good night, Gideon."

"Damn it, Hannah, you're not making any sense tonight. You talk as if you have to transform yourself into some sort of super woman before you'll risk going back to bed with me."

"Before I risk going to bed with you or any other man. I'm going to learn to set the rules. The games will be played my way, and I will be the one who always wins or at least I'll break even. Come back and see me in a year or two, Gideon. No telling where I'll be by then."

"You can't send me away that easily, lady."

"Why not? Because you saved my life that day in the cove? You can't hold that over my head as a means of getting me into bed. Besides, I've already thanked you for that."

"Well, what about what I'm doing for your brother? You haven't thanked me for that." The rash, challenging words were out before he could stop them. Gideon swore silently as he saw her eyes narrow. Why the hell hadn't he kept his mouth shut?

"You've made it perfectly clear that your business with my brother excludes me. The last time I got involved I made a fool of myself. I wouldn't dream of interfering again. Not unless you use your consulting position to hurt him somehow. Did you make the deal with Nick as a way of convincing me I owed you another couple of nights in bed?"

"No, damn it!"

She nodded, satisfied. "I didn't think so. After all, you're probably not that desperate for a woman. There must be plenty of females available in Tucson. Lots of sun-streaked blondes who like to hang around successful businessmen. No, it's as I said. You're here for your own, private reasons. I don't think those reasons really include me except in a peripheral way. Let's not argue, Gideon. There's nothing more to discuss. Dinner was lovely. Thank you and good night."

"I don't believe this."

"That's because you're so accustomed to winning."

"This isn't a game we're playing."

"Everything that has a winner or a loser can be classified as a game."

She slipped out of his arms. He made no attempt to stop her. Hannah moved out of reach, aware that she was seeking a sense of safety by putting some distance between herself and Gideon. She knew that the only reason she had succeeded in sliding away from him just now was because he was too surprised by her actions to stop her.

"Hannah, listen to me."

She smiled bleakly. "You thought it would be so easy, didn't you, Gideon? Don't worry, you'll live. Maybe you'll even discover that you don't have to win every time." She was standing by her desk, idly toying with a page from her aunt's journals. Earlier she had left the book open to an entry detailing the women's cult on Revelation Island. "You know, these Revelation women certainly had a foolproof method of handling men. Nothing like being the chief intermediaries between the gods and the males to keep the males in line. You should read what went on during these all-night celebrations. They had a huge, carved vessel that they filled with a fermented liquor they made themselves. Everyone drank from it during the ceremony. The theory was that when it was empty the most important goddess could be reached. I'm afraid Aunt Elizabeth got tipsy right along with the rest of the women. I don't think she mentions that in her books but it's here in her journal." Hannah broke off in surprise as she realized that the page she was looking at was from a much earlier section of the journal.

"Hannah, I don't give a damn about Nord's studies on some female cult." Gideon stepped closer, his expression intent and forbidding. "I want to talk about us."

"When it comes to us, the conversation is closed for the evening, Gideon." She flipped the pages in the journal, searching for the one she had been reading earlier. "I could have sworn I left this open at a different place. Maybe a breeze came through. But I didn't have the window open." With a curious sense of unease she glanced around the room. Something was wrong and she couldn't quite put her finger on it.

"What is it, Hannah?" Gideon was alert now, watching her in a different way.

"I don't know. It's just a feeling." She wandered over to look down into a box of books she still hadn't unpacked. "I left this carton closed."

"It's closed now." Gideon followed her, glancing down at the cardboard box which had all four edges wedged under each other.

She drew in a breath, calming herself. "But not the way I left it. I didn't feel like struggling to get the corners locked together that way so I just left the edges folded shut. Gideon, I think someone's been in here tonight."

"Hell. And we've been standing here in the living room yelling at each other as if we were involved in a charming little domestic quarrel."

"Hardly yelling."

"Get out into the hall."

"But, Gideon..."

"Now." He was already yanking her toward the door, opening it and stuffing her outside. "Scream if you hear anything at all or if I'm not back in three minutes."

"What are you going to do?" She stared at him in confusion.

"I'm just going to check to make sure we haven't trapped someone in the bedroom." He was gone before she could argue.

Feeling foolish and suddenly quite worried, Hannah obeyed, listening intently to the sounds of Gideon's movements. The search didn't take him long. It was a very small apartment. He was back at the door within a few minutes, his expression thoughtful.

"It's all right. If there was anyone here, he's gone now."

"Why would anyone be interested in that carton of books?"

"I doubt if he was. Probably didn't know what was in the box when he opened it. You'd better have a look at your valuables and see if anything's missing. Whoever he was, he was neat. I can't see any obvious signs of the place having been tossed. There aren't even any signs of the door being forced."

Hurriedly Hannah went through her drawers, checked her stereo, counted her few items of jewelry and made sure the small stash of emergency cash was still hidden in the freezer.

"The freezer? You keep cash in the freezer?" Gideon looked appalled.

"It's for emergencies."

"It's probably the second place a burglar would look. Right after he'd checked your bedroom drawer."

"Well, he didn't find it, did he?" She closed the refrigerator door with triumph.

"No. He doesn't seem to have found anything, in fact. Hannah, are you absolutely sure that box was closed a different way?"

She grimaced. "I'm having a few doubts now. If someone had been through the apartment there ought to be more evidence. I didn't think the average burglar was this neat."

"I don't think he is."

"What about the average corporate spy, Gideon?"

"Huh?" He swung around to face her, his brows drawing together. "Corporate spy? You think one of Ballantine's people went through this place?"

"If I ever find out Ballantine had my apartment searched, I'll sue until kingdom come."

"You won't have to sue. I'll take him apart. He's got no business dragging you into this."

The new level of tension in Gideon was almost palpable. Hannah experienced a flicker of uncertainty. It occurred to her that Gideon Cage could be a dangerous man. She had sworn to herself that she would not get involved in his battles and that she would keep an emotional distance between them, but some of her old habits were proving hard to break. She felt an unfortunate urge to protect Gideon from himself.

"I was only talking off the top of my head, Gideon. It's highly unlikely that Ballantine would have my apartment searched. What could he possibly hope to find? He'd hardly expect you to store corporate secrets around here. The truth is, you were undoubtedly right about my incipient paranoia this evening. Nothing is missing. All I have to go on is the fact that I remember leaving the journal open to a different page and that box closed in a different manner. Neither of those two facts is enough to warrant hysteria. I'm sorry I mentioned them."

"Now you're trying to convince yourself that no one was in here after all?"

She smiled brightly. "Doing a good job of it, aren't I? You said yourself that any burglar worth his salt would have found my cold cash. And even if he hadn't thought the stereo sufficiently high tech he would have been interested in the bits and pieces of jewelry I've got. As for Ballantine, he simply has no reason to want this place searched."

"Unless he knows I'm here."

"Even if he knows you're here, why would he want to have a look around my apartment?"

Gideon ran a hand through his hair, looking frustrated and concerned. "I don't get it."

"Neither do I. But I expect it's because there's nothing to get. Closing the door probably caused enough of a draft to turn the pages in the journal."

"What about the carton?"

She lifted one shoulder. "I must have forgotten how I left it. I'm sorry, Gideon. A woman living alone sometimes gets a bit nervous about small details."

"You're still nervous, aren't you? All your rationalization hasn't really convinced you that no one was in here tonight."

"As I said. A woman sometimes gets nervous. There's certainly nothing here to warrant calling the cops. Don't worry, Gideon. I'll be fine."

Thumbs hooked into his belt, Gideon sauntered over to the desk to look down at the journal. "You'll feel better if I spend the night."

She went still. "No, I will not feel better. I will feel like a fool."

His head came up, his gaze hard. "I'm not going to seduce you."

"I know," she said easily. "I don't intend to let you."

"I'll sleep on the sofa."

"It's too short."

"I'll manage."

"Gideon, there is absolutely no need for you to stay with me tonight."

"It's nearly midnight and I haven't got a hotel room."

"Damn it," she muttered, "that's hardly my fault. You should have arranged one earlier."

"Please, Hannah."

That stopped her. She was braced for an argument, not a plea. She glared at him. "Please, what?"

"Let me stay." He waved a hand to indicate the sofa. "I'll sleep out here. You don't have to worry about being assaulted in the middle of the night."

"Why do you want to stay?"

"Because I came all this way to be with you."

She drew a long breath. "I don't think this is an emotionally healthy situation, Gideon."

"Is that guidance counseling talk? Emotionally healthy situation?"

"It's common sense, which is what guidance counseling is all about."

"Go to bed, Hannah. I promise I'll behave myself. It's raining outside, I'm tired, and I don't even have a hotel reservation. I'm being as humble as I can. Let me stay."

She tipped her head to one side, examining him cautiously. "You ought to try groveling a bit more often. It suits you."

"Remember what you said earlier, Hannah. You're not in my league yet. Don't start something you can't win."

"Is that a threat, Gideon?"

"It's a plea for common sense and intelligence. Go to bed, honey."

She went, a small smile of triumph on her face.

THE SHRILL RINGING of the telephone woke Gideon shortly after seven the next morning. He sat up, stiff and sore from the effects of the sofa, which had definitely been too short. For a moment he sat with his elbows on his knees, glaring around the room as he tried to locate the phone. It was hidden behind a pile of books he vaguely recognized as having come from Elizabeth Nord's cottage. The phone was on its fifth or sixth ring by the time he got to it.

"Make it quick. I am not in a good mood."

"I don't care what kind of mood you're in," Steve Decker said. "I'm just glad to be able to find you at all. Gideon, you're not going to have a business left to run if you don't stop dropping out of sight whenever the notion strikes you."

"I told you I'd be back in a couple of days." He glanced at his watch. "Tomorrow in fact. How did you find me?"

"Mary Ann said you'd bought a ticket to Seattle. I figured there was only one reason you'd go to Seattle. This is Hannah Jessett's apartment, isn't it?"

"You know it is. Get to the point, Steve. Why are you dragging me out of a warm sofa at this hour of the morning?"

"Sofa? You slept on a sofa?"

"Forget it. Just tell me why you're calling."

"I'm calling, Gideon, because you're not the only one who's taken to dropping out of sight lately. Ballantine's left his office again. My contact says he's disappeared."

"We're going to have a tough time fighting the war if nobody shows up, aren't we?"

"This is serious business, Gideon. As far as I can tell, you're chasing tail when you should be here

making decisions on everything from the Surbrook
deal to the annual bonus plan. And I don't like hearing that Ballantine's gone again. The last time he disappeared, he went to Seattle, too."

"Chasing tail? Does Angie know you talk like
that?"

"Damn it, Gideon...."

"All right. Calm down. Maybe Seattle is where the
final battle will take place. Have you thought of
that?"

Decker held his tongue and slowly counted to ten.
"Our kind of battles take place in your office, Gideon. You damn well know it."

"You're right, as usual, Decker. Try and hold things
together until I get back, okay?" He hung up the
phone before Steve could respond. Gideon turned to
find Hannah watching him silently from the hall. She
was wearing a robe patterned with huge tropical flowers and her hair was nicely tousled. He liked the way
she looked in the mornings.

"What was that all about?" she asked.

"My assistant. He was phoning to say Ballantine's
dropped out of sight."

"You people certainly keep tabs on each other,
don't you? Where is he?"

"I don't know and I don't particularly give a damn.
The last time he did this, though, he came to Seattle to
see you."

"Well, he hasn't seen me this time." She yawned
and then glanced at the journal on her desk. "At least,
I don't think he has." She headed for the kitchen.
"Want some coffee, Gideon?"

"Hannah," he said slowly, "you don't really think
he was in here last night, do you?"

"No." Memories of blue eyes behind a diving mask floated back into her head. "No, I think that's highly unlikely. I don't think anyone was in here last night. My imagination has been a little overactive lately. Go get dressed, Gideon. I'm not used to having men run around my apartment in their Jockey shorts."

Chapter Twelve

"ARE YOU SURE you want to spend an hour and a half in here?" Hannah paused at the door of the athletic club and eyed Gideon dubiously.

"Your brother took me here yesterday. They've got a good pool."

"An hour and a half is a lot of swimming."

Gideon leaned around her, shoving open the door. "Stop trying to get rid of me, Hannah. I'm not going back to Tucson until tomorrow."

"You are a very stubborn man." She turned and walked briskly through the door. He followed in her wake.

"Around you a man doesn't have much choice. He's either stubborn or he's nowhere."

"Are you sure the front desk will let you in?"

"Nick said he'd okay it."

"You and Nick seem to be getting along just splendidly these days."

"You're right. Splendidly." Which was a lot more than he could say for the way he was getting along with Hannah, Gideon thought. He scrawled his name in the visitor's book and watched her disappear into the ladies' locker room to change her clothes. He hadn't expected to spend the night on the sofa. He'd been so sure of her and of the welcome he'd eventually find in her arms.

He was beginning to think that all his problems were Elizabeth Nord's fault. Hannah had become obsessed with the journals. Last night, after Hannah had gone to bed, Gideon had read a few pages in the book that was open on the desk. Nord, herself, had been obsessed with the cult she had been describing. The journal had been a personal one, devoid of the air of scientific objectivity that characterized her published writings. Nord had seen the cult on Revelation Island as the chief source of political and social power in the group. She had been fascinated with it and had been allowed to participate in the rituals.

Her female informants had apparently accepted her completely because she was a woman. They had talked freely of their surprisingly liberal sex lives, which had included a fair amount of interest in lesbianism as well as male-female relationships. Gideon had always assumed that the more primitive the culture the more the men controlled the sexual activities of the women. Of course, Gideon reflected in amusement, Nord's famous descriptions of the liberated lives of the ladies of Revelation Island was one of the things that had made several generations of undergraduate students read *Amazons* with some enthusiasm.

There had been no mention of "Dear Roddy" in the pages Gideon had read. He wondered vaguely what had happened to the man. It didn't take much guesswork to come to the conclusion that Roddy, whoever he was, had been left behind in the dust as Elizabeth Nord moved forward in her career.

Gideon knew what it was like to leave others behind in the dust. He'd done it often enough himself. It didn't surprise him that Elizabeth Nord had done it also. Anyone as successful as Nord probably got very good at it. What was beginning to worry Gideon was that Hannah seemed to be trying to emulate her aunt. Gideon decided he didn't like the idea of being the one left behind.

Hannah emerged from the locker room a few minutes later dressed in a vivid yellow and turquoise outfit that made him blink in amused astonishment.

"You can't come into a place like this unless you're properly dressed," she informed him. Her eyes moved briefly over his swimsuit. Gideon couldn't tell if she was remembering their time together in the Caribbean or not. He hoped she was.

"You don't have to explain that getup to me," he told her. "This is supposed to be a free country."

"You don't like it?" She glanced down at herself.

"I like you better in nothing at all."

"Go take your swim, Gideon."

"Where are you headed?"

"Into that room with all those horrible machines. The therapist here has worked out a program for my knee." She peered through the glass doors that separated the machine room from the lobby. "Just my luck. Vicky and Drake are here. You'd think they'd get tired of pumping iron day in and day out."

Gideon moved up behind her, curious. "Vicky? The infamous Victoria Armitage? The lady who has done so much to inspire you lately?"

"That's her. The one with red hair and the emerald green leotard cut up to her armpits."

Gideon studied the other woman for a moment. "Great pecs."

Hannah made a rude noise and pushed open the door. "That's exactly what my brother said."

Gideon stood at the door watching Hannah laboriously strap herself into a stainless steel machine that almost immediately began prying her legs widely apart. From where he was standing he had an excellent view. She looked up, saw him staring at her crotch and stuck her tongue out at him. He waved and walked off toward the swimming pool.

She was still in the workout room, albeit struggling with a different machine, when Gideon finished his swim and came back to check on her progress. He could tell from the damp stains on her yellow leotard that she had been working hard. Her face was set in lines of deep concentration and he realized that she was talking to Victoria Armitage as she worked. Gideon assumed that the man on the stationary bicycle was Victoria's husband, Drake. He looked in the same excellent physical shape as his wife. Long contours of well-proportioned muscles shaped his shoulders and back. There was strength in the man's body, although Gideon thought he looked weak in other ways. Something about Drake Armitage's handsome mouth and eyes made Gideon wonder how he was able to hold his own with the flame-haired Vicky. Victoria's beautiful features held no trace of weakness. For the first time Gideon began to see why Hannah saw her as both a challenge and a nemesis. There was a sense of energy and disciplined determination radiating from Victoria Armitage that was somewhat daunting. If she tackled her career the way she was tackling those weights Gideon could understand why she was so successful at such an early age.

For Hannah the sight of Vicky Armitage was probably the same experience Gideon had when he looked at Hugh Ballantine. There was a certain implacableness in both that let everyone in the vicinity know they could either stand and fight, in which case they might get clobbered, or they could turn and run. People such as Vicky and Ballantine didn't negotiate or compromise very well.

But, then, Gideon remembered as he pushed open the door of the machine room, people had often said the same thing about him.

"Gideon! Finished your swim already?"

He tried to decide whether Hannah looked somewhat relieved to see him. Perhaps she was tired of battling both the machine and Vicky Armitage. "I've had enough for one day," he said agreeably, nodding pleasantly at Vicky, who gave him the once over with unabashed professional interest.

"This is Dr. Victoria Armitage," Hannah said coolly. "And her husband, Dr. Drake Armitage. I believe I've mentioned them. Gideon Cage," she went on to inform the other two. "An acquaintance of mine who's visiting from Tucson."

Drake inclined his head in an easy fashion from the bicycle. "You swim, huh? Do any weights?"

"No," Gideon said.

"You need the weights to build strength. Swimming alone won't do it."

"I'll remember that."

Vicky smiled at him but her eyes still glittered with a certain fire that told him she'd been in the midst of an argument with Hannah when he'd interrupted. "We were just discussing Hannah's aunt's work. My father was also an anthropologist. Taught for several years."

"I see." Gideon kept his response bland. He didn't like the militant look in Hannah's eyes. She kept flexing her knee on the machine as the conversation continued.

"Vicky's father wrote a couple of papers discrediting Nord's work," Hannah said quietly.

"Unfortunately, it's almost impossible to successfully challenge someone as established as Nord was," Vicky said, shifting the weights on her machine. "No one paid much attention to his papers, although he did get them published."

"Nord was such a giant in her field that anyone who wanted to discredit her work would have to come up with some very convincing evidence." Hannah kicked out on the machine with furious energy. "Apparently your father didn't have that kind of evidence."

"My father was able to prove beyond a shadow of a doubt that she couldn't possibly have been right in her analysis of the power structure on Revelation Island. She was out to prove what she wanted to prove and she skewed her findings accordingly. The female cult she found so interesting was nothing more than a simple social institution similar to a nineteenth-century sewing bee."

"The hell it was," Hannah said.

"Prove it. Turn the journals and papers over to qualified professionals who can interpret them properly."

"Now, Vicky," Drake began mildly, "there's no need to badger Hannah. The library is hers. She can do whatever she wants with it."

"Thank you, Drake." Hannah reached down and unfastened her leg from the flexing machine. "I'm glad someone realizes that."

"Don't mind Vicky, she's just frustrated because that research grant from the Carter Foundation has been delayed.'' True to form, Drake moved in to smooth the troubled waters left by his wife. "I've told her there's nothing to worry about. I've spoken to the head of the foundation myself and he's assured me everything's on track. We'll have the money by the end of the second quarter. Vicky and I will take off for some field work next spring.''

"I detest having to depend on these silly foundations run by a bunch of amateurs who think they have the right to judge what's worthy of research.'' Vicky leaned heavily on the weight machine, her irritation obvious.

Hannah smiled grimly. "You can't be too choosy, Vicky. You'll have to take the money from whatever source you can find. That's life in the academic world.''

"It's a bunch of bullshit,'' Vicky muttered.

Hannah looked up, her eyes unnaturally bright. "I'm finished Gideon. Let's go have lunch.''

"Fine with me.'' He watched her get cautiously out of the machine. It was obvious the workout had left her knee sore. Instinct told him she wouldn't appreciate him giving her a hand in front of the Armitages. He nodded again at Vicky and Drake and followed Hannah out of the room.

"I know I shouldn't let her get to me,'' Hannah sighed on the other side of the glass doors, "but sometimes she drives me straight up the wall. Drake is decent enough and he tries to keep things polite when he's around, but you can see that Vicky is hard to stop.''

"She'll go far if she doesn't ruin her chances with her mouth.''

"She's got Drake to handle the social side of life. I'll be out in a few minutes, Gideon." Hannah ran the back of her hand across her perspiring forehead and moved toward the locker room.

They ate in the chic café attached to the athletic club. Gideon ordered salmon and watched Hannah order a hamburger.

"At these prices you're ordering a hamburger?"

"Best burgers in town. I eat here whenever I can get Nick to take me. The chef has all sorts of fancy certificates but underneath he's really just a good fast-food fry cook."

Gideon didn't argue. "How do you want to spend the afternoon?"

"I assume you're going to hang around?"

"I'm a glutton for punishment."

She nodded. "In that case we might as well go on down to the Pike Place Market. I can pick up some vegetables."

"Sounds exciting."

Hannah raised her eyebrows. "Anytime you get bored, you know what you can do about it."

"I think you've been hanging around Vicky Armitage too much. You're starting to have a similar problem with your mouth."

"I feel," Hannah said softly, "that I spend most of my time lately trying to hold my own against the rest of you." The hamburger arrived, a huge, wonderfully greasy thing stacked with onions, tomatoes, lettuce and jalapeño peppers. Hannah took a giant bite and then said, "By the way, thanks for not helping me out of the weight room as if I were a little old lady."

"Maybe we communicate better than you think, Hannah."

PIKE PLACE MARKET was alive with activity in the daytime, Gideon discovered. It didn't resemble the night version he'd seen the evening that he'd walked back to his hotel from the restaurant. The nooks and crannies that had been filled with shadows, winos, and other assorted creatures of the evening were now filled with vendors selling everything from home-grown raddish sprouts to handmade leather goods. The vegetable stalls were stocked with red tomatoes, yellowing papayas, green limes, and purple cabbage—all artfully displayed, drawing a great deal of attention from tourists and their cameras, and painters and their brushes.

The fish markets displayed the Pacific Northwest salmon for which they were famous and added a few of the large, phallic-shaped geoduck clams as attention getters. Nobody passed up a stack of geoducks without staring. Once you'd stopped to stare, an aggressive fishmonger moved in to sell you a pound of shrimp and a couple of slices of halibut.

"Do you want to eat out tonight?" Hannah asked as she paused in front of a long row of bright yellow peppers.

Gideon looked at her, remembering the quiet evenings they had spent in Elizabeth Nord's cottage. "Not particularly." At least she was accepting the fact that he would be sharing dinner with her. One step at a time, Gideon told himself.

She said nothing but turned to order two massive artichokes. Gideon trailed behind her as Hannah went on to buy a papaya for breakfast the next morning. Perhaps, if he handled her carefully, he wouldn't have to wake up on the sofa tomorrow morning. Just one night, Gideon told himself. Just one more night in bed. He was sure he could reestablish what they'd had together on Santa Inez Island if he could just get Hannah back into bed.

By the time he eased the car out of the crowded downtown area, Gideon was feeling confident again. Hannah sat beside him, apparently relaxed. Her sacks of vegetables and fish were in the back seat. The whole scene seemed quite comfortable and intimate. Gideon was sure Hannah had lowered some of her defenses.

He carried the groceries into her apartment with a feeling of anticipation. Gideon was still aware of a growing sense of satisfaction when the knock came on the door. Hannah propped her cane on the arm of the sofa and went to answer it.

"Well, hell," she said. "Don't you use the buzzer any more?"

"I was hoping for a slightly warmer welcome," Hugh Ballantine remarked. "Besides, the door was open."

Gideon felt everything inside him turn to chilled steel. Slowly he set his grocery bag on the counter and walked to the door of the kitchen. Ballantine looked over Hannah's shoulder and saw him.

"Does this mean," Ballantine asked Hannah very casually, "that you aren't interested in my offer?" But his eyes never left Gideon.

"It means," Gideon said evenly, "precisely that. Did you really think you could get to me through her?"

"It was worth a try."

"No," Gideon said. "It wasn't worth a try. It's going to cost you."

Hannah found her tongue, her eyes filling with a quiet rage. "Stop it, both of you. Do you hear me?

You're like a couple of boys squabbling over an ice-cream cone.''

"Stay out of this, Hannah," Gideon said. "It doesn't concern you."

"Doesn't concern me? This is my apartment, in case neither of you had noticed. I haven't invited either of you here. You have both tried to use me to further your stupid battles with each other. You say it doesn't concern me? All right, I'll go along with that. Get out. Both of you."

Gideon didn't look at her. "Easy, Hannah."

"Out!" Her voice was tight with fury. "I will not be the ice-cream cone in the middle of this. You will not use my home as your battleground. I want you both out of here this instant or I will call the cops and have you removed. Do I make myself perfectly clear?"

"Perfectly," Ballantine said. His mouth crooked faintly in his characteristic smile but his vivid blue gaze held no trace of humor.

"Go on," Hannah charged forcibly, her eyes burning into Gideon. "Get out. Your main interest in life is making war with him. Don't let me stop you. Go play your male games in the street. I want you both out of here."

Gideon finally jerked his eyes from Ballantine's face to Hannah's. He took one look at the fierce determination in her features and knew he would have to leave. Without a word he picked up his windbreaker and walked to the door. Ballantine stepped aside. The door slammed shut behind them.

Gideon hooked the jacket over his shoulder and started toward the stairs. "I don't suppose," he offered casually, "that you'd be interested in talking?"

"Probably not. But you can try."

"You wasted your time trying to use Hannah, you know."

"Oh, I don't know." Ballantine followed slowly down the stairs. "It was worth the trip just to see her throw you out."

"I'll be going back. You won't."

Ballantine took a deep breath of the cool, crisp air. The day had turned out sunny, and some of the warmth lingered as evening began. The two men stood facing each other at the foot of the stairs. Ballantine smiled whimsically.

"If I'd pulled it off, it might have worked."

"What might have worked? Using Hannah?" Gideon shook his head. "Not a chance."

"She's gotten to you, hasn't she?"

"That's beside the point. It wouldn't have worked because she would never betray the man she's sleeping with."

Ballantine raised his eyebrows. "Not even if the guy had used her?"

Gideon started walking, not surprised when Ballantine fell into step beside him. The tension they were both radiating under their laconic poses was an invisible screen that kept a couple of feet of distance between them. "Is that what you tried to tell her? That I used her?"

"It was the truth. I can see how it might have been after that business with Accelerated Design. Kind of flat for you, wasn't it? Seducing Jessett's sister probably seemed an interesting idea. But you didn't count on finding her too interesting, did you, Cage?"

"As usual, Ballantine, when it comes to analyzing people you don't know what the hell you're talking about. Let's try and stick to business."

"I'm listening."

"You can have Surbrook."

Ballantine's head came around, shrewd blue eyes hard as ice. "Bullshit."

Gideon shrugged. "Okay, if you don't want it, forget it. I'll go ahead and take it. It's a good, solid little firm. I'll find some use for it."

"What are you talking about, Cage?"

"I'm telling you that I've decided not to fight you for Surbrook. The price is getting too high."

Ballantine sucked in more fresh air. "What would you tell your backers?"

"That the game wasn't worth the candle."

"I don't believe you, Cage. You're not going to back down."

"Why not?" Gideon watched a black-and-white cat dart across the quiet street in hot pursuit of a squirrel. The squirrel saw the cat out of the corner of its eye and every time the cat got close the squirrel simply moved farther away. The presence of the hunting feline did not stop the squirrel from gathering dinner.

"You know damn well, why not. Back off from this and I'll just keep coming at you. You can't back off forever. If you do you'll achieve the same result as if you simply put up a fight and lost. Either way your investors are going to start having doubts. Those doubts will turn to panic. They'll desert the sinking ship so fast you'll never know what hit you."

"Like I said. Take Surbrook if you want it." Gideon watched the squirrel edge out of reach of the cat.

"I'm not falling for this, whatever it is, Cage. You'll stand and fight. You've never backed down from a confrontation in your whole career."

"I am from this one."

"Why?" Ballantine demanded.

"Other things have become more important."

"That woman back there in the apartment? I don't believe it. Nothing is more important to you than the reputation of Cage & Associates, least of all a woman. Besides, how long do you think she'd want you once she finds out you're on a skid?"

"Let's not bring Hannah into this. As I recall, she specifically asked to be left out of the war. I think she's got a point. I'm removing myself from the war, also."

"You can't. You're trapped."

"Only if I let myself be trapped." Gideon sighed. "Face it, Hugh. You can't hurt me the way I hurt your father."

"Jesus. You even admit it."

"That I destroyed him financially? I've never denied it. There was a time when I would have sold my soul to the devil for your father. I'd have done anything for him. The bastard knew that. He used it. Then he calmly slit my throat and left me to find my own way out of the ditch."

"You're lying."

Gideon sighed inwardly, wondering why he was even bothering to try to explain. Normally he didn't attempt to explain himself to anyone. People inevitably interpreted explanations as a form of weakness. "You didn't know your father as well as I did. Not back in those days. I did know him. Knew how ruthless he could be. But I thought I had some protection because I was his protégé and then his partner. I owed him. He'd given me more than I ever dreamed I'd have. He was the father I'd never had."

"Can the drama, Cage."

Gideon lifted one shoulder negligently. "All right. I won't bore you with the unpleasant details. When he walked away and left me in that mess I swore I'd make him pay. You could say I dedicated my whole life to it. I lost a lot along the way."

"If you're referring to the fact that Sharon left you, I'm not buying it. Everyone knew the two of you were having problems long before you and Dad broke up the partnership."

"Those problems got a lot worse when I set my sites on making Cyrus Ballantine a nonplayer in the corporate world." Gideon remembered the fights and the endless recriminations over the twenty-four-hour days he began putting in after Ballantine had walked away with the assets of the corporation.

Sharon had been restless and unhappy before the disaster. When he'd married her she'd been a prize, a glittering jewel from the right side of the tracks who was just what he needed to crown his growing success. When he'd been younger, women like her had seemed to be from another planet—totally unavailable to a boy who made a living selling hubcaps and running errands for Cyrus Ballantine. By the time he met her he was making real money for the first time in his life. He knew where he was going and he was sure the sky was the limit. Sharon had agreed with him.

Even though he'd reached the point where he could have his choice among a variety of cool, blond beauties, Sharon had still seemed unique. Not only did she have the looks, she had the background. Good family, good schools, just the right amount of third-generation money. There had been an initial physical attraction that had lasted through a three-month affair and six months of marriage. There had been some problems, but Gideon was sure they could have been worked out. Then the crunch came.

After the financial crisis, Gideon knew he wasn't going to be able to hold Sharon. She was angry, and bitter at him for what had happened. There had been too many embarrassing articles in the paper, too many humiliating moments at the country club. She was the wife of a loser instead of a winner. She blamed him for making her look like a fool to her family and friends. Eventually she took a lover, making little effort to conceal the fact from her husband. It was as if she were trying to punish Gideon. But by that time Gideon didn't care as much as he should have cared. He was immersed in his plans for revenge. There were times when Gideon wished he had time for a lover himself. But the task of going after Ballantine proved to be a harsh mistress.

"So you went through a divorce," Hugh said. "Is that supposed to matter to me?"

"No."

"I don't believe for one moment that you saw my father as a substitute parent. You would never have done what you did to him if you'd felt that way about him."

"Hugh, I did what I did to him precisely because I felt that way."

"I'm not buying any fake psychology, so skip the personal analysis. It makes no difference."

"Have you ever looked into the whole story of what happened when your father's corporation fell apart?"

"He told me what happened. He explained how you'd been screwing around with the banks and the Feds for two full years before the whole thing caved in on you."

"It was your father who was playing games. But he was smart enough to know that it might all fall apart. So he stashed the profits out of the country. On the day the government walked in, he was boarding a plane for the Bahamas. I was the one left sitting there with a very dumb expression on my face."

"The way you're going to be sitting when I get finished with you."

Gideon watched the squirrel decide it had had enough of evading the cat. With several long bounds it headed for a tree and climbed it in seconds. The cat gave up and went off in search of easier prey. "No, Ballantine, I don't think so. Once was enough."

"I'll take everything you've got. All your backers and clients. Your reputation's going to be shit by the time I've finished with you."

"We'll see." Gideon came to a halt and faced the other man. "I think this conversation has reached its logical conclusion. Good night, Ballantine."

Ballantine stood braced on the sidewalk. The wind ruffled his hair, enhancing the farm-boy image that served him so well in business. It was easy to underestimate Hugh Ballantine because he just didn't look like the shark he was evolving into. But Gideon didn't underestimate him. He'd known the man's father.

"You won't back down, Cage. You'll fight. You've got too much to lose."

"You've got something to lose, too. But I don't suppose you're interested in hearing about it. I sure as hell wasn't when I was your age." Gideon turned and started back up the sidewalk to Hannah's apartment building. He could feel Ballantine's eyes on his back.

HANNAH SAT STARING at the page of her aunt's journal she was trying to read. She'd put away the groceries, no longer interested in fixing dinner. She'd considered substituting a strong drink for the artichokes and clams she'd planned on sharing with Gideon but even that hadn't sounded appealing. The apartment felt cold although she knew the heat was set high enough. She rubbed her upper arms with her palms and wondered where Gideon had gone with Ballantine.

She had been right to send both of them away. She wanted nothing to do with the self-destructive battle they were fighting. Gideon had chosen his own path and as far as Hannah was concerned he was free to go to hell in his own way.

She would not judge him. He was a powerful man who had forged a place for himself in a rough world. He had known what he was doing and he'd been willing to pay the price. But she would not let him involve her. She must not let him involve her.

Hannah remembered the cold way the two men had eyed each other in her apartment. She had known then that she wasn't really important to either of them except in whatever way each could use her. As far as Hugh Ballantine was concerned, it didn't matter. But when it came to being unimportant to Gideon, things were different. But they shouldn't be different.

The words on the page in front of her blurred slightly. Hannah struggled to concentrate. Her aunt had walked away from "Dear Roddy" without a qualm. Now she was in the middle of the landmark study of her career. Even at the time Elizabeth Nord had realized she was on to something very significant.

Her excitement echoed down through the years, captured for her niece in the pages of the journal.

She shouldn't be worrying about Gideon, Hannah told herself fiercely. What happened to him was no concern of hers. She must learn to put her natural empathy and compassion aside. She must endeavor to become more like her aunt. Elizabeth Nord had not needed anyone by the time she left Revelation Island. She was a complete individual, secure in her work, her philosophy, and her own company. Nord had been worthy of the necklace she'd inherited. Hannah touched the dull stone around her neck. Elizabeth Nord had not wasted her time worrying about the fate of others.

The knock on the door caused Hannah to flinch. She hadn't been expecting it. Slowly, with a feeling of inevitability, she got up from her chair and went to answer the summons. She opened the door to find Gideon in the hall, his jacket still hooked over his shoulder. Something in his eyes made her want to forget all the lectures she had been giving herself and take him into her arms. It cost her, but Hannah managed to resist.

"Well? Any blood on the street outside?" she asked.

"No."

"Good. It might have ruined my reputation with the neighbors if word got around that I entertain hoods."

He stepped through the door and dropped his jacket on a chair. "Hood, singular. You don't entertain Ballantine."

"Where is he? What did you do with him?" She closed the door and stood with her back to it, her hands gripping the knob for support.

"I didn't do anything with him. As far as I know he's still standing down there on the sidewalk."

"Did the two of you trade a lot of macho insults?"

Gideon looked at her, his eyes unfathomable. "Not exactly. Not any more macho than the insults you traded with Vicky Armitage this morning."

Hannah's head lifted in shock. "That's an entirely different kind of thing."

"Is it?"

"Of course it is. What are you going to do now, Gideon?"

"Have dinner and go to bed."

"Don't sound so damn casual about it," she stormed. "I told you and Ballantine earlier that I won't be used by either of you. I meant it."

"I need you, Hannah. If you think that means I'm using you, so be it. I'm not in the mood to argue with either you or Ballantine this evening. I think I'm becoming a pacifist."

"Pacifist, my foot. It isn't in you to be a pacifist."

"I read a page in your aunt's journal this morning that said something about everybody having the capacity for the whole range of human emotions, drives, and motivations. It's a matter of circumstances and the norms of whatever society a person is born into that determines the way he develops. The implication is that a man can change."

"You want me to believe you're changing?"

"Right now I don't really care what you believe. I need a drink."

"What about me?" she whispered.

"I also need you."

She watched him walk into the kitchen. A moment later a cupboard door clanged and then there was the sound of liquor being poured over ice. He needed a drink and he needed her. For tonight at any rate. What had been said between Gideon and Ballantine out there on the sidewalk?

She was a fool to let Gideon stay, Hannah told herself. If she had any sense at all she would kick him out. He was a disruption in her life that she simply didn't need right now. But there had been a look in his eyes when he'd come through her door a few moments ago, a look that forced her to acknowledge she was still vulnerable.

She was a long way from reaching the lofty, unemotional peak of inner certainty that Elizabeth Nord had reached, Hannah decided as she trailed slowly toward the kitchen. She wasn't even up to the standards of the women who had run things on Revelation Island.

Hannah grimaced, wondering how long it would take to throw off her chains and become an Amazon.

Chapter Thirteen

"GIDEON, WHAT HAPPENED out there?" Standing in the kitchen doorway with her arms folded and her eyes shadowed, Hannah watched him finish splashing a healthy dose of Scotch into a glass.

"Nothing of any earthshaking significance. You want some?" he held up the bottle.

"No thanks. What did you say to him?"

Gideon leaned back against the counter and took a long swallow. "I told him he could have Surbrook."

Hannah gazed at him in amazement. "That company you're both squabbling over? You told him he could have it? Just like that?"

"Yeah."

"And he didn't believe you." It wasn't a question.

"I don't think it was a case of him not believing me," Gideon said thoughtfully. "I think he didn't *want* to believe me."

"There are times, Gideon, when you're rather perceptive for a shark. I think I'll have a drink after all." She watched as he turned back to the counter to pour her one. "What did he say?"

"That I was lying. He assumed I was up to something."

"Your track record in that department is fairly impressive."

He swung around, her glass in his hand. As he shoved it into her fingers, Gideon's expression tightened with leashed anger. "I don't lie."

Nervously Hannah swirled the Scotch in her glass. "I didn't mean you had an impressive track record when it comes to lying. I meant you have one in the area of being up to something. I've had first-hand experience of how you can mislead someone when it suits your purposes, Gideon."

"Come off it, Hannah. You're the one who resorted to cheating that first night. You can hardly blame me for not spilling my guts about my plans for your brother's firm."

"Let's just say you're very good at not telegraphing your moves. So why should Hugh Ballantine think you're being particularly straightforward with him?"

"No reason." Gideon took another swallow of the Scotch. "I made the mistake of trying to explain some things to him."

"What things?"

"Just small stuff. I took a shot at telling him how I'd felt about his father. Why I'd done what I did to Cyrus."

Hannah bit her lip to conceal the wave of compassion that washed through her. Poor Gideon. He really had gone out on a limb. "You told him Cyrus Ballantine had been a father figure to you?"

"Christ. You said something like that once before. Is it that obvious?"

"No. But I've known you for several weeks now, Gideon. I've heard you talk about Cyrus and I've seen what the need for revenge did to you. It takes a very powerful motive to put a man on the track you've been on for the past nine years. It makes sense that the reason you hated Cyrus Ballantine so completely was that he had betrayed you on a personal level as well as a business level."

Gideon's mouth hardened. "There are some serious disadvantages to sleeping with a guidance counselor. A little knowledge of psychology is a dangerous thing."

"Just be grateful I'm not a psychiatrist. A real shrink would have a field day analyzing you. And you're not sleeping with me. Not currently."

His eyes met hers. "Aren't I?"

She took a slow, steadying breath. "Did you really try to give Surbrook to Ballantine?"

"I tried."

"I could have told you it wasn't going to be quite that easy."

"Lately, nothing," Gideon said, "has been easy."

"If it's any consolation, I'm sure you've shaken him to the core. That would be the one move he wouldn't expect from you. He'll go crazy trying to figure out what you're up to now."

"I don't want to waste time playing games with Hugh Ballantine. As far as I'm concerned, he's had his chance."

"I see." Hannah tried a sip of the Scotch. "You made one attempt to end the war and if that doesn't work, the hell with it, right?"

"I've made one more attempt than you've made."

Her eyes narrowed. "What are you talking about?"

"You haven't made any effort to end the friction between yourself and Vicky Armitage."

Angry color stained Hannah's cheeks. "That's different."

Gideon smiled grimly. "You sound like a little kid defending herself for getting into a fight with another little girl."

"You don't know what you're talking about." Hannah moved abruptly away, stalking back out into the living room to stand in front of the window that opened onto her postage-stamp-size balcony.

"Hannah, when it comes to waging war, I'm an expert. I'm learning that it's not so easy to call off a battle once it's started. But the one person I don't want to fight with this evening is you." He came up behind her and turned her slowly around to face him. "I want you. I've been wanting you since the moment I met you, and a few days on that damn island only made the wanting worse. Is it absolutely necessary for you to fight me tonight? Couldn't we have another truce like the one we had on Santa Inez? I need a little peace and comfort."

She trembled under his hand and looked up at him through her lashes. The taut strain in him was etched around his eyes, making her want to lift her fingers to soothe away the lines. She was too soft where this man was concerned. He didn't need her softness. But he would take it, soaking it up like a sponge. Hannah was not at all sure he could ever learn to give it back except in isolated moments of passion.

"Gideon, what is it you really want from me? Just a little peace and comfort?"

"You make those things sound as if they're not very important. But they are important, Hannah. I've only recently started realizing just how much I crave them." He bent his head and brushed his mouth across hers. "I can't seem to get enough."

"And what do I get in return?"

His fingers tightened in her hair. "I don't know. What *do* you get in return? You keep responding to me, so you must be getting something." He kissed her again, his lips moving deliberately on hers, seeking some sign of her own need. "Let me take you to bed, Hannah. I need you."

She felt the glass being removed from her hand, heard it clink lightly as it was set down on the table next to Gideon's. Then his arms were around her, tugging her against him. With a soft sigh she let the need in him envelop her. In that moment she couldn't completely analyze the reasons for her own response, but she knew she wanted him. She could accept that. A woman had a right to physical gratification. She just wished she didn't also long to offer the comfort he said he craved.

"Ah, Hannah, you're so sweet. So soft. I've been wanting you so damn much." His fingers twisted deeply in her hair, holding her face still for his deepening kiss. When Hannah lifted her hands to his shoulders and parted her lips he groaned, moving into her mouth with a hunger that could no longer be concealed or denied.

Hannah gave herself up to the heavy, seductive warmth Gideon was offering. She had been missing his touch, even while she had told herself she must live without it. But tonight everything was as it had been on the island. He needed her and she needed him. What did she get out of it? Not as much as she wanted, but more than she'd ever had with any other man. Perhaps she wasn't as strong as she should be yet. Or perhaps she was stronger than she had thought.

He pulled her gently down onto the sofa, pushing her beneath him as he lowered himself. Gideon's fin-

gers fumbled slightly as they found the fastenings of
her clothing. There was an urgency in him that com-
municated itself to Hannah, making her want to give
him what he needed. She found the buckle of his belt
and undid it.

"Yes, honey. Yes, please," he muttered in her ear.
His hands moved on her, stripping the clothes from
her body in quick, impatient movements.

His own clothing came off in a similar fashion,
winding up in a heap on the floor beside the sofa. Gideon's mouth claimed Hannah's as he sprawled on
her. She was vividly aware of the masculine strength
in him as his knee came between her thighs. Her nails
sank into his shoulders as he let her feel the waiting
need in his lower body. She knew her own body was
already dampening in anticipation. When Gideon's
thumb moved over one nipple he found the peak hard
and excited. His fingers explored lower, discovering
the ready response between her legs.

He didn't hesitate. Her name was a thick groan
against her mouth as he guided himself to the waiting
entrance and then surged forward. When she gasped
at the deep intrusion into her body he swallowed the
small sound.

"Wrap yourself around me. I want to feel you
holding me the way you did when we were on Santa
Inez. Take me, Hannah."

She obeyed with an eagerness that knew no bounds.
The driving force of his body against her own was a
primitive summons that called forth the response he
wanted. Hannah was on fire with the consuming need
to satisfy and be satisfied. She tightened her legs
around his lean hips. There was perspiration across his

back; she could feel it under her palms. There was more moisture on her skin between her breasts.

There was nothing of sensual subtlety or erotic skill in this coming together. It was an urgent coupling, a quick, flaming search for physical union and release. The lack of finesse did nothing to lessen the powerful impact. Hannah heard Gideon biting off her name as his body shuddered and locked into hers. She tightened around him as she followed him over the edge. For an instant they both hung suspended in the throes of the climax and then Gideon sagged along the length of Hannah's body, his weight crushing her deeply into the sofa cushions. She traced a small pattern on his shoulder, her mind blessedly unconnected with everything around her except the man whose body was still joined with hers.

"This sofa," Gideon finally mumbled, "is going to be the end of me." But he made no attempt to shift his position.

"You seem to be surviving."

"I'm capable of putting up a valiant struggle when the need arises."

She smiled. "So I see."

He lifted his head to look down at her. There was a directness in his gaze that belied the lethargy in his body. "Hannah, come back to Tucson with me."

The request took her totally by surprise. It had been the last thing Hannah had been expecting. Floundering, she said the first word that came into her head. "Why?"

"Isn't it obvious?"

"You mean," she asked carefully, "that you want the affair to continue and it would be simpler for you if I came to Tucson."

"Much simpler."

Her head moved uneasily on the flowered cushion. She couldn't seem to think straight. "I'm not sure it would be simpler for me, Gideon."

"You don't go back to work at the college until fall. That gives us all of August and part of September. There's no reason we can't spend that time together."

"This is my home."

"You could learn to be at home in Tucson. You could spend the rest of the summer sitting out by the pool working on your book. Come with me, Hannah. I want you with me."

"To use as a sounding board while you go through the rest of your mid-life crisis?"

He lifted himself away from her with an abrupt movement. Sitting up on the edge of the couch he looked back at her. "Why do you always have to question everything I say or do? Why can't you just accept that we have something good together?"

"I've told you, Gideon, that I'm not sure I'm strong enough to handle you yet." She wasn't at all certain she could spend the summer with him and then blithely return to work in the fall. Hannah felt the tightening in her stomach as she contemplated trying to extend the affair. Fear and anger and resentment were at war within her, battling the need and the fierce attraction she felt for this man.

"You're only using that as an excuse. Why are you trying to fight me, Hannah?"

"Because if I don't protect myself from you, no one else will," she said simply.

He reached out to touch the tip of her breast, his fingers lazy and possessive. "Just relax, Hannah, and let it all happen. This isn't a war you have to wage with me. It doesn't have to be like that.''

She moved, struggling to a sitting position beside him. Awkwardly she scooped up her jeans and shirt, holding them clutched in front of her. "Have you really thought this through, Gideon? Or is it just something you've decided you want on the spur of the moment?"

"I know I want you with me."

"I'd probably spend the rest of the summer giving you advice on how to run your business. You wouldn't enjoy it."

His mouth lifted in a slight smile. "I can find ways to shut you up when I get tired of hearing the advice."

"I don't think it's a good idea for either of us, Gideon," she said very seriously.

"You mean you're unsure of yourself. You're afraid of me."

"No, I am not afraid of you," she snapped, "but, yes, I'm unsure of myself. I have some decisions to make this summer. I don't think I can make them with you in the vicinity."

"It's those damn Elizabeth Nord papers, isn't it?" Gideon lifted his hand to touch the necklace around her throat. "That woman is having more of an effect on you now that she's gone than she ever had when she was alive."

"She's making me ask some questions and find some answers," Hannah agreed quietly.

"A part of you wants to become like her. You told me once that she was the kind of woman who didn't need anyone, not a lover or a child or even a close friend."

"She was strong. Totally self-sufficient. Like you," Hannah added. "And until I have that same kind of strength I think my safest course is to steer clear of people like you."

"You can't steer clear of me, honey. I want you too much to just let you go off in search of yourself. Especially when I don't like the direction you've chosen to follow."

She tugged on her shirt. "What's wrong with the direction I've chosen?"

"It scares the hell out of me."

Her head came around in astonishment. "It scares you?"

"Yeah."

"You don't want a strong woman for this summer affair you're planning, is that it?" She stood up and tugged on her jeans. "You want a pleasantly weak, malleable sort of female."

"You're already strong enough, Hannah. What scares me is that if you keep drifting in your current direction you won't care what happens to me any longer."

She stared at him. "Maybe that way I'll feel safe. Safe enough to come and stay with you for a while in Tucson."

"I don't want you locking yourself safely away in some invisible cage, damn it. I want the real Hannah Jessett. The one who tries to tell me what's good for me and how to run my business. The one who melts in my arms at night."

"So far, it sounds as if you haven't changed one bit. You want an affair conducted on your terms. Well, I've got other plans for the summer. When you can tell me what I'll get out of it besides free use of your pool for the rest of the season, maybe I'll consider the offer." She turned and headed for the hall, intent on getting under a hot shower. Her body felt sticky and sweaty and she knew she carried the scent of him on her.

"Hannah." He was on his feet behind her, not bothering with his clothing. Gideon caught her before she reached the bathroom. His hands came down on her shoulders, spinning her around. "I don't know what it is you want from me, but I'll try to give it to you within reason. Give me a chance, honey. You don't have to turn yourself into an Amazon to feel safe with me."

She shivered from the almost overwhelming desire to surrender. It would be so simple, so inviting, to just throw herself into his arms and allow herself to be swept away for the summer. The necklace suddenly seemed very warm and heavy against her skin. Unconsciously she touched it and remembered all that it had stood for in the past. Her life was changing this summer. If she didn't find out what lay along the new paths she was exploring she would always wonder what she had denied herself. Gideon's eyes followed the movement of her fingers to her throat. She saw the glittering dislike in his gaze.

"I need time, Gideon."

"How much time?" he demanded.

"I don't know. I want to do some thinking. I can't seem to think very clearly when you're around."

"If I leave you alone you'll go straight back to those damn journals and papers. You'll start thinking again about whatever it is you're trying to prove to yourself and Vicky Armitage."

"So? As soon as you're alone you'll start thinking about the war you're conducting with Hugh Ballantine. I'm not going to be hustled into something I'm not at all sure I want, Gideon. You've already hustled me enough. I agree with Ballantine. You're tricky. You might not lie to me, but you're quite capable of trying to manipulate me. Manipulating people is second nature to you."

"I am not trying to manipulate you, damn it."

"Gideon, you're so good at it that you don't even know when you're doing it." Wearily she turned away. He released her reluctantly but the aggressive tension in him filled the hall.

"Hannah, come with me to Tucson. We'll spend the summer working it out."

She halted at the odd combination of raw appeal and arrogant command in his voice. He sounded almost as torn as she felt. She wanted to give him what he wanted. But she could also see a hazy future that promised personal security and power on a scale she'd never before known. All she had to do was reach out and grab it. One thing was clear to her in that moment. She couldn't have both Gideon and that as yet uncharted future. Hannah braced one hand on the door jamb but she didn't turn to face him.

"I have to think, Gideon. I need time." Without waiting for his response she went into the bathroom and closed the door behind her.

GIDEON LEFT on an early morning plane for Tucson. Hannah took him to the airport and saw him off in near silence. He had spent the night on her sofa, alone. That morning he had been as silent as she, as if he knew there was nothing else to be said. In the departure lounge he suddenly hauled her close and kissed her hungrily.

"I'll give you a little time, Hannah, but not much."

"Why are you so impatient, Gideon? Because you're not accustomed to a woman having doubts? She's supposed to leap at the chance of having an affair with you?"

"I'm impatient because I'm scared of losing you. That should be simple enough for you to understand. Goodbye, Hannah."

She watched at the lounge window until the jet lifted into the sky and then slowly turned and made her way out of the airport. Interstate 5 was crowded on the trip back into the city. The congestion made her uncomfortable. She seemed overly conscious of the small spaces between the Toyota and the rest of the cars around it. Alertness on the freeway was one thing: paranoid nervousness was another. She had been regaining her self-confidence in driving, Hannah thought, but there were times when she seemed to be having a relapse. When she happened to glance to the side while driving over an interchange she felt a moment of queasiness. It was a long way down if one went through the guardrail.

Deliberately she pulled her imagination back from the brink and concentrated on watching for the proper exit as the downtown highrise buildings came into view. After a moment or two she had herself back under control.

When she reached the street where her apartment building was located she parked the Toyota with a sense of relief, the same relief she always experienced these days after finishing a trip in the car. Then she made her way up the stairs, trying to take satisfaction from the fact that she hardly needed the cane at all.

The apartment seemed very empty. Hannah locked the door behind her and set down the cane. For a few minutes she stood gazing out the window. Gideon was gone again.

This time she could have gone with him. The choice had been hers. Hannah didn't doubt that he wanted her with him for the summer. But, then, she hadn't doubted that he had wanted her on Santa Inez.

Elizabeth Nord's journal still lay on the desk. Slowly Hannah wandered over and sat down in front of it. Somehow, she felt certain, the answers all lay within the old, leather-bound volume. Somewhere in this book was the key she needed to make the choices that lay ahead of her.

Going with Gideon would have foreclosed on some of those choices. Hannah knew that with a sure instinct. She would not be free to choose while he was around. Gideon would fill up too much of her life, demand too much of her attention, and force her to concentrate too much on him. Nord had been right to refuse "Dear Roddy's" proposal of marriage. Whoever Roddy was, he would have trapped her and used her. Gideon wouldn't use Hannah in the same way, but he would use her, nevertheless.

Hannah looked down at an entry dated early in the year of 1942.

> The war is coming close. I know I shall have to leave soon. But I desperately need more time here. I am beginning to worry about some discrepancies, which are occurring in the information my informants are giving me. They're

relatively minor and probably aren't significant, but they are starting to become a concern. Why does Laneoloa give me one explanation for tasting the menstrual blood of a new cult initiate while Kanaea provides a different reason? Also, I'm beginning to doubt the emphasis on lesbianism among the group's members. When I expressed great interest in it at the beginning of my studies, my informants gave me a tremendous amount of detailed information about the female sexual rites practiced during certain ceremonies. Yet I saw no indication of such sexual practices during the ceremony last night. I don't understand why certain details are not coinciding properly.

The next entry was dated three days later. It read:

The islanders have decided to abandon the village and the island. I have explained to the women that there is every possibility the Japanese will be landing soon. Preparations are being made tonight to hide the sacred vessel. My informants have told me that it must not leave the island, and in this the men seem in agreement. I have recommended that it not be hidden in the village as there is too much likelihood of looting. Tonight, during a special ceremony, a location will be chosen. Damn this war. There is so much to be learned here on Revelation and I am so afraid that afterward all will be changed. Men and their idiotic notions of settling conflicts. What have they done to us this time?

The next entry was written hastily and dated a few days later:

I am on a ship headed for Hawaii. The islanders have gone their own way and I hope they will be safe. The navy has provided me with transport. I am told the Japanese took Revelation Island this morning. A few minutes ago a young man who looks as though he has already seen too much war approached me. It seems that military intelligence would like a first-hand report of the terrain on Revelation. Their information is sketchy and comes from old atlases. I suppose this means that an attempt will be made to take Revelation back from the Japanese. I cannot bear to think of the slaughter that must ensue. My poor island will be bathed in blood. I will tell this young man who already has so much age in his eyes what I can. I fear it will not do much to lessen the carnage.

Hannah stared at the page in front of her, imagining her aunt's feelings as she had sat jotting the notes in her journal. Elizabeth Nord had known even then that nothing would ever be the same on Revelation Island. All the data she would ever have for writing *The Amazons of Revelation Island* was in her hands at that point. A small, unique culture would be lost to the world from that moment on, recalled only in the text of *Amazons*.

There were further notes, mostly hurried observations and a few last-minute recollections that Nord had obviously wanted to get down on paper before she forgot them. Hannah read them quickly, looking for the time when Nord had decided to write the book. When she found it several pages later, Hannah slowed her reading once more.

I have been going through the elaborate notes I made regarding the initiation ceremony. There is no longer any doubt in my mind about the discrepancies. At least two of my informants have given me differing explanations of the portion of the ritual in which the young girls are initiated into the cult. Is it possible they have lied to me?

Hannah skipped ahead a few paragraphs and found another notation of a discrepancy in the explanations of Nord's female informants. It was a small point having to do with a matter of dress but it was clear that it had bothered Nord.

There is so much information to be considered. I suppose it is not at all strange that I have gotten a few things mixed up, but it is so unlike me to make a mistake of this kind. Yet why would my informants deliberately mislead me?

Time slipped past in the journals as Nord made the decision to write her book and began putting the extensive data into order. "I have come across a particularly valuable reference," she wrote late in 1942.

It is a missionary's journal from the last century and contains some notes on the people of Revelation Island. I am ecstatic over the discovery. Perhaps I will find information that will help substantiate some of my own findings. There may also be some details that will help me clear up some of the curious discrepancies I have noted recently.

The next entry was of a different nature:

Roddy stopped by to see me this afternoon. He has changed little during the past few months. He has made it plain that he thinks I made an error in turning down his proposal of marriage. I, on the other hand, have never been so glad of a decision in my life. He is also convinced I have wasted my time on Revelation Island.

In an entry dated the following day Hannah could almost feel the concern underlying the sentences.

I have been through the missionary's journal and have found it most upsetting. The Reverend Helmsley also noted some odd discrepancies in the explanations given to him by the Revelation Islanders. His informants were all male, of course, but he speaks of his wife having made contact with some of the women and of their accounts differing markedly. I have begun to realize that because I was a woman, I did not communicate well with the men of the island. I relied heavily on the women for information. A pattern is emerging here and it makes me uneasy.

Three days later, after what was obviously intensive study, the pattern became clear to Elizabeth Nord. Hannah read the relevant passages with stunned amazement.

There is no longer any doubt. I have been a victim of my own bias. The record left by Reverend Helmsley has removed the last of my doubts. The islanders have deliberately deceived me on several occasions. I do not think it was maliciously done. Rather it is as if they simply make a practice of telling outsiders what they think they wish to hear. I was a woman who wished to find the power structure on the island centered around the females. It was probably easy enough for my informants to figure out what I wanted to hear. They then took pains to exaggerate their explanations. It is not an unheard-of phenomenon in fieldwork. I should have been alert to it. My notes are not all lies and nonsense by any means, but I am forced to reconsider my conclusions concerning the basic role of women in the social structure of the islanders. It would appear that it is not all that different from the role of women on neighboring islands. While unique in some respects, it is fairly traditional in many others.

Hannah read further, suddenly growing afraid of what she would find next.

I fear that I am faced with a decision. I can write *Amazons* as I originally intended, describing a fascinating culture based on female power, or I can write what appears to be the truth. If I do the latter, my book will merely be one more in a long line of studies concerning South Pacific island societies, adding little that is new or illuminating. But if I write the book as I originally intended, a great deal of good might be accomplished. I will provide a whole new view of human nature, especially the nature of women. It will astound anthropologists as nothing else has done in recent years except for Mead's work on Samoa. Perhaps it will cause the so-called male experts to reevaluate their own biases and to view the women of other cultures with new eyes.

The decision, Elizabeth Nord concluded, was truly hers. By the end of 1943 Revelation Island had been retaken from the Japanese. As Nord had predicted, there was little left to disprove her conclusions. The islanders were scattered now, their culture forever destroyed by the forces of modern civilization. Even if they could all be successfully brought back to their village at the end of the war, there would be no way to undo the influences of modern life to which they had been exposed. Another unique pattern of society had been wiped out. That meant, as Nord realized, that no one would ever be able to contradict what she chose to write.

It is my chance to force a new view of culture into the field of anthropology. My chance to shake old beliefs and prejudices concerning the supposedly subordinate role of women in primitive societies. I am going to seize the opportunity. Once *The Amazons of Revelation Island* is in print no professional student of human beings will be able to take for granted that the role of women in society is a biologically determined one. This glaring exception must always give the student pause, force him or her to question his assumptions about the nature of power in any society, cause questions to be asked concerning the roles of the sexes. Once questions are being asked, all things are possible. I will write the book the way I want it written.

Hannah closed the journal with a feeling of disorientation. Elizabeth Nord had lied. She had deliberately skewed her findings to establish an anthropological myth that had lasted for years and was still in existence. And in the process she had established herself as a giant in her field.

Chapter Fourteen

YOU HAD TO hand it to Aunt Elizabeth, Hannah decided, even her deceptions were practiced on a larger-than-life scale. The enormity of the Nord lie was awesome. Hannah sat stunned in the fanback chair, gazing unseeingly across the room. The journal still lay on the desk where she had left it when she'd gone to fix herself a cup of coffee.

It wasn't coffee she needed but it seemed indecently early in the day to be pouring medicinal scotch.

The whole underlying premise of *The Amazons of Revelation Island* was a fabrication. For generations of college students it had been required reading, the landmark book of one of America's most eminent anthropologists. Elizabeth Nord's stature had been of such towering height that the carping criticism of people such as "Dear Roddy" had been generally dismissed.

Whatever had happened to poor old Roddy? Hannah thought about the man and wondered anew what he must have been like. There was no doubt that in the beginning of his association with Nord he had been a typically condescending, overbearing, patronizing male of the species *academius*. He had probably been intelligent enough to see the brilliance in his young associate. At first he had apparently treated her the way he would treat a precocious child. But when the child began to surpass him in accomplishments and publications, that condescending attitude had shifted into something else. He had become resentful, petty, and critical. He had even gone through a stage of trying to appropriate her future for himself by asking her to marry him. In the end Dear Roddy had drifted into relative obscurity, just one more anthropologist in an overcrowded field.

The fact that he had been right about Elizabeth Nord's interpretations of the social structures of Revelation Island was an ironic twist of fate. Hannah wondered how he had felt as he watched Nord's position in the academic world become unassailable.

She got up from the chair, suddenly consumed with a desire to know more about Dear Roddy. Hannah wondered how he had coped with his bitterness and the knowledge that Nord's greatest claim to fame was based on a lie. Yanking a World War II-style bomber jacket out of the closet, she grabbed her cane and headed downstairs to the street. She needed the resources of an excellent academic library, a library that would be much more comprehensive than the one belonging to the small college where she worked.

She would take the bus to the University of Washington, Hannah decided. It was much more economical and efficient to use public transportation. The fact that it gave her an excuse not to drive the Toyota was not lost on her but she didn't dwell on it. Driving back from the airport had been enough of an adventure for one day.

Two hours later she sat in a study carrel piled high with old anthropological journals and collected readings in the field. With the help of a reference librarian she had tracked down the scattered essays and papers that had dared to criticize Elizabeth Nord. There weren't a great many of them that had been published since World War II but the pre-war materials provided richer digging. Finding Dear Roddy in the pile was going to take some work, but Hannah knew that at one point at least he had been associated with the same university as her aunt. In the early days they had actually collaborated on some papers.

The first reference that looked positive was a short paper done by Roderick Hamilton and Elizabeth Nord for an obscure journal that had long since ceased publication. It was a discussion of certain aspects of the building of ceremonial canoes on a small South Pacific island.

Roderick Hamilton. Sure this was "Dear Roddy," Hannah continued her quest, finding other papers that had been published over the years. Shortly before the war her aunt's name stopped appearing under Hamilton's. Her own publications became more frequent while his became less and less so.

There were a couple of stinging critiques of Nord's work by Roderick Hamilton in the 1950s, but none of them seemed to have inspired much controversy. By the late sixties there were a few pedantic pieces by him, mostly rehashes of his pre-war work. By 1970 there were no further citations.

The man had been right about Elizabeth Nord but no one had listened. Hannah could just imagine how that would have grated on him. She closed the last journal and walked back to the reference desk.

"I'd like to see if there is an obituary of Roderick Hamilton," she explained to the librarian. "He was an American anthropologist."

"What university was he affiliated with?"

Hannah told her the name of the school that had been listed in Hamilton's last paper. The librarian began reaching for several reference books on academic personnel. Ten minutes later she found the obituary. Hannah turned the book around on the desk so that she could read the short entry. There wasn't much to it. Roderick Hamilton had died ten years earlier after a long career in anthropology. Some of his early works were cited as having been influential. None of his later work was mentioned. His greatest claim to fame was that he had collaborated with Elizabeth Nord at one time. Hamilton had been a widower when he died. He was survived by a daughter. Hannah stared at the name: Victoria Hamilton.

It was too much of a coincidence. Victoria Hamilton had to be Victoria Armitage. Frowning, Hannah went after the information she needed. It wasn't hard to find. Victoria Hamilton had graduated with honors and the results of her early fieldwork started making its way into print shortly after she married Dr. Drake Armitage.

Good old Drake, Hannah reflected. No wonder Vicky stuck with him. He knew how to play the academic game, how to get the right kind of attention, how to make certain people know how brilliant Vicky was. He had known how to get her published. Unlike Elizabeth Nord, who had refused to ride to fame on the coattails of a husband, Vicky had chosen to marry a man who could smooth the way for her.

But, as far as Hannah knew, Victoria Armitage hadn't resorted to creating a myth in order to establish her name.

Depressed, Hannah thanked the reference librarian and walked out of the elegantly old world library building. Outside, the sun was shining on the prestigious brick university structures and the acres of wooded campus. Students ranging in style from Mercer Island preppies to kids fresh off the farms of eastern Washington lolled in the red brick plaza. She picked her way through them and started down to "The Ave," as University Way NE was casually termed. The street was lined with everything from leftover counterculture shops to trendy boutiques. Even during the summer there was plenty of activity. She crossed the footbridge, resisted the temptation to duck into the art gallery, and strolled slowly along the Ave. There were, Hannah remembered, a couple of excellent coffee houses tucked away amid the clutter of stores and ethnic restaurants.

She found the quiet corner she needed not far from the huge University bookstore. She tried to order plain coffee but soon discovered that was next to impossible. One had to select between café latte, cappuccino, or espresso. Ensconced at a table with a small cup of very dark, thick liquid in front of her, Hannah tried to come to terms with what she had learned. When she didn't have much luck with that line of thought, she found herself dwelling on the subject of Gideon Cage.

Theoretically, Gideon was not a part of her current dilemma. He was safely back in Tucson by now. But he kept slipping into her mind, entangling himself with the chaos that was already there. Slowly, Hannah forced herself to finish the expensive espresso and then go back out onto the street to find a bus that would take her home.

During the trip back to Capitol Hill she sat slouched in a seat, staring out the window at the endless green that enfolded Seattle. Her fingers toyed absently with the necklace she wore. Nothing seemed to be clarifying itself. Perhaps she was still in shock.

When she reached her apartment she was going to call Gideon. He had been there at the beginning with her when she had uncovered the journals. He alone, besides herself, knew about Dear Roddy. She needed to talk to someone. The phone in Tucson was answered on the third ring. Gideon's voice sounded impatient.

"This had better be important, Decker. I'm half way into a shower."

"Gideon, it's Hannah."

"Hannah." There was a distinct pause and then Gideon said quietly, "What's wrong?"

"Nothing, really. I called to see if you'd gotten home safely."

There was another pause. "You did?"

"Well, no. I mean, I assumed you'd gotten home safely. What I actually called about was Dear Roddy. Remember him?"

"Hannah, you sound odd."

"I'm feeling odd. You do remember Roddy? From my aunt's journals?"

"I remember him."

"Well, I looked him up this afternoon at the University library. Roderick Hamilton was Vicky's father. Isn't that a coincidence?"

Gideon hesitated thoughtfully. "I guess it explains her interest in those journals."

"It also might explain why she always argues against my aunt's work."

"Possibly. But I think Vicky tends to argue because it comes naturally to her," Gideon said. "It probably drives Armitage crazy at times."

That stopped Hannah for a moment. "I didn't re- alize you'd made such a thorough study of the woman."

"Once you get past the great pecs you can't help but notice the loud mouth. That woman would chew a man alive in bed."

For some reason Hannah was annoyed. "What about me? I do a fairly good job of arguing on occa- sion, too!"

"Yeah, but I can usually keep you from doing it in bed. What's this all about, Hannah? Are you really calling just to tell me you've found out who the mys- terious Roddy is?"

"Was. He died a few years ago and no, I'm not calling just to tell you that. There's more."

"Out with it. For Christ's sake, Hannah, you sound as if you're in shock."

"I am. I just got to the point in my aunt's journals where she admits she knew she was wrong about the Amazons. She decided to write the book, anyway."

Gideon exhaled on a long, low whistle of astonish- ment. "She admitted she was off base about the whole female thing?"

"Yes."

"But she wrote the book the way she had originally planned to?"

"She lied. Deliberately. It's the most incredible thing, Gideon. I can't quite take it in."

"What are you going to do about it?" he asked bluntly.

"That's one of your strong points, Gideon. You have a way of getting right to the bottom line. The truth is, I don't know what I'm going to do about it."

"What about us?"

"I don't know what I'm going to do about us, ei-ther. I feel totally confused at the moment."

"Hannah, listen to me," he ordered urgently. "Pack a bag and come on down here. You don't have to do your thinking all by yourself. You can do it here."

"I don't think that's such a good idea, Gideon."

"You've just admitted you can't think straight. How do you know whether it's a good idea or not?"

"Instinct. Goodbye, Gideon. I'll talk to you later."

Hannah hung up the phone before he could argue further. She might not be at her most brilliant that af-ternoon but something told her she wouldn't find herself getting any more intelligent while sleeping in Gideon Cage's bed. Hannah looked at the snapshot of her aunt's cottage on Santa Inez.

That was what she needed, she decided, the quiet solitude of a beach cottage. She needed to think things through in an environment that held the essence of Elizabeth Nord. Hannah made up her mind and picked up the phone to call a travel agency.

The door buzzer sounded from downstairs just as she finished making the reservations. Hannah sighed and went over to the intercom.

"Who is it?"

"Hugh Ballantine."

There was something in his voice. It was too flat and unemotional. Hannah considered her options and then decided there really wasn't much she could do except politely let him inside.

"Come on up."

He was at her door a moment later, hands thrust deeply into the pockets of his suede jacket. The red hair was tousled and the blue eyes didn't appear quite

as open and friendly as they had the time he had taken
Hannah to dinner.

Blue eyes, Hannah thought as she stepped aside and
let him into the room. Why did he have to have blue
eyes? She was not going to start becoming paranoid
about blue eyes as well as freeway driving, she vowed.

"What can I do for you, Hugh?" She didn't sit
down.

He stood watching her as if he was trying to figure
something out. "You're the key."

"To Gideon? You're wrong. How many times do I
have to tell you, I'm not involved."

"You've changed him."

"Impossible. Nothing short of a nuclear explosion
would change Gideon Cage. We both know that."

Ballantine shook his head. "He says he's going to
run. He says he won't stand and fight. Claims he's
going to hand Surbrook over to me on a silver plat-
ter."

Hannah considered that. "Do you believe him?"

"I don't know what to believe right now. That's
why I came back to see you."

"I'm afraid I'm not going to be able to help you.
Gideon's gone back to Tucson. If you want to pursue
this, you'll have to call him there."

"I don't want to talk to him. The last time you fixed
it up so that we had to talk to each other I got very
confused."

She tilted her head to one side and frowned. "Hugh,
are you drunk?"

"It's a possibility, but I don't think so. Not yet.
Maybe later." He turned away from her and stalked
across the room to the fanback chair. There he threw
himself down without waiting for her invitation and

rubbed his hand across his nape. "Do you know what kind of bull that bastard tried to make me believe?"

"Something about him having seen Cyrus Ballantine as the father he never had?" Carefully Hannah seated herself on the arm of the sofa. She wasn't quite sure what to do with Hugh Ballantine.

"A real sob story. I wondered if maybe you helped him make it up."

"I see."

Hugh looked at her. "Did you?"

"Nope. Came up with it all on his own, I'm afraid. But I don't think it's a story. I think it's the truth."

"You believe him because you're sleeping with him."

Hannah got to her feet. "I think you'd better leave, Hugh."

He winced. "Sorry. It's just that I'm trying to work out what he's up to and I can't figure it. Something's missing and I think that something is you. You're the key."

"You keep saying that."

"Because it's the truth."

"I am not the key," Hannah repeated quietly. "This thing is between you and Gideon. You'll have to work it out together."

"Why is he backing away from the Surbrook deal?" Hugh eyed her accusingly as if she could provide the information he needed.

"Maybe because he doesn't feel like going to war over a stupid little aerospace manufacturing firm."

"Saving the ammunition for a bigger battle?"

"I don't know," Hannah said honestly. "I can't read him any better right now than you can. There's always been a part of him I couldn't quite analyze."

"He's lying, you know. About my father, I mean."

"I don't think so, Hugh. It would take a great deal to make Gideon hate as thoroughly as he hated Cyrus Ballantine. It would take, I think, a real sense of betrayal."

"Cage is capable of utter ruthlessness."

Hannah sighed. "I know this doesn't make much sense, Hugh, but being casually and utterly ruthless is different from actively hating someone. Gideon was more than ruthless in his dealings with your father. He wanted revenge on Cyrus Ballantine."

"Why won't he stand and fight over the Surbrook deal?"

"How should I know? His war was never with you. He doesn't hate you."

"But I hate him," Ballantine stated.

"Do you?"

"Absolutely."

"Then in the end you might win."

Ballantine's blue eyes grew harshly brilliant. "Do you believe that?"

"It's possible. Are you sure that's what you want, Hugh?"

"To win? Oh, yes. I'm sure it's what I want. Nothing else in the world is that important to me."

"Then nothing I can say will stop you." Hannah walked to the door and held it open. She knew she should keep her mouth shut, but she couldn't quite resist tacking on one last warning. The old guidance counselor in her wouldn't lie down and die. "Just take a minute to consider your future. Ask yourself if you want to end up like Gideon Cage. He's a lonely man, Hugh. All of his victories are hollow these days. He's where you'll be in ten years if you're successful in crushing him."

Hugh got reluctantly and carefully to his feet. "He's not lonely. He's got you."

"No," she said. "He doesn't have me. I'm on my way out of town and I'm not going to Tucson. I'm clearing out of the war zone. Good luck, Hugh. I am not giving out any more free advice. No one listens to me, anyway."

Ballantine moved slowly to the door. "You won't help me go after Cage?"

"No."

"He told me you wouldn't," Ballantine said. "He's very sure of you."

That irritated her but Hannah concealed her annoyance behind a shrug. "Cage is sure of most things."

"I don't suppose you want to come out with me and watch me finish getting myself drunk?"

"Not particularly." But she softened the refusal with a gentle smile. "I've got some problems of my own to work out. I'm afraid you and Gideon will have to solve your own."

"You really believe that bullshit about him thinking my father betrayed him?"

"Gideon is quite capable of manipulating people and events but he doesn't tell outright lies. Good night, Hugh."

"Good night, Hannah." Ballantine looked vaguely wistful. "I wish you felt like coming out and getting drunk with me."

"Some other time, perhaps." She closed the door softly in his face.

STEVE DECKER forgot himself so far as to actually
throw the notes down on his boss's desk. His face was
red from the effort he was making to control his frustration as he faced Gideon.

"You can't do business this way and you know it,
Gideon. We've got to take Surbrook. We've got to
stop Ballantine at every turn or one of these days he'll
stop us. What do you mean you want me to pull the
offer for Surbrook?"

"Just what I said." Gideon examined the notes in
front of him. "Surbrook isn't worth this much
money."

"That's got nothing to do with it. We've gone too
far to back out now."

"I don't want that firm, Steve."

"Why not? Admittedly it's going to cost a little
more than it should but ultimately we can make up for
it. It's a sound company. And by taking it we stop
Ballantine for a while."

"I'm no longer interested in stopping Ballantine.
I've got better things to do. Did you review the file on
Accelerated Design?"

Decker yanked off his glasses and polished them
disgustedly on his shirt. "I reviewed it. I don't know
what the hell for. That deal's over and done."

"We've got another deal with Accelerated Design," Gideon said patiently. "We know every weak
point in the firm, right?"

"Sure." Decker shoved his glasses back on his nose
and glowered at Gideon. "That's how we pulled off
the last deal."

"So who better than us to help Jessett get his company back on its feet?"

Decker's mouth fell open. "What are you talking about? We're not in the management consulting business."

"We are now." Gideon folded his hands behind his head and rocked back in the chair. "I'm putting you in charge of our first major consulting project. It's a promotion, Steve. Make that clear to Angie for me, okay? I want you to go to Seattle and look over the operation. Jessett is more than willing to cooperate. He'll give you whatever you want in the way of information. Take the time you need and come up with a step-by-step scenario for doing what has to be done. If he's going to need more cash, we can handle that, too. This should be a piece of cake, Decker. Jessett's no idiot. Left to his own devices I think he could probably haul himself out of the muck just fine. But with our assistance he can do it faster, cleaner, and cheaper."

"But, Gideon, this isn't our kind of work."

"Think of it as an experiment. Who knows, maybe we'll have an aptitude for it." Gideon leaned forward again, reaching for a file.

Decker stared at him in helpless frustration. He knew he was being dismissed. Slowly he turned toward the door.

"By the way, Steve," Gideon said behind him.

Decker glanced back apprehensively. "Yes?"

"Take Angie with you when you make the scouting trip to Seattle."

Decker blinked owlishly. "She'll appreciate that."

"Good. I've been trying to convince her for five years that I'm really not such a bad guy."

"Is that why we're getting involved with Accelerated Design again? Because you're trying to convince

another woman you're not such a bad guy after all?"
As soon as the words were out, Decker was shocked at
his own temerity.

"Get going, Decker."

"Yes, sir." Decker escaped with a clear sense of
having come much too close to a very dangerous edge.
Not like him to do dumb things like that. Not like him
at all. He was obviously more upset than he'd realized about his boss's strange change of mind. Then he
thought about being able to tell Angie she could go
with him to Seattle and his mood lifted. Angie was
going to be excited. She loved to travel and they hadn't
gotten to do much of it since he'd been working for
Gideon Cage. If this new line of work Cage was initi-
ating meant more travel, it was a cinch Angie would
back the decision one hundred percent. She'd be very
pleased with his promotion, too.

Gideon didn't look up until Decker was out of the
door. Then, slowly, he closed the file he'd opened and
eased back in his chair. On rare occasions Steve Decker
could be disconcerting. Normally the man's intuition
was confined to dissecting profit and loss columns, but
once in a while he saw further.

Gideon studied the ancient sea chart across the
room, the one that depicted monsters waiting for un-
wary ships that sailed too close to the edge of the
world. That's what he was doing, Gideon decided.
Sailing very close to an unseen edge as the priorities in
his life began to rearrange themselves.

Chief among those priorities was Hannah Jessett.
Once he had her in place perhaps everything else
would settle down into some kind of rational order
again. He picked up the phone and dialed her num-

ber. He'd been trying to reach her all day but there'd been no answer. It was nearly five o'clock.

Giving up in disgust, Gideon thumbed through the Accelerated Design file until he found Nick Jessett's number. He was in luck, the younger man was still in his office.

"How's it going, Gideon?"

"Fine on this end. I'm sending someone up there to get the ball rolling on the Accelerated Design analysis. His name's Steve Decker. I think you'll like him. He knows what he's doing."

"Decker, huh. Is he the guy who pulled the data on us together the first time around?"

"Right."

Nick chuckled wryly. "Well, he should know what he's doing then. When does he get here?"

"I'll send him up on Monday. His wife will be with him." Gideon cleared his throat. "I was wondering if maybe you and Hannah could take them out to dinner? I think Angie would like Hannah."

"Be fine with me except that Hannah's out of town again." Nick hesitated and then added cautiously, "Didn't she tell you?"

Gideon tried to loosen his sudden deathgrip on the phone. "No, she didn't tell me."

"Oh."

"Where did she go, Nick?"

"Left yesterday morning for Santa Inez Island. I'm sorry, Gideon. I thought you knew. I guess it was a sudden decision on her part. She's been acting a little strange lately."

"I just talked to her two days ago. She didn't mention leaving town."

"I think she was upset," Nick offered. "All I got was a phone call asking me to be sure and water her plants if she didn't get back within a few days."

"A few days. Jesus. How long is she going to stay down there?"

"Beats me. You know her well enough by now to realize that she's got a mind of her own."

"I'm beginning to think that whoever first decided to let women have minds of their own made a big mistake."

"I'll go along with that." Nick made a clear effort to change the subject. "These academic types sure have it soft in the summer. Here's Hannah flitting off to the Caribbean for a second vacation and when I mentioned it to Vicky Armitage yesterday in the club she tells me she and Drake are heading for Hawaii this week. A few weeks ago they went to Mexico. It's unfair. Maybe I chose the wrong field. I should have researched careers that provide extensive time off."

"Well, don't plan on any time off in the near future. Decker will be keeping you busy," Gideon said absently.

"I'll keep an eye out for him. Want me to make hotel reservations at this end for him and his wife?"

"Don't worry about it. My secretary will handle it. You say Hannah took off yesterday morning?"

"Yeah."

"I'll get back to you, Nick." Gideon hung up the phone. For an instant he didn't move. Then he was on his feet, grabbing his jacket and heading for the door.

"Going home early today, Mr. Cage?" Mary Ann asked brightly.

"It's five o'clock," he growled.

"For you that's early." She reached for the cover of her typewriter. Gideon was gone before she had finished covering the machine.

Behind the wheel of the Porsche Gideon sat glowering at the road. His hand was swift and savage on the gearshift as he sent the car surging up into the hills toward home. She had gone back to Santa Inez without even telling him she was leaving.

There was only one explanation. Hannah had made her choices for the future and they didn't include him. She was going to follow in Elizabeth Nord's footsteps and in the footsteps of those other women who had once worn that goddamned ugly necklace.

He couldn't let her do it, Gideon realized with stark clarity. He couldn't allow her to just walk out of his life this way. She had no right. He needed her and she belonged to him. She had no business trying to turn herself into the kind of cold, aloof Amazon queen her aunt had been.

Hannah had no right to turn herself into the kind of remote, untouchable, one-dimensional human being Gideon Cage knew he had allowed himself to become during the past nine years. This time around it was Hannah who needed saving.

Chapter Fifteen

IT WAS THE MAP that bothered him. Gideon found himself glancing at it again and again that evening as he made the airline reservations for the following day. Every time he looked at the tourist version of Santa Inez Island he remembered the narrow, winding roads that followed the cliffs above the sea. Then he thought of Hannah driving those roads to her aunt's house.

She would get one of those silly pink-fringed jeeps, he was sure. But he wondered how much good the frivolous-looking vehicle would be when it came to making her feel secure about her driving. He hadn't forgotten her quiet tension when he'd skimmed around a curve or dodged an oncoming taxi. When she'd driven him to the airport he'd sensed how uncomfortable she still was behind the wheel of a car. Traces of the terror she had experienced the night of her accident lingered in her mind. Perhaps they always would. Gideon didn't like the idea of Hannah driving the Santa Inez roads alone.

He didn't like the idea of her being anywhere alone. The raw truth was that it panicked him. She could so easily put him out of her mind and out of her life. All those other women on her family tree who had succeeded on their own terms had somehow passed along their genes to Hannah, together with that damned necklace. Gideon felt like breaking something. He dialed another airline instead.

She wasn't cut out to become the hard, remote, coldly brilliant creature her aunt had been. Nord had been capable of sustaining an academic myth for a lifetime. Hannah was different. Hannah was softer, gentler, and compassionate. More honest. And there was a passion in her that Gideon couldn't believe had existed in Elizabeth Nord. If it had, it had been totally channeled into her work.

The frightening part was that Gideon knew what it was like to channel passion and every other emotion into work. It could be done. Nord had probably done it. He, himself, had done it. Maybe all those fierce Amazons on Hannah's family tree had done it.

But Hannah was wrong to think such people were whole and complete within themselves. He knew better now. Such isolation had its advantages, but they were bought at a high price. Nothing came for free in this world. Lately Gideon had become well aware of what his power had cost him. He couldn't allow Hannah to pay the same price. There was no altruism in his decision. The simple truth was that he needed her, wanted her too badly to watch her turn into an Amazon who would leave him behind.

Gideon sat impatiently on hold, waiting for the airline ticket agent to answer, and wished he could get the image of Hannah weaving around Santa Inez's road in a pink-fringed jeep out of his mind.

It wasn't as though she couldn't drive, he reminded himself. She had driven him to the airport, hadn't she? True, she was overly cautious and wary on the freeway, but she'd handled herself all right. He had known she wasn't comfortable or relaxed behind the wheel then, but she hadn't been panicked by driving.

But it wasn't a freeway on which she'd had that accident a couple of months ago. It was a narrow, crooked mountain road. A road not unlike the roads on Santa Inez. The ticket agent came on the line just as Gideon's mind began to play with the notion of the similarity between mountain roads and island roads.

"Early tomorrow evening? Is that the earliest you can get me to Santa Inez? Hell, it'll be getting dark. No, no, I'll take it. Go ahead and book the seat. Are you absolutely positive you haven't got an earlier connection out of Miami?"

"I'm sorry sir. There's no way to shorten the layover in Miami. All our other flights are full. We're the only airline with afternoon flights from Miami to Santa Inez. If you'd care to stay over in Miami and leave the next morning, we could—"

"Forget it. Wait list me on your earlier flights and go ahead and book this one," Gideon said grimly.

"Fine, sir."

It wasn't fine but Gideon couldn't think of any reasonable way around the problem. He might as well be calm about this. Hannah wasn't going anywhere. She'd drive from the airport to her aunt's house, pick up some groceries along the way, and then sit on the beach and think.

The beach. Something else to worry about. Memories of the beach brought back too many details of the morning he'd awakened to hear her crying for help as some bastard played water games. Gideon had long since decided that morning ranked as the worst of his life. Far worse than the morning he'd awakened to find himself surrounded by the results of Cyrus Ballantine's treachery. He had survived treachery. He wasn't sure what he would have done if he'd allowed Hannah to be killed.

Logically, the guy in the diving outfit had to be long gone. He wouldn't have hung around Santa Inez after nearly getting caught trying to drown or rape a tourist. He had been white with blue eyes, not one of the locals. He couldn't have expected to blend in with any crowd except the tourist crowd.

Just one more thing to worry about, Gideon decided. As if he didn't have enough. He should forget the bizarre stuff such as jeep accidents and marauding rapists. The thing he really needed to worry about was what Hannah was thinking, planning, and deciding about her future.

Damn Elizabeth Nord. Damn the necklace and damn the journals. If it wasn't for them, perhaps Hannah would have accepted her relationship with him more readily, Gideon thought as he stared broodingly at the map. Damn Victoria Armitage while he was at it. Her presence had been a major factor in all this.

Actually, all things considered, Vicky Armitage's presence had been the largest single factor. Hannah had been disturbed by the other woman for a couple of months before Gideon had even come on the scene. Since about the time of the accident, in fact.

Gideon felt the first tendrils of an uneasy thought that he pushed at once to the back of his mind. He had to pack.

He was up at dawn the next day after a restless night. It was going to be a long trip, what with airport layovers and awkward connections. The initial flight out of Tucson left shortly before eight. Gideon was standing at his black slate dressing table, checking his pockets for keys and wallet when he finally decided to put a call through to Seattle. He might as well make it and put his mind at ease about something. It was a cinch he wasn't going to find much else to ease his mind today.

Finding Nick Jessett's phone number took a while, but Gideon eventually located it on a business card he'd picked up in the other man's office. Nick's home number was scrawled on the back. Gideon dialed with a sense of urgency that was accompanied by a feeling of idiocy.

"Nick?"

"What in the hell?" Jessett sounded half asleep. "Gideon? Is that you?"

"Sorry to get you out of bed."

"You'd be sorrier if you could see what's still in the bed."

"Your sister says you haven't had time lately for that sort of thing thanks to Cage & Associates."

"Younger brothers don't always confide everything to their big sisters. What do you want, Cage?"

"Just some dates. I know this is going to sound stupid, but you said something yesterday about the Armitages having taken another vacation this summer. A few weeks ago, you said. Can you remember exactly when?"

"Jesus, Gideon. It's six o'clock in the morning."

"Try, Nick."

"All right, all right, I'm thinking. It must have been about the same time Hannah went down to Santa Inez. We all missed Vicky's pecs at the club for a few days right about then. Does that help?"

Gideon took a deep breath and told himself he was being an ass. "Yeah. It helps. Thanks, Nick."

"Hey, Gideon? What's going on?" The sleepiness vanished from Nick's voice.

"Nothing. I'm heading for Santa Inez myself in a few minutes."

"Is that right? What a surprise." Nick sounded anything but surprised. "If you're going down there to use sweet reason on my sister, I think I should warn you that she's been acting a little strange lately. Not entirely sweet or reasonable. Something's bothering her about those damn journals."

"I'm going to try to convince her that she should be more bothered by me than Nord's journals."

"Good luck. Why did you want to know about the Armitages' vacation?"

Gideon wondered how much to tell him and then decided not to inflict his own irrational fears onto anyone else. There was nothing Nick could do anyway. "It's not important, Nick. I knew Hannah was upset about the journals and I wondered how long Vicky had been pestering her, that's all."

"But what's the trip to Mexico got to do with it?"

"I'll tell you when I get back from Santa Inez. Go back to bed, Nick."

"That's the most intelligent thing you've said so far this morning. By the way, when you see my sister tell her she'd better hurry back if she wants those plants of hers to live."

"You're supposed to water them."

"I know but I realized yesterday that I've lost her key off my ring. I can't get into the apartment unless I break the lock. Say, Gideon, about my sister and those journals..."

Gideon hung up the phone before Jessett could launch into any more questions. Nick could be tenacious when the mood took him. Rather like his sister.

Two hours later, sitting in his plane seat, Gideon mulled over breakfast as he mulled over the information Nick had given him. Neither breakfast nor information was very palatable. He prodded the scrambled eggs and thought about the motivational power of revenge. It was strong, even stronger than most forms of ambition or desire. No one knew better than Gideon Cage just how far a thirst for revenge could drive a man. There was no reason to think it couldn't drive a woman just as far.

He was being fanciful, looking for ghosts where there were none. No, that wasn't strictly true. There were a couple of ghosts involved in this mess. There was the one of Elizabeth Nord, for instance. And then there was the one of Dear Roddy. Each ghost had a current champion. Vicky and Hannah were both being manipulated by the past.

The part that put Gideon's nerves on edge was that Hannah probably wouldn't understand just how badly Vicky might want to avenge her father. For that matter, Gideon didn't know himself. But the possibility existed and that alone was enough to fill him with a restless uncertainty. He wouldn't relax on that score until he was with Hannah. The fact that the Armitages were taking their vacations right about the time Hannah was slipping off to the Caribbean probably meant nothing, but he couldn't seem to convince his instincts of that.

Gideon thought again about the island's crooked roads and Hannah's tension when she drove. The one thing he tried very hard not to think about was how

Hannah's accident might have occurred a couple of months before.

In another few hours he would be with her. Then he could stop worrying about her safety and start working on the task of making her understand that she wanted him as much as he wanted her.

SHE HAD NEVER driven a jeep before in her life. Hannah had chosen the pink-fringed vehicle without considering that fact. There had been no question in her mind about which rental car to select, though. She had known from the start that she wanted the frivolous-looking jeep. She tossed her luggage and the carefully wrapped Nord journals onto the passenger seat and climbed in. She was determined to master the intricacies of the clutch and gearshift by the time she reached her aunt's cottage.

The cliff roads were a different matter. She admitted unashamedly that she missed being a passenger while Gideon fielded the wild taxis and negotiated the narrow roads. There was a cool competence about Gideon that could be very reassuring at times.

She had no real problems on the way to the beach cottage, however, and by the time she'd parked the jeep Hannah was feeling more confident. She carried her luggage, a sack of groceries, and the journals into the house, making two trips because of her cane. In another couple of weeks she would be able to do without the cane entirely. Her knee felt infinitely better.

The first night she thought about Gideon a great deal, far more than she'd intended. She knew she associated the cottage with their brief affair and probably always would. Time had stood still for a while

there on the island. She might never know that kind of
passionate peace again.

At dawn the next morning, Hannah forced herself
to take stock of her situation. She was there to make
some crucial decisions, not to relive her fleeting time
with Gideon.

Ahead of her lay the task of making up her mind
about what to do with the bomb that had been
dropped in her lap. Hannah walked down to the cove
thinking about the information locked in the journals
she had brought with her. Once the journals were
made public they would cause a sensation. The truth
this time could not be dismissed as minor carping or
the opinions of hostile professionals. Elizabeth Nord
had deliberately lied and she, herself, had admitted it.

But what good would it do to make the information public, Hannah asked herself as she came to a halt
on the beach and stood gazing out at the multifaceted
water. Scholars would enjoy themselves tearing apart
her aunt's reputation, but would anything really be
changed? The myth of the Amazons was old history
now. Debunking it might prove interesting to the academic community, but the real damage would be to
her aunt's stature in the profession. It was up to Hannah to decide whether to allow her aunt's name to be
dragged in the mud. No one else had ever been powerful enough to do it. People such as Roderick Hamilton had tried and failed. It was ironic that Elizabeth
Nord was so strong that only she herself could jeop-
ardize her reputation.

Beyond that issue lay another, more personal one.
Hannah fingered the necklace and thought about the
woman who had worn it before her. Elizabeth Nord
had been a very powerful woman. Hannah wondered

if she could ever have that much power. It took guts to boldly create a myth and live it for a lifetime. Hannah looked back at the house and thought of her aunt living there in splendid isolation.

It would take guts to write the book that would compromise her aunt's reputation. It occurred to Hannah that her aunt wouldn't have minded in the least. She would have found the whole thing amusing. There was no question of protecting Elizabeth Nord. Nord didn't need or want protection. She hadn't needed it when she was alive and she needed it even less now. In a flash of insight, Hannah knew that if her aunt had been there she would have encouraged her to write the book. The warmth of the necklace seemed to emphasize the truth of that conclusion. None of the women who had worn it had worried about the past. None of them had cared about the opinions of their contemporaries. They were too serenely secure in themselves, too magnificently aloof from the rest of the world.

No, it wasn't the prospect of writing the book that made Hannah uneasy. It was the thought of what would happen afterward. Nothing would ever be the same. She knew that with a deep certainty.

Writing the book wasn't going to be a single, isolated event. It was an act that would change the course of Hannah's life. She would be committed after that. It would be an act of will that would forever alter her path. Hannah knew the truth of that with deep intuition. Once started down that road, she would keep going, seeking power and success with the same driving intensity with which others around her sought it. Writing the book would not satisfy her, Hannah knew. She would have to continue, proving to herself and to

Vicky Armitage that she was as formidable as her aunt had been.

The book was nothing in and of itself. But it was the first step down a glittering road that could lead to real power. She wouldn't be able to stop. There would be no room in her life for a man except for fleeting physical affairs. She would need all her emotional energy for herself. No longer would she waste compassion or empathy on others. Guidance counseling would not interest her as a career. It was too "other" oriented.

Hannah touched the necklace again. By the time she had finished the book, she would be concerned with no one but herself. She would be like Vicky Armitage in some ways and like Elizabeth Nord in others. She would be a young Amazon.

Hannah turned to walk along the water's edge, her bare feet finding firm purchase in the wet, packed sand. The lures lay stretched out ahead of her, beckoning with shining, mesmerizing power. She would be rich, Hannah decided. Making money would be high on her list of priorities because money was a source of power. There was money to be made from the Elizabeth Nord journals if she played her cards right. Wealthy collectors or a rich research foundation would pay considerable sums to obtain the valuable library Nord had left. The book Hannah would write before she sold the library should bring in a healthy sum on its own.

No, she decided, there was a better way to play it. She would not sell the library for cash, but would exchange it for a director's position on the board of an important research foundation, the kind that provided money to the Victoria Armitages of the world. From there she could wield influence over the kind of research that received funds. She could begin to control people such as Vicky Armitage. If they wanted foundation grants they would be forced to deal with Hannah Jessett. If the sale of the Nord biography brought in sufficient money, Hannah realized, she would be able to set up her own foundation. All things were possible if you were thoroughly committed to the end result.

The people who controlled money were the ones who controlled research. Yes, Hannah thought, that was the route to take. She would use her aunt's legacy to buy her way into a position of power and from there she could climb as high as she wished. She would ultimately have more control over the field of anthropology than any single professor with a Ph.D. could hope to have. Ph.D.s were a dime a dozen. The people who controlled research money were a far more important group. She would join that group.

Everything started with writing the book.

The sun climbed higher in the brilliant blue sky as Hannah continued to contemplate the future that lay before her. As the day wore on, things began to fall quickly into place. The haze of uncertainty that had masked her future was clearing with breathtaking rapidity. She had been right to come back to the island. Things were so much more obvious here, so self-evident. How could she have wasted so many years of her life floundering? Where had this stark, sharply etched vision of her future been hiding all this time? She felt as if she saw clearly for the first time in her life.

Hannah was suddenly consumed with energy. It burned in her, simmering in her veins. She wanted to run, but the first tentative attempt almost ended in disaster. She managed to steady herself in time with the cane and then laughed at her own exuberance. Glancing back at the cottage, she imagined Elizabeth Nord standing on the porch, smiling at her.

"Look at me, Elizabeth. You were right. All those times you told me to follow my own instincts, you were right. It just took me a while to figure out what I wanted. But now I know, Elizabeth Nord. I want what you had. And I'm going to get it. In my own way, I'm going to get it. My God, but you had guts, Aunt. You lied your way to fame and fortune. You lied your way into power. And now I'm going to use the myth you created to find my own way to power. You'll be proud of me, Aunt Elizabeth. And so will all those other women who once wore this necklace."

She shut up abruptly, realizing how foolish she would look to anyone who might see her. But there was no one around to watch. Hannah was free to talk to her aunt if she chose. Grinning, Hannah started back toward the cottage. Nothing could get in her way. All she had to do was follow the path that had opened up ahead of her. It stretched endlessly toward the horizon, narrow and sure and full of brilliant promise. The heat of the rising sun had warmed the necklace around Hannah's throat until it almost burned against her skin.

She had been right to return to the island.

It wasn't until the evening of the following day that Hannah began to come down from the euphoric high she had been experiencing as her future crystallized. Perhaps it was the advent of darkness that quieted her overexcited spirit. Or perhaps she was just tired from trying to contain such energy. *Tired from too much energy.* That was a paradox, she told herself, but somehow it made sense. She poured herself a glass of wine and decided to take another walk along the edge of the cove. Then she would go back to work on Elizabeth Nord's journals.

Feeling quite decadent walking barefoot along the water's edge with a glass of wine in one hand, Hannah drank in the balmy, scented air and let her mind skip from one thought to another. It was going to rain this evening. The usual afternoon thunderstorms seemed to have been postponed by a couple of hours. Or maybe this was a major storm approaching. Whatever the reasons, the dark clouds were filling up the sky and obscuring the moon's light.

There were things to be done soon. She would have to make some contacts to determine the best way to go about selling the idea of her book to a publisher. An agent would undoubtedly be necessary.

She was wondering how to go about finding an agent when another stray thought drifted into her head. To her surprise, Hannah found herself thinking about what Gideon Cage was doing that evening.

Making a firm effort to push the thought aside, Hannah tried to concentrate on the business aspects of bringing out her book. But the word "business" meant Gideon Cage. A few weeks ago when she had walked along this beach he had been with her. It was Gideon who had pulled her from the clutches of the diver who had tried to drown her.

Hannah stopped walking and took a long sip of wine. She didn't like thinking about either the diver with the blue eyes or Gideon. Both were too disturbing. But it was easier to dismiss memories of the diver than of Gideon. The assault was in the past. Gideon was still very much in her present.

"Damn you, Gideon. Go away. I'm not going to let you interfere any longer. You chose your path, now let me choose mine."

But the uneasiness wouldn't fade. Maybe she was just getting spooked by being out here alone at night, Hannah told herself. She finished the wine and decided to head back to the house. It wasn't really late but the isolation of her aunt's cottage was suddenly very evident. She would feel better back inside with the doors locked.

Irritated with her jumpy mood but unable to talk herself out of it, Hannah started toward the front steps of the cottage. She was still some distance away when she thought she caught a shadowy movement in the stand of palms. Her jumpiness shifted into outright alarm. Hannah quickened her pace toward the house.

It was ridiculous. There was no one hiding in the palm grove. Her imagination, fueled by memories of the near fatal incident in the cove, was working overtime. She began to wish that the cottage contained a phone, though. It would be soothing to know that she could reach help in an emergency. She would have one installed when she moved in on a permanent basis, Hannah thought as she started up the veranda steps.

The tap of her cane on the bottom step almost but not quite concealed the small scuffling noise that came from the palm grove. Hannah froze. It took an effort to turn and search the shadows. She was acting like a child who felt safer hiding under the covers than looking for trouble in the darkness. Taking a deep breath, Hannah forced herself to calmly watch the palm grove until she was certain there was no one there.

She wished she had a gun in the house or stashed in the jeep. But of course she didn't. Innocuous, insipid, sweetly earnest guidance counselors didn't own guns. She wouldn't know how to use one even if she had it put in her hand.

That would change, Hannah thought. She would buy a gun and learn how to use it. If she were going to live out here alone she would need to have some protection. But the prospect of protection lay in the future. Tonight she would have to think of something else.

Because there was someone out there.

Hannah had operated on her instincts often enough in the past when it came to offering advice to others. She decided that she would be a fool to ignore those instincts now. The house was not a safe refuge. The louvered windows could be pried open easily and the lock on the front door was a joke to someone who lived in the city. The lock on her apartment door in Seattle was three times stronger than the one Elizabeth Nord had placed on her cottage door.

Hannah hesitated no longer. She hauled herself up the steps with the aid of her cane, slipped into the front door and found her purse. It contained the keys to the jeep. Before she stepped back out onto the porch she switched off the light. There was no reason to silhouette herself.

The jeep seemed very far away even though in reality it waited just at the bottom of the steps. Hannah climbed inside with a sigh of relief and shoved the key in the ignition. She would spend the night in a hotel. In the morning she could come back and have a look around. Then she would see about getting a local locksmith in to put some decent protection on the doors and windows.

The engine caught immediately and Hannah turned the wheel. The pink fringe swayed playfully in the darkness above her as she sent the jeep out of the driveway and toward the main road into town. The rocky cliffs above the sea were mercifully concealed in shadows as Hannah drove along their upper edges. She would not look to the side or down. She would concentrate on the road ahead.

There were no lights in the rearview mirror until the car behind her was almost on top of her. Then they flashed on with blinding brilliance.

Hannah had an instant of startled terror that mingled with an old horror left over from her accident. Flashes of memory came back to her. *This was the way it had been.* A car surging out of the darkness behind her, blinding her with headlights, and then sideswiping her car viciously before roaring off into the night.

Perhaps it was the rush of memory that saved her life. Perhaps it was sheer luck. Whatever the reason, Hannah shoved the brake peddle to the floor instead of giving in to the impulse to swing the wheel and swerve to the side.

The car jerked out from behind her and shot past, managing to catch the hood of the jeep with a rough, savage scraping sound. The little pink jeep rocked with the force of the impact and jolted toward the edge of the cliff in spite of Hannah's fierce war with the brakes. There was a timeless moment of utter silence as the vehicle shuddered on the edge of the cliff. Hannah felt her fate being decided by careless gods.

Then she was clawing at the seat belt. She shoved open the door and threw herself out onto the road as the finger of one of the island gods reached out and casually flipped the jeep off the cliff.

Hannah lay on the pavement, gasping with pain and clutching her left leg. She'd landed on the injured knee when she'd thrown herself out of the jeep. In that moment of shock and agony she knew a rage that was unlike anything she had ever experienced in her life. Fury roared through her.

Above her the skies opened, spilling a torrent of rain onto the narrow road where Hannah lay. The crashing sound of thunder faded into the distance to be replaced by the angry throb of a car's engine.

Hannah knew that whoever had tried to kill her was returning to make certain that he had succeeded.

Chapter Sixteen

GIDEON DIDN'T BELIEVE in premonitions but he had a great deal of faith in his instincts. He'd depended on them too many times on the street and later in business. When the dark gray sedan that was parked by the edge of the road loomed up out of the rain he knew there was trouble. The car was too close to the Nord cottage, the night was too wild with the storm that had swept in right after his plane had landed, and Gideon was too certain that accidents were becoming too frequent in Hannah's life.

The only thing that gave him hope as he pulled his rented car over to the side of the road was that there was no sign of a silly pink jeep. Ignoring the warm, pounding rain he climbed out of the compact and slowly approached the dark sedan. There was no sign of anyone around, but the knowledge didn't do much to untwist the knot in his stomach. There was a feeling of wrongness here and he'd long since learned to respect that sensation. After a glance into the car which told him absolutely nothing, Gideon walked around it. He spotted the scraped and dented rear fender immediately.

Then he glanced over the cliff and saw the pink-fringed jeep on the rocks below. For a sickening instant Gideon simply stared down at it, wanting to deny the evidence, willing to trade everything he'd ever had to change reality and knowing all the while that you can't make deals with the universe.

The sickness in him turned into a cold chill that at least allowed him to function. He stripped off his jacket and started down the jumble of rocks that led to the beach. He had to know the worst, had to see for himself if his soft, sweet Hannah was lying broken inside the jeep. Then he would destroy whoever had been in the dark sedan. There was no doubt in Gideon's mind that the other car had forced the jeep over the edge. For the second time in his life the violent desire for revenge swept through Gideon. He would do whatever had to be done to make the people in the car pay.

Scrambling on the rain-slick rocks, Gideon reached the jeep. The closer he got the more he tried to prepare himself for the sight of Hannah crumpled on the rocks or trapped inside the jeep which was lying on its side. Nothing he did could unfreeze the coldness in his guts, but he found no sign of her at the bottom of the short, tumbled cliff. It took all his willpower to look into the front seat. The seat belt clasped nothing. It was lying undone. Hannah always wore a seat belt. It had saved her life during the first accident.

For the first time since he'd looked down from the road above and seen the jeep Gideon allowed himself a small measure of hope. He tried to kill it almost at once because it left him feeling jittery. It was, however, just barely possible that she'd survived the crash and managed to crawl out of the jeep. She'd survived a car accident once before, he reminded himself.

He was turning away to scan the cliff face when he spotted the rakish leather-trimmed photojournalist bag, the one with all the buckles and pockets. It had been thrown out of the jeep and lay on the sand near the water's edge. The skewed lights of the jeep illuminated it. With a final glance up at the dark sedan, Gideon turned to walk through the rain toward the bag.

He picked it up and went through it. Hannah's wallet was still inside. Whoever had driven the sedan hadn't been the type to indulge in casual looting. Gideon dropped the bag down onto the sand. Someone who passed up a wallet in circumstances such as this might have been intent on offering assistance. Or he might have had other things on his mind.

Gideon looked back at the jeep and tried to imagine which way Hannah might have gone if she'd unbuckled herself after the accident and crawled out. She would have been shaken and badly bruised at the very least, probably far more severely injured. The rocks would have seemed much too formidable to climb in that condition. She would have headed toward the beach, perhaps with some idea of walking to a point where she could more easily scale the cliff to the main road. The beach stretched invitingly to the left but twisted into a jumbled maze of rocks and slippery sand to the right. Someone trying to walk away from a serious accident would probably have turned to the left.

That analysis left unanswered the question of what the person or persons in the dark sedan had done. If they had come down the cliff and found the jeep empty they would probably have reasoned much as Gideon had. They certainly had not driven off in search of assistance. That left Gideon with the conclusion that whoever had been driving the sedan had gone in search of Hannah.

The storm was letting up a little already. A weak moon offered some visibility as the clouds began to disperse. Rain still fell in wind-driven sheets here and there. There was no point searching in the glove compartment of the jeep for anything so useful as a flashlight. Rental agencies weren't that thoughtful. In any event there was a chance that a light might be more dangerous than useful. It would advertise his position for several yards. Gideon wasn't sure he wanted his position advertised. Not until he'd figured out who had been in the dark sedan.

A fierce urgency drove him as he started along the beach in the only direction in which Hannah would have gone if she'd managed to escape the jeep. The waves that broke along the sand glistened with an iridescent whiteness less than a yard from his shoes. Gideon broke into a ground-covering jog. The storm-ruffled sea created enough noise to shield the sound of his footsteps.

Every inch of the way Gideon kept his eyes moving, scanning the open expanse of sandy beach for a dark, huddled form. Surely she couldn't have gone far. She would be suffering from shock at the very least. In the chancy moonlight and the intermittent rain there were no clues to tell if someone had come this way ahead of him. He could only follow the logical route and hope.

The beach began to narrow. The cliff walls grew closer as Gideon moved along the water's edge. He was going to run out of sand fairly soon. It looked as if the beach ended in a formidable tumble of rocks at this end just as it had at the other end. If someone else had followed Hannah, he couldn't be far ahead. Gideon slowed and moved into the deep shadows of the cliff.

He thought again about the photojournalist's bag lying on the sand. There was another possibility that he didn't want to contemplate. Once before someone had attempted to drown Hannah. If whoever had followed her down the cliff had found her unconscious or injured in the jeep, it would have been a simple matter to pull her free and drag her into the water to finish the job.

Savagely Gideon shoved that thought aside. If someone had found Hannah and killed her, he would have already made good his escape in the dark sedan. No. If there was anyone else here on the beach, he was still around. And that meant Hannah might still be alive.

Sinking into the darkness near the cliffs, Gideon kept moving. The protection offered by the rock wall wasn't all that different from the kind afforded by a dark alley. It had been a long time since he'd used the shadows for concealment. These days he was accustomed to camouflaging his movements behind corporate sleight-of-hand. But some things you never forgot, he discovered wryly. It was sort of like riding a bicycle.

From the shadows he could watch the stretch of beach between him and the water. Anyone moving across it would be a dark figure silhouetted against the lighter sand. He was almost to the wall of stone at the far end of the beach when he saw a shadow of movement. Gideon went utterly still, waiting.

The figure detached itself from the rocks at the closed end of the beach and started slowly back toward the wrecked jeep. It wasn't Hannah, Gideon knew at once. The shape and movement were that of a man. He moved cautiously, obviously still searching for someone. Gideon watched him for a few tense seconds and then carefully began to parallel the other man's movements back up the beach.

Sticking close to the cliff, Gideon kept moving, narrowing the gap between himself and the man. Whoever he was, he didn't appear to be armed. His hands moved freely, unencumbered by the bulk of a gun. Maybe he was simply a concerned motorist who was trying to find the other victim of the accident, Gideon told himself. Then the man swung around to survey the beach behind him. The pale moonlight fell on Drake Armitage's face.

That took care of the concerned motorist theory. Gideon waited impatiently as Armitage scanned the beach once again and then resumed his walk back to the jeep. When Armitage's actions made it clear that he had stopped searching and was intent on getting back to the vehicle, Gideon slipped out of the shadows and began closing the distance between them rapidly.

As if warned by some instinct, Drake whirled at the last second, his mouth half open on an unvoiced protest. But it was too late to dodge. Gideon's momentum carried him straight into Armitage and sent them both thudding down onto the sand.

"You bastard!" Armitage's choked off cry wasn't followed by any further conversation. He heaved upward, intent on using the strength in his upper body to dislodge his attacker.

Gideon rolled to one side, trying not to give Armitage a target. Then he snapped a hand across Drake's throat, connecting solidly enough to make the other man gasp painfully. Armitage tried to throw himself onto Gideon, attempting to pin him onto the sand. But Gideon shifted again and brought his knee up into the other man's groin. The one rule about street fighting was that there aren't any rules.

The blow was a little off center but it was sufficiently brutal to send Armitage over backward. Gideon moved in and caught the full force of Armitage's foot on his thigh as the man kicked out savagely. Stupid, Gideon told himself as he struggled to reestablish his balance. In the old days he would never have made that kind of mistake. Maybe he'd spent too many years in corporate street fighting after all. Or maybe he was getting old. He had five or six years on Armitage, and in this kind of thing that counted.

But age brought some knowledge of treachery, and what good was knowledge if it wasn't put to use? Gideon let the kick take him farther out of reach than Armitage intended, falling onto his back and trying to present a reasonably tempting target.

Armitage didn't need any invitation. With a muttered shout of triumph he jerked to his feet and tried another kick, this time aiming at Gideon's head. The younger man apparently operated on the theory that if something worked once, you could use it again. But in street fighting predictability could get you killed. Gideon grabbed for Armitage's ankle and yanked his opponent off balance. Armitage yelped in rage.

Gideon was on top of Armitage before the other man had hit the sand. Two blunt, chopping blows made Drake's head snap first to one side and then the other. By the time Armitage had shaken himself free of the cobwebs Gideon had a pocket knife pressed against his throat. Drake's eyes opened very wide in the moonlight. It was hard to tell for certain because moonlight washed out their color, but Gideon was almost sure Armitage's eyes were blue. He tried to remember the day in the athletic club when he'd been introduced to the younger man.

"It's not the best knife I've ever used for this kind of work," Gideon said as he dug the blade a little into Armitage's throat. "Just a pocket knife, I'm afraid. But it will do the job, believe me."

"You're crazy." Armitage didn't move.

"Possibly. Especially at the moment. Where's Hannah?"

"Jesus, I don't know. I was looking for her. Her car went off the cliff. I was trying to find her."

"Her car went off the cliff because you used your car to push it off, just like you did a few months ago."

"That's a lie, damn it. We were just trying to help. For Christ's sake, Cage, why would I want to hurt Hannah?"

Gideon ignored the question. "We? I assume that means Vicky's somewhere in the vicinity? Of course she would be. She wouldn't send you out alone on something this crucial. Where is she?"

"I don't know, I tell you. We split up looking for Hannah. We wanted to help her, Cage. She's probably hurt, maybe unconscious somewhere."

"Thanks to you." Gideon let the point of the pocket knife sink a little deeper.

"Listen to me," Armitage pleaded, "we saw her jeep get into trouble. We were right behind her on the road. When we went past Vicky said we should turn around and go back to see what had happened. By the time we got back the jeep was at the bottom of the cliff. I figured Hannah must have gone over with it so

I came down here to have a look. But Vicky thought she might have crawled out up on the road. She's searching up there.''

Gideon didn't want to think about that possibility. He'd seen the expression in Victoria Armitage's eyes once when she'd looked at Hannah. If Hannah had escaped from the jeep before it went over the edge, she would probably be wounded and frantic. An easy target for an Amazon.

"Come on." Gideon got to his feet, pulling Armitage up beside him.

"What are you going to do?" Apprehensively Drake eyed the knife that still hovered too near his neck.

"I'm going to find Hannah. And if she's dead I'm going to come back here and put this knife into your throat."

"You *are* crazy. Will you listen to me? Vicky and I only want to help."

But Drake's defense of his actions and those of his wife came to an abrupt halt as a gunshot echoed through the darkness.

"Shit. Vicky's got a gun." The coldness in Gideon's belly turned to ice. "When this is all over, I really will kill you, Armitage, and I'll take my time about doing it."

"No, you've got to understand, we had to do something. Everything had gone wrong. Nothing had worked. Vicky said we had to do something—"

Gideon didn't bother to let him finish. He used the edge of his hand on the back of Drake's neck, choking off the other man's words along with his consciousness.

Then Gideon started running down the beach, searching for a route back up the cliff.

CRAWLING OFF THE ROAD and into the tangled vegetation on the opposite side had been the hard part. Hannah had been certain that her reinjured knee would collapse under her. The pain was intense. Surely anything that painful had to be incapacitating. But fear was another great motivator, she discovered. It ranked right up there with revenge when it came to giving a person strength and determination. She was learning a lot about willpower these days.

The distant roar of the engine of the returning car had grown steadily louder through the rain as Hannah laboriously pulled herself off the road. She felt like an injured animal that had been carelessly hit on the highway and was now trying to drag itself off into the bushes to die.

No, damn it, she was not going to die. Her leg was on fire, but other than that she was relatively unscathed. She had a few bruises on her hands and face from her impact with the road, but the sturdy cotton twill of her fatigue pants and bush shirt had protected her from too much damage. When this was over she would have to write a letter of commendation to the folks who ran the mail-order house from which she'd ordered them. It wasn't often these days that you got your money's worth from a product.

The ludicrous thoughts probably meant that she was suffering from some kind of shock, Hannah decided. It wasn't rational to be thinking of writing thank-you letters to mail-order outfits at a time like this. On the other hand, it did serve to take her mind off her knee for a few seconds.

She was well into the tangle of tropical foliage when she heard the car come to a halt on the edge of the road. Hannah lay gasping for breath, clutching her knee, and tried to figure out what to do next. She had no idea whether whoever was in the car would come looking for her, but it was a pretty good bet they'd want to make sure they had killed her. With any luck they'd assume she'd gone over the cliff in the jeep.

Then she heard the voices.

"I'll go down and make sure."

A man's voice. One Hannah recognized but didn't want to acknowledge. Then came the woman's voice and Hannah decided that there was no use in pretending she didn't know Victoria Armitage's loud, harsh tones.

"I don't think she's down there, Drake."

"Got to be. Where else could she have gone?"

"We didn't actually see the jeep go over. She might have had time to get out."

"No way. Her reflexes aren't all that good, especially with that leg of hers. You've seen her move lately. She still uses the cane."

"I don't know, Drake. I have a feeling she's not down there."

"I'll go look."

"All right," Victoria agreed. "I'll check around up here. You're right about one thing. Wherever she is, she can't have gotten far."

"The first time she managed to get herself to a hospital." Drake sounded thoroughly disgusted. "And the second time, Cage got in the way."

"This time we'll make sure of her."

"God, Vicky, I wish you'd get this business finished once and for all. It's getting damned spooky."

"Don't lose your nerve now, Drake. There's no way she'll get out of this. I'll take the gun."

Hannah closed her eyes in horror. A gun. Vicky was coming after her and she was armed. Frantically Hannah opened her eyes and glanced around. The rain offered some protection but it seemed to be lessening. Tropical storms didn't last long. She'd better take advantage of the downpour while she could. It would hide her movements for a while.

Gritting her teeth, Hannah levered herself to her feet. There was no point fooling herself that adrenaline and fear would completely overcome the pain and weakness in her left leg, but she made an attempt, regardless. There was no choice. Dr. Englehardt had done a good job on the knee. He'd said so, himself. If the job hadn't been good enough, she'd sue when she got back to Seattle.

Slowly, painfully, Hannah made her way deeper into the undergrowth. The terrain became rough quickly, and sizeable chunks of granite were as abundant as frangipani and ferns. Using both hands to help herself along, Hannah opted to use the boulders as protection. They looked as though they'd be better able to deflect a bullet than the delicate, flowering shrubs.

The rocky hillside provided a number of handholds. Unfortunately, it also provided a number of loose pebbles and debris. The rain was still heavy enough to conceal most of the noise Hannah was making but it wasn't going to go on much longer. She had to find a decent hiding place before the storm ended.

Some of the delicate tropical bushes weren't quite as innocent as they appeared, Hannah discovered as she put one palm firmly around a vine bristling with thorns. Stifling a groan of anguish, she released the vine and stared at her hand. Rain washed across her palm, carrying traces of something that might have been blood. Then again, it might simply have been mud. Hannah went back to the task of finding a hiding place.

The obvious one lay amid a jumble of craggy rocks. It was a cave, surrounded by thick vegetation. It loomed up out of nowhere, its dark mouth yawning invitingly in the rain. It offered shelter and shadows. With the age-old instinct of the wounded and the hunted, Hannah headed toward it.

She was about to collapse into the dark interior when something made her think more clearly. The cave was a little too obvious. If Vicky Armitage spotted it, she was likely to come to the same conclusion as Hannah, and Hannah would be a sitting duck of a guidance counselor trapped inside.

Biting back a groan of despair, Hannah paused to catch her breath and search her surroundings. Above the cave, an uneven mixture of thick vegetation and rocks stretched upward and backward. If she could get above the cave entrance she could keep climbing into the hills.

Hannah set herself to fighting her way around the mouth of the cave. If her leg hadn't been hurting so badly it wouldn't have been such a difficult task. The terrain wasn't so rough that it couldn't be handled easily by someone with two functioning legs. Vicky had too functioning legs, Hannah reminded herself. Vicky would be humming right along behind her on two legs toughened up by a great deal of running. She would also have a gun in her hand.

Damn it to hell. Vicky not only had a Ph.D., she had a gun. Life could be very unfair at times.

Hannah dislodged a few pebbles as she hauled herself around a boulder. The rain was definitely slackening now. If Vicky were close enough, she might have heard the small clatter. But there was no shout and no shot so Hannah kept climbing. There was nothing else to be done at the moment.

A huge fern blocked her path. Hannah wondered if she could go through it. She didn't think she had the energy to circle around it. The fern proved obliging enough. It collapsed beneath Hannah's weight and when she crawled over it, she found herself in the jumble of plants and rocks above the mouth of the cave. She lay trying to catch her breath and wondered how useful the struggle had been.

The question remained unanswered. A drift of departing rain swept across Hannah's prone body and, when it passed, Vicky Armitage materialized. Hannah blinked painfully as the other woman stepped cautiously out into the open near the cave. It was true. Vicky did, indeed, have a gun. Fretful moonlight revealed its dark bulk in her fist. Hannah had full confidence in the other woman's ability to use it. She lay utterly still on the damp, muddy earth and wondered how much luck any one guidance counselor could possibly have.

Vicky wasn't worrying about being taken by surprise. She was obviously being cautious simply because she didn't want to overlook any possible hiding places. She was probably quartering the terrain or walking it in concentric circles. Whatever technique she was using, Hannah was certain it would be brilliant and methodical.

The moon emerged more fully as the clouds scattered and departed. It occurred to Hannah that, if she got out of this, she owed two letters to the mail-order firm where she had purchased her clothing. Not only had the tough cotton protected her during the escape from the jeep but the khaki green shade of the shirt and pants was making her a part of the night-shrouded vegetation. As she thought about her clothing, Hannah also thought about her belt.

It was two inches wide, guaranteed to be made of sturdy British harness leather and finished with a hefty brass buckle. Just the thing for trekking into the tropics. It wouldn't be much use against a gun but there might be other uses for the heavy belt. Slowly, trying not to make any noise, Hannah reached under herself and undid the buckle. Watching Vicky all the time, she inched the belt free. She looped the end of it around her wrist just as Vicky turned and spotted the dark entrance of the cave.

As Hannah had anticipated, Vicky headed at once for the dark, yawning hole. But she stopped short outside.

"Hannah?"

There was an unnerving, unhealthy excitement in Vicky's voice. It sent a strange chill down Hannah's spine. The woman was enjoying this. Hannah didn't move.

"Hannah, you should have listened to me. You should have given me Elizabeth Nord's journals and books. You were a stupid little fool, and now it's going to cost you. Because I'm the one who's going to end up with those journals. I'm going to find the truth in them."

Silence reigned for a moment. Hannah held her breath. Then Vicky took a step closer to the cave.

"Nord ruined my father with her lies. Do you hear me? He was a brilliant man and she ruined his career. He tried to help her in the beginning, tried to give her a hand up in the profession. She used him and then she turned on him. He told me so many times how it had happened. She *used* him! Do you have any idea of what she did to him? He died a weak, pitiful man. He became an alcoholic at the end. She killed him, Hannah! Just as surely as if she'd put a gun to his head. She didn't even give him a quick death. It took him years to die. Years of watching his reputation dwindle and disappear. Years of getting second-rate teaching posts. Years of having the best journals turn down his papers. Years of knowing he was right and Nord was wrong and having no way to prove it."

Hannah risked a very careful breath as Vicky moved closer to the cave.

"Come on out, Hannah. I know you're in there. Just like you to run and hide. You're like your aunt, aren't you? You'd have used your connection with Nord to write the one book people would be sure to read about her. No one gave a damn about anything my father wrote about Elizabeth Nord. And you'd have made sure Nord's lies were handed down to another generation. But I'm not going to let that happen. My father knew she'd lied. He told me she had. But no one would listen to him. They'll listen to me, though, Hannah. By God, I'll make them listen. I've known from the time I was fifteen years old and watched my father start to drink himself to death that I'd make people acknowledge the truth. And I'll use Nord's own journals to tear apart her reputation. I'm not going to let a weak little nobody like you get in my way."

Hannah watched Vicky move into the cave. This was the only opportunity she was likely to get. She pulled herself to the edge overlooking the cave entrance. It might help if she had some sort of distraction to offer Vicky when the other woman emerged from the cave. Suddenly the necklace seemed very warm on Hannah's throat.

Hannah yanked at the old chain. It snapped and the pendant came free in her hand.

"Damn you, Hannah, where are you?" Vicky came back to the cave entrance. Hannah could see the top of her head as she looked down at the other woman.

Hannah hurled the necklace into the shrubbery across from the cave. It tinkled lightly as it struck a rock. Vicky's hand came up in a classic firing stance and the gunshot split the night. Hannah thought she might be permanently deafened.

Then she was pushing herself over the side, falling heavily to land with a jolting thud on top of Vicky. The shock winded both women, but it was Vicky who took the brunt of it. She collapsed beneath Hannah, the gun falling from her hand.

Almost instantly Hannah realized that she wasn't strong enough to overpower the other woman, even with the advantage she'd had. Vicky Armitage had spent too many hours in the weight room of the athletic club and too many hours running. Her physical strength and endurance were formidable and they were both finely tuned.

But the rage that had first gripped Hannah as she lay in agony on the road washed back through her veins. She felt Vicky twist beneath her and knew she

was trying for the gun. At the same time Vicky shoved
violently with her elbow, catching Hannah painfully
in the ribs. For a sharp second Hannah wondered if
something had been broken. But there wasn't any time
to find out.

"Damn you, you stupid little bitch!" Vicky twisted
again, and this time she succeeded in dislodging Hannah.

Hannah gasped and fell to the side. She saw Vicky
struggle to her knees and loom over her. The beautiful face was a mask of rage. Vicky swung at her again,
a vicious punch that carried the full weight of her well-
developed shoulders behind it.

Hannah managed to jerk her head aside and took
the blow on her shoulder, which promptly went numb.
But it was her left shoulder, and the sturdy leather belt
with its dangling brass buckle was wrapped around her
right wrist. Hannah flung out her hand.

The belt cut through the air with the force of a small
whip. Vicky wasn't expecting any kind of weapon and
the heavy buckle caught her by surprise, snapping
across her cheek. She screamed in pain and rage and
scrambled backward for the gun.

Panicked by the knowledge that the pistol lay only
a yard away, Hannah vaulted herself to her knees.
Agony laced through the left one. But her fear and
fury enabled her to ignore the pain. She swung again
with the heavy leather. The second blow lashed across
Vicky's arm, not doing much damage but causing the
other woman to jerk back out of range. Hannah decided to keep trying for Vicky's face. Any woman, especially one as good looking as Victoria Armitage,
would instinctively try to protect her face and eyes.

The theory worked for one more swing of the belt. Then Vicky made a dive for the gun. Hannah threw herself onto her opponent and found long nails scratching at her eyes. Frantically she ducked her head and tried to wrap the leather around Vicky's throat.

Vicky realized what was happening and shoved heavily at Hannah. When Hannah's weight eased she made another grab for the gun.

But Hannah had rolled on top of it. The metal cut into her breast as she lay gasping on the soggy ground. Desperately she reached beneath her and grasped the handle.

"Stop it, Vicky. Stop right there or so help me God, I'll shoot. I swear it."

Vicky halted abruptly as Hannah lifted the gun with both hands and pointed it at her. Savagely she looked from the weapon to Hannah's face. "You don't know how to use that thing."

"Are you kidding? I'm Elizabeth Nord's niece, remember? She was a font of useful information for a young girl. A real role model."

Vicky glared at Hannah in bitter frustration, but she didn't try to take the gun away from her. Just as well, Hannah realized. She was shaking so badly it would have been like taking candy from a baby.

Then another hand was reaching down to remove the gun from Hannah's grasp. A familiar, masculine hand that was accompanied by a familiar, laconic voice.

"I'll take over now, Hannah. You've been through enough for one night." Gideon's fingers closed around the weapon. "So have I, come to think of it."

For a few seconds Hannah lay staring up at Gideon's grimly set face, wondering if shock had made her hallucinate. But he seemed very solid and very real. She released her hold on the gun.

"The necklace," Hannah whispered. "I have to find the necklace."

Chapter Seventeen

"YOU SCARED the living hell out of me, you know that, don't you?" Gideon ran savage fingers through his hair and stopped his pacing long enough to stare down at Hannah, who was ensconced on her aunt's sofa. "I can't even remember the last time I was that terrified."

"Not even during some of your biggest business deals?"

"Take a little advice from a very short-tempered man, Hannah. Don't make jokes at this particular point. I'm still recovering. My sense of humor will probably be the last thing to return to normal." Gideon began stalking back and forth across the floor in front of her. "When I heard that shot I thought I'd go crazy. I still can't believe you managed to get the gun away from Vicky."

"I was angry at the time. Lots of adrenaline."

"Uh-huh." He halted again. "I know the feeling. Jesus, what a mess." He shot her a curious glance. "Would you have used the gun?"

"Probably. If I could have figured out how to work it in time," Hannah admitted.

"You didn't know?" He looked dumbfounded. "What was all that snappy chatter about having learned from your aunt?"

"I saw very little of my aunt when I was growing up, Gideon. When she did come to visit she didn't take the time to teach me how to use a gun. But I've seen a lot of television. The trick to holding a gun on someone is to look and sound like you're going to use it. You've got to have dramatic presence.''

He shook his head. ''You're certainly in a good mood considering what you've been through.''

''I expect it's relief. Makes me bubbly.'' Hannah gingerly massaged her left knee, which was stretched out in front of her and propped on a pillow. ''The pain pills the doctor gave me may also be a contributing factor.''

Gideon walked restlessly over to the sofa and crouched down beside her. ''How's the leg?''

''It hurts.''

''Did the doctor think you'd done any more serious damage?''

''No. He thinks it'll be all right in a couple of days. It's just going to be damn sore for a while.''

Gideon looked at the leg for a while and then at her. ''You would have had to figure out how to use that gun, I think. Vicky was past being rational or easily intimidated. The way she was eyeing you gave me the impression that nothing short of a small cannon would have stopped her.''

''I know. She was crazy with anger.'' Hannah leaned back as Gideon began to gently knead her knee. ''But, then, I was very angry, myself.''

''What did you do to her face?''

''That gash? I wasn't fighting fair. I used my belt buckle on her. She was so strong, Gideon. And I wasn't exactly in my prime with this damn leg. I figured that, under the circumstances, I was allowed a few cheap shots.''

"Given the fact that she was the one with the gun, I'd hardly say you were wielding an undue advantage. Besides, when you're in that kind of fight, you don't worry about playing fair. You worry about winning."

She smiled weakly. "Advice from an expert?"

"Damn right." Gideon massaged the knee in silence for a while. "When I saw that jeep at the bottom of the cliff, I thought I'd lose my mind."

"It was the same way it had been that night coming back to Seattle from my friend's home, Gideon." Hannah gave up the attempt to maintain a bright, flippant attitude. It was wearing. "The lights coming on suddenly in the rearview mirror, startling me. The car so close behind mine. Then that quick swerve to sideswipe me. When the lights hit the mirror, nearly blinding me for an instant, I remembered. I still don't recall everything, but I remember those lights and then the car crowding me off the road. Last time I swung the wheel without thinking, I was so shocked. But this time I kept the wheel straight and used the brakes. Unfortunately it wasn't enough to keep the jeep on the road after it got swiped."

"It bought you the time you needed to get out," Gideon said. "Thank God for small favors."

"What happens now?"

"You mean with Vicky and Drake? The island police seem to have no problems believing our side of the story this time. There's plenty of evidence, including Drake singing his fool head off to the arresting officers. His charm isn't going to work down here. These people have seen too many tourists. They aren't easily charmed by them. They just tolerate them. I don't know if we can make the other charge stick, though."

"The one against Drake for trying to drown me?" Hannah grimaced. "Too bad he didn't mention that when he was busy trying to convince the cops he was just an innocent bystander."

"If we can get him on this charge, I'll be satisfied. Vicky was so angry that she said a little too much to the cops, also. I just want both Armitages out of your life."

"I suppose they were the ones who searched my apartment that night you and I went out to dinner. I wonder why they didn't take anything?"

"I doubt if they intended to take anything. Stealing the journals would have been too obvious. How could Vicky have popped up on the academic scene in a few months with all of Nord's private journals without raising a few questions? I imagine she just went into the apartment out of a burning curiosity to see what kind of data you'd brought back with you. Your brother says your key is missing from his ring. It would have been simple enough for Drake to have taken it sometime at the club."

"What good would killing me have done?"

Gideon's mouth hardened. "Once you were out of the way your aunt's books would have wound up sooner or later in a library or a research foundation. Then Vicky would have had access to them. But she probably counted on being able to talk your brother into letting them handle the Nord papers after your death. They'd made a point of socializing with him and were on friendly terms. It wouldn't have been hard to convince Nick to let them have a bunch of books and notes he couldn't have cared less about."

"Drake must have deliberately wangled those visiting professor jobs at the college where I work."

"It wouldn't have been hard, given Vicky's reputation and his own political sense."

Hannah nodded in agreement. "The Armitages were big time for my little college. I'm sure the faculty was thrilled when they offered to spend the fall quarter in Seattle. I suppose it's fortunate the Armitages never knew that Elizabeth Nord had retired to Santa Inez or else they might have hounded her down here. Aunt Elizabeth always guarded her privacy. No one except her family knew where she was for the past few years."

"Vicky and Drake knew you were the key they needed when they saw her obituary and realized that everything had been left to a niece in Seattle." Gideon showed his teeth in a silent snarl. "I want them out of your life."

"Suits me. I've never been hated the way Vicky hates me. The ludicrous part is that I was envious of her. I thought I understood the power of the desire for revenge, but I've got to admit she carried it to new heights."

"She blamed your aunt for her father's failure to become a luminary in the world of anthropology. The truth was, her father just didn't quite have what it takes. From what Nord says in her journals Dear Roddy was a competent man but not a brilliant one. She didn't do anything to actually hinder his career, she simply left him behind while she went to the top."

"She went to the top with a lie, Gideon."

He smiled. "But she did it on one hell of a grand scale, didn't she? You've got to admire that kind of nerve."

"I know. The rest of her work in anthropology is legitimate research," Hannah said. "I'm sure of it.

She was a brilliant woman and she would have been a leading light in the academic world even without the Revelation Island book."

"I don't doubt it for a moment."

"I don't think she invented the myth of the Revelation Island Amazons just to further her own career. I think she did it because she wanted to shake up her fellow researchers. She wanted them to think twice about the kinds of conclusions they came to when they looked at women in various social groups. It's so easy to pigeonhole the sexes and so much damage is done because of those easy assumptions. In her day those assumptions were especially narrow. Who knows? Maybe we owe some of the current freedom women enjoy to that myth my aunt created. *Amazons* has been such an influential book over the years. It's hard to blame Nord for what she did."

"Hard for you to blame her. Vicky Armitage had no problem."

Hannah snorted. "If it hadn't been for my aunt, young women such as Victoria Armitage probably wouldn't even have thought of going into anthropology in the first place."

Gideon's grin flashed briefly. "I guess that's one view."

"You know what really bothered Vicky most?" Hannah went on thoughtfully.

"What?"

"Her father's weakness. She wanted to idolize him and couldn't. He simply didn't have the academic stature she wanted him to have. In the end he became an alcoholic, she said. She hated that."

"So she turned her hatred against Elizabeth Nord for having made her father into the weak man he was? That's kind of complicated."

"Makes sense, though," Hannah said. "The sad part is that on the subject of Revelation Island, Vicky's father was right. Nord faked the research. It must have torn Hamilton apart when no one would listen to him."

"Hannah, the reason no one would listen to Hamilton at that point was that his work was already failing to compare with Nord's. You've said yourself that by the early forties her papers were the ones being published and admired. His were pedantic and pedestrian by comparison. People were beginning to ignore him even then. If he hadn't begun to slip behind her in terms of the recognition and respect of his colleagues, he wouldn't have looked petty and vengeful when he attempted to discredit her work on Revelation Island."

"She realized at one point why he offered to marry her," Hannah said thoughtfully. "She suspected that he was just trying to use her. If she had married him and taken his name their work probably would have continued to be published jointly. It would have been the Hamilton name that carried the clout and because he was the man in the team, Vicky's father would probably have been respected as the senior researcher. In husband-and-wife teams it's often the husband who gets most of the credit."

"That didn't stop Vicky from marrying Drake. Even I can tell that it's Vicky who has the brains."

"But no sense of diplomacy. You need that to survive in the academic world, Gideon. Vicky needed Drake and she was smart enough to know it. Drake was the one who could talk people into giving her grants. Drake was the one who knew how to function at the faculty club parties, shake the right hands, talk to the right people. He would have paved the path for her and Vicky's own intelligence would have done the rest. The alliance would have lasted until Vicky figured she didn't need him any more. I'm not sure she would have realized that she'd probably always need him. Ultimately her ego would have made her dump him and that would have been a mistake."

"Vicky on her own would be awesome," Gideon decided.

"Yes." Hannah thought about just what Vicky had been like on her own. "Very awesome."

"On the other hand," Gideon murmured, "you can be rather formidable, yourself."

"You should talk. I saw what you did to Drake Armitage. You're a nasty street fighter, Gideon. But I suppose I already knew that. The military world doesn't know what it missed when you decided to go corporate. The leg feels better, thank you."

"What about the rest of you?"

"I think the adrenaline is beginning to slow down. I don't feel so jumpy. God, that's a weird feeling. Is it always like that after a battle, do you suppose?"

Gideon rocked back on his heels, studying her. "It takes people different ways. But it's always rough afterward. A kind of shock, I guess."

"You looked calm enough. Didn't holding a knife to Drake's throat leave you shaky?"

"What made me shaky," Gideon said distinctly, "was hearing that gunshot. I lost a few years at that point. It was then I decided I was definitely getting too old for that kind of excitement. You want to know what really unhinged me, though?''

Hannah made a face. "I already know. You thought I'd gone crazy just because I wanted to find the necklace.''

"I came to the obvious conclusion that the experience with Vicky had definitely done some permanent damage to your brain.''

"That necklace is very important to me, Gideon.''

"I figured that. Anyone who could think only of finding a piece of cheap jewelry after just fighting for her life has got to have an odd set of priorities.''

"You don't understand.''

"No, I don't. But I'm not going to argue about it. Probably a function of shock. People do odd things when in shock. You've got your precious necklace and I've got you. All things considered, I'm willing to call it even.''

Hannah looked up at him uneasily, her mind beginning to focus on other things now that she was calming down. "What made you come down here, Gideon? Why did you follow me?''

His gaze was very steady. "You know the answer to that.''

"You'd figured out that Vicky and Drake were dangerous?''

"No. I didn't start thinking in those terms until after I'd already decided to follow you to Santa Inez. I didn't want you down here on your own, brooding in your aunt's house, poring over those journals with her ghost hovering around you.''

"That's a pretty melodramatic image.''

"Sometimes when I get nervous about you I get melodramatic.''

Hannah drew a deep breath. "Does having me spend the rest of the summer in Tucson mean so much to you, Gideon?"

"We're talking about more than a few weeks and you know it."

"Are we?"

He got to his feet and moved slowly toward the chair across from the sofa. "Please don't be evasive, Hannah. We know each other too well for those kinds of games."

"I'm not sure we do, and I'm not playing games, Gideon. I came down here to decide some very important things in my life. What happened tonight with the Armitages doesn't change anything. I still have to make some decisions."

"You don't have to make them here."

"Yes, I do have to make them here. I was right to come back to the cottage. This is where I need to be while I work it out."

"Work what out, for God's sake?" Gideon's face was hard now, his eyes remote and too brilliant. He was locked in another battle and he knew it.

"For one thing, I have to decide whether to do the book about my aunt."

"You don't have to be here to decide that."

Hannah's mouth lifted wryly. "I told you, you don't understand."

"Explain it to me," he challenged.

"I can't." It was the truth. She didn't know how to put into words what she knew writing the book about Elizabeth Nord would do for her and how it would change the direction of her life. Gideon would be furious if he realized that what he wanted was in jeopardy simply because of the Nord journals. He was dangerous when he was furious.

Gideon leaned forward intently, his elbows on his knees. "The real reason you ran down here was to get out of my reach, wasn't it?"

She hesitated. "That was part of it, I guess."

"It didn't work."

"No."

"So stop running, Hannah. Come back to Tucson with me."

"No."

"Christ, Hannah, why are you being so damned stubborn?"

"Because I need time to think. I came down here to do exactly that and I intend to finish what I started. You'll have to go back to Tucson alone, Gideon, because I can't think as clearly as I should when you're around. I've told you that several times."

"Doesn't the fact that you can't think clearly around me tell you anything?"

"It tells me I need to be alone for a while." The necklace burned on her throat and Hannah automatically lifted her fingers to touch it. "I have to make my own decisions."

"You're involved with me. Your decisions affect me. Can't you understand that?" He watched her toy with the necklace and frustrated malevolence flashed briefly in his eyes. "Come back to Tucson with me and I'll replace that stupid thing with a diamond."

Hannah stared at him and then burst out laughing. "Oh, Gideon," she said, recovering slowly, "you know that was a dumb thing to say."

He sighed. "I know. I'm desperate. Besides, you'd look lousy in diamonds. They wouldn't go with the safari clothes."

"I'm afraid not."

"Hannah, please don't fight me on this."

"I have to have time. I'm going to stay down here and contemplate a great many things while you go back to Tucson."

He watched her in silence, knowing she meant every word. "How long?"

"How long will it take me to decide? I don't know."

"It's not that damn Nord book you're going to think about. It's us."

She thought about it. "Yes, in a way." But it was all tied up with the book.

"Not 'in a way.' It's definitely us you'll be thinking about."

"Yes."

"Hannah, let me stay."

"You've got a business to run."

He swore softly. "I'm not sure I do. By now Ballantine has probably hired away my staff and fed my reputation to the other corporate sharks in the sea."

"Ballantine can't crush you, no matter what he does. You're too strong, Gideon. He could succeed in wiping you out financially and still not crush you. Don't you see, Gideon? That's the real reason you can afford to step back from a fight with him. He could never do to you what you did to his father. There is something inside you that would never be defeated. It's got nothing to do with your business or your reputation. It's much more fundamental than that. One of these days Hugh Ballantine will probably realize it and call off the war. He's too smart to beat his head against a stone wall forever."

"I don't give a damn about Hugh Ballantine at the moment. You're the one who's driving me over the edge. I don't want to leave you down here by yourself."

"You have no choice," she said simply.

He looked at her and knew she spoke the truth. "Damn it to hell."

GIDEON DELAYED the inevitable as long as possible. He paid a few more visits to the island police clearing up details and making sure the Seattle authorities were notified. He insisted on taking Hannah back to the doctor for another examination of her leg. He bought groceries. He cleaned up Hannah's kitchen. But in the end there were no more excuses. The next day he left Santa Inez Island. He drove himself to the airport feeling frustrated, angry and, deep inside, fearful. He had rarely known real fear in his life.

There was something going on in Hannah's stubborn, proud head that he simply didn't understand. It was so completely female that it seemed alien. He wanted to stand his ground and fight, but for the first time in his life he didn't have the vaguest idea of how to combat the enemy. So he left, knowing that for the moment he had no choice. He would have to take his chances.

Hannah felt a wave of sadness tinged with relief as she watched Gideon's car disappear out of the cottage drive. Slowly, leaning heavily on the cane again, she made her way back into the house. This was the only way. There had been no choice.

The rest of the day passed slowly. She spent the time resting her leg, sipping iced tea and trying not to think about anything at all. The thinking could wait until tomorrow.

The next morning dawned with the promise of stifling heat. Hannah put on a pair of olive green walking shorts and a short-sleeved camp shirt. When she walked out into the living room the first things she saw were the journals.

They waited for her. They always seemed to be waiting for her. No matter which way she turned the journals were there, beckoning, insisting, and promising.

Writing the book would change everything. She would be choosing a path that would consume her in some ways, endow her with power in others. But it would be a path that would not allow anyone else as strong as Gideon to get too close. She would walk it alone, the same way her aunt had.

Elizabeth Nord had traveled her path willingly enough, Hannah thought. In fact Nord had gloried in it. Hannah could revel in it also. All she had to do was write the book. Her life would never be the same.

But neither would it be if she chose to go to Gideon. Her life would be changed. His personal strength was a danger to her in some ways. He could overwhelm when he chose, and in his natural arrogance he would probably choose to do exactly that on frequent occasions. She would have her hands full loving him and at the same time holding her own around him.

Loving him. The words tripped through her brain, startling her. She hadn't been thinking in such terms, hadn't wanted to think that way. Love was a perilous business, something a smart woman didn't risk unless she could be sure she was loved deeply in return. Nord had understood that and had stayed clear of the emotion. Gideon, too, had managed to avoid the weakening force of love. There was no guarantee that he would ever get to the point where he could love someone else completely. There was too much that was remote and private in him, too much that was hard and strong and independent.

She could be like that if she wrote the book. The necklace was hot on her skin. *Free.* Totally, gloriously free. Never again would she become mired in the problems of other people. Never again would she allow the weaknesses of others to drag her down. Never again would compassion and empathy compromise her own personal strength. All she had to do was write the book.

Hannah stood irresolutely on the veranda, considering a walk down by the cove. She had wanted to be alone, but suddenly she was afraid to be alone. Changing her mind about the walk, she went back into the cottage and found the keys to the new jeep Gideon had rented for her.

Driving, she quickly decided, was never again going to be a totally relaxed experience for her. Two accidents in such a short period of time were enough to traumatize even an Amazon, and Hannah wasn't at all sure she was made of Amazonian material. Nevertheless she forced herself to drive back along the cliff road into town. She was not going to let herself be housebound. But she didn't look over the side when she came to the point in the road where the jeep had gone over the edge. Willpower was a good thing, but there was no sense pushing it to the limit.

In a pink stucco waterfront hotel that had been built during the Dutch colonial era Hannah found a pay phone and some privacy. She hesitated a few moments and then called her brother. He came on the line immediately, his voice sounding both relieved and anxious.

"Hannah! You're driving me bonkers this summer. I just had a call from Gideon who, by the way, sounds madder than hell. He told me what had happened. You're all right this time?"

"I'm all right. A little sore and bruised in places but I'm okay." It was good to hear her brother's voice.

"I can hardly believe that business about the Armitages. Gideon said you got into a knockdown, drag-out fight with Vicky."

"You were right about the pecs on that woman. She's as strong as a horse."

"Must be hell on wheels in bed. Wonder how Drake handled her?"

"Trust a man to think of that first. Don't forget he spent a lot of time on the weight machines, too. I've got a feeling he could hold his own. While you were noticing Vicky's pectorals, I had occasion to admire Drake's biceps. Listen, Nick, I'm not calling to talk about that."

"What are you calling about?"

"Just to hear your voice."

He chuckled softly. "Feeling lonely down there?"

"In a way."

"You shouldn't have sent Gideon back to Tucson."

Hannah wrinkled her nose. "He told you about that?"

"He said your stubbornness was equalled only by your idiocy."

"That man certainly has a way with words."

Nick's voice softened. "Are you really okay, Hannah?"

"Yes." It was true. She was fine. "I just have some thinking to do."

"Because I can be down there by tomorrow if you need me."

"Thanks, but I'm all right, really."

"Gideon isn't."

"No?"

"You've got him running scared."

"I think that's overstating the case," she said dryly.

"I don't. You forget I know the man in some ways you don't. I've seen him in action on the corporate level. I have a great deal of respect for anyone, male or female, who could terrorize him."

"Gideon is no more terrorized than you are. He's just mad because he hasn't gotten his way."

"Maybe that's why he's so damned nervous. He's used to getting his own way, Hannah."

"I know. Goodbye, Nick. I'll call you when I'm ready to leave the island."

"Take care."

"I will."

"I love you, sister."

"Same here, brother." Hannah hung up the phone feeling better.

She wandered through the narrow, twisting alleys outside the hotel, browsing in the shop windows without really noticing what she was looking at. At one point she followed a cobbled walk that led back to the courtyard where she had bought the souvenir map for

Gideon. Seeing another stack of the same maps left her feeling strange. She turned away and went in search of a glass of lemonade.

By noon the day had fulfilled the promise of heat. There were damp patches under the arms of Hannah's camp shirt as she drove back to the cottage, and she wished for the first time that her aunt had installed air conditioning instead of the picturesque ceiling fans. It was hard to think in this kind of heat.

No, she decided as she changed into a swimming suit. It wasn't any harder to think here than it had been in Seattle. She was finding deep thought difficult for other reasons. She'd had enough pop psychology to recognize that on some level she was trying to avoid the issues, which had seemed so clear cut shortly before the Armitages had run her off a road for a second time. She was trying to avoid thinking about her feelings for Gideon Cage.

Two paths lay before her. Following one meant never having a second chance at the other. The certainty of that was what made the decision so frightening. The weight of the necklace around her neck seemed to impress the stark reality of the choice into her very bones. She had to choose.

She walked down to the cove, past the palm grove and into the crystal water. She savored its freshness on her perspiration-damp skin as she swam slowly out to a point where she would be able just barely to stand with her chin above the water. Small wavelets slapped playfully at her face. Then she stood, allowing herself to be enveloped by the wonderful coolness.

She loved islands. She would always love islands, just as Elizabeth Nord had always loved islands. Hannah could become as powerful in her own way as her aunt had been. The link between herself and her aunt was real.

The necklace was warm, even here in the water, but now it was a comforting, familiar warmth, a pleasant heat she was beginning to take for granted.

Two paths. One, the bright, beckoning path of unequaled personal success. That path stretched backward as well as forward. When she turned around and looked back along its length she could see the other women who had worn the necklace. They were proud, strong, coldly brilliant women whose genes she bore in some small measure. She could be like them. There was absolutely no doubt in her mind. Once she had taken the crucial step, she would be happy with that decision. Completely satisfied. That promise was as clear as the water around her. There would be no regrets.

The second path did not stretch backward, it went forward but it was unclear and unfocused. There were twists and turns in it that she could not see. There was no predicting what lay ahead if she went to Tucson. Going back to find Gideon would require strength, but it would be strength of a different kind than that needed on the other path.

Writing the book would make all the difference. You couldn't have it all. You had to make choices.

Hannah swam for a while again, floating in the hot sunshine, diving under the surface when the heat became too much. At least her experience with Drake in the cove hadn't soured her on swimming, she thought at one point. Here in the water her leg ceased to hurt her. She felt whole and strong again.

Gideon was a hard man. If she went to him she would have to be prepared for the core of toughness in him. There were so many risks. He might change his mind about her. He might never learn to love. She might not be able to tolerate or moderate his sometimes destructive power. He could turn it against her.

She considered that last bit, floating again on her back. It didn't worry her as much as it should have under the circumstances. Not because she was feeding herself some silly line about having enough love for both of them, but because she simply wasn't genuinely scared of the risks she would be taking if she went to him.

She could handle Gideon Cage. The thought surprised her.

Hannah waded slowly out of the water and stood on the beach fingering the necklace. For her the choices were almost excruciatingly clear. On the one hand she was being given what most people never got, a second chance to grab what she had missed a few years ago. She could have everything Elizabeth Nord had had.

Picking her way carefully, Hannah walked out along the rocky outcropping that sheltered one end of the cove. Standing at the far end she looked down at a roiling surf that had spent forever trying to invade the quiet, sheltered waters on the other side of the rocks. It was more exciting out here than it was in the safety of the cove. Foaming water splashed her, daring her to take the risk of swimming here rather than in the quiet waters. The waves rolled hugely, their energy communicating itself to her.

She wanted it all, Hannah thought. But life wasn't like that. You couldn't have it all. Choices had to be made. She would have to choose what she wanted most.

Hannah took the necklace from around her throat and held it out over the rough surf. The water below was very deep.

She drew a deep breath and feminine voices from at least three centuries called her, warning her. Hannah ignored them. This was her decision. She threw the necklace into the sea. It flashed in the sunlight and disappeared forever under the waves.

Then at last she knew the truth. It almost shattered her.

There was not nearly as much power in the necklace as there was in herself. Her future was in her own hands.

Chapter Eighteen

Vegas wasn't going to work this time. The cards weren't going well but that didn't surprise Gideon. He wasn't paying proper attention. All he could think about with any concentration was Hannah. Nodding distantly to the croupier, Gideon left the blackjack table and went in search of a drink. It wouldn't be hard to find. There was a choice of lounges and bars surrounding the gambling floor of the huge casino.

Gideon selected a familiar location, a dark, shadowed table that partially concealed him while allowing a view of the hectic activity out on the floor. Beneath magnificent chandeliers designed to illuminate an endless night, people in Bermuda shorts rolled dice next to women in evening gowns. The professionally polite croupiers didn't blink an eye at either extreme. Vegas was nothing if not egalitarian when it came to taking people's money.

The glass of Scotch warmed in Gideon's fingers. In a few minutes he would try another blackjack table, but it was hard to work up any genuine enthusiasm for the idea. Vegas no longer functioned in its assigned role. It no longer provided the shot of adrenaline or the short, temporary fix he got from winning. What really bothered Gideon was that he didn't even seem to care when he lost. He felt no pang of regret. There was only a deep desire to settle the future with Hannah.

He had come to Vegas for a few days because he couldn't stand the waiting. Hoping that the glitter and the fake excitement would take his mind off Hannah, Gideon had quietly slipped out of Tucson. But he might as well go back. Vegas wasn't going to work.

"Lucky as usual, Cage?"

Somehow the voice at his elbow didn't surprise him. Gideon didn't move. He kept his eyes on a man in lizard skin boots and a white Stetson who was playing blackjack. "Ballantine, don't you have anything better to do than follow me around?"

Hugh Ballantine sat down, putting himself between Gideon and the view of the man in the lizard skin boots. "No. Not at the moment." He sipped the martini he had brought over to the table. The vivid blue eyes were shadowed and watchful. "I phoned your office and your secretary said you were out of town. I asked her if you were in the Caribbean or Seattle. She said neither."

"So you knew exactly where to look." Gideon gave up trying to watch the blackjack player and resigned himself to looking at Ballantine. "Why?"

Hugh shrugged. "I wanted to talk to you."

"Why?" Gideon asked again, wondering at his own patience.

"She believes you."

"Who? My secretary? Of course she believes me. She's paid to believe me."

Ballantine shook his head. "Hannah. Hannah believes you."

Gideon felt his insides tighten. "About what?"

"About the past."

"Why are you here, Ballantine?"

"I think I started believing your version of what happened after I realized that, even though she had a lot of reasons to hate your guts, Hannah believed you."

"Don't do me any favors. I don't give a damn whether you believe me or not. If you've come all this way just to tell me that, you've wasted your time. In the end it just doesn't make any difference."

"I know. Nothing makes much difference to you, does it?"

Gideon didn't bother to answer. He took a swallow of his drink instead.

Ballantine leaned forward suddenly. "Tell me about him."

"About who? Your father?"

"Yes, damn it."

"He was your father, not mine. You must have known him better than I did."

"That's not true, Cage and you know it. I wasn't his real son. You were. I knew that from the time I was in high school. Why the hell do you think I avoided anything that was even remotely connected with the business world for so long? I couldn't compete against you."

Gideon eyed him. "I don't recall you even trying."

Ballantine smiled slightly. "There was no point. You were older, stronger, tougher, shrewder. You were everything Cyrus Ballantine wanted in his son."

"He had a strange way of demonstrating his paternal affection."

Ballantine looked at him. "That's why I couldn't believe your version of what happened nine years ago. I couldn't believe Dad would do that to you."

"And you still don't."

"Hannah does."

"She's only got my word for it."

"That seems to be enough," Ballantine said.

"Are you trying to tell me Hannah's feelings on the subject are enough for you?"

"Let's just say she's put doubts in my mind."

Gideon paused and then said calmly, "I can remove those doubts by telling you that Hannah has been wrong about me on other occasions. There's no reason to trust her instincts this time."

"Tell me about him, Cage."

Gideon sighed. "What do you want to know?"

"Anything. Everything. He was foreign to me. A stranger. I wanted to know him but he was always busy. Always gone. Always working on something important. And then there you were to help him with the busy, important things that kept him gone so much of the time. I just want to know something about him."

"You set out to avenge a man you never knew?"

Ballantine's mouth curved wryly. "He was my father."

"You want to know the truth? You're more of a man than he ever was. Cyrus Ballantine would never have changed the whole direction of his life to avenge a man he never knew. He wouldn't have bothered to do it for someone he knew well. Your father was brilliant, manipulative, and entirely self-centered. He'd have laughed himself sick if he had known that the two of us would go to war because of him. Cyrus fought his own battles but not those of other people. He did, however, have an odd sense of humor. It would have amused him to know that neither of us has been able to get him out of our lives. He'd have liked the idea that he was still manipulating us in some way."

"You hate him, don't you?"

Gideon thought about it. "No. Not any more."

"When did you stop?"

"I don't know. A long time ago. When did you stop hating him?"

Hugh looked down at his drink. "I didn't know I hated him until I transferred all the hate to you. Hannah told me I blamed you for killing him because I didn't want to find any weakness in Cyrus. I didn't want to admit that he could be destroyed physically and emotionally just because he'd been destroyed financially."

"Hannah has a lot to answer for," Gideon mused. "She's got a bad habit of handing out advice even when no one asks for it."

"She's got a talent for it. She sees things in people."

Gideon sighed. "I know."

"She could do a lot with that kind of ability," Ballantine said quietly. "She could use it."

"What are you talking about?"

"She could be dangerous," Ballantine said simply. "She's honest and up front about handing out the advice but it wouldn't be hard for her to be less direct. Add a dose of Machiavelli to Hannah Jessett and you'd have a very dangerous combination. She's the kind of woman who could manipulate others fairly easily in subtle ways. It's a useful skill."

It was Gideon's turn to smile wryly. "I know. But I don't think she's ever realized it. Maybe she wouldn't care if she did. She's more interested in being dangerous in other ways. She's got a ghost of her own to exorcise."

"A ghost like Cyrus?"

"In a way."

Ballantine was silent for a while. Gideon decided that it felt odd sitting there across from the man who had sworn to ruin him. But maybe no odder than whatever Ballantine was feeling.

"I wanted to be you," Ballantine said finally. "I guess I wanted to be the man who was even smarter and tougher than my father."

Gideon took a deep breath. "Change your mind?"

"I don't know yet."

"I told Hannah that when I looked at you, I saw myself looking back. The man I was nine years ago. You can be whoever you want to be, Hugh, but if you want some free advice, I'd suggest being yourself. Your father and I aren't particularly good role models. Just ask Hannah."

"Maybe I'll do that."

Gideon put down his glass. "No, you won't. That was just a figure of speech. You won't go near Hannah looking for advice or anything else. She's already given you as much as you're going to get. You can have Surbrook, Ballantine. God knows you're going to pay enough for it. And you can have as many of my clients as you can steal. But you can't have Hannah."

Ballantine cocked a brow. "You think you can have her?"

"When I really want something, I usually get it."

"And you really want Hannah," Ballantine said calmly.

"Yes."

"How are you going to get her, Cage? You can't buy a woman like Hannah. I know. I tried. Do you have any idea how much I offered?"

"I saw the letter."

"So how are you going to get her?"

"That's not your problem."

"No, but I'm curious." Ballantine regarded him with deep interest. "The only way you'll get her is if she comes to you. Think she'll do that, Cage?"

Gideon's fingers tightened around the glass. "I've told you, it's not your problem, Ballantine."

Hugh got to his feet, a tinge of humor in his blue eyes. "Just trying to take a few lessons from a master. A wise man never passes up the opportunity to learn. Know what I think?"

"No, and I don't particularly care."

"I think you haven't got the vaguest idea of how to go about getting Hannah. You're just praying she'll decide she wants you. Because if she decides differently, you're not going to be able to do a damn thing about it."

Gideon smiled but there was no trace of amusement in the expression. "Don't go near her, Ballantine."

Hugh considered the advice. "Hannah told me that if I wasn't very, very careful I might grow up to be just like you. It was a sobering thought." He turned and walked away.

Gideon watched him go. Then he finished his drink and headed back to the card tables. He needed something to loosen the savage tightness that gripped him and it was clear the Scotch wasn't going to do the trick. He would try the cards again.

Time passed in Vegas the way it always did, in perpetual night. Two evenings after the encounter with Ballantine, Gideon decided that there wasn't much point remaining for another cycle of eating, gambling, swimming, and sleeping. He was bored, restless, and tense. As a means of taking his mind off Hannah, Vegas wasn't working. He sat at a blackjack table with a drink beside him and tried to find some measure of interest in the ace and jack he had just been dealt.

"Feeling lucky?"

Gideon closed his eyes as the clear, quiet, slightly amused voice flowed over him. Then slowly he turned to look at Hannah. She was standing to his right, slightly behind him. The chandeliers created a soft nimbus around the riot of tawny brown curls. She was wearing a safari dress in olive green silk that was trimmed with gold buttons on the epaulets, pockets and cuffs. She was leaning a little on her cane, smiling at him, and she looked wonderful. He saw the anticipation in her eyes and allowed himself to hope that at last everything was going to be all right.

Without a word Gideon folded his cards and left the table. He took the three steps it required to bring him to Hannah and then he just stood there looking down at her.

"I thought you'd never get here." He reached out and pulled her into his arms. "My God, lady, I've been waiting forever."

He kissed her then, a quick, hard, kiss full of desperation and relief and hope. Hannah responded and then Gideon knew for certain that it really was going to be all right.

THE ROUND BED sat on a red-velvet platform in the center of the suite. It was wonderfully, outrageously tacky, just like the rest of the hotel room. The canopy overhead was mirrored, and when Hannah looked up she could see herself and Gideon reflected in garish decadence. The red-velvet spread was pushed to the foot of the bed and the gold sheets were in chaos. Gideon was lying on his stomach, half asleep, his leg and arm making Hannah a prisoner. She wasn't struggling very hard to free herself, although she was far from sleepy. She lay quietly on her back, her arms behind her head, and smiled up at the scene in the mirror.

"You make me nervous when you smile like that." Gideon didn't open his eyes.

"How did you know I was smiling?"

"I can feel it."

"Oh."

"What are you thinking about?" Gideon lifted his lashes slightly, the gold flecks in his eyes glittering as he watched her.

"Nothing that should make you nervous."

"I'll be the judge of that." He raised himself up on one elbow. "Tell me what you're thinking about?"

"Revelation Island."

He groaned. "At a time like this?"

Hannah's smile deepened. "The great part is that I can think about it at a time like this. It wasn't so long ago, Gideon, when I was convinced I couldn't. That's why I went back to Santa Inez. I thought I would have to choose."

"Between me and Revelation Island?"

"In a way. I was sure that choosing to write my book would change everything, and it will, but not the way I thought it would. I know now that I can control my future."

"Nord and the book kept getting in my way," Gideon muttered. "Every time I tried to find a path to you I found them blocking it. I was afraid I was going to lose you to them."

"You almost did." She turned on her side to look at him.

Gideon frowned. "I just realized you're not wearing the necklace."

"No. I threw it away."

He looked shocked. "But you said it was important to you."

"It was. But it isn't any longer. It's a long story, Gideon. Sure you want to hear it right now?"

"Yes. But I think I already know part of it."

"What part?" Hannah studied his face.

"That necklace scared the hell out of me. I came to think of it as somehow associated with the changes you were going through. I could feel you slipping past me just as I was finally figuring out what I wanted. I was trying to find a way of getting to you but you were busy striking out in a whole different direction. I was terrified it was going to be a direction that didn't include me."

"It wouldn't have included you or anyone else," Hannah said. "Just as the direction you've been going in for the past nine years hasn't allowed room for anyone. I was going to be as strong as you and my aunt and Vicky. I was going to be very powerful and very free. It was heady stuff, Gideon. It was as if I'd gone to visit the same sorceress the three of you had visited and she'd made me the same offer. I could have the power and success I needed to prove to myself that

I was as strong as Aunt Elizabeth had been or as Vicky Armitage was. I could fulfill the promise I had shown in college. All I had to give up in exchange was any real involvement with other people and other things. All I had to do was focus completely on what I wanted, and it would be mine.''

Gideon's fingers tightened on her shoulder. ''It's a lousy bargain, Hannah. I know. The price is very high.''

''It has its compensations. My aunt was happy with her choice.''

''You'll never known for certain. You said yourself you didn't know her that well. No one did.''

Hannah's mouth curved. ''That's the paradox, isn't it? You can't know well someone who has chosen that kind of path in life. I guess we can't argue the matter. Neither of us can prove anything one way or the other. But I think, on the whole, she was satisfied with her choice.''

''I wasn't satisfied with my choice,'' he pointed out roughly. ''I told myself I was, but you knew the minute you met me that I was lying through my teeth.''

''You probably weren't satisfied because you didn't willingly choose your route to isolation and power. It was more or less forced on you. You were a successful man nine years ago, a reasonably ambitious man who had the skill and the talent to take most of what he needed and wanted in life. But you hadn't closed off the rest of the world. You had that father-son relationship with Ballantine, for one thing. It was important to you. You also had your interest in map collecting. You got married. Then Ballantine betrayed you and all at once you only wanted one thing. Your focus became very narrow, very fierce. You wanted revenge, and to get that you had to have more than your natural share of power. That's when you made your bargain with the sorceress.''

"There is no sorceress, Hannah. There are only choices. We all have to make them. That's what you were doing down on Santa Inez, wasn't it? Making a choice between me and...and something else that could have been yours. Something that would have made you into a woman like your aunt. If you had chosen that other path you would have left me behind and never looked back. That's why I've been going out of my head here in Vegas. I knew there wasn't going to be much I could do to keep you from becoming an Amazon. And I also knew that Amazons don't need men like me.''

"Just as you haven't really needed any one woman for the past few years,'' Hannah said with a touch of wistfulness. "There's something to be said for not needing anyone else, for being entirely self sufficient. The sky's the limit, then. There's a certain kind of freedom in that, Gideon.''

"There's a certain kind of hell in that.''

"Do you think you've really changed?'' she asked.

"You're the one with the good people instincts. You tell me.'' He leaned over to kiss her lightly, his mouth warm and lingering. But his eyes didn't lose their intensity.

"Sometimes it's hard to be sure about someone when you're too close. It's tough to be objective,'' Hannah whispered. "From the beginning I could see a part of you very clearly. But there were other sides of you that were always hidden.''

"Maybe that's because I didn't understand them myself. Or because I learned to hide them a long time ago."

"Maybe. The point is, I couldn't be sure what the hidden part of you really meant. I didn't know how strong it was or even what influence it would have over you. When we first went to Santa Inez together I thought you might be capable of changing."

"So you decided to take the risk of allowing me to become your lover. Then you got scared, didn't you?"

"I was not frightened," she said indignantly. "I merely came to the conclusion that I'd been deluding myself. You were never going to soften and as long as I was around you, I would be playing the unrewarding game of hitting my head against a stone wall. Besides, at that point I'd gotten into my aunt's journals and I'd found the necklace. I was beginning to see that there were other possibilities in life."

"So about the time I started opening up my life to let you in, you were busy deciding you didn't want to be bothered." Gideon sounded thoroughly annoyed.

"If you hadn't turned out to be such a persistent kind of male, we might never have seen each other again after Santa Inez."

"You sure as hell weren't going to come running down to Tucson, were you? As far as you were concerned you'd given me one too many chances."

"I felt I was the one taking all the risks, and I was not at all sure I had enough stamina or power to hold my own against you."

"Does it have to be a battle between us?" he asked softly.

"There are definitely going to be times when it will be open war," she told him easily.

"All you have to do is to take me to bed and the battle will be over before it's even begun."

Hannah laughed. "If you expect me to believe that, you're not nearly as bright as I once thought you were. No woman could control you with sex, Gideon."

He grinned. "You could try."

"Don't look so hopeful."

His grin faded. "Do you really want to be able to control me?"

"No. But I want to be strong enough so that you can't control me, either."

"Ah, Hannah, I only want to love you." He sprawled on top of her, kissing her with renewed hunger. Hannah wrapped her arms around him and decided that as long as they took such comfort and pleasure in each other they could both forget about controlling each other. After a moment Gideon raised his head. "What conclusions did you arrive at down there on the island, Hannah? I'm not dumb enough to question my luck, but I'll admit I'm curious."

"I decided that I wasn't willing to make the bargain. I wanted my chance with you. I wanted my chance at having it all. I wanted to write the book and I wanted to continue with my guidance counseling. I wanted a lot of things I knew I couldn't have if I went the route my aunt took. The funny thing was that when I threw away the necklace, I knew everything was going to be all right. I could still write the book and it wouldn't change everything the way I had come to believe it would. I could write it for different reasons."

"Is that what you're going to do? Write the book?"

"Any objections?"

"None. As long as you don't kick me out of your life while you do it."

"Never." Her arms tightened around him. "I have always believed in maintaining a balance in life, Gideon. For a while there I thought I might try a different approach, but now I know I've been right all along. Interested in taking a trip?"

"Another one? I seem to be doing nothing but getting on and off planes since I met you. Where do you want to go now?"

She smiled. "I thought we might go to Revelation Island and see if we can find the spot my aunt marked on that old war map."

"When am I supposed to find time to run Cage & Associates?"

"You'll find a way. You have a talent for business."

AMAZON: THE LIFE OF ELIZABETH NORD generated considerable interest among both academicians and laymen when it was published eighteen months later. There were several critical reviews questioning the author's credentials for writing the book, and a few people were scandalized by the emphasis on the young Nord's romantic relationship with Roderick Hamilton.

But the fact that Nord had deliberately misrepresented the culture of Revelation Island fascinated everyone in and out of the academic community. So many people had been forced to read *The Amazons of Revelation Island* in college and remembered it as a classic text that widespread interest was guaranteed from the moment Hannah's book hit the stands. The shocking facts of the deception kept those in the academic world arguing for months. The cheerfully done passages describing Nord's romantic life as well as the truth about the sex lives of the Revelation Islanders held the attention of everyone else. No one was disappointed. The new biography resurrected a great deal of interest in all of Nord's books. Her name became even more of a household word. Elizabeth Nord would have found the whole thing very amusing.

Not long after the book appeared, Nick Jessett wrote his sister a letter complaining good-naturedly about having to fend off reporters. He enclosed part of a column that had been written by the book review editor of the student newspaper published on the campus where Hannah was employed as a guidance counselor. It read in part:

Hannah Jessett Cage was unavailable for comment, but it was learned from her brother that she has donated the valuable Nord Library to the university which financed Elizabeth Nord's work on Revelation Island. Accompanying the collection was an unusual ceremonial vessel reputed to be the one described in Nord's landmark work, *The Amazons of Revelation Island.* According to Jessett, his sister and her husband recovered the vessel earlier this year with the assistance of a World War II map of the island.

The former Ms Jessett is presently vacationing in the Caribbean with her husband, Gideon Cage. Cage is the president of a newly formed management consulting firm headquartered in Seattle. The author intends to return to her position as a guidance counselor at this college after her vacation.

Harlequin® Historical

FLASH: ROMANCE MAKES HISTORY!

History the Harlequin way, that is. Our books invite you to experience a past you never read about in grammar school!

Travel back in time with us, and pirates will sweep you off your feet, cowboys will capture your heart, and noblemen will lead you to intrigue and romance, *always* romance—because that's what makes each Harlequin Historical title a thrilling escape for you, four times every month. Just think of the adventures you'll have!

So pick up a Harlequin Historical novel today, and relive history in your wildest dreams....

HHPROMO

HARLEQUIN®

my **Valentine** *1993*

The most romantic day of the year is here! Escape into the exquisite
world of love with MY VALENTINE 1993. What better way to celebrate
Valentine's Day than with this very romantic, sensuous collection of four
original short stories, written by some of Harlequin's most popular
authors.

ANNE STUART
JUDITH ARNOLD
ANNE McALLISTER
LINDA RANDALL WISDOM

THIS VALENTINE'S DAY, DISCOVER ROMANCE
WITH MY VALENTINE 1993

Available in February wherever Harlequin Books are sold. VAL93

Where do you find hot Texas nights, smooth Texas charm and dangerously sexy cowboys?

Crystal Creek

DEEP IN THE HEART

Wedding Bells—Texas Style!

Even a Boston blue blood needs a Texas education. Ranch owner J. T. McKinney is handsome, strong, opinionated and totally charming. And he is determined to marry beautiful Bostonian Cynthia Page. However, the couple soon discovers a Texas cattleman's idea of marriage differs greatly from a New England career woman's!

CRYSTAL CREEK reverberates with the exciting rhythm of Texas. Each story features the rugged individuals who live and love in the Lone Star State. And each one ends with the same invitation...

Y'ALL COME BACK...REAL SOON!

Don't miss *DEEP IN THE HEART* by Barbara Kaye. Available in March wherever Harlequin books are sold.

CC-1

ROMANCE IS A YEARLONG EVENT!

Celebrate the most romantic day of the year with MY VALENTINE! (February)

CRYSTAL CREEK
When you come for a visit Texas-style, you won't want to leave! (March)

Celebrate the joy, excitement and adjustment that comes with being JUST MARRIED! (April)

Go back in time and discover the West as it was meant to be . . . UNTAMED— Maverick Hearts! (July)

LINGERING SHADOWS
New York Times bestselling author Penny Jordan brings you her latest blockbuster. Don't miss it! (August)

BACK BY POPULAR DEMAND!!!
Calloway Corners, involving stories of four sisters coping with family, business and romance! (September)

FRIENDS, FAMILIES, LOVERS
Join us for these heartwarming love stories that evoke memories of family and friends. (October)

Capture the magic and romance of Christmas past with HARLEQUIN HISTORICAL CHRISTMAS STORIES! (November)

WATCH FOR FURTHER DETAILS IN ALL HARLEQUIN BOOKS!